Her eyes filled with tears. I was furious with Sedic. What was he playing at? Did he want to alienate everyone who cared about him in one fell swoop?

As if she could read my thoughts, Lila said quickly, 'It's not his fault. He said I was to wait for him to get in touch after you arrived. He said maybe he'd come down to Jogja to visit. I just couldn't wait.' She struggled to control the disappointment on her face. 'Is he coming later, perhaps? Maybe in a few days?'

I couldn't bear to upset her any more, but it would have been cruel to give her false hope. 'I'm not sure,' I said.

She was puzzled. 'But you are Nicola, the girl he is going to marry? I thought you were both working here for seven months. That's what he said. I've been looking forward to meeting you so much.'

'I'm so sorry,' I said again. 'I don't know what Sedic is planning to do. He broke off our engagement three weeks ago. I came out here alone . . .'

Also by Gill Paul in Coronet:

Enticement

About the author

Gill Paul is a successful businesswoman who has lived and
travelled all over the world. Born in Scotland, she now lives
in London, running her own publishing company.

Compulsion

Gill Paul

CORONET BOOKS
Hodder & Stoughton

Typeset in Times
Hewer Text Ltd, Edinburgh

Printed and bound in Great Britain by
Mackays of Chatham plc, Chatham, Kent

Hodder & Stoughton
A division of Hodder Headline
338 Euston Road
London NW1 3BH

For Gray and Fo

ACKNOWLEDGEMENTS

Political events depicted in the novel are loosely based on the overthrow of Indonesian President Soeharto in 1998 but artistic licence has been taken, especially with regard to the timescale and order of events. All international companies and products described are completely fictional and no resemblance is intended to any existing or previous companies or products.

With grateful thanks to Katie Bailey and Dr Gavin Yamey for medical advice; to Mark Hampton for information about international finance; and to Fiona Williams for Indonesian detail.

My agent, Vivien Green, and my editors, Carolyn Caughey and Kirsty Fowkes, gave valuable feedback and support, as did my trusty panel of advisors: David Boyle, Carol Cornish, Susan Hill, Marion Jansen, Murdo Macdonald, Dee McMath and Karen Sullivan. Special thanks to all of them.

Chapter One

━━━━◦◦◦━━━━

'Shit!' I said out loud, then bit my lip. It's better to avoid expletives when you work in a children's unit, but I was carrying a Styrofoam cup of scalding coffee that was slopping onto my fingers. There was a phone ringing urgently down the corridor and I sensed it was mine before the pager in my pocket began to chirp. I shoved open the office door and clattered my hip on the edge of the desk as I rushed to answer. Coffee splashed on some case notes spilling out of the filing tray.

'Dr Drew?' It was a nurse calling from Casualty, asking if I'd go down to look at a baby who had just been brought in. The mother was worried about an unusual stillness, a lethargic manner, although there were no other physical symptoms. I shrugged on my white coat and stethoscope and ran down the back stairs, then zigzagged through X-ray.

The Ormesley is an ancient hospital set in several different buildings connected by narrow alleys that never see sunlight. Confused outpatients and visitors are invariably clustered in front of improbable arrows labelled Haematology or Radiology, Lady Margaret or Rainbow wards, unsure whether they're being directed through a door to the left or further down the lane.

It was only ten o'clock so Casualty was fairly quiet. An old man with long straggly hair snuffled in a plastic chair and a woman with a cut on her forehead was crying in the corner. The sister directed me to cubicle 10, I pulled back the pale blue curtain and there, sitting by the trolley, was a woman in her mid to late thirties holding a baby wrapped in a long white woollen coat that had a chunkiness that made me think it was hand-knitted. I stepped into the cubicle and stopped abruptly a few feet away from the mother and her baby. I could see that the woman was smartly but not expensively dressed. The baby looked well cared for but there was a languidness about its posture, an uneasy quietness. And I got an uncanny sensation, a pressure on my diaphragm like a hand pushing upwards, a feeling I've had many times in my medical career and have never been able to explain. In that instant I knew, as surely as I knew anything, that the baby was not going to live much longer.

To cover my shock, I lifted the notes the nurse had given me, then I smiled and introduced myself. The little girl was called Emily. When her mother pulled back the coat, I saw a fuzzy coconut head and dark brown eyes, a body that was long-limbed and marginally underweight. The mother was articulate and concerned but not over-anxious.

'I'm sure it's nothing,' she told me. 'It's just that she hasn't taken a proper feed for a couple of days. She lies with a nipple in her mouth, staring into space.'

'Any breathing difficulties?' I asked, and she shook her head firmly.

'She's three months old?'

'Three and a half.' The pallor was creamy, the lips a slightly purply shade of rose. She didn't object or seem to notice when I lifted her from her mother's arms. I unfastened the pop-studs of her towelling all-in-one and lifted the miniature vest to listen to her chest and just after the first of the two heart sounds, I heard the whooshing noise that indicated a systolic heart murmur. Why had no one picked it up at the postnatal or six-week baby checks? How could everyone who had seen that baby so far in her life have missed something as fundamental as that? I felt a rush of fury at the carelessness of whoever had been responsible; someone's mind hadn't been on the job.

I continued the examination, listening to the baby's lungs, palpating her abdomen to look for liver enlargement, checking temperature and scanning her skin for rashes. Then I explained that we needed to run a couple of tests and asked the sister to organise a chest x-ray, ECG and echocardiogram.

By the time I ushered the mother into my office that afternoon, her composure was rattled, her eyes pleading, and she fidgeted constantly, plucking at the wool of Emily's coat.

'Sit down,' I motioned, and she lowered herself into the chair, careful not to disturb Emily who was now sound asleep, her little chest rising and falling.

'Have you found anything?' the mother asked, her voice unsteady.

'I'm afraid our tests show that Emily has a hole in her heart.' I watched her shoulders tense and her expression freeze as this information sank in. She looked like a nice woman and I felt very compassionate towards her.

'What . . . is that serious?' she gasped.

'It's the reason why she's listless and has lost her appetite. The blood isn't being pumped efficiently round her system, so she's conserving her energy.'

She cuddled Emily tighter within the woollen coat and began to rock her slowly. 'But . . . you can fix it, can't you? I mean, I've read about all the operations you can do now . . .'

'It may well not require surgery. The majority of septal defects close by themselves by the time the child is three. If Emily's doesn't, then we might operate and yes, you're right, it's a very successful procedure.'

'But what can I do now?' She was listening intently to my words, trying to commit them to memory.

'I'm going to put her on a course of medication that will help her almost immediately. We'll admit her for a few checks and keep an eye on her until we see the treatment working. You can stay as well.' I glanced at the notes. 'Although I see you've got two more children under five at home. That must be a handful.' I smiled, but she didn't smile back.

'My husband can look after them. He'll have to take time off work. How long will you keep Emily here?'

'Just a few days. Not long. Until we see her picking up strength and feeding well again.'

'And then, when I go home, what can I do? How can I help her? Will she be able to . . . you know, crawl, walk, play, do the normal things?'

3

'She's not going to be an invalid.' I looked at the baby and bit my lip for a second. My instinct that she wasn't going to make it felt stronger by the minute, but I couldn't possibly say so. Instead, I explained about special measures she should take: dietary advice, exercise, keeping Emily away from cigarette smoke and people with viral infections. We talked for over an hour and she cried a lot but asked intelligent, pertinent questions.

'What about the other two children? Should I keep them away from her? They can be a bit boisterous but I can't supervise them constantly. I mean, I'll do my best.' She had dislodged a strand of wool from the hem of the coat and was winding it round and round her finger.

'She's not that fragile. Honestly. I'll find some reading material so you have as much information as possible, but you must remember that almost all hole-in-the-heart babies go on to lead perfectly normal lives.' I knew I must be very late for my ward round now but resisted the urge to glance at my watch. There was no way I could rush this meeting to a close before I had answered all her questions.

'Is there a phone I can use?' she asked at last. 'I need to call my husband.'

'Of course. I'll get a nurse to arrange that for you and to carry out the admission procedures, then I'll come and see you later.'

As I hurried down the corridor to the paediatric wards, I had a bad taste in my throat, like sour, undigested food. There was no clinical evidence to suggest Emily's case would be any different from other ventricular defects I'd treated but I'd felt dishonest and two-faced as I talked about the prospects for most hole-in-the heart children because I knew it wasn't going to be that way for this baby.

I popped back to the ward at ten to seven to check that they were settled for the night and then I had to rush down the stairs and out of the main entrance, late for meeting Sedic. As soon as I emerged, I could see him sitting on a wall behind the car, swinging his legs to and fro, a brown paper package in his lap. He waved and smiled and the corners of my mouth curled upwards. There was something so winning about his smile, the way it brightened his whole appearance. It always made me want to hug him.

He leapt off the wall, landing easily on the tarmac, and walked towards me with his easy stride, a man who was comfortable inside his own skin.

'I've got a present for you, Nicky.' He waved the parcel. 'Some friends of mine have just opened an artists' co-operative shop near the studio.'

He reached me and pulled me into a tight embrace, lips squashing against mine then nuzzling my neck. One hand gave my bottom an absent-minded squeeze. 'Go on, open it.'

I pulled out a purple satin evening bag with tiny seashells sewn all over. 'It's lovely,' I exclaimed, glancing inside and wondering how on earth it would hold all my paraphernalia. I never seemed to travel light.

'You always use that enormous leather bag, like a school satchel, and it ruins the look of all your evening clothes. You're like a kid playing at dressing up and getting it a bit wrong. The fairy princess in Doc Martens.'

'Thanks a lot,' I laughed, opening the car door.

'Can't I drive?' He reached for the keys.

'Sure. Let me just get my "school satchel" from under the seat.' I'd taken to leaving it there, hidden under a flap of carpet, because the hospital lockers were always being broken into.

Sedic cupped his hands over my bottom again as I bent over and I nudged him away, laughing. 'Stop it, you! If any of the parents of my patients are watching, I'll lose my professional gravitas.'

I handed him the keys. 'Gravitas indeed.' He raised his eyebrows. 'Yeah, right.'

I walked round to the passenger side, my thoughts back with baby Emily. Sedic must have detected my mood. 'What's up?' he asked, reversing out of the parking space. 'Bad day?'

'It's a baby that was brought in this morning. She's got a hole in the heart that no one had spotted before. Normally I wouldn't worry about cases like that but . . .' I hesitated.

'You've got a bad feeling?' He glanced at me.

5

'I know she hasn't got long to go.' It was a relief to put it into words. Sedic reached across and squeezed my hand.

'Did you tell anyone else what you think?'

'I've asked the night sister to keep a close watch and we're running more tests tomorrow. It's very rare to die from ventricular septal defects but it's as though she's not trying. Maybe I'm wrong. I hope I am.'

He didn't respond for a few moments as he concentrated on turning right across two lanes of traffic. 'You know you're not wrong. Don't you think you should have warned the mother that things aren't looking good, and tried to prepare her a little?'

'You can't prepare mothers for their babies dying. She was too shocked by the diagnosis to take anything else in.' I paused. 'It's a sensitive situation. Years ago, when I was a junior doctor, I got hauled in front of the Senior Registrar after I told a nurse that I thought a car accident victim wasn't going to make it. If it got back to the relatives that I'd written him off before even examining him, they could have claimed that we didn't try as hard as we could to resuscitate him. Which wasn't true, of course.'

'I know. We've talked about this before. I just think it's a terrible burden on you, carrying it all by yourself. There must be a way you could let trusted colleagues know so you can all be extra-vigilant around these patients.'

I shrugged. 'What could I say? That I've had a premonition about this one? It's not very scientific.'

Sedic rubbed my thigh sympathetically. 'Poor old you. I guess having dinner with my father and Leona is the last thing you feel like doing tonight.' I shrugged. 'I don't mind. I just hope Leona's not going to spend the evening putting me down. You haven't seen Peter for a while, have you?'

'Six months. He must want something from me, to have asked us out tonight.'

'Like what?'

'Like doing some work for him.'

'And you don't want to?'

'God, I hate it. It's just that I haven't sold a painting for ages now and it's not fair that you're still paying for everything. At least if I do a trip for Peter, I'll get a few hundred quid to chuck in the pot.'

I sighed. 'Sedic, we're getting married. We're a modern couple. When we've got kids, it might have to be the other way round, but for the moment it doesn't matter a hoot that I earn a bit more than you.'

He chuckled. 'I'm still a bloke, darling. You know we're all hunter-gatherers at heart.'

'What I don't understand is why Peter keeps asking you to do these trips when he knows you're reluctant. Surely there must be plenty of other people he could send?' Sedic shrugged dramatically. 'It's an Italian thing. Family are the most trustworthy. He knows I'll go out there and follow his instructions to the letter: collect this piece of machinery, take it somewhere else, pick up the cash, take it to the bank. I just do it robot-fashion. Also, he uses me for the more sensitive transactions. Maybe clients trust me more because I'm the boss's son. I dunno, Nicky. You're right. Anyone could do what I do for him and I wish to God he would find someone else.'

'Just say no. I'll back you up.'

He exhaled with a rush of air. 'But we're getting on so badly at the moment. I think he's close to writing me off because I've refused him so many times this year.' I could see that his earlier high spirits had deflated.

'What will you say if he asks you tonight to make another trip?'

Sedic shook his head. 'I'll see.' Then he exclaimed, 'Christ! I'm getting in a bad mood just thinking about it. Let's not go! Let's turn round and go home and just not show up!'

I laughed. 'We're nearly there now. You can't be so rude.'

'Why not? He's done it to me plenty of times." His tone was petulant. I reached across and ran my fingers through his hair, scratching his scalp.

'Usually when flights were delayed.' He frowned. 'Tell you what, we'll leave early. I'll say I'm on call first thing in the morning.'

We turned into the street where the restaurant was located and Sedic slowed down to look for a parking spot. 'Hah!' he yelled triumphantly and slotted the car in neatly right outside the entrance. 'Will you do something for me?' he asked, eyes gleaming. He squeezed my leg. 'Take your knickers off. That'll give me something interesting to think about when Dad's irritating me. Will you?'

'Not here,' I grinned. 'People can see.' A doorman was watching us from the entrance to the restaurant.

He leaned over to kiss me then whispered in my ear, 'Go to the ladies' as soon as we get inside.'

It was very exciting being Sedic's partner. Situations could become sexual at any moment, often when I least expected it. 'OK,' I agreed. 'But let's go in now. We're late.'

Sedic's father, Peter Molozzi, stood up and waved ostentatiously as we walked down the curved green glass stairs to the dim restaurant below. I kissed him first, then bent to greet Leona, his partner, dodging between her huge wooden earrings and the chopsticks that held her topknot in position. She tilted her cheek but made no effort to kiss me back. I peeled off my jacket and dropped it on the seat then murmured 'Excuse me a moment,' and hurried to the toilet at the back of the restaurant. Everything was black – floors, ceilings, cubicles, washbasins, toilet bowls, towels. A cloakroom attendant sat watching so I felt I had to pretend to use the toilet rather than just slipping my knickers into my handbag, then I washed my hands with the liquorice soap, thinking what a ridiculous conceit it was for somewhere they serve food. Peter reckoned he was being modern and trendy when he chose such places, but the meal was generally lousy.

When I returned, there was already an atmosphere at the table, hovering like static. It never failed to astonish me quite how uncomfortable Sedic appeared to be with his father. Undercurrents fizzled, meanings became layered upon meanings, expressions were scrupulously guarded. I was never sure if this was a recent development, since he'd begun to turn down work for Peter's companies, or if there had always been this tension. I'd certainly never seen them behaving in a relaxed fashion with each other. I caught Sedic's eye and winked briefly, to let him know I'd done as he wanted. Leona intercepted the gesture and regarded me coolly.

'Better now?' she asked, staring with owl eyes set in a sharply delineated skull. She was wearing a low-cut black knitted dress and the ridges of her ribs formed a ladder below her prominent collar bones.

'Yes, thanks. Sorry about that, I've been desperate all the way here.' I wriggled into my seat, opposite Sedic's father, who smiled at me.

'You're looking well. Have you cut your hair?'

'No. I think it's grown since I last saw you. It was just after Christmas, wasn't it?'

Leona interrupted. 'Peter, how about some champagne?'

He clapped his hands together – 'What a good idea!' – and turned to summon a wine waiter.

Sedic was gazing abstractedly at the other diners. Peter seemed to be in an animated mood, while Leona was controlled and distant. I watched Peter discussing the wine list with the waiter and was struck yet again by how little family resemblance there was. Possibly a jut of the chin or the angle of the forehead. They were both of medium height and dark, but Peter's looks were Italian, with round hazel eyes and wavy hair, while Sedic's eyes were almond-shaped, his hair thick and spiky, his skin the smooth beige of his mother's Indonesian family.

'How's the painting, Sedic?' Leona asked. 'Have you been working on anything new since the Whitechapel show?'

'Yes, I have, in fact.'

I listened with interest. He didn't like to talk about work in progress, so I'd usually wait until he offered to show me recent canvases or discuss ideas.

'Could I come and have a look? I've had a cancellation at the gallery for the first three weeks of October and if you've got some suitable material, I could slot you in.'

I gasped, but Sedic seemed unmoved. 'Sure, come by the studio when you're next in the neighbourhood.'

Peter joined in. 'Early October's a good time for getting

reviews. People are just back from their holidays and they're in a good mood with the world. You also get the early Christmas shoppers buying presents. But it only gives you a couple of months to get ready. Do you think you could have at least twenty new paintings framed up by then?'

'So long as you decide the work I'm doing is "suitable".' There was a harshness in his tone that I couldn't fathom. He'd been desperate to follow up his small East End show with something bigger in central London but Leona had never offered to let him use her gallery before.

'I'm sure I'll like it,' she said. 'Your work has been improving dramatically over the last couple of years. Since you two got together, in fact. Being in love must stimulate your creative juices.'

The words and the tone were patronising. Here we go, I thought. Leona liked to make it obvious that she found me devoid of artistic judgment. It was a kind of intellectual one-upmanship. Sedic said she was intimidated by me being a doctor but I wasn't so sure. I couldn't figure out what kind of partner she would have liked to see him with. Another artist? Maybe anyone but me.

'What's the catch?' he asked sharply.

'No catch at all,' his father replied. 'We've been meaning to offer you a show for ages and it seemed like perfect timing when this opportunity arose. I do have another unconnected proposal for the two of you that I was going to explain over dinner. But let's order first.'

Sedic glanced at me and rolled his eyes slightly. I couldn't tell if he was pleased about the offer or not. Peter asked each of us what we wanted to eat then relayed it unnecessarily to the waiter. I noticed that he seldom looked at his son, even when addressing him directly. His eyes hovered in the middle distance somewhere beyond Sedic's shoulder.

'Have you just flown in, Peter?' I asked. 'Where was it this time?'

'The Caribbean.'

'You do have businesses in glamorous places.'

Leona was fiddling with one of her earrings, trying to replace a butterfly clip that had worked its way loose. 'Damn stupid thing. Can you help me, Sedic?'

Scowling, he took the silver clasp from her. She bent her head to one side and he held her earlobe between his fingers and slipped the clip onto the back without saying a word. As she straightened up, she patted his knee.

'Thanks, darling. You've got such wonderfully steady hands.'

The waiter popped the cork from the champagne and we all watched as he tilted our glasses to fill them, then Peter proposed a toast to the exhibition and we took a sip. Another waiter brought a basket of bread and Leona lit a cigarette. Peter glanced at her then began to explain his proposal.

'Nicola, I'm not sure how much you know about my business interests.' I shrugged and smiled blankly. 'I have a number of companies around the world, particularly in the Far East. I expect you've read in the papers that some of the economies out there are running into trouble so I'm having to do a lot of shuffling of my financial affairs. As a currency drops in value, exports become cheap and imports are expensive. Sometimes we need to sell off existing stock as quickly as possible before it becomes ridiculously devalued. I won't go into detail but the bottom line is that I need someone I can trust to go out there for the next six months or so to look after my interests.'

'Uh-uh. Not a chance.' Sedic shook his head emphatically and I bit my lip.

Peter held up his hand. 'I knew that would be your first reaction, but hear me out. Now, I've got a portfolio of different types of business, from the art dealership to a casino and a vineyard – all sorts of things. Each one has an individual management team but there's no one else I can trust to take an overview, or make decisions about diverting resources from one to another. Sedic is the only person I can rely on in a crisis. He's family and this will be his inheritance one day, so I know he'll always act in our best interests. You can understand, Nicola, why I'm so keen to persuade him?'

'I suppose so.' The tension round the table was palpable. Suddenly it reminded me of the atmosphere in an intensive care unit full of humming monitors and whispering nurses. No one was drinking any longer.

'I'm fully aware that Sedic is fed up working for me. He just wants to paint, and I'm sure he wouldn't want to leave you behind for that length of time, so the pressure is on me to make my offer as attractive as possible.'

I thought it was odd that he was addressing me although it was his son who would have to be convinced.

'You two are getting married next year and you'll want to start a family, so it seems to me you'll need a house with a garden. I know what property prices are like in London, so I'm prepared to give you a helping hand with the deposit when the time comes. The figure I had in mind was two hundred and fifty thousand pounds.' He paused for effect.

I glanced at Sedic but he was staring at his plate. Leona was examining her nails, nudging back the cuticles nonchalantly. It was a substantial sum that would make a massive difference to the kind of property we could afford. It would also mean we could start our family sooner, which was important to me since I'd just passed the age of thirty. These were the first reactions to flash through my brain.

'Then I wondered if we could find a job for you as well, Nicola. I made some enquiries through a medical equipment company I'm involved with, called Medimachines, and there's a clinic in the centre of Jakarta that would love to have a Western doctor over for a six-month consultancy. They were jumping at the chance. It's a busy accident and emergency clinic and my colleague tells me a lot of the patients still believe in witch doctors and folk medicine. I thought maybe you'd find that interesting.'

'It sounds fascinating,' I said politely, 'but I don't speak any Indonesian. How could I treat people I couldn't talk to?' Peter smiled. 'Bahasa Indonesia is the official language but there are over two hundred other ones in use, so most Indonesians don't understand each other. They're used to interpreters and sign language. Sedic will tell you.' Sedic didn't say anything. 'The nurses all speak English so they could translate. I don't think you'd find language a problem.'

'But what about my job here?'

'It's just a suggestion, but maybe they would give you a sabbatical if you could convince them it would be good experience. You'd learn all about tropical diseases and snake-bites and whatever else. I'd have thought it might be quite a challenge.'

I considered this. 'I suppose they might agree.'

'I'd organise a house for you with a pool, fully staffed. You'd have cars and drivers to take you around. The lifestyle out there is very comfortable for Westerners.'

'When would you need us to go?' I asked, trying to keep the excitement out of my voice.

'Immediately after Sedic's exhibition in October. That will give us enough time, for you to make the arrangements and for me to organise the house and so forth. But I need to know your decision in the next week because if you don't want to go, I'll have to find someone else. I'm flying out of London on Saturday but you can leave a message with Leona.' He turned to Sedic. 'Then we could start getting everything ready for that exhibition. We should send out the invitations well in advance to make sure all the journalists book it into their diaries.'

'Of course the exhibition's contingent on us going to Jakarta,' Sedic said on the way home. 'Or me, at least.'

'I can't believe he'd do that!'

'I know him better than you.'

'Look, if you really don't want to go, then we won't do it. I'm sure you could get an exhibition somewhere else and we'll just start our family in a smaller house. We don't have to let him control us like this.'

Sedic didn't reply.

'Do you want me to find out whether it's possible to get the time off work? If you're going, I'd much rather come with you. It would be horrible to be separated for that length of time.'

He nodded briefly, or at least that's the way I remember it. 'Let's not talk about it any more tonight.' He shifted in his seat. 'Actually, I've got other things on my mind.'

'Such as?'

'Such as something I want you to do when we get home.' He brushed a hand lightly across my chest, teasing, and I grinned and waited. It was a favourite erotic game, telling me his sexual plans in advance. 'I want you to walk in front of me, without saying anything. When we get inside the building, you've to lift your skirt up around your waist and hold it there. Keep moving, don't look back.'

I felt hot. 'What if one of the neighbours comes out?'

'They won't.'

I stepped slowly up the staircase, conscious of him following just a few steps behind so that my bare buttocks were at his eye level. Sedic had always been excited by looking. He liked to scrutinise every part of my body, twisting me to view from different angles, missing nothing. It's a very intense experience. The first time we went to bed together, he undressed me then laid me down on top of the bed cover and scanned my skin as though he was memorising every curve, hair and freckle. I tried to wriggle away when he moved down to look at my feet, because they're so ugly and deformed, my least favourite part of my body, but he caught one in his hand and examined it carefully then planted a kiss on the instep. It's flattering to be with someone who notices everything about you, but a bit unnerving at times.

Near the top of the stairs, he said quietly, 'Bend over.' One hand held my hips as I leaned forward to rest my elbows on the landing a few steps further up, then I felt his other hand guide his penis between my legs. He must have unfastened his trousers while we were walking up. As he pushed inside me, all my worries about the neighbours coming out of their apartments disappeared. The light clicked off on its automatic timer and I squeezed hard with my muscles to pull him deeper inside.

Chapter Two

Next morning there was a 'beds crisis' meeting at the hospital. These tended to be tetchy point-scoring sessions, with each department arguing for more intensive care beds to be allocated for their patients. I got there early and grabbed a chair to the side of the room, sitting back to watch as bad-tempered, sleep-deprived colleagues shuffled for position. As in other hospitals, the hierarchies were male-dominated and the higher the men got in the ranks, the less they exhibited any pleasant characteristics or people skills.

My head of department greeted me and positioned himself a few seats further along, then I looked up as my ex-boyfriend Geoff, an orthopaedic surgeon, entered the room. I smiled but he barely nodded in my direction before choosing a place near the front. It was two years since I'd left him for Sedic and the only conversations we'd had since then had been formal and work-related.

The meeting began with the Head of Nursing giving some long-winded outline of the reasons for the current crisis, and my thoughts drifted back to Geoff. It was bizarre to think that I might have married him if it hadn't been for a chance meeting with Sedic in a bank. Everyone had assumed we would marry: we were medical school sweethearts who went on to good jobs in the same hospital; we'd have had a safe, sensible life of cosy dinner parties, annual holidays in Tuscany or Provence and, before long, a couple of kids. My parents were both GPs, his were lawyers, and we'd have repeated their lives in symmetrical mirror image.

Geoff spoke up, interrupting to complain about some building work that had closed one of the operating theatres, and I
mused on how serious he'd become. From this angle, I could
see his waistline settling into comfortable middle age and his
scalp shone through a thin patch on the crown of his head.
I couldn't imagine how I had ever found him attractive or
interesting enough to consider spending my life with him. The
sex had always been routine: same sequence of foreplay, same
positions. There must have been fun bits in our relationship
but it was hard to remember them now.

Without being aware of it, I suppose I was ripe for romantic
adventure when Sedic and I met, or at any rate itching for some
kind of change. It hadn't felt that way at the time. It had been
agonising, terrifying, stressful and wonderful all at once, like the
classic thunderbolt of Italian literature. We looked at each other
and fell in love almost straight away.

He was standing in front of me in the bank, arguing with a teller
who refused to cash his cheque. I remember he was wearing a
black beret and a long caramel cotton coat with lots of pockets,
and he was gesticulating dramatically, shifting from foot to foot,
bobbing his head to one side. The lengthening queue listened
with interest.

'OK,' he said cheerfully. 'Let's try this from another angle.
How does a person with an Italian bank account withdraw
money when they visit London? What's the normal procedure?'

The cashier spoke quietly and he listened to the response. 'I
don't have a cash card but if you call my bank in Rome they'll
guarantee the cheque is good and I'll reimburse you for the
call. What have you got to lose?'

At that stage, I assumed his accent was Italian, although
his English was fluent. The teller pointed at the queue, which
now stretched to the street doors, and, as he turned to look,
he caught sight of me. Immediately, he swivelled to face me
and gave a huge intimate smile, as if I was some old friend he
was delighted to see. Puzzled, I checked if there was someone

behind me, but there was no doubt the smile was directed at me. I couldn't refrain from smiling back – it was almost a physiological response – and immediately afterwards I felt foolish and ruffled.

He gathered his cheque book and papers from the counter and stuffed them in the pocket of his coat, then went to sit on a chair by the side. The queue stuttered forwards. I could sense he was watching me, aware of a vague shadow in the outer reaches of my peripheral vision. I examined the bills I was paying, checking that the figures were correct, the account numbers were on the back of the cheques, and the stubs filled out. My turn came and the cashier stamped the paying-in slips noisily.

As I walked back towards the cash machines, I concentrated on folding the bills into my wallet. I had inserted my cash card and was tapping in the code when the man appeared by my side.

'Hello,' he smiled. I smiled back politely. He had shiny black eyes and very white teeth, like a healthy puppy.

'Can I take you for a cup of coffee?' he asked. He placed a friendly hand on my forearm.

'Aren't you waiting for them to call your bank in Italy?'

'No, I give up. I'll try somewhere else. How about it?'

I noticed there was a tiny chip missing from the corner of his front tooth. 'I can't just go for coffee with a stranger I meet in a bank,' I said, smiling again so my words didn't seem too unfriendly.

'Why on earth not?' He shrugged exaggeratedly. 'I've just moved back to London and I hardly know anyone. How am I supposed to make new friends in this town? You look nice so I'm asking you for coffee. Will you come?' He held his palms flat as if to communicate his trustworthiness.

I felt flustered and glanced at my watch without registering what it said.

'If you don't have time now, I could meet you later. Where do you work?'

I extracted the banknotes from the machine and slipped them into my wallet, conscious that I'd withdrawn exactly the amount he'd been unsuccessfully requesting from the cashier. 'I really can't.'

He took a step back and appraised me with a seductive smile. 'You think it wouldn't be proper but you're still tempted. Your instincts tell you that I'm not a mugger or a serial killer, just a genuine guy who's trying to be friendly, but that old lesson about not talking to strangers was impressed on you once too often when you were younger. So how do you ever meet new people in your life? Would it be different if we'd met at a party or in a wine bar? I don't see the difference, do you?' He grinned wider. 'You're changing your mind. Your shoulders are relaxing and you're thinking about unfolding your arms. Come on, five minutes, one cappuccino and I'll stop pestering you.'

'I don't really meet new people,' I explained in answer to his question.

'Ah, but you just have,' he announced and, much to my embarrassment, he slung a casual arm round my shoulders as he led me out through the glass doors onto the street.

I always thought of the days that followed as the hurricane days. He insinuated his way into my body then my mind, bossy and playful, loud and daring, pushing through my reservations and inhibitions with careless abandon.

When I told him about Geoff, he said firmly, 'You're not going to marry him,' and within a week he was inciting me to break up the relationship.

'But I want to have children,' I had counter-argued, weakly. 'I'm going to be thirty next year so I can't wait forever.'

'I'll give you as many children as you want. I'd love to fill you up with children,' he said, stroking my belly. 'We could have pink ones, green ones, black ones and yellow ones.'

'I'm serious,' I said.

'So am I,' he replied.

It was surprisingly easy to break up with Geoff, just like waving a friend off on a long sea voyage. He reacted with a pompous indignation that merely underlined my instinct that we'd been two people behaving as society expected, rather than lovers.

*　　*　　*

Geoff glanced round suddenly, as if he sensed I was watching him, and I hurriedly looked away and tried to concentrate on the speaker's words. The tone of the discussion had taken on a decidedly competitive edge.

'Dr Drew, how many IT beds are you occupying just now?' the Head of Nursing asked me abruptly.

'Only three, but I need another tomorrow for a post-operative six-month-old.'

'Can't you take one of the current three out of IT to make way?'

'Not a chance,' I shook my head. 'Absolutely no way.'

She glared at me but didn't argue the point. No one else was willing to relinquish a bed either, and the meeting broke up in confusion as two people's pagers went off simultaneously and some of those at the back of the room began to slink away.

My boss and I hovered in the corridor afterwards, buying cups of murky tea from a vending machine.

'Well, that was a complete waste of time,' he remarked, and I agreed, hoping he wouldn't ask for my opinion on anything. I hadn't followed the proceedings very closely.

'Can I ask you a hypothetical question?' I ventured. 'Sedic and I have been offered the chance to go to Indonesia for six months and I was wondering if there would be any chance of taking unpaid leave?' He sighed heavily so I hurried on. 'I know it would be difficult for you to find a short-term replacement but it might be very good experience for me. I'd be working in a hospital in Jakarta, learning all about tropical diseases and so forth. What do you think?' I tailed off.

'Would you be in paediatrics?'

'No, I think it's a general A & E hospital. I don't know the details yet. We haven't decided to accept. I just wondered . . .'

'Why Indonesia? What's the connection?'

'Sedic was born out there. He lived there till he was eight then, when his mother died, he was brought to Europe by his father. He still goes back regularly on business trips for some companies his father owns in the Far East.'

'It would certainly be an experience. I don't know anything

about medical practice out there but I expect it's very different from what you're used to.'

'Will you think about it and let me know if it would be possible?'

He tossed his half-drunk tea into a wastebin. 'I'm sure we could find a way if it's a choice between that and losing you altogether. But we're not talking about next week, are we?'

'End of October, early November. We need to make a decision fairly quickly, though. I'll keep you posted.'

All day, between ward rounds and paperwork, I was speculating about what it might be like in Jakarta and coming up with more reasons why it was a good idea to go. I'd never seen that part of the world; it would be interesting to learn about the culture that Sedic had been born into; and I'd always enjoyed the tropical diseases classes while I was training so it would be fascinating to get a chance to treat them at first hand. Behind all these benefits, there was another, more powerful instinct at work, a sense that it would be good for Sedic and me to have a proper adventure together before we settled down.

I called in to see Emily and her mother a couple of times and found them resting calmly.

'She took a feed this morning, about ten minutes. That's better, isn't it?' the mother asked hopefully.

I nodded. 'How's your husband coping at home?'

'Oh, it's good for him to see what I have to put up with day to day.'

I laughed and she smiled back, although worry was etched around her eyes.

On the way home, I stopped at a bookshop and picked up a guidebook to Indonesia. The photographs inside showed misty hillsides lush with palm trees, smoking volcanoes, men leading bullocks through waterlogged rice terraces, a vast Buddhist temple, exotic birds, lizards and flowers. I hadn't realised there were so many different islands, each with their own peoples; the bone structures and skin colours varied widely.

'*Selamat siang*,' I called to Sedic as he walked in the door. 'Am I pronouncing that correctly?'

He shook his head and threw his jacket across a chair. 'Couldn't be worse.' He glanced at the cover of the book. 'Looks as though you've made up your mind already.'

I stretched up to kiss him hello. 'Not at all. I'm just doing some research. I think the hospital would give me the time off, though, if we decide we want to go. I asked today.'

Sedic walked into the kitchen and pulled a bottle of wine from the fridge. 'Fancy a glass?'

'Sure,' I nodded. 'There's steak and salad for supper when you're ready.'

He handed me a glass of cold wine and I took a sip, watching him pour his own.

'You don't have any idea what kind of job Peter might have found for you out there. It could be deadly boring. And I've got no idea what he wants me to do. Funny how he expects us to make such a big decision without any real information, don't you think?' He took a slurp of wine, grimaced and peered at the label on the bottle.

'I suppose we could ask him to provide a few more details before we commit. And if we get out there and we're not happy, we could turn round and come home again. Or we could set off on our own and explore the Far East. There's loads of places I'd love to see. Vietnam, Cambodia and the Philippines would all be within easy reach.'

'That's not a reason to accept Peter's offer. We could go to those places on our own without being beholden to him.' He perched on one of the kitchen stools and began flicking through the guidebook I'd bought. I sat down opposite.

'Is that the reason for your reluctance? Because you'd feel beholden? We'd be working for him but that doesn't put us in his debt.'

'It's a ridiculously generous offer. That lump sum would make a big difference to us and he knows it. It's a carefully calculated figure.'

'What are you saying?' I couldn't understand his objection.

'Just that nothing's ever straightforward where Peter's concerned.'

I pursed my lips. It seemed stupid to pass up this chance to live overseas and receive a generous cash payment, just because of Sedic's pride. 'Tell you what, why don't we call Leona and say we might be interested but that we need to see a firm offer. Details of the work we'd be doing, salary, terms and conditions. That's only fair. Then when we have all the information we can decide.'

Sedic shrugged and topped up his glass.

'There's something I've never understood. Why doesn't Peter have an Italian name? Surely it should be Pietro?'

Sedic smiled grimly. 'He's too cosmopolitan, darling. It's Pietro in Italy, Peter in England, probably Pierre in France and Piotr in Russia. He likes to fit in wherever he goes.'

'How confusing! I wonder what name he signs on cheques?'

Sedic didn't answer. 'What time do you want to eat? I'm a bit peckish.'

I'd put the steaks under the grill and Sedic was mixing his special-recipe salad dressing when the phone rang. He picked it up and listened for a moment then passed the receiver across. 'For you. The hospital.'

I made a face, checked the meat was browning evenly, then walked over to take it. I wasn't on call that evening so it shouldn't be a summons to go in, but maybe they'd mislaid some notes or wanted to consult me on a patient's condition.

'Nicky? It's Cameron.' Cameron Wilson was a paediatric colleague, a friend of Geoff's, an able and trustworthy doctor. 'I'm afraid I've got bad news about one of your patients and I wanted to warn you before you came in tomorrow.'

I felt suddenly cold. 'It's Emily, isn't it?'

'She died just over an hour ago. I was called to the ward because she had severe breathing difficulties. We had trouble ventilating and then she went into cardiac failure. We tried to re-suss for twenty minutes but she was well and truly gone.'

I sobbed and it caught it my throat like a barb. 'Oh no!' Sedic looked up, alarmed. Tears gathered behind my eyes and I blinked to try and stop them.

Cameron continued. 'It all happened so suddenly. I thought it was a routine septal defect but there must have been some other weakness. I expect there'll be a post mortem so I decided I'd better warn you.'

I reached across the counter and pulled a tissue from the box to blow my nose before I spoke. Sedic squeezed my hand, his eyes questioning. 'I had a feeling she wasn't at all well but there were no unduly worrying clinical signs. I checked on her at four this afternoon. Maybe there's something else I could have done.' I caught Sedic's eye and saw he'd realised what had happened.

'Don't start beating yourself up. You did everything by the book. We both know how babies can deteriorate from perfect health one moment to life support the next.'

'I should come in and talk to the parents.' I wiped a stray tear from under my eye.

'They've just left,' Cameron explained. 'I said the usual stuff. No one knows why these things happen, no reason why any other children should be affected. The mother blames herself because she smoked a couple of cigarettes during the pregnancy.'

'Oh no, poor thing.' Tears started to trickle out again and I smeared them with the back of my hand.

'They've got two other children. They'll get over it.'

'I hope you didn't say that.'

'Course not.' He paused. 'Are you OK?'

I pressed a tissue against my eyes. 'Just a bit shocked.'

'Let's talk in the morning. Come and see me first thing. And don't worry. You did all you could.'

As I hung up, Sedic wrapped his arms round me and I stood there, listening to our steaks crackling and spitting under the grill.

'You told me I should have warned someone,' I mumbled into his shoulder. 'And you were right. But how? What on earth would I say? How will I cope next time this happens and the time after that? How?'

Chapter Three

———◆◆◆———

Around a week later, Peter telephoned me at the hospital.

'I've got some of the information you were asking for about the post in Jakarta. I think you'll be pleased.'

'Oh yes?' I said politely. Sedic and I hadn't discussed the trip again after deciding to ask for more details. I'd been working evening shifts so we'd barely seen each other, and Emily's death had been at the forefront of my thoughts.

'The hospital where you'd be working has four medical wards and an outpatients clinic. Surgical cases are referred elsewhere. The suggestion is that you'd work a forty-hour week, on shifts to be mutually agreed with the clinic, starting from early November. If possible, they'd like you to stay until the end of May, so that would be seven months altogether. Salary will be on a par with what you're getting here but we'll also cover return flights, the cost of the house and two live-in staff members, a car and a driver.'

I scanned my desk looking for a pen to write these details down but couldn't see one amongst the clutter of paperwork. 'Who would my contract be with?'

'Medimachines is funding your post as a goodwill gesture because the hospital has bought so much equipment from us. They're delighted and very keen to hear from you about the latest approaches to diagnosis and treatment in the West. Why don't I get my office to draft a contract and send it over?'

'Yes, OK, but what about Sedic? What would you want him to do?'

Peter paused. 'Just the usual. He knows what's required. Liaison between different companies, arranging imports and exports. The fact that he speaks the language and can negotiate directly with customs officials and government officers would really give me the edge right now. My other manager out there, Phil Pope, isn't very fluent.'

'Will you give Sedic a call to discuss the terms? He'll be at home this evening.'

'Good. I will. I also want to congratulate him. Leona says she's seen his latest work and it's terrific. Should make a wonderful exhibition and she's confirmed it for October.'

'That's excellent news.' So Sedic was wrong. They were booking in the exhibition before we'd agreed that we would go to Indonesia.

'You've both got an exciting few months ahead.'

As I drove down to Soho to meet some girlfriends after work, I was wondering about the ways in which medical practice might differ out there. Would they use the same diagnostic tests? Did the hospital have labs to check samples? How up-to-date would their pharmacy be? What if I found they were using substances that were banned in the West? There were all sorts of potential conflicts. Then, of course, there were religious differences. When I had treated Muslims at the Ormesley, I found the women were very shy and modest about their bodies, some of them unwilling to strip for examinations. I'd have to read up about their habits and taboos so I didn't put my foot in it on the first day.

I was crawling through the one-way streets of Soho looking for a parking place when suddenly a vibrating sound started up just by my right ear. I glanced round to see a fat bee about the size of a furry black grape hovering improbably in mid air. It chuntered past my shoulder and collided hard with the front windscreen, fell winded onto the dashboard, then began to clamber frenetically along the divide where glass met plastic.

Keeping a wary eye on the insect's progress, I wound down the window on my side; exhaust fumes blasted inwards but the bee ignored the turbulent change of atmosphere. It was emitting a noise in short electric bursts, like someone touching two live wires together, twitching its way up the convex curve of the windscreen. I couldn't pull over without incurring the wrath of the impatient procession of cars behind me, who would have no room to overtake.

After some anxious minutes, I spotted a narrow space up ahead in Soho Square and managed to manœuvre the car into it, holding my breath. I stretched across and pulled a brochure from the top of my bag, bent it into a rigid gutter shape and tried to shuffle the bee in the direction of the window with a contorted wrist movement, but as soon as the glossy paper touched it, the creature emitted a loud burst of sound and took off in a mid-air trajectory directly towards my face.

I yelped, dropped the brochure and flailed, hitting the bee with the back of one hand as I opened the door with the other, clattering it loudly against the car parked alongside. I squeezed out and glanced at the spot where my hand had made contact with the bee to see if I'd been stung. I could still feel the sensation, although there wasn't a mark. At that moment it flew through the car door, barrelling past my arm so fast I could feel the displacement of air, and disappeared into the evening rush.

I stood for a moment, heart drumming, then glanced round to see if anyone had witnessed the disturbance. The street was busy with office workers heading home, messenger bikes delivering canisters of film, *Big Issue* sellers gossiping in the park, but no one was paying any attention to me.

As I locked the car, I noticed that one of the back windows was open about an inch. That must explain how the bee had got in, but when could the window have been opened? I hadn't had any back-seat passengers for a while, or none that I could remember. I unlocked the door again and stretched in to wind it shut then relocked it and hurried down the street clutching my bag.

Anna was waiting at a table on the narrow pavement outside the wine bar. I kissed her hello and as soon as I sat down, we saw Claire's curly chestnut hair appear round the corner. One hand was clutching a mobile phone to her ear and the other was trying to hold onto a wraparound skirt that was flapping open in the sluggish breeze. She let go of the fabric to wave and it billowed behind her, exposing her plump, very white thighs. She clicked off the mobile, grabbed the skirt again and hobbled towards us, holding it firmly across the front of her legs.

'Sorry I'm late,' she gasped. As she kissed me, her arm nudged the table and wine slopped from our glasses. 'Marco wanted my saxophone for a gig tomorrow so I had to take it out to Notting Hill and the tubes were hell.' She wriggled onto a canvas chair and folded the skirt decorously across her lap.

'How did I guess it would be something to do with Marco?' Anna murmured.

I poured her a glass of wine. 'I'm glad you made it. I've got an offer that I hope you won't be able to refuse.'

Claire pulled a strand of hair across her mouth and looked coy. 'Oh, yes?'

'You've been telling us for ages that you're fed up with the bedsit, so I wondered if you'd like to stay in my flat for seven months. Rent free. I need you to look after it for me.'

'But where are you going?' Anna and Claire stared at each other in astonishment and I smiled mysteriously.

'It's not definite yet, but Sedic and I have been offered jobs in Indonesia, very well paid, with a big cash bonus at the end.'

'Jesus, you're not getting involved in heroin smuggling, are you? You do know they have the death penalty out there!' Anna raised her eyebrows.

'As if! No, I'll be working in a hospital and Sedic is managing some business for his dad. The Ormesley have said they'll get someone to cover for me till next June.'

'That's so exciting! Wow, I'd love to stay in the flat.' Claire bounced in her seat. 'When would you actually leave?'

'Here's your hat, what's your hurry,' I smiled, excited. 'Not till the end of October.'

'Sedic must be delighted you're going to spend time in his home country,' Anna remarked.

'I wouldn't say so. He's not mad keen on the trip, but the package was too great to turn down.'

'Does he have any family still out there?'

27

I shook my head. 'I don't think so. Maybe some distant ones. I'm not sure, actually. I must ask him.'

The sound of circusy music drifted up the street, getting louder until it drowned our conversation. Two men in embroidered waistcoats and plus-fours were approaching along the pavement, singing, shaking maracas and squeezing a huge accordion. The notes were so loud and blurred, you couldn't distinguish a tune. Anna pressed her hands to her ears. I bent to fumble in my bag for some change but by the time I'd extracted a few coins, the manager of the wine bar was hustling the muscians further up the street. When they were a block away, I recognised the song as the Dr Zhivago theme, 'Some day, my love . . .'

'The other good news is that Sedic's having an exhibition in Leona's gallery before we go.'

'That's in Mayfair, isn't it?' Claire asked. 'Posh people with more money than sense. Can I come to the opening? I love watching that type.'

I grinned. 'Of course you can come.'

'Has Sedic got work that's suitable for a Mayfair gallery?' Anna wondered. 'I would have thought his stuff was a bit radical for them.'

I shrugged. 'Leona seems to think it's fine.'

'She knows best, I suppose.'

I glanced at Anna, wondering what she was getting at. Maybe she wasn't keen on Sedic's work herself. She raised her wineglass to drink and, as I watched her, a thought came into my head out of the blue. It was a voice, my own voice, speaking as though I was at work, making a clinical pronouncement. 'She's pregnant,' the voice said. I couldn't see any telltale signs, no slight bulges or bleached pallor, but I knew it was true. I'm never wrong about pregnancies. Why hadn't she mentioned it? Either she didn't know yet or she'd decided to keep it secret for a while.

'What is it?' she asked, and I realised I was staring.

'I was just wondering if you feel OK? You look a bit peaky.'

'I'm all right. We're stressed out at the office, that's all.'

She reached across to pick up the wine bottle and I touched her hand to restrain her.

'Maybe you shouldn't be drinking. It's the worst thing for stress.'

'Is it?' Claire chipped in. 'It's always worked for me.' She began to tell some story about drinking tequila slammers with Marco the previous weekend.

I was only half-listening, wondering if I should say something to Anna. Surely she wouldn't be drinking if she knew? Maybe it would be better to speak in private, in case it wasn't welcome news. The thought crossed my mind that she might be annoyed at my interference. Perhaps I should leave her to find out and announce it in her own time? But then I remembered baby Emily. One of the effects of her death had been to convince me that I should always voice my instincts in future, even if it got me into trouble.

Claire's voice cut through my deliberation. 'I don't think I've ever seen you drunk, Nicky. What are you like?'

I laughed. 'Sedic says my conversation gets more creative. I'm not entirely sure what he means by that.'

'Your conversation is always creative,' Anna rebuked. 'What a strange thing to say.'

'I know what you're like drunk,' I told her. 'You start using the F-word as an adjective at least three times in every sentence. It's so obvious because you never swear when you're sober.'

'I just fall over,' Claire remarked gloomily. 'I wake up next morning with bruises in the most obscure places.'

Anna winked at me. 'Isn't that one of the symptoms they list in the Alcoholics Anonymous questionnaire?'

'Could be,' I teased. 'I think that's one of the ones they consider a definite diagnosis.' Claire pouted huffily.

I offered to give Anna a lift home and as soon as we'd pulled out of Soho Square, I broached the subject that had been on my mind all evening.

'Have you and Rob talked any more about when you want to start a family?' I asked, watching her out of the corner of my eye.

'Yes and no. We go round in circles. I think we should

move to a bigger flat first and he doesn't think we can afford it.' She looked round at me, curiously. Anna never misses a trick. 'Why do you ask?'

'It's just that I got a feeling this evening that you might already be pregnant. Is it possible?'

She was quiet for a moment. 'I suppose so. I'm a couple of days late, but that's not unusual. What makes you think that?'

I sighed. 'I honestly don't know. There aren't any physical signs. I just sense something different.'

'Oh, my God.' The news was sinking in. 'Can it really be true? I've got some testing kits at home so I'll do one tonight and call you later.'

'How will you feel?'

'If it's positive? I don't know. Nervous? Excited? Scared? Rob will be ecstatic.'

'Good, I'm glad. Congratulations.' I patted her knee.

She was staring out of the car window, her mind elsewhere. I felt a little pang of jealousy then stopped myself. My turn would come soon.

Sedic was watching TV when I got home, sprawled across the sofa with a beer bottle in his hand.

'Did Peter call you?' I asked, after kissing him hello.

He nodded and grunted in a tone that I took to mean yes, without taking his eyes off the television programme.

'He rang me at the hospital. It sounds like an interesting set-up out there. And I spoke to Claire tonight and she'll be happy to look after the flat while we're away. So what did Peter say about your job?'

'Same old, same old.' An overweight blonde in a very short skirt was being interviewed on the screen. It looked like some sort of documentary on prostitution.

'And the money?'

'Five hundred a week.'

I gasped. 'That's good. You must be pleased.'

'It's a bit of a bargain for him. Usually I'd get that amount for one trip lasting three or four days and now he'll expect seven days for the same price.'

I perched on the sofa beside him and took a sip of his beer.

'You can't work seven days a week. I won't let you.' The scene changed to show kerb crawlers driving down a dark city street. 'Peter's sending me a written contract to look through and he wants our final decision by Friday. Is he sending you a contract as well?'

'I've never had one in the past, so I don't know why he'd start now.'

I lay down on the sofa, curled into the shape of his body, and he clasped his arms round me.

'We're going to have such fun, you and me,' I whispered. 'A real proper adventure.'

I wriggled against his crotch and felt him stiffen in immediate response, but then the phone rang.

'That'll be Anna,' I explained, getting up. 'She's calling to tell me she's pregnant.'

In bed that night, after we'd made love, I remembered Anna's question.

'Do you have any relatives in Jakarta? Aunts or cousins or whatever?'

'No, there's no one. If there had been, I could have stayed with them instead of coming to Europe with Peter.'

I stroked his hair. 'I was just wondering if we could go back and explore your childhood hangouts when we're out there. We could figure out where your house used to be and visit your old school. Maybe we'd find some neighbours who'd remember you as a child.'

He rolled over to face away from me and huddled the duvet round him. 'The neighbourhood's probably been demolished and had skyscrapers built on top of it. Jakarta's changed beyond recognition in the last twenty years. It's a big commercial city now.' I smiled and snuggled behind him, spoon fashion. 'There'd be no harm in trying. I'd like to see exactly where you come from.'

There was no answer and, seconds later, his body gave the little involuntary spasm that signalled he was drifting into sleep. I shifted my arm so I didn't get pins and needles. It was always hard to get him to talk about the early period of his life. Subsequent events had been so traumatic that he'd blocked it off, but gradually, in our first few weeks together, I'd managed to extract the story. The events trickled out in fragments and I could tell there were some parts he'd never articulated before. Facts came easily enough, but the memories of what he'd felt as a child were dredged up from a more inaccessible place.

'Peter was living in Jakarta in 1970, setting up one of his businesses, and he hired my mother as his housekeeper,' he told me. 'Her husband Faisel was the gardener and they lived in the servants' quarters of his house, along with their fourteen-year-old daughter Anika. I've only got Peter's version of what happened next, but at some stage he and my mother began sleeping together.'

I frowned. 'What's Peter's version then?'

Sedic snorted. 'He's implied to me once or twice that she got pregnant on purpose to extort money from him. I find it hard to reconcile that with the cheerful, loving mother I remember, but I suppose it's possible. People are very poor out there.'

'So did Peter give her money?'

'Mmm,' he nodded. 'He bought us a house and gave Mum a monthly allowance to bring me up. I think we must have been relatively well off because I remember family trips to the Thousand Islands and visits to the old schooners in the harbour. I was sent to a good school and had a very happy childhood. My strongest memories are playing with my sister Anika. We used to paint pictures together. She'd do elaborate backgrounds and I'd add the people, cars and animals to them.' He paused and I rolled over to give him a hug, pressing my skin against his. 'I wish I had some photos or something to remember them all by . . .'

I waited.

'It was all so sudden. Maybe that's why I remember everything so clearly. Every single emotion is vivid, although I was only eight years old. I said goodbye to Mum one morning and Anika walked me to school as usual. Towards the end of the school day, a secretary came into our classroom and said that the headmaster wanted to see me and I thought I was going to get a row because I'd tipped over a tray of paint in the art class. Instead, I arrived in the headmaster's office and Peter was sitting there. He told me that I was to go with him because Mum and Faisel and Anika had been in an accident. I started to scream. He was a stranger to me. I mean, I hardly recognised him. I'd only met him a handful of times over the years.'

Sympathetic tears sprang to my eyes. 'What kind of accident?'

'I don't think he ever told me at the time – maybe he thought I couldn't deal with it – but it seems there had been an explosion caused by a faulty gas canister and the house just collapsed on top of them. Some areas of Jakarta are built from such flimsy materials they crumple like a pack of cards whenever there is an earthquake and I guess my family's house was like that.'

'So you didn't see them again?'

He sighed deeply. 'They'd gone. Just like that. Peter took me back to a hotel that evening and we sat in the restaurant but I refused to eat any dinner. I just sat there feeling shell-shocked. Afterwards we went into the hotel bar and he gave me money to play the pinball machine and bought me a cola. I forgot what had happened for a while and began to enjoy myself, then it came back to me that my family had just died and I was overcome with guilt.'

I squeezed his arm. 'Kids deal with grief in very strange ways. They often go a bit wild and hyper.'

'Peter kept telling me how brave I was so it became a point of honour not to cry. The next day we drove to the airport and I was distracted by the excitement of getting on a plane for the first time. I must have been so bloody shallow.'

'No, I don't think so. Kids have brilliant defence mechanisms. When there's a situation they can't deal with, they just switch off. In hospital, when I tell children bad news, they often start playing with their toys, or want to watch TV or demand some icecream. Once I had to explain to a little girl that she wasn't going to get better and she just nodded and fell asleep. It's a way of protecting themselves when they can't handle any more. Like you playing pinball that night or getting excited about an aeroplane ride.' I combed my fingers through his hair, feeling overwhelmed with protectiveness. 'So Peter took you back to Italy?'

'Yeah. I stayed with Gina, his Italian girlfriend, and her two older sons, but they used to beat the shit out of me whenever they got the chance. Peter was always away on business trips and when he came back he'd want to test my Italian, or my maths, or whatever. Then he broke up with Gina and we moved to Switzerland to live with Hanna, but she detested me right from the start.'

'How could anyone detest a motherless little boy?'

'I expect I was a bit naughty. Maybe she just hated children. She made such a fuss that I was sent to boarding school in Geneva.'

'So that was another language you had to learn?' I knew he spoke four or five.

'I got by, but it meant I never made any close friends, always the outsider. Then, when I was sixteen, Peter met Leona and we moved to London to live with her. That's twelve years ago now, his longest relationship to date. She's tough enough to be a match for him, that's my theory.'

'All the same, it was nice of Peter to bring you over to Europe. I suppose he could just have left you out there to stay with friends or go into an orphanage.'

'To be honest, I don't think he had much choice in the matter. It would have looked bad in the eyes of the Indonesian authorities if he had ignored his responsibilities. You have to remember that Peter had business interests to protect out there.'

'Surely it wasn't a purely cynical decision?'

Sedic exhaled loudly and raised his eyebrows. 'Of course it was cynical. He didn't want to be seen to shirk his duty and I suppose he foresaw that I might be useful to him one day. That's why he gets annoyed when I refuse to make trips. He never misses an opportunity to point out that if it weren't for him I'd be working in the fields, planting rice, or foraging for scraps in rubbish tips. He acts as though I owe him for the expense of my upbringing.'

I wondered if he was exaggerating. Peter had gone to a lot of trouble in educating him and flying him around Europe. They were just having a classic father-son conflict because Sedic didn't want to follow in his footsteps. 'Do you ever wonder what your life might have been like if you'd stayed in Indonesia?'

'Oh, sure, every time I go out there.' He rolled onto his side so our bodies were pressed against each other and looped his arm round my waist. 'I'd have been a lazy, wife-beating, expectorating swine who'd expect my dinner to be on the table when I got home in the evening. Not much different, eh?' He kissed the tip of my nose.

'But maybe you'd have been shown more love.'

'Don't give me any of your psychobabble,' he rebuked.

After our conversation, I had resolved to provide a stability he'd never known. A home where he could relax, someone who was always on his side. He moved in with me shortly afterwards, we found a studio space in the East End where he could paint, and I bought canvases, oils and frames to get him started. It had surprised me, six months later, when he asked me to marry him because I hadn't thought he was the conventional, settling-down type. I suppose he wanted to find the family life he'd lost when he was eight. That suited me. I already knew I wanted to be his family.

Over the next few weeks, Sedic spent more and more time at the studio getting his work ready for the exhibition. Sometimes, when he was on a roll, he'd spend the night there and just come home for a few hours' sleep in the morning. He seemed excited, as if everything was going well, and I was happy to see him busy and fulfilled. If only this exhibition was a success, it could make all the difference to his career.

Peter's contract had been very standard, with exactly the terms he'd outlined on the phone, setting my starting date as 4th of November. I signed it and sent it back and, almost by return, we received two plane tickets in the post for flights to Jakarta on the 31st of October. Then there were numerous arrangements to be made. I informed the hospital and popped into the travel clinic for my cholera and typhoid innoculations. Claire was delighted when I confirmed that she could stay in the apartment.

By the last week of September, I was so busy at work and Sedic was so preoccupied with his painting that we seemed to communicate solely by notes left on the kitchen counter and messages on the answer machine. One night I got home with a load of shopping and nudged the front door closed with my hip. Plastic carrier bags were cutting like steel wire through my finger joints and the car keys gripped between my teeth swung and hit against my chin. I staggered across the main room to the kitchen and dumped the bags on the floor by the fridge. A red light was blinking in the corner and I removed the keys from my teeth then pressed the play button on the answer machine. It was Sedic's voice, with the mock-ingratiating tone he used to ask a favour.

'Nicky, it's me. I left my stupid wallet somewhere and had to borrow money from old what's-her-name in the shop across the road. Could you slip over and give her a tenner before she shuts? I said you would. Thanks, honey, see you later.'

I checked my watch. It was only nine so the shop would still be open. I was briefly annoyed, because it would leave me short of cash to pay the cleaner in the morning, but he had a lot on his mind. Then I glanced into the front room and caught sight of a dark shape on the sofa under the window. The light was fading, so I walked over for a closer look. There was the purple leather wallet, stuffed with receipts, old bus tickets and miscellaneous scraps of paper. I flicked it open and delved into the notes section to pull out a ten-pound note, and a white business card fell out. It was small and flimsy and the words were in clumsy capital letters, as though it had just been run off on someone's laser printer. 'CELIA WING, PARTY ORGANISATION' it read, then there was a mobile phone number. I turned it over but there was nothing on the other side.

I pushed the card back inside, making a mental note to ask him about it later, then hurried downstairs and across the road. Ella was just lowering the metal shutters over the shop windows. She was wearing a red and white flowered summer dress and her blue-knotted flesh bulged out of the neckline and sleeves, while her swollen feet were crammed into white peeptoe sandals.

'Hello, dear, you look bushed,' she greeted me. 'Did you have a busy day?'

'We've got a lot of asthma attacks just now. The air quality's terrible.'

'Poor wee souls.' Ella padlocked the last shutter and stood up, clutching her lower back. 'Ooh, I'm a bit stiff today.'

'I hear that useless partner of mine borrowed some money from you this morning,' I said, waving the note. 'Is this right?'

'Oh, I never mind with him,' Ella laughed. 'He's such a charmer, you'd forgive him anything, wouldn't you?' She took the note and stuck it in a pocket.

'I'm not sure about that. Anyway, thanks for bailing him out!' I turned quickly to skip back across the road. If I engaged in any further conversation, it would quickly turn to one of Ella's ailments and how the doctors couldn't seem to diagnose it properly. Her clicking hips, or her mysterious palpitations, or the recurrent itchy rash under her bosom. Lose some weight, I was always tempted to say. Like three stone.

Coming back into the apartment, I looked around and thought once again how lucky I was. Sedic's taste had made it a stunning home. When he moved in, he'd brought colour to brighten my monochrome walls and stark furnishings: ochre and vermillion cushions, huge, arresting pictures, the sunny Mediterranean shades he painted the bathroom, and the mosaic tiles in the kitchen. The bookshelves held huge illustrated tomes on theatre and art, music and mythology. My CD rack was now full of zippy jazz, Chopin nocturnes, southern soul, music that touched you deep inside. I put on a Louis Armstrong CD and wandered into the kitchen.

As I was preparing the ingredients for a salad, I wondered again about Celia Wing. I hoped Sedic wasn't planning to use her to organise the opening night party. If the business card was anything to go by, she wouldn't be professional enough to handle the customers of an important Mayfair gallery. Surely Leona wouldn't let him engage someone downmarket? I had assumed the gallery staff would make the arrangements, but I wasn't sure how it normally worked.

I tossed some watercress, carrot, beetroot and cherry tomatoes in a bowl then pulled a cooked chicken from the fridge and began to slice segments of white flesh. A floorboard creaked behind me to the right and I turned to see Sedic creeping across the room, smiling. He raised a finger to his lips to stop me speaking then removed the carving knife from my hand and placed it to one side.

One palm cupped my bottom, while the other pulled my head towards his for a long, insistent kiss. His hands stroked downwards to wriggle my skirt up and he pushed me back against the corner where the counter met the stainless steel of the sink. Narcotic lust overwhelmed me, as it always did.

He pulled my knickers down round my ankles, where I kicked them off, then lifted me in one swift movement so I was perched on the corner, one leg resting on the draining rack. It was hot, dark sex, his thrusts shoving me against the kitchen cupboards behind. When I opened my eyes, his teeth were clenched with determination.

'You're so fuckable,' he murmured as he pulled out. 'You have no idea.'

I started to swing my legs round to climb down but he pushed them back. 'Stay there, let me look at you. Your cheeks are all red.' He kissed me and smiled, stroking a thigh with his finger.

'Do you know what I like about you?' he asked. 'Efficient anatomy.'

I laughed. 'That's romantic. What does it mean?'

'You have to finish some girls off by hand.'

'Don't be crude,' I giggled, pleased with the compliment anyway. 'What else do you like about me?'

He considered this for a moment. 'Flexible hips.' We both laughed, looking at my ungainly position, legs splayed in opposite directions. I shifted round and swung them to the ground, then stood up and pulled him close for a hug.

'I love you,' I whispered, ruffling his hair.

'Yeah, that's another thing I like about you,' he whispered back.

We made love again when we went to bed, and afterwards I lay awake in his arms, excited about his exhibition, the trip to Indonesia, my new job. I remember feeling as though my life was utterly perfect and there was no one else in the world I'd rather be.

Chapter Four

On the morning of the exhibition opening, Sedic was distant, jumpy as a frog, trying on jacket after jacket then leaving the rejected garments piled on our bed in apocalyptic chaos. He selected the outfit he wanted me to wear, a black linen dress that stopped an inch above the knee. He even chose the shoes to accessorise it with and suggested I carried the purple bag. Left to myself, it wouldn't have been the outfit I'd have chosen but I agreed to wear it because this was going to be his evening after all, and he did have better taste in clothes than me. I packed it into a holdall so I could get changed at the hospital after my shift.

'Don't come too early,' he instructed. 'Charles Blatchley wants a private view before we open. Get there between half seven and eight. Then afterwards, I've got an interview with someone from the *Independent*. I don't know how long it will take.'

I reacted as I always did in the face of his manic moods. I moved around behind him, unobtrusive, making coffee, ironing shirts, smoothing the edges.

'Are any of your friends going to be there?' he asked.

'Claire's coming with me. I'm not sure if Anna will make it, though. She hasn't been very well this week. Morning sickness.'

He frowned. 'You'd think she'd make the effort.'

I turned on the taps to wash up the breakfast dishes. 'I'm sure she'll come along another evening. It will be thronged with people tonight so you'll hardly be able to see the paintings. Anyway, openings are just about the glittery art set drinking Leona's wine and bitching to each other.'

I could understand why he was so agitated. I would never have the confidence to expose myself the way artists are forced to. Your ideas, personality, intelligence and the workings of your mind are all set out on canvas with an invitation to judge the creator. Sedic might act brittle and nonchalant, but beneath the skin he was just as vulnerable and scared of rejection as anyone else. Perhaps more so.

'Leona thinks there's a good chance Charles Blatchley will buy something. She says the paintings are very much his taste.'

'I can't wait to see them,' I smiled, but when I turned round, he'd left the room.

'Where are my black shoes?' he shouted from the bedroom and I dried my hands on the dishcloth and went into the front room to retrieve them from behind the sofa where I'd noticed them the previous evening.

I left the ward half an hour early, showered and changed, then went to meet Claire at the tube station as we'd arranged. Waves of commuters barged out of the lifts and dispersed across the road towards the late-night grocery store with its crates of scrawny vegetables.

I glanced at my watch and realised I was absent-mindedly fingering my engagement ring. It was a postmodern style that Sedic had chosen, white gold with slivers of diamond chips like broken glass. I slipped it over the knuckle and back down my finger again, watching the station entrance. Claire should have called to warn me if she was going to be late. I pulled the pager from my bag to double-check but no messages were displayed on the screen.

Two lifts opened their doors at once, spilling passengers into the ticket hall. Someone's briefcase jabbed the back of my calf and my knee bent reflexively. The crowd pushed past without looking at me and then the hall was empty again. I couldn't wait any longer, so I turned to walk back to the car, peering irritably over my shoulder. Arrangements made with Claire had a habit of becoming complicated. Meeting places were misunderstood, times half-heard, intentions scrambled. After one final look, I started the car and accelerated down the hill.

It had been a scorching Indian summer day and the air was viscous and stale, as though it had been exhaled too many times and any goodness used up long ago. Noises were especially loud: planes droning overhead, buses chuntering past, children shrieking, overexcited by the sunlight. My thighs were rubbing together under my dress and I splayed my legs wide and pushed the fabric down between them. My skin felt sticky and I could feel the armpit seams of the dress dampening.

Just past Great Portland Street, a taxi pulled to a halt, blocking my path, in a road reduced to a single lane by rows of cars parked bumper to bumper along either side. A couple began to unload bags, boxes and suitcases onto the pavement, so many it looked as though they were returning home from years spent overseas. I raised my hands, palms outstretched, in a gesture of incredulity. The woman nodded and held up a finger to indicate they would only be a minute. She opened her bag to pay the driver and a piece of paper flew out, so there was a further delay as she hopped comically, trying to stamp on the errant scrap dancing in the breeze.

Nerves fluttered in my throat and I had to swallow hard to calm them. I was anxious that something might go wrong, that the exhibition wouldn't be as successful as Sedic hoped. He'd worked so hard for this and it could be make or break. Good reviews and a couple of high-profile sales would set him on the fast track, but a bad press could thwart his progress. I wished Claire was with me. I'm always a bit shy at parties where I don't know many people and Sedic would be far too busy mingling with the other guests.

Finally the taxi moved and I drove on, across Oxford Street. Crowds of late-night shoppers pushed in front of the car. When I pulled into the street where the gallery was located, the clock read quarter past, later than he'd told me to arrive, and worry about the time galvanised me, so I pulled up in a residents' parking bay, deciding to risk a ticket. I remembered that Sedic had asked me to carry the purple bag rather than my leather satchel, so I quickly transferred some cash, a credit card and my keys. I slid the larger bag under the flap of carpet, checked my reflection in the driving mirror, then hurried down the road towards the glittering glass and chrome doors of the gallery, smoothing the black dress over my thighs.

The first impression was of a clinical brightness after the sultry honey dusk outside. I glanced into the room but couldn't make out individual faces until my eyes adjusted. There was a decadent aroma of harsh tobacco, fruity wine and oily perfume. The voices sounded whispery and blurred like wind blowing through poplar trees. A flashbulb ignited as someone took a photo, and I smiled seconds too late, so the picture would show a bizarre contortion, not one expression or another. Sedic once said that the attraction of my features lies in an animation that can't be transferred to celluloid. All I know is I never recognise myself in photos.

More flashbulbs popped and I kept the smile pasted to my face as I descended the two or three steps to the gallery floor and accepted a glass of sour citric wine from a tray. David Hockney was just in front of me, examining a painting, easily recognisable in his grey trenchcoat and brown felt hat. I watched for a moment, trying to read his reaction to the work, but he moved to the next canvas without a flicker. I turned to look for Sedic, or one of the many friends who should be present, and that's when I got the uncanny impression that several people were staring at me: a woman with a black Cleopatra bob, who turned away as our eyes met; a fat blond man in pale-blue-rimmed spectacles who didn't. There was a glint of jewellery and lots of dark panda eyes.

I began to move through the crowd, still searching for a familiar face, and then a hand gripped my elbow and lips spoke close to my left ear.

'It'd be best if you left now, dear, take my word for it.' The voice was husky, with a smoker's rasp, and an accent that seemed to mix many different places. I turned to look at the speaker and caught a whiff of cheap scent.

'What do you mean? I've just arrived.' The woman was like a carnival parody, with bright blue makeup smudged in circles round her dark eyes, shocking pink lipstick smeared over the edges of her lips, two round spots of blusher sitting on the fleshy pouches of her cheeks. The hair was bleached to straw, nicotine-yellow with black roots, and pulled up into a fountain ponytail on top of her head. Her tee-shirt displayed a crêpey cleavage and loose-skinned, yellowy arms.

'Don't say I didn't warn you,' she whispered, conspiratorially. 'I'm off now myself.'

An instinct made me look up to the balcony that looped round one end of the room. Sedic was standing with a group of four or five people, staring down at us. I raised an arm to wave and curved my lips to smile but stopped halfway. There was little reason to doubt that he saw me.

His gaze tracked down to my feet then back up to my face again and he said something to a companion, who looked at me and laughed. Sedic's expression seemed cold and contemptuous. Something crashed in my head, like a piano falling downstairs.

I turned to look for the woman who'd advised me to leave and saw the ponytail moving quickly through the crowd towards the door. Sedic was watching her as well. Then I steered my way towards the spiral staircase that led up to the balcony, conscious that people were interrupting their conversations to watch my progress. Something very odd was going on. As I reached the top of the stairs, a security guard blocked my path.

'I'm sorry, miss, but no one's allowed up here.'

'I'm the artist's fiancée,' I explained, pointing to where he stood just ten feet away.

'All the same, I can't let you through. They keep the money in the safe in there. Your fiancé will come down and join you when he's finished talking business, I expect.'

I glanced across at Sedic and the group he was talking to laughed with a sudden burst of sound.

'Sedic,' I called, and he turned, his eyebrows raised in a kind of supercilious expression. 'Can you ask him to let me through?' He shook his head slowly. 'What's wrong?' I asked. 'I'm sorry I'm late but Claire didn't show up. Surprise, surprise.' I was having to raise my voice so it would carry. 'Are you coming downstairs?'

Sedic took one step towards me and spoke quietly but distinctly, each syllable like a stab wound. 'If you leave now, you might manage to salvage some dignity.'

Tears pricked my eyes. 'What do you mean? Why are you angry with me?' He didn't reply. 'Who was that woman?' I asked.

'I thought she must be a friend of yours,' he replied coldly.

'I've never seen her in my life but she just told me I should leave. What's going on? What am I supposed to have done?'

'Oh, just go, Nicola. Don't you have any pride? Get out of here.' He turned and walked quickly into one of the offices behind him and shut the door with a decisive click. He was like a stranger. I'd never seen that granite expression or heard such a scathing tone from him before.

'Please can I get past?' I begged the security guard, taking another step upwards and trying to slip through. 'I must talk to him.'

'Sorry, miss.' He folded his arms and looked over my head.

I wobbled slightly on my heels and turned precariously to descend the stairs. My face felt frozen and a huge lump had formed in my throat. I was still clutching a glass of wine, so I took a gulp, then stepped carefully down into the room again. The chattering faces and clinking glasses seemed to be on the other side of a thick sheet of perspex. I walked through them in a daze, greeting a couple of acquaintances automatically, circling the room, trying to decide what to do.

'Where's Sedic?' a man asked me. I peered hard but couldn't recognise him or the woman he was with, although they seemed to know me.

'He's up in the office.'

'Isn't he coming down? I wanted to have a word.'

'Later,' I replied, and they walked on.

'I like your bag. Where did you get it?' It was a girl I knew Sedic had had an affair with before he met me.

'Sedic bought it for me.'

'Oh, look at the seashells.' She fingered them. 'I must ask him where he found it.'

I kept looking round every time I heard the gallery doors open, willing Claire to arrive. I desperately needed someone to talk to. Sedic hadn't reappeared on the balcony but the friends who'd laughed were still there and I felt as though they were watching me. Everyone was watching me, waiting to see what I would do next.

I only glanced at a couple of the pictures, making out bright earthy colours, hard shapes, tangled contours, and a little nugget of terror branded itself on the inside of my skull.

'This hasn't happened. I'm not here. It's a dream. I'm in the wrong place.'

At last it all became too much. A cacophony of voices followed me as I walked unsteadily across the room, put my empty glass on a tray and stepped out into the blowsy night.

Chapter Five

I turned to the left outside the gallery and swayed slightly, feeling drunk although I'd only had the one glass of wine. Something flapped against the side of the building. It was a programme for the exhibition, with a coloured picture on the outside. I picked it up. 'The Moments After', the title read and Sedic's name was printed below in huge letters. I couldn't make out the image in the dim light but there were jagged shapes and an awkwardness in the composition of fleshy pinks and grey–blues. 'Moments after what?' I wondered.

Back in the car, I sat with my head resting against the steering wheel. Was I doing the right thing in leaving? Maybe I should stay and talk to him when the crowds had dispersed. He was being nervous and temperamental and he needed me to remain calm and supportive. But he'd been vehement in his insistence that I should leave. Was he angry that I'd arrived late? That was the only motive I could ascribe to his attitude, but it seemed an excessive reaction. I'd never known him be cold and hurtful like that, and the fact that it was directed at me was incomprehensible. What had happened since this morning when he kissed me goodbye as I headed off to work?

Another group of guests arrived and pushed open the gallery door but there was still no sign of Claire. I made my decision, turned the key in the ignition and pulled out into the road. A taxi honked, making me jump. Jagged fear pricked my skin and a little hard knot griped in the base of my stomach.

Was there anything I had done to merit this treatment?

What did he mean when he asked, 'Don't you have any pride?'

Fortunately the roads were quiet now because I drove automatically, without concentration, my head buzzing with illogical, random, unspecific thoughts. Was he ill? Had he had a breakdown? Had I totally misread the situation? Was it all a joke? His few words ricocheted in my head like bullets.

I turned the car into our road and slowed down to hunt for a parking space. When I glanced up, there was a dim glow emanating from the apartment. He must have left the kitchen light on. For some reason, I felt apprehensive climbing the stairs, unsure what I might find. Streaks of moonlight penetrated the tall windows of the front room casting long white rectangles on the wooden floor. Down the corridor, the bathroom door was ajar, the light switched off. I pushed open the bedroom door and noticed that the duvet was pulled smooth across the bed.

I wandered back to the kitchen and poured myself a glass of wine from a bottle that was open in the fridge. It was starting to turn acidic and I shivered a little. Sedic had forgotten to cork it after he poured our drinks last night. Then I noticed a light blinking on the answer machine and rushed towards it, pressing the play button.

'Sedic, where the bloody hell are you?' It was Leona, sounding very cross. 'Charles Blatchley's here already, looking round. I told you he was coming early. Get here as fast as you can, for God's sake.'

What could have happened to make him late? If he'd missed the meeting with one of London's most important art collectors, that might explain his bad mood.

There was a click then another message. 'It's Claire. Sorry I was late, I'll explain when I see you. I just missed you at the gallery. Sedic said you didn't stay long. He's in a foul temper. Hope you're OK. Give me a call on the mobile when you get in.'

I slumped on one of the kitchen stools and leant on an elbow. Could it somehow be my fault that Sedic missed the meeting? Is that why he was angry with me? I picked up the receiver and dialled Claire's mobile but was immediately transferred to the answering service, so I left a message asking her to call me as soon as she could.

I pulled the bottle of wine from the fridge door and carried it through to the sofa by the windows in the front room, then I kicked my shoes off and knelt on the seat, curling my feet beneath me and huddling against the back to watch out of the window. The wine didn't seem so sour now, quite palatable in fact. The moon was almost full, surrounded by a white haze, and I remembered the superstition that it's bad luck to look at a full moon through glass. Or was it the new moon that was bad luck? Better not to risk it. I knelt to release the catch and pull down the window and night-time city sounds entered the room: a bus trundling up the hill, a distant police siren, a whispering rustle of rats and burglars and people sifting through dustbins. The light was mesmeric, as if the moon was emitting magnetic pulses of energy. The temperature had dropped a little but was still unseasonably balmy. The wine began to dull the painful edges and I felt a little more confident.

I hadn't done anything wrong and he was being absurdly unreasonable. It was just a tidal wave of anxiety about the exhibition and he was taking it out on me, as the person closest to him. In the past, he had been prone to occasional bouts of depression which lasted a few days at a time. He never wanted to talk until he was starting to pull out of it, then we'd sit and discuss whatever events might have precipitated the onset.

Maybe that's what I should do when he got back later, I decided. Rather than bombard him with demands for an explanation, I should wait until he was ready to talk. He was as tense as a time bomb, desperate for the exhibition to be a success. If he gained some recognition from it, and began to earn real money, it would take one of the pressures off our relationship. I would be able to work part-time for a few years while raising our children, without worrying about how the bills would get paid.

It was after eleven when the phone rang and I sprinted through to pick up.

'Hi, it's Claire.'

'Where are you?'

'I just left the pub. A crowd of us went for a drink after the exhibition closed.'

'Is Sedic with you?'

'He was in the pub, at another table, but he headed off about ten minutes ago.'

'Really?' My spirits lifted. 'I guess he'll be home soon in that case.'

There was a pause. 'I don't think he's coming back to yours tonight.'

'Why not?' I asked. 'What's the matter?'

Claire sighed. 'He's being a total bastard, that's all. Shall I come up to your place? I could get a cab and be there in quarter of an hour or so.'

'Yes, do come. You can stay over if you like.'

I jumped up when I heard the rattling of the cab turning into the road, like bottles vibrating in the door of an old fridge. I pushed the buzzer to let her into the hall and opened the door to listen to her trudging up the stairs. We hugged in the doorway and I breathed in the scent of her hair, a mixture of fruit shampoo and pub haze.

'I'm so sorry I was late for meeting you,' Claire began. 'Marco had left his car keys at my place so I had to take them over to him. I thought I'd have plenty of time but the tubes were outrageously slow. I waited for fifteen minutes at Piccadilly, can you believe it?'

'But if you were in town already, why didn't you just meet me at the gallery instead of getting a tube out of the centre so I could give you a lift back in?'

'That's what we'd arranged. It seemed more complicated to change it.'

'You could have paged me.'

'Yeah, I know, I only thought of that later.'

She could be unbearably frustrating. 'Come on. Let's go in and have a drink.'

'How come Anna wasn't there?' Claire asked as she watched me pouring the wine.

'She's not feeling very well,' I explained vaguely. Anna

hadn't mentioned her condition to Claire yet. She was still getting used to the idea herself.

We curled at opposite ends of the sofa clutching our glasses and I looked at her. 'I want you to tell me exactly what you said to Sedic and what he said to you because I've got no idea what any of this is about. Is he mad because I turned up late?'

'God no! I explained that was my fault. I got there about quarter to nine, I think, maybe a bit later. The place was totally mobbed but Sedic was talking to some people near the front door. I tapped his arm and asked where you were. I said, "She's going to kill me for being late." He kissed me hello, all arty and affectionate, then he kind of gave this dramatic shrug and said that you'd left about ten minutes earlier. I asked why, what happened, thinking there must have been some emergency at the hospital, and he said, "What do you expect? She's never been interested in my work. I'm surprised she turned up at all."'

'He said what?' I shrieked. 'Was he drunk or something?'

Claire considered the question. 'Not drunk, I don't think. Perhaps a bit hyper with all the excitement. I said to him, "You know that's a piece of crap. She couldn't have been more supportive." And he gave a kind of sneer and said, "That's what you think." Lots of people were congratulating him, shaking hands, slaps on the back, you know how it is. I had a quick look round at the pictures then went to the pub with a couple of friends, and around half ten, Sedic arrived.'

'Who was he with?'

'Leona and those boys that work in the gallery, a journalist woman, his friend Henry, a couple of Americans, an older couple. I was too pissed off with Sedic to go over and talk to them.'

'Was there another woman there? Apart from you and the journalist and Leona.' I wasn't sure why I had asked this question.

'Yeah, one of the Americans and a grey-haired woman. Why?' Claire looked at me suspiciously. 'You don't think he's seeing someone else, do you?'

'No, it's not that.' I frowned. 'Did you get a chance to ask him any more about why he's angry with me?'

'I didn't have to ask. He was telling everyone in a loud voice that you tried to stop the exhibition going ahead.'

This was so unexpected that I jerked upright, spilling my wine. 'Why on earth would I have done that?'

Claire looked surprised now. 'I suppose because of the subject matter of the paintings.'

'What do you mean?' I breathed, very still.

Claire hesitated. 'Haven't you seen them?' I shook my head. 'Oh, my God.' She reached over and gripped my hand. 'I thought you must know. Why on earth are you wearing that dress?'

'Sedic told me to wear it. Why?'

'What a bastard,' Claire whispered. 'It's in one of the paintings. They're all of you, Nicky, and they're not very nice. Personally, I wouldn't have been at all surprised if you'd tried to stop it going ahead.'

Air molecules floated in the moonlight, cell walls pulsed and atoms vibrated. I felt suddenly microscopic and a long way away.

Chapter Six

I woke the next morning feeling parched and nauseous with a taste in my throat like rancid poison. My first thought was to wonder whether I was due to go in to work; then I noticed the space in the bed beside me, and images flooded my head of the inexplicable scene at the gallery and the paintings that were supposed to be of me.

For Sedic to stay out all night wasn't unprecedented but something else seemed amiss in the creamy morning light. I looked round at the familiar shapes, textures and colours in the room. The louvred shutters across the windows; the little picture of Rama and Sita he'd brought me from his last trip to Indonesia; the chair painted with bright Andalusian flower patterns; the pine chest of drawers. My eye paused at the chest and I realised with a start that the sculpture of the lovers was missing from the top. It was a large fluid piece in grey pumice; round heads and voluptuous shoulders melted into each other, arms curved gracefully round and the lower bodies merged into one whole. The texture was airy and satisfying, making it a beautiful object to hold and run your hands over. Where could it have gone? Why would he have moved it?

A pressure nagged inside me, like a finger pressing on a bruise. I jumped out of bed and opened the cupboard doors. Right side mine, left side Sedic's. On the left, empty hangers rattled between a couple of old suits and a few shirts. All the jackets he'd tossed on the bed the previous morning had gone. I hurried through to the bathroom. The shelf above the sink was bare of his bristled shaving brush and special soap, the black and silver toiletries and the purple toothbrush. I was aware of my heart thudding.

I strode up the steps to the front room and saw straight away that the painting above the fireplace was still there. Sedic's favourite, it was a large study of wise, vibrant Indonesian women in a market, full of movement and colour, the foreground taken up with strange swirling vegetables and spices you felt you could almost smell. He wouldn't have left without it; he must just have gone to stay somewhere else for a few days; the thought calmed me a little. Claire lay asleep on the sofa, making tiny sighing sounds under the sheet, her leg trailing over the edge.

I went into the kitchen and flicked through the card index by the phone, stopping at the number for Sedic's friend Henry.

'Oh hi, Nicola,' he drawled, all bleary and slow. 'Sedic's not here. I don't know where he went.'

'You must know,' I insisted. 'Claire says you left the pub together. Where did he say he was going?'

'He didn't mention that. We just said goodbye at the tube station.'

'Which tube was he getting? Did you think he was coming home?'

'I don't know. I got the bus outside. I'm sorry, but I can't help you. I've got no idea what he's up to.'

I didn't believe him but didn't want to alienate him either. 'Don't you have any clues? You're his best friend. Surely he talks to you.'

There was a pause. 'I know he's upset that you tried to ban the exhibition. He's worked very hard on these paintings.'

'Henry, that's rubbish,' I insisted. 'I didn't try to ban it. I didn't know anything about it.'

'I thought he got a lawyer's letter from you yesterday.'

'Not from me, he didn't.'

'Look, this is between the two of you. I don't want to get involved. You should talk to each other and sort it out.'

'That's what I'm trying to do. How can I, though, when I don't know where he is?'

'He's bound to go to the gallery later. Why don't you leave a message for him there?'

'I'll do that, but if you see him first will you tell him that if he's received a lawyer's letter, it's nothing to do with me?'

I hung up and stared at the phone. There was something very odd about this lawyer's letter story. When would he have received it? The post had already been delivered when I left for work yesterday. Maybe it would have gone to the gallery but, if there was such a letter, who had it come from? Sedic couldn't possibly believe it was from me. He knew I hadn't seen the paintings and that, even if I had, I would never do anything to spoil his exhibition.

I tried to think where he might have gone. Sedic was so gregarious, he had several friendships I knew nothing about. One day he'd mention a Roger and I'd ask who's Roger and he'd evince surprise. 'Just about my closest friend in the world; I must have told you about Roger.' I trawled through the card index looking for inspiration. It was only half eight and the gallery wouldn't open till eleven at the earliest. I found Leona's home number and dialled but it didn't even ring before I was connected to a machine giving the gallery number. Next I tried his old friends Shirley and Tom.

'Hi, Nicola, how did the opening go?' Shirley asked brightly, and I could hear a toddler chattering in the background.

'Fine, I think. I don't suppose you've seen Sedic, have you?'

'Not for a couple of weeks. Why, what's happened?'

'He didn't come home last night. We had a bit of a tiff, I suppose, although I've no idea what it was about.'

'He's probably just being temperamental because he's wound up about the opening. He'll be home later, all boyish and irresistible, and you'll forgive him straight away. I know what you two are like.'

'I hope so,' I whispered. 'Let me know if you hear from him.'

I felt too humiliated to call any other friends and broadcast our problems more widely. Suddenly I remembered the leaflet in my bag and tiptoed through to the front room to retrieve it. Claire had rolled onto her back and was snoring gently.

I laid the glossy paper on the kitchen counter and stared at the coloured image, about ten centimetres tall. Two inverted V shapes represented, on closer inspection, the bent spread legs of a naked woman, lying back on a pillow. It was painted from the perspective of someone whose eyes are level with her feet, staring up through her legs. The genitals were sleek, neatly folded, surrounded by artfully trimmed hair. Sedic liked women to be well-groomed. He had always teased me if I didn't keep up to date with the feminine waxings, filings, pluckings and polishings.

Looking beyond the stylised genital area, the rest of the figure was foreshortened, the nipples uneven as if one breast hung differently from the other, the face unrecognisable, just a double chin and open mouth. Was it supposed to be me? There were no immediate similarities. Maybe Claire had just assumed the pictures depicted me because of their intimate nature. Sedic had painted nudes before but usually from memory and imagination rather than from models. His style was to use grand sweeping shapes rather than detailed figurative representation. I pondered the title 'The Moments After' again. Could it mean the moments after sex? Surely he couldn't have produced an entire exhibition on that subject alone? It didn't seem terribly profound and his work was usually more challenging than that.

My hands were shaky as I poured some coffee beans into the grinder and switched it on. The clatter echoed off the tiled walls and woke Claire in the next room.

'What time is it?' she called.

'Ten to nine. Do you have to be somewhere?'

'Shit! I'm teaching at nine o'clock.' Claire scurried through with the sheet draped round her. 'I've got to get to Camden.'

I sighed. 'OK, you get dressed while I call the school and tell them you're going to be a bit late, then I'll drive you up there.' I abandoned the coffee and pulled on the skirt and blouse I'd worn to work the day before.

Claire was distracted and chirpy in the car. 'I'm putting

together a show with these kids, but what a racket,' she explained. 'There are maybe three with some talent and the rest are doing it to get out of sports.' She's not the most sensitive person and we were almost at the school before she noticed that I was subdued and unresponsive. 'Don't worry about Sedic,' she advised. 'No doubt he'll come crawling back later today, begging forgiveness, but I think you should give him a bloody hard time. You don't treat people like that, especially not friends of mine.'

I hugged her and the mass of curly hair tickled my face. 'Thanks for coming over last night,' I said, then Claire jumped out of the car and hurried through the playground, skirt flying behind her.

I detoured to call in at the hospital on my way home. A four-year-old patient, Andrew, had had some bone marrow tests the previous day and I wanted to see if the results were through. All the signs pointed to leukaemia, but this kid was a fighter.

As I walked along the corridor, I saw Cameron sitting at a desk filling out some charts.

'You're here early for a day off,' he waved, and I went in and perched on the edge of one of his chairs.

'I was wondering if Andrew's results have come through?'

'Not yet.' He shook his head. 'Lunchtime probably. Do you fancy a coffee? I could use one.'

'You stay there,' I motioned. 'I'll go and pick them up.' Cameron had been on call all night and he now faced an eight-hour shift, while I had the next three days off. Rather than go down two flights of stairs to the canteen, I popped into the nurses' station at the nearest ward and persuaded them to give me a couple of coffees from the pot on their hotplate, promising to bring the cups back later.

Cameron took a sip as soon as I handed it over. 'Busy night last night. Did I tell you I met your replacement? Anne Gleneagles. She's older, a bit dry, not going to be much fun, I'm afraid.'

'Oh.' I hated the idea of someone else taking over my wards and my patients, imposing their own style of care, sitting at my desk in my office.

Cameron was watching me. 'You must be getting really excited. It's only about three weeks till you go, isn't it?'

'Three weeks on Tuesday.'

'Have you arranged a leaving party yet? We should give you a proper send-off. I'll speak to everyone if you like.'

I hesitated. 'Can you leave it for now, Cameron? I'm not sure what's happening.'

'What do you mean?'

I didn't plan to tell him but I suppose I needed someone to talk it through with. 'Sedic and I have fallen out. Something very strange has happened. I went to the opening of his new exhibition last night and he refused to talk to me, just told me to leave. Then Claire came round later and she said all the pictures are of me and they're crude and disgusting. It's a bizarre, horrible mess.'

'Didn't you see the pictures yourself when you were there?'

'Not really. I wasn't looking properly. Nothing leapt out at me.' I frowned. Maybe Claire was wrong about them. I hadn't thought of that possibility.

'Perhaps you should go back and have a look before you leap to any conclusions.'

'I suppose so. Yes, I think I will. But something's definitely going on because he told his friends that I'd tried to ban the exhibition then he didn't come home last night.' I gazed at Cameron, hoping he would be able to think of a rational explanation.

He sipped his coffee slowly. 'Forgive me for saying so, but it all sounds very childish. How long have you been together?'

'Two years.'

'And he can't pick up a phone and talk to you? Surely if he thought you wanted to ban his exhibition, he could have phoned you? There's more to this than meets the eye. I think you should go down to the gallery and find out. I'd come with you for moral support if I wasn't on duty.'

I stared at my fingernails, a huge lump in my throat, not trusting myself to speak.

'What will you do about Indonesia? You're kind of committed now, aren't you?'

I shook my head. 'I can't think that far ahead. I've got to find out what's going on and make things up with Sedic first of all.' I couldn't bear to imagine there was a chance we might split up over this. It was unthinkable.

Cameron was watching me curiously. 'It was a dramatic life choice you made, rejecting the nice-and-safe partner for the wild-and-unconventional one. I've often wondered what you're really looking for. Maybe you need to find someone with a mixture of qualities.'

'Who knows why any of us do anything?' I stood up. 'I'd better go now. You need to get on with your charts and I want to find my wild-and-unconventional one and try to sort things out.'

It was another filthy hot day but an autumn chill hovered under the surface warmth. Reflections from the gallery's glass exterior caused a silvery pattern to dance and shimmer in the air. One of Leona's dark-haired assistants hurried over as I walked in. He stared through me, appearing not to recognise me, although I was sure we'd been introduced a few weeks earlier.

'Would you like an iced tea? Or maybe a cappuccino? I'm sorry about the mess but we're still clearing up from the opening last night.' A tray of dirty wine glasses was balanced on a shelf and the acidic smell filtered across.

'I just want to have a look around, if that's OK.' I glanced into the gallery space. There were no other visitors at that hour.

'Would you sign our visitors' book, please?' He held out a pen.

For a moment, I considered using a false name, in case Sedic was annoyed that I'd come back on my own, then I realised how ridiculous that would look. He might even arrive while I was there. Why was I nervous about seeing him? My mind felt muddied and unable to react logically. I signed on the left of the page, leaving the columns headed 'Company' and 'Comments' blank.

The boy handed me a sheet of paper listing the prices of

pictures and told me to call if I needed anything, then headed towards the back of the gallery with a jerky walk that thrust his hips from side to side.

Just opposite the door was the picture that had been reproduced in miniature on the leaflet I'd picked up. I faced it from a couple of feet away and saw immediately how much detail had been lost at the smaller size. It was a searingly disturbing picture of a woman, from an angle that left her no dignity. Flesh swung loose from muscle, sacks of it collected beneath her thighs and spread in furrows around her middle. The breasts were cruelly distorted, pale beige nipples aslant. The expression on what could be seen of the face was dull and brainless. She was a lumpen manatee, a poor creature for fucking. The lines of paint led the eye first to the open mouth and then to the seamless purply genitalia surrounded by neat orange-tinted fuzz. I peered closely but there was nothing about it that looked like me.

A typed card was stuck to the wall alongside the picture, with the title: 'Lost at Sea'. It made sense of the blubbery texture of the woman, who was like some dumb aquatic creature, but it seemed a very angry, aggressive picture, quite unlike the work he'd displayed in East London.

I moved on to the next canvas, the one I'd seen David Hockney examining. At first glance, it was a craggy mountain landscape of odd knolls and angular crevices, with a series of little pools in the foreground that were ridged as though the surface had been ruffled by a breeze. Fine concentric lines curved across the roughened brown earth, looping like the contours on an ordnance survey map. Angular struts of rock clambered down to the pools on the right, the fourth strut bent awkwardly under the third, but there was something odd about the composition. My chest tightened. Could it possibly be some abstract representation of my feet, or was I being hyper-sensitive? That shiny bald hillock to the right could be a bunion; just by it, the little white crater might be a corn; the ridged and roughened earth, my stubborn hard skin; the struts of rock my bumpy misshapen toes; the pools my toenails.

I stood back to examine it from a distance and became more convinced. The part of my body I hated the most and strove to disguise in clumpy shoes and boots was now displayed in Technicolor on a gallery wall. He knew how I felt about my feet; this picture could only be a deliberate attempt to hurt me, particularly viewed alongside the typed card on the wall, which read 'Site of Outstanding Natural Beauty'. But why on earth would he do that?

I felt short of breath and began to move round more quickly, observing less closely. In isolation the next canvas could have been seen as a beautiful abstraction of dimpled white orbs streaked with glittering silver lines like snail trails. The thick brushstrokes gave it a three-dimensional texture and lusciousness. Blood tingled in my cheeks and I knew they must be reddening. In the next, a creamy white waterfall emerged from bracken-covered hillside; swollen purple fields undulated and short, bristly branches poked through the snowy hollow of an unshaved armpit. There was a sound like the sea in my ears. I realised my face was becoming more recognisable in each picture: that was the mole on my right cheek, the silhouette of my nose. I rounded a corner and straight ahead, on the opposite wall, there was a huge canvas, the one Claire had mentioned, in which I was wearing the black dress and carrying the purple bag.

Barely breathing, I stepped slowly towards it, the features coming gradually into focus, then I stopped a few feet away, so appalled I thought I might faint. I crouched on my heels and peered up at the painting. The face drew your attention first, its expression trying to be girlish and coy, but the eyes signalling fear of rejection, humiliation and discomfort. The reddish-blonde hair was cut in my shoulder-length bob style, but dishevelled and greasy-looking. The curve of her arms, holding up the dress, led your eye down to another focal point, a dark, messy hollow between the legs that she was straining to push towards you in a gesture that begged 'Take me!' Rounded sacks of fat bulged from her thighs – surely they were fatter than mine? – and bunions protruded from the strappy high-heeled sandals. It was a mixture of a little girl striving to be grown-up and to please, and a gauche, ungainly and very desperate woman.

I sat down on the gallery floor, my legs bent awkwardly,

gulping quick dizzy breaths. I cupped my hands across my face, partly to hide from the pathetic gaze of the painted woman, partly to try and think. How could he humiliate me like that? What was he playing at? A clicking of heels approached across the wooden floor and a hand touched my shoulder.

'Are you all right?' Leona's voice asked. 'Do you want a glass of water?'

I nodded without removing my hands from my face and the heels clipped away again. I felt chilled and very lonely.

'Here you are.'

I took the glass and sipped the water. It tasted chalky, like tap water rather than bottled.

'Why don't you come upstairs to the office? You can lie down until you feel better.' Leona grasped my arm, and I rearranged my legs and rose to my feet. She was the last person I felt like talking to but I didn't know what else to do at that point. I gripped the railing hard as we climbed the steep curving staircase. Leona shifted a bundle of papers onto the floor so I could lie down on a cream canvas-covered sofa and I swung my feet across the arm.

'James has only just told me you were here or I'd have come down earlier.' My eyes were closed but I could feel Leona watching me closely. 'Is this the first time you've seen the pictures?'

I nodded. 'Although I hear I'm supposed to have sent a lawyer's letter trying to ban the exhibition.'

Leona tutted. 'That's just a stupid story Sedic made up for that journalist's benefit. I told him not to, because she'd see straight through it, but he's desperate to get publicity for his work somehow.' I felt as though I was going to cry and turned my face towards the back of the sofa. 'I suppose he wasn't sure how you would react to it all.' There was a click then a fizzling sound as Leona lit a cigarette. She blew out the smoke and a nauseous wave of it reached my nostrils.

'Oh, I think he must have known perfectly well how I'd react.'

Leona took a deep drag and exhaled noisily. 'I hope you're not going to be stupid about this. Art is art, and you have to be a bit controversial to make a breakthrough in our world.'

'Since when did humiliating pornography count as art?'

'You're such a baby.' Leona's voice was distant and bored. 'What on earth are you doing with someone like Sedic when you don't understand the first thing about painting? Don't you know who he is? Did you think you could change him into a househusband to do the cooking and bring up your babies for you?' I didn't reply. 'I'm not saying you haven't been good for him. He's a lot calmer since you've been on the scene, but it would be nice if you took more of an interest in his work.'

'That's not fair!' I protested. 'It's his choice. He prefers not to discuss work in progress.'

'Didn't you ever find that a mite strange?'

I shook my head. 'I don't know what I thought.'

'You're taking this all very personally and you shouldn't, you know. Most of these pictures have nothing to do with you. In the rest, you might be the model but you're not necessarily the subject. He's used you, sure, but that's what artists do. I think it was Oscar Wilde who said that a true writer would betray his own mother if it made a good story. Something like that.'

I swung my feet round to the floor and sat up. 'Aren't you worried by the misogyny of these images? There's a real hatred of women and a disgust for their bodies. It makes me feel' – I sought the right word – 'unclean. I'm really surprised at him.'

Leona stubbed out her cigarette fiercely, making the bracelets on her arm jangle. 'This might be Sedic's big chance to make his name. It would be churlish of you to try and hold him back because you're squeamish about the subject matter. You don't even understand what he's trying to express.'

'I don't think I want to. Why did he let me walk in last night, wearing that dress as he'd told me to, the one in the picture, without some kind of warning? And then he wouldn't even talk to me once I was here. He ordered me to leave. It was awful.' I shuddered at the memory.

'Just don't overreact. Talk it through with him, let him explain. Once you're in Indonesia, you'll have time to work things out.' Leona extracted another cigarette from a case on her desk and regarded it thoughtfully.

'I don't think I can go now. Everything has changed.'

'Now you're being silly. You have to go. You've signed a contract, for one thing. It's all arranged and you'll have a wonderful time. Stop thinking about yourself all the time and make an effort to understand the man you're planning to marry.' She put the cigarette back in the case again.

I felt claustrophobic, as if the atmosphere of the gallery was poisoning me. Not just the smoke, but the brutality of the paintings and the steely monetarist calculation that was foremost in Leona's attitude. I stood up. 'I'd better go. If you see him later, will you ask him to call me, please?'

'I'm sure he'll call you later.' Leona's tone was smug. 'Why not have a look at the rest of the pictures before you go? You might learn something. You might even want to buy one.' She cackled with a fruity smoker's laugh.

'Thanks for the water,' I said, then pulled the office door shut behind me. I stepped slowly down the stairs, curving my feet inwards to keep my balance. Suddenly I felt nervous that Sedic would arrive and I'd have to decide what to say to him. I needed space to think it all through before I saw him again.

James was waiting at the bottom. 'Are you feeling better now? Shall I call you a cab?'

'No, thanks.'

As I walked back towards the door, my eyes were drawn to a series of still lives on a wall I hadn't looked at before. I stopped in front of one. It was an arrangement of a green wine bottle lying on its side, an old-fashioned silver cigarette lighter with the top flicked open, a haphazard pile of ropes and a burnt white candle lying in a pool of wax. The caption read 'Maintaining Interest'. I felt crystal pains in my joints, a dull ache as though I was succumbing to a virus. I turned away from the pictures, and hurried out of the gallery and down the street towards my car.

Chapter Seven

———◆◇◆———

I watched Anna, rapt in concentration as she grated Parmesan on top of the tortelloni. Some of the creamy flakes missed the bowl and floated onto the counter like dandruff. I noticed that half a dozen grey hairs streaked her head, just above the ear. Dark pigmentation tends to fade first, but Sedic didn't have any grey hairs yet.

'How's the morning sickness?'

'It's not just the morning. It comes and goes throughout the day.'

'Are you taking anything?'

'A friend at work has given me some herbal teabags with ginger and they seem to help.'

'Really?' I raised an eyebrow. 'Make sure you keep snacking during the day to keep your blood sugar up. Dry biscuits are good if you can't face anything else.'

'I'm just crossing my fingers that it will pass by three months. Anyway, tell me about you. Claire says you didn't know anything about the kind of pictures Sedic had been working on. You must feel very shocked.'

'I didn't really take them in last night with everything else that was going on, so I went back to have a proper look this morning.'

Anna clattered the pepperpot down on the table. 'And?'

'I don't know what to think. Some of them are recognisably me, and they're cruel and ugly.'

'Claire says they're all about sex. Obscene pictures of

women in suspenders and chains, grasping money in their teeth.'

I thought back. 'I don't remember seeing those.'

'She says the face is often yours but the bodies are grossly distorted, with hideous sagging flesh. She found them quite unbearable to look at. It's as if he finds women disgusting, especially ageing women.' She pushed the bowl of pasta into the centre of the counter and served some onto our plates. We perched on the kitchen stools to eat.

'I guess I'm still in shock. It's so out of character that I keep feeling as though it can't have been him, that there's been some mistake. Maybe he has an evil twin brother who's responsible.'

'Or maybe there's another side of him that you've never seen. You've said to me before that he's a very private person. Perhaps he's got a secret life you don't know about.' She gave me one of her penetrating looks.

'But I keep coming back to the fact that he wanted to hurt me. There's no getting away from it. That must have been his aim.'

'Maybe he's making some kind of artistic point by super-imposing your face – the woman he loves – on grotesque bodies. Is that possible?'

I put down my fork, feeling queasy at the fattiness of the cheese. 'The bodies are me as well, at least partly. He used my feet, my poor feet. That's the worst thing.'

'What's wrong with your feet?' she asked.

'Have you never noticed? I've got terrible feet.'

'Show me.'

I kicked off my mules and held them out, twisting the ankles from side to side. 'I inherited them from my father. The bones are deformed, causing a very high instep, and the stress of walking pushes weight towards the big toe, forming bunions and curling the toes like claws. I may have to have an operation one day when it gets too pronounced. But Sedic knows how sensitive I am about them. I hate anyone seeing them. It's OK with you, but I get completely paranoid about going to shoe shops and I always wear those big clunky styles.'

Anna was peering down critically. 'They're not that bad. Everyone hates their feet. I've got bunions as well.' She slipped off a shoe to demonstrate. Her feet were long and slim, but with awkward lumps at the base of the big toes.

'But don't you see? It has to be a personal attack on me. Why else would he have done it? Who would want a picture of my feet on their living room wall?'

Anna took a forkful of pasta and chewed thoughtfully. 'What makes me angriest is the way he let you arrive last night, wearing that dress, without an inkling about anything. He just threw you to the sharks.'

'And he spread a rumour that I'd tried to ban the exhibition, in some bizarre publicity stunt. I mean, he should have told me and I could have joined in, maybe chucking some wine around and shrieking a bit.' I tried to smile.

Anna banged her fork down. 'I'm sorry, but you don't do that to someone you're supposed to love. It's a complete betrayal. And who knows what that journalist made of it all? Claire says he was sounding off to her in the pub.'

I had forgotten about the journalist. 'Why, what was he saying to her?'

'Claire didn't elaborate.' Anna was looking towards the fridge and I followed her gaze then realised it was unfocused. There was a tiny tickle on my forearm and I looked down to see an insect so small it was barely distinguishable, just a speck of brownish black. Astonishing how sensitive the nerve endings were, to pick up such minute stimuli. I squashed it between my thumb and forefinger.

'Was he talking about me?'

'Nicola, he's a complete bastard. He has no loyalty to you or to anyone, but it will backfire because he'll be the one that looks bad in any press coverage, not you.' Anna's cheeks were pink with anger.

'I think that's what he wants,' I mused. 'He'd love to be the bad boy of the art world. Anything, so long as people are talking about him.'

'You're not going to start making excuses for him, are you? You do realise he's gone too far?'

I clutched my head in my hands. 'When you're planning to spend the rest of your life with someone, you don't walk away at the first sign of trouble. Surely he deserves a chance to explain himself?' Anna looked sceptical so I continued. 'You have to understand that he's like a child. Sometimes he pushes me to see what he can get away with and it's up to me to set the limits.'

She placed a hand over my forearm. 'Nicola, you have to start thinking about yourself. You've had a terrible shock. You should take it easy for a few days and look after yourself.'

I sighed loudly. 'I just need to talk to him. I know there can't possibly be an innocent explanation for all this but it would be easier to deal with if I knew what he was thinking.'

She squeezed my wrist hard. 'Just keep your wits about you. Don't let him off the hook. I know you. If you see him, you'll sleep with him and if you sleep with him, you'll get back with him and all this will be brushed under the carpet. You're too forgiving sometimes.'

There was a big part of me that found that thought comforting. What I wanted more than anything was to be able to turn the clock back and for none of this to have happened.

That night, the second after the exhibition, Sedic didn't come home again. I lay awake, watching the figures click round on the digital clock by the bed, and at eight o'clock in the morning I threw on a tracksuit and hurried across the road to the shop. Ella was sorting the papers into bundles and inserting the Saturday supplements, her vast bottom thrust in the air, threatening to split the seams of her skirt.

'How're you doing, my precious?' she called cheerfully.

'Oh, not too bad. I've got a couple of days off.' I picked up *The Independent* and handed her the money.

'How's that naughty boyfriend of yours?'

I stared at her, wondering if she could possibly have heard about the exhibition. Surely Ella didn't follow events in the art world? 'Why's he naughty?' I asked.

'He's a cheeky so-an-so. Always making personal comments,

he is.' She patted her hips and chuckled. 'You've got your hands full with that one.'

'You can say that again,' I agreed and swivelled my eyes comically. Astonishing how you can conform to expected stereotypes when your life is falling apart.

Back in the kitchen I extracted the paper's Arts section and spread it on the counter. Theatre, Music, Books. One page had a long article maligning the Royal Academy Summer Exhibition, saying it was for self-important Sunday afternoon dabblers with minimal technique. 'Who wants to see yet another wave breaking on a rock? Who cares to watch the artist's mother pouring a cup of tea?' Sedic would love it. He'd submitted a couple of pictures but neither had been selected. On the next page there was an interview with a thriller writer who lived on the oceanfront in Malibu, and boasted that he'd never sold less than a million copies of any of his books.

I closed the supplement and put some coffee beans into the grinder. They must have a longer lead-time for arts coverage. The exhibition would probably be reviewed next week. I poured boiling water into the coffee pot and carried a tray into the front room with the rest of the paper. There were few stories of interest: 'Nose grown in laboratory', 'More surgeons investigated in transplant scandal', 'Six babies born in Italy from frozen eggs'.

An image buried in the middle pages caught my attention. There was a mass of tangled limbs, almost unrecognisable in newsprint. The headline above ran, 'A spiteful way to leave your lover'. I read the story so quickly I couldn't take it in and had to skim back to the beginning before I was sure I wasn't imagining it.

'Artist Sedic Molozzi chose an original and vindictive method of breaking up with his girlfriend,' it read. 'His latest exhibition, entitled "The Moments After", features pictures that show her in a range of humiliating sexual poses.' It claimed that I had 'stormed out' soon after arriving at the opening night party. 'Asked about the hatred and misogyny of the pictures, the artist explained, "It's an honest depiction of what men feel when love has died but they're still trapped in a situation. I couldn't think

how to tell her it was over so I let the pictures do it for me."'
The journalist described Sedic as nasty and twisted and his actions
as despicable, adding that the pictures were clichéd. It finished,
'Dr Nicola Drew did not turn up for work at Ormesley Hospital
yesterday but friends say she feels hurt and betrayed. "Bastard"
was a word that featured in most of their verdicts.'

I reread it several times, my hands shaking so the newspaper
rustled and creased. My foot twitched and nudged the coffee,
making it slosh onto the floorboards. My face burned with a
mixture of embarrassment and rage. How could he say all that?
This kind of coverage must be what he'd intended, but could
it be true that he'd planned the whole exhibition as a way
of telling me he no longer wanted to be with me? It seemed
extraordinarily complicated. Or was it all a massive stunt? In
that case, why hadn't he contacted me? Neither explanation
seemed wholly convincing.

Suddenly it occurred to me that he might have stayed in
his studio for the last two nights. It wouldn't have been
very comfortable but there was an old sofa in the corner.
The kitchen and bathroom facilities were minimal and light
flooded in through the glass roof but it was the obvious place
if he wanted to be alone. There was no telephone. I glanced
at the clock and decided to drive over there.

The street was littered with detritus from a fruit and veg market
the day before: cardboard boxes, oozing tomatoes, torn cabbage
leaves, plastic bags and crumpled drink cans. I parked right
outside the squint wooden door alongside the security-barred
frontage of a building supplies retailer. Paint had flaked off in
uneven patches and the wood underneath was weathered and
ridged like driftwood on a seashore. I pushed it open and walked
into the dark stone hallway.

There was a festering sewage stench – they were always
having trouble with the drains – so I breathed through my
mouth as I climbed the stairs two by two. The only light filtered
in through frosted glass windows on each landing. Some of the
doors had nameplates but I knew the rest were empty. Sedic's

studio was on the top floor, six flights up. As soon as I reached it, I knew he wasn't there because a huge bolt stretched across the door, fastened with a small shiny padlock like the kind cyclists use. I knocked anyway and called his name, then I took hold of the padlock and rattled it. The edge of the bolt embedded in the door frame wiggled loose in the rotting wood. I examined it. Just a tiny wrench would probably pull it free. One of the screws was dangling uselessly and the other didn't look very secure. I pulled gently and could feel it moving in its socket.

Without thinking it through, I looped my fingers behind the bolt, just where it entered the frame, and pulled hard. It came loose with a cracking sound as the wood splintered apart. I twisted the bolt downwards to clear the frame then pushed the door open.

The heat was sweltering, like a glasshouse in a botanic garden, and the air was thick with dancing dust particles and the sharp smell of turpentine. I looked at the sofa first, and it was obvious from the rumpled yellow sheet and indented pillow that he'd been sleeping there. A mug by the bed was half-full of milky coffee that had formed a skin on top but hadn't yet curdled in the heat. I walked into the kitchen alcove, just a tiny cubicle with a stone sink and a shelf for a kettle, teapot and cups. A chipped plate and two glasses were stacked in the sink and Sedic's shaving soap and brush were balanced on the side. He didn't like electric shavers.

There was a bulging black rubbish bag on the floor and when I pulled it open, a cloud of tiny black flies rose into the air. A takeaway pizza box was balanced on top and a milk carton with today's date. I closed the bag again, trying to arrange it exactly as it had been before.

I prowled round the studio ticking off a mental inventory. His clothes were piled behind the sofa and a couple of suits were suspended from the top of a stack of blank canvases. At the end of the room, bright brushstrokes scrawled across a large canvas and I went over to look. It featured the same huge inverted V shapes and swollen curves of many of the gallery pictures but not in any conjunction that could form a human body. The geometry was fractured and rearranged, and the overall effect was more cheerful and positive. There was a sense of movement and balance. On a table alongside, gobs of paint had dried to molten plastic on his palette but the tubes of colour were immaculately arranged and his brushes were cleaned. He liked order when he was working.

I thought I heard the street door bang far below and turned nervously, listening for footsteps on the stairs, but none followed. It was then I noticed the statue of the lovers, sitting on its own on the floor, looking smaller than I remembered. It must be significant that he'd taken this rather than any of the other pictures or sculptures in the flat – a symbol of the withdrawal of his love, perhaps? But then I looked back at the picture he was working on and realised it had a similar fluid motion and satisfying form. His latest model was made of pumice rather than flesh.

I decided to leave a note and opened my handbag to pull out a spiral-bound notebook and biro. I sat on a wobbly wooden chair and sucked the end of the pen for a moment then scribbled quickly. 'Sedic, I saw the piece in *The Independent* this morning. Hope the publicity will do you some good. Don't you think it's time we talked about all this? I'm around over the weekend, back to work on Monday. Please get in touch.' I hesitated, wondering whether to write the word 'Love' but just signed my name instead.

Then I had to decide where to leave it. Maybe if I closed the door behind me and slipped the bolt back into the frame, he wouldn't realise I'd broken in, then I could push the note under the door. I went outside to try but the wood was so splintered it wouldn't grip the metal bolt any more. I considered adding a postscript apologising for breaking the lock but decided against it. I tore the sheet of paper from the notebook and propped it on his pillow then left, pulling the door shut behind me.

Chapter Eight

It hadn't occurred to me that other friends might have read the article in *The Independent*, so I was staggered by the number of messages displayed on the answer machine. The red light was blinking furiously like a warning light on the controls of a diving aircraft. As I stood staring at it, wondering if one of the messages might be from Sedic, the phone rang again. I listened as my voice told the caller to speak after the tone, then an unfamiliar accent filled the kitchen. It sounded like an older woman calling from some kind of bar or club, because there was tinny music and a blur of voices in the background.

'Sedic, it's Celia. Time's running out and you'd better get the money to me this weekend. A service has been rendered and all that. Don't be a prick about it.' She hung up.

I picked up the phone and dialled to find out the previous number then jotted it down on a corner of the newspaper. It looked like the code for a mobile. Then I pressed to play back the messages. There was a long rambling one from Claire, apologising for giving the journalist that quote about me being hurt and betrayed, then asking if I'd like to go to a party that evening; my mother was next, sounding anxious, checking that I was going to visit as planned the following weekend; Cameron Wilson said he'd read the article and wanted to see if I was OK; Sedic's friend Shirley said the same thing; Claire rang again to ask if I'd give her a lift to the party; and then I listened once more to Celia's message. I couldn't work out if the tone was playful or threatening, but this time I recognised the voice. I was pretty sure it was the husky accent of the woman who'd approached me at the exhibition. Seconds later, I remembered where I knew the name from: the card that had fallen out of Sedic's wallet, belonging to Celia Wing, party organiser. What did she mean about a service? What could she possibly have done for him? I shuddered. It seemed sinister and inexplicable that he should be involved with someone like that.

The front door buzzer sounded and I jumped. The thought passed through my head that it might be her, come to collect the money he owed her.

'Nicola, it's Peter,' the voice crackled. 'I need to talk to you. Can I take you out for a spot of lunch?'

'Come on up,' I said, cursing as I pressed the entry button. I wanted to be alone that afternoon. I'd been thinking of going back to bed for a nap, or just to think in peace. I rushed into the front room and picked up the tray of coffee things, mopping up the spilt puddle with the sleeve of my tracksuit. I folded the newspaper and tucked it under my arm then kicked my slippers out of sight under the dresser; I had just carried the tray through to the kitchen when he knocked at the door.

He pulled me into a stifling hug and kissed both cheeks, holding on longer than I felt comfortable with. I edged away and he followed me in.

'What a surprise!' I said brightly. 'I didn't know you were in town.' He was wearing a purply brown suit and tie and carrying a beige raincoat over his arm.

'I flew in this morning,' he said, shaking his head sadly. He hung his coat over the back of a chair. 'Leona told me what's happened and I felt I had to come over straight away to apologise to you on behalf of my family. I'm devastated about it.' He sat down on the arm of the chair. 'What must you think of us?'

'It's not your fault,' I frowned.

'I'm furious with Leona,' he exclaimed, sounding very Italian. 'She should have put a stop to this when she first saw the pictures. At the very least, she could have warned you.'

I spoke cautiously. I didn't want to get dragged into a position of criticising his partner. 'She's been very helpful. She explained to me that I shouldn't take it personally. She said artists may use people as a model but it doesn't mean that they are the subject.'

'All the same, he had no right. I don't suppose he's here?' He looked round accusingly.

'No, I haven't heard from him since. Have you seen the papers this morning?'

'Definitely libellous. I think you should sue. I'll give you the number of a good lawyer.' He reached into his pocket.

I stopped him. 'No, thank you. I want to forget all about it.'

Peter stood up and walked across the room to put an arm round me. I'd never been alone with him before and felt extremely awkward. 'Promise me one thing, Nicola. Don't write my boy off. He needs you so much. I know you must be hurting but please try to understand him and give him another chance. I'll do anything I can to help if you'll just try to forgive him.'

I shrugged off his arm and busied myself folding the newspaper on the counter. 'It should be your son saying this to me.'

'I know, but he won't. He's too proud. Come out for lunch with me and let's talk and see if we can figure out a way to resolve this terrible situation.'

I took him to a local bistro full of Saturday shoppers, with the menu chalked on a blackboard at one end. We ordered goat's cheese tarts with salad and a bottle of Sauvignon. Peter began to talk about Sedic's childhood and I listened, fascinated, to some anecdotes I'd never heard before.

'He was always such an angry little boy, kicking out at anyone who tried to help him. Gina's sons did their best to include him but he'd break their toys and tear up their homework as soon as they turned their backs.'

Sedic had told me they used to beat him up. Maybe that was why. 'But you can understand that he was disturbed after what he'd been through – the deaths of his mother, stepfather and sister, moving to a new country with you. His life had been massively disrupted.'

'That's true, of course. We tried to be patient but everything

I gave him, he would destroy. We took him to a psychiatrist in Rome who prescribed some transquillisers but they never worked. He just fell asleep after he took them and was as bad as ever when he woke up.'

'Do you remember what they were?' I asked, but Peter shook his head blankly.

'That was twenty years ago, but I'm telling you now because it seems he's still following the same pattern. Whenever someone is good to him, he has to hurt them and push them away. It happened with Gina and her sons, then Hanna in Switzerland. We sent him to a fantastic boarding school but he kept running away. I supported him when he got into art school but he dropped out after a term. You can see how self-destructive he is.' Peter put down his fork and regarded me seriously. 'He has everything going for him – a beautiful, intelligent woman ready to marry him – and he self-destructs again.'

I frowned. It all seemed a bit too glib.

Peter continued. 'One time, I spoke to a counsellor about this, and she said maybe he's scared that if he lets himself love someone too much, he might lose them and risk repeating the pain he went through when he was eight all over again. Whereas if he pushes them away first, it's easier to cope with.'

'I'm familiar with that psycho-analytical theory, Peter, but it doesn't fit the facts. We'd been happy together for two years. Why would he suddenly reject me now, without any warning?'

He shrugged expansively. 'All I can say is, you're not alone. He's been doing it to me all his life. When I first asked if he wanted to learn about the business, he was very eager and he picked it up extremely quickly. I even talked about making him a partner and passing the whole set-up to him when I retire. Then wham!' He clapped his hands together hard. 'Out of the blue, he drops me! Doesn't even return my calls, refuses to help any more. It was very hard, because I'd come to rely on him.'

'After the East End exhibition, he wanted to concentrate on his painting more and consolidate on the success he'd had there.'

Peter looked disbelieving. 'I asked him to make – what? – two trips a month at most. Six to eight days out of every thirty. Did that really stop him painting? On the contrary, I thought it would subsidise his art. I've always encouraged him to paint. Why do you think I talked Leona into giving him this exhibition?'

I shook my head blankly. What he said made sense.

'Maybe it's unhealthy for a father and son to work together. Maybe it couldn't have lasted forever.' He drained his wineglass and regarded me seriously. 'It's just vitally important to me that he goes to Indonesia. I need him out there for the next six months or I stand to lose a lot of money. After that, I swear I'll never ask him to help with the business again unless he wants to.'

'Peter, I can't predict what he's thinking of doing. I have no idea what's going on in his head.'

'You have more power over him than any of us. If you tell him that you're going anyway, even if you pack up and leave without him, I know for a fact that he'll follow you. He's crazy about you, completely besotted, but the strength of his feelings terrifies him because he's such a complicated, mixed-up kid.'

I felt as though I was going to cry and cleared my throat. 'He's just dumped me. He told that journalist he wants to break up with me.'

'That's rubbish! I've seen the way he looks at you and I've heard him talking about you to Leona. He's so proud of you. You're his touchstone, his centre of gravity. He might be throwing a tantrum right now and behaving like an impossible child, but he won't let you go without a fight. Believe me.'

There was so much conflicting advice coming at me from different directions that it was hard to reach inside and get in touch with my own instincts. I was floundering, casting around for some certainty to cling to, and here was Peter offering the reassurances I most wanted to hear. 'But what if I go to Jakarta alone and he doesn't follow me?' I asked.

'He will. No question.' Peter gulped the rest of his wine. 'If you have to be there on your own for a couple of weeks my local manager, Phil Pope, will show you round and introduce you to people. You'll have a lovely time. What are you going to do if you stay in London? The hospital have got someone else to fill your job so you'd be moping around at a loose end in a dreary British winter. On the other hand, you could be on a beach in the tropics, exploring another part of the world. I've found you a wonderful house, the arrangements are all made and the contracts with the clinic are signed. It seems quite straightforward to me.'

I looked at him curiously. Was there an undertone in his reminder of my contractual obligations? Peter was a shrewd man. I wouldn't say I trusted him, but what he said made sense.

'I want to try and find Sedic this weekend and talk to him. I'll let you know what he says and we'll take it from there.'

'Don't expect him to be conciliatory just yet. I'm sure you know my son better than that. Be firm and resolute and he'll follow you. He needs you to be strong. It's the best tactic if you want to save your relationship.'

Before we parted, Peter gave me a folder containing my work permit, details of the house he'd arranged and some forms to fill out so they could pay my salary directly into my bank account. As he'd said, it was all arranged, but I still didn't know what to think or what was the best course of action.

As soon as I got back to the flat, I unfolded the newspaper and dialled the mobile number I'd scribbled down earlier. It was answered on the third ring.

'Is that Celia Wing?' I asked.

'Who's that?'

'My name's Nicola Drew. I'm Sedic's girlfriend. I think we met at his exhibition the other evening.' I held my breath.

'You've got the wrong number, dear,' she said, and hung up.

I redialled straight away and spoke as soon as she answered. 'You just left a message for Sedic on my answer machine,' I said. 'I wanted to let you know he's away from home at the moment but I'll ask him to ring you if you like.'

'I've never heard of anyone called Sid-Dick,' she drawled.

'It was your voice on my answer machine.'

'I don't think so, dear,' she said, and hung up again.

This time, when I rang back, an automated voice told me the number was unavailable and that I should try again later. Why would she deny knowing him? I had absolutely no doubt now that the voice on the phone belonged to the woman with the fountain ponytail who'd warned me to leave the gallery. I took my personal address book from my handbag and carefully transcribed her number under W for Wing.

Chapter Nine

───────◦◦◦───────

I kept the windows shut and the doors locked even though the air was stale with the plastic smell of warm car seats. It's a rough neighbourhood and sporadic groups of revellers staggered past on their way to parties, clutching carrier bags of booze. The girls wobbled on high heels and some boys kicked a tin can in an impromptu football match. Even at midnight, the light was grey and hazy rather than dark, but gradually a stillness settled, the noises faded and the street emptied.

I was sad and apprehensive but determined. Anger had been pushed to the background, behind my need to understand. I'd sit there all night if I had to. The minutes seemed to pass slowly, then I'd notice that half an hour had gone by, as if the recent full moon had altered the atmosphere and was playing tricks with time.

I had no idea what to expect, but I tried to rehearse all the potential scenarios in my head. If he arrived with a group of friends, I'd get out of the car and ask quietly if we could speak in private. If he didn't come back at all, I'd return the following night. What if he had a girl in tow? I clenched that image between my teeth till my jaws hurt.

I don't know what time it was when his white-tee-shirted figure appeared round the corner from the direction of the tube station. His elegant, loose-limbed walk always makes him seem taller than he is. I watched him get closer, so beautiful in the moonlight, and when he noticed me, I unlocked the door and climbed out of the car. He stopped and regarded me, his eyes huge in their sockets.

'How are you?'

'Fine,' he replied.

I paused, trying to gauge his mood. 'Please can we talk?' I asked.

'There's nothing to talk about.'

I opened my mouth to disagree but the icy glaze of his expression stopped me. 'Congratulations on your exhibition,' I said instead. 'It seems to be going well.'

'Is that all you came to say?' He sounded impatient. 'Because I'm tired and I want to go to bed.' He stepped towards the door.

'Sedic, why don't you come home?' I pleaded. 'I miss you.'

He shook his head, but he wouldn't look at me. 'I think I've made it quite clear what I want.'

I felt as though I was watching myself from the other side of the street, as if the scene was a complex and frustrating dreamscape. 'I don't understand. What happened? What did I do?'

'Nothing,' he said. 'There's nothing I can say to you right now. Things change, that's all.'

'Have you met someone else?' I dug my fingernails into my palm waiting for the answer.

'You really don't have much imagination, do you?'

I struggled to find a clinical professional mode. This wasn't going to work if I disintegrated into a heap of emotion.

'So you're telling me that you're leaving me, just like that?'

'Past tense,' he said. 'I've already left.'

'Sedic, stop this. Talk to me. Tell me what's happened.'

'I thought you said in your note that you'd read the *Independent*.'

'And that's the truth, is it? That you wanted out and you didn't know how to tell me? Am I supposed to believe that?'

'Believe what you like.'

'What about Indonesia?' I asked. 'Your Dad came to see me this afternoon and he's desperate for you to go.'

'He'll get over it.'

'But I'm committed. I've signed a contract and they've arranged a replacement for me at the hospital.'

'Don't be ridiculous. Of course you don't have to go now. He can't make you. You're such a fucking stickler for the rules.' He turned away and shook his head quickly. 'Nicky, you can't go to Indonesia. Someone like you would never survive out there. You're too straight; they'd run rings round you. Just talk to the hospital and sort yourself out and stay in London, for God's sake.'

'Sedic, we need to talk about this properly. Can I come in?'

'It's obvious I can't stop you,' he said nastily.

'I'm sorry about the lock. I'll get it fixed.'

'Not my problem,' he said. 'You pay the rent. I'll only be here for a few more days while I'm looking for my own place then I'll call to arrange a convenient time to pick up the rest of my stuff from your flat.'

'Our flat,' I stressed, tearfully. 'Yours and mine. Why are you being like this?'

'You paid for it, you can keep it. I'm not interested in your flat and I'm not interested in you.'

The words were designed to sting. I gave a little yelp. Sedic turned and pushed open the door and it swung shut behind him with a rush of wind. I hesitated for a few moments then locked the car and followed him. It would be too awful to walk away now without getting an explanation from him but my feet dragged on the stairs. He was in a recalcitrant mood, unlikely to soften. If we were at home, after a row, I'd give him space to calm down but if I left now, I didn't know when I would see him again.

He was in the kitchen, brushing his teeth at the sink and he'd taken his tee-shirt off. I watched the angles of his shoulder blades moving under the unmarked skin, the bumpy ridge of his spine, the glimpse of dark hair in his armpits. I was so attracted to him, it was like a physical pain. He spat out the toothpaste, rinsed his brush under the tap then cupped some water in his hand to slosh around his mouth and spat again, before putting the brush in a cup on the shelf. I moved aside to let him walk past and his hip brushed mine in the narrow doorway. He sat down on the sofa and bent to unlace his shoes.

'Celia Wing rang for you,' I said in as calm a voice as I could manage. 'She says you have to get the money to her this weekend.'

'Oh, for fuck's sake,' he shouted, making me jump. 'Stop being so bloody controlling. You think you own me because you've paid for this and that but it doesn't fucking work that way.'

'She was a bit stroppy on the machine, says that a service has been rendered and called you a prick.'

'I'll deal with it,' he said, pulling off his socks.

'Is she a friend of yours?'

'That's none of your business.'

'What kind of service could someone like that possibly have done for you?' The thought made me feel sick.

'Just fuck off.'

He stood up and unzipped his trousers then stepped out of them. He was wearing the blue and white boxer shorts I'd given him. He pulled back the grubby yellow sheet and lay down on the sofa and arranged it on top of him, then folded his arms across his chest. Our eyes met and I held his gaze and for a split second I thought I could read sadness in his expression, maybe a modicum of regret, but he was the first one to look away.

'What on earth happened, Sedic?' I was fighting back tears now. 'I know you used to care about me. You can't have faked it all. So how did it just vanish into thin air? How can you be so cruel after all we've been to each other?'

'Life moves on. I fell in love one day then I got bored and fell out of love again.' His voice caught slightly and he stared fixedly at the wall opposite.

'I still love you,' I said, aware my voice was trembling. 'I'm sorry if you don't want me to. I miss talking to you and being with you and making love with you.'

He pulled himself up on an elbow and regarded me evenly. 'Take your dress off then,' he said.

'What?' I breathed. There was a buzzing in my head and I wasn't sure if I'd misunderstood.

'You heard me. Take your dress off.'

I was torn between wanting desperately to make love with him so I could pretend everything was all right, and fear of his unpredictable mood. Our lovemaking had always been erotic and exciting but never cold, and it felt desperately sad that he appeared to be offering me a heartless fuck, like some casual conquest. What did he want? Should I try and kiss him? If I was affectionate, how would he respond? Would he push me away? Was this some kind of test?

He looked amused as he watched me weighing up the options. He pulled back the sheet, inviting me, and I could see there was a lazy hard-on poking against his shorts. It would have been so easy. He waited. I looked into his eyes again but the expression was closed; no warmth there.

'I'm going now,' I whispered at last, and he shrugged as if he didn't care either way. 'Call me when you want to talk.'

I ran out, yanking the door shut behind me and hurried down the stairs before I could change my mind. I unlocked the car and the emotion I'd been trying to contain burst out. I clenched my fists round the steering wheel and howled with a raw animal grief that shook my frame.

There was a movement on the opposite pavement and I saw a figure looking across curiously, as if they were about to come over. Hastily I wiped my eyes on a yellow duster I found in the glove compartment then started the car and sped off.

When I got home, I curled up on the sofa and cried till my eyes stung and my chest ached so much I was breathing in great heaving gasps. I went over that decision again and again. If I'd stayed, would it have made him weaken? I remembered Anna's words – 'If you sleep with him, you'll get back with him' – and wondered if it would have worked that way. I'd never refused him sex before, not ever, not anything, no matter what.

I analysed every word of our conversation, over and over. There weren't many of them, after all. He'd said, 'There's nothing I can say to you just now,' implying there might be at some future date. He didn't seem to want me to go to Jakarta. The mention of Celia Wing made him angry. The financial inequities between us were still frustrating him. And he was still physically attracted to me. Could I have been right about the flicker of sadness or was I fooling myself?

For a long time, I sat in a mental blur, without a single clear thought in my head but too rattled to consider sleep. Everyone seemed to have a different agenda for me – go to Jakarta; stay in London; forget about Sedic; give him space and he'll come crawling back. Some birds began squawking outside the window, seeming louder and more obstreperous than ever before, as if they might be trying to influence my decision.

It was unimaginable to stay in London, in our flat, without him; to drive to work each morning and come home to an echoing emptiness; to walk round each street corner wondering if I'd bump into him with another girl. On the other hand, maybe Sedic was right and I wasn't tough enough to survive in a foreign country on my own. Then I considered Peter's theory that if I flew out first, Sedic would follow, but after the scene this evening, that seemed unlikely.

No. I had to accept that whatever I did, I was alone now. It was going to be a long time before I recovered from this shocking rejection but maybe if I went to Indonesia, I could put some distance between myself and the unmanageable emotional turmoil of the last few days. By the time the misty grey light of morning seeped through the blinds, I knew what I was going to do.

Chapter Ten

———◦◦◦◦———

The plane took off from London mid-evening and headed east into time zones already ahead of ours, so at midnight by my watch the whole of Turkey was in the still dead hours of early-morning blackout. Stewardesses moved round the cabin pulling down blinds, because over Iran, we were flying into pink-streaked dawn without having slept. I dozed intermittently but woke as we began to skim the Indian coastline, too high to see more than terracotta land and sparkling sea. A miniature TV screen showed our position on the map, heading due south over India then turning east towards Malaysia. As they served breakfast in our cabin, it was early afternoon for people on the ground below.

The confusion of time zones mirrored the clutter in my head. Images of the patients I had said goodbye to the day before – stoic white-faced Andrew whose leukaemia had been confirmed, and Mumtha, my little bald amputee learning to walk on a prosthesis – mingled with the faces of friends and colleagues at my leaving party. I ran through all my financial arrangements, anxious that I might have forgotten a standing order or left a bill unpaid. I'd gradually begun to unwind the complex tentacles of a life shared with Sedic, cancelling his cash card and the rent for the studio, and closing down the credit card account he had access to. I'd sent a formal note outlining these practicalities but there hadn't been a single word in response. My parents had been furious and very alarmed when I told them my engagement had been called off and that I was travelling alone.

Anna and Claire had been tiptoeing round, treating me like
an invalid, in a way that just increased my sense of isolation.
Everything felt complicated and unreal.

We touched down in Singapore and I wandered the sophisticated terminal for an hour, amongst shops selling impossible
electronic gadgets and bouquets of white and fuchsia orchids in
Cellophane-covered boxes. I found a door to an outside terrace
and gasped as I stepped from air-conditioned sterility into dusty
equatorial heat, like the blast in the face when you open an
oven door. Planes taxied round the runways and an old man
was sweeping the floor meticulously, several minutes to each
square foot, his head bent in concentration.

After takeoff from Singapore, we crossed the Equator and
immediately hit turbulence. According to my guidebook, the
east coast of Sumatra is notorious for plane crashes and shipping
tragedies, as air and weather fronts clash and seas are rough.
Behind me a woman was crying noisily. It felt as though
we were leaving civilisation and heading into an altogether
wilder place.

The touchdown in Jakarta was bumpy and uncertain and I
became apprehensive about the customs formalities. Peter had
warned me there might be trouble because of the working visa
in my passport and that I should offer a fifty-dollar bribe to
smooth the way, but I couldn't imagine how I would do that.
Smile and hand it over? Should I say anything? Would they even
speak English? In fact, the official barely looked at my passport
before waving me through. I piled my cases onto a trolley and
was heading towards the green channel when a uniformed man
caught my eye and waved me over. He smiled when I pulled
up the trolley beside him, took it from me and walked off. I
followed, assuming with alarm that my luggage was going to be
searched for contraband. Would they object to the few medical
supplies I'd brought? Or the two bottles of wine?

Instead of walking into the customs area, the man pushed
my trolley through automatic glass doors into the main airport
terminal. I rushed after him, confused. There was a sign with
my name on it so I waved at the Indonesian man holding it,
presumably the driver who had been booked to meet me, then

gestured frantically towards the trolley that was fast disappearing with my luggage. The driver pursued my cases and I ran behind. There was a rapid exchange and the trolley was handed over, but then my driver pulled a few coins from his pocket and handed them to the man, who nodded his appreciation. The driver turned to me.

'Are you Dr Drew?' he asked in English. 'My name is Dadong.'

'How do you do.' I shook his hand. It was cool and slim.

'Is this all your luggage?' I nodded, still bemused.

'The car is this way,' he gestured, and led me out of the airport building into the sauna atmosphere outside. It was early evening and the light was a heavy creamish-grey; the air was thick and damp and the temperature oppressively warm, like a foggy day in London but hot, if such a thing was possible. Sweat filmed my skin and my shirt stuck to me before we reached the car, only twenty yards away. It was a dark green kind of people carrier that looked as though it had rolled off the assembly line that morning, so perfect was the gleam of the paintwork.

Dadong opened the rear door with formal courtesy and I climbed into the cool interior then turned to watch as he arranged my cases in the back. Other drivers stood around in clusters, smoking and talking, brightly patterned shirts hanging loose over their trousers, but my driver was neat in a smartly-pressed pale khaki shirt and trousers of a slightly darker shade, belted at the waist. He must be married, I thought to myself. Surely a man wouldn't iron his own shirt quite so impeccably? His black hair was short and well-kept, his features fine.

He climbed into the driver's seat and started the car.

'Will you be my driver while I'm here or were you just sent to pick me up today?' I asked.

'I will be your driver,' he replied.

'That man in the airport – was he trying to steal my luggage?'

'No, no,' he explained. 'He's a porter.'

I frowned. 'But what was he doing inside the customs area?'

'That's how they get work,' he told me and I relived the

scene from that perspective. It looked as though I had been conned into hiring a porter when I hadn't needed one. I felt foolish, a naïve tourist. He must have seen me coming.

We pulled out of the parking area in front of the boxy sixties terminal building and slid onto a loop road lined with vivid fuchsia-pink and red flowering bushes.

'Your English is very good,' I commented. 'Where did you learn?'

'I picked it up,' he said. 'I've worked for a lot of English people here.'

We were approaching fast-moving streams of motorway traffic but Dadong didn't slow down at all. He pulled out into the nearest lane, causing the other cars to rearrange themselves and make room. I soon found out that he never gave way to other cars, in any circumstances. He drove smoothly and confidently, as though ours was the most important vehicle on the road and we had a God-given right to preferential treatment. Astonishingly, other drivers didn't honk or complain, but manoeuvred deferentially to let him pass.

'Was it hot today?' I asked.

'It's always thirty-one degrees in Jakarta,' he told me.

'What, every day?'

'Every day,' he confirmed.

Wherever I looked, the foreignness of the country was apparent. Some scrawny goats were grazing on the central reservation of the motorway. People in conical straw hats trudged through water-logged fields. A rickety yellow bus sped past with passengers clinging to the roof or hanging precariously out of the doors. Everything is going to be different here, I thought.

We stopped at a toll booth and Dadong wound down his window and handed over some change, without saying a word.

'You must let me give you the money,' I said. 'And however much you had to pay that porter in the airport.'

He shook his head. 'No, I deal with that. I claim the expenses back from the company.'

'Which company?'

'Medimachines is my employer.'

'Are you sure that's OK?' I asked.

'That's how it works.'

We were entering the city now, and the rice paddies were replaced by tower blocks inscribed with international brand names: Seiko, Hambro, Shell. The traffic slowed to a crawl and I peered ahead at the three lanes of solidly packed, barely moving cars.

'Do you think there's been an accident?' I asked. 'Why is it so slow?'

'It's always like this,' he told me. 'There are too many cars here.'

'Do we have far to go?'

He looked at his watch, which I noticed he wore on his right wrist. 'We'll be there in half an hour,' he said with authority.

Concrete walkways straddled the road. The car windows were tinted but when I looked out at the drivers crawling along beside us, they stared back with interest. Up ahead, four skinny boys zigzagged on foot through the traffic, stopped by a car and three of them began to sing while another shook a tambourine. The voices were enthusiastic rather than tuneful and I guessed from their heights they were only about five or six years old. A window wound down and some coins were handed to the tallest boy. They moved on to the next car then drew level with us. Before they could begin singing, Dadong opened his electric window and handed them some coins then closed it again, but instead of moving on, the boys clustered by my window, peering in, smiling eagerly and holding out their hands.

'Should I give them some money as well?' I asked.

Dadong reopened his window and spoke to them rapidly, in a level tone, and immediately they darted off through the traffic, tambourine clattering.

'What on earth did you say to them?' I asked.

He closed his window. 'I told them their singing was terrible.'

'No, you did not,' I laughed. 'Why did it scare them so much?'

In the mirror, I saw him smile for the first time, obviously pleased with himself. 'Sometimes when gangs of kids crowd round your car, they let down the tyres or scratch the paintwork. Then if you get out of the car to confront them, they might have a knife.'

'Not those kids, surely? They looked far too young.'

'Yes, but maybe their brothers are waiting round the corner. Who knows?'

When we reached the next corner, an intersection where tall concrete pillars supported another road overhead, there were half a dozen women in short skirts and high heels standing on a triangular piece of kerb. They wore bright-coloured wigs and lurid makeup and I stared, fascinated. Something about the scene felt peculiar and finally, it was the strong jaws and muscular legs that made me realise they weren't women at all. I gawped. It seemed a strange place for a group of transvestites to meet for a chat.

'What are they doing?' I asked Dadong and he replied without looking.

'Waiting for business.' His tone was disapproving.

We pulled off the freeway at the next intersection into a narrow rutted road lined by shops. 'Best Jeans' one was called; bamboo furniture was piled high outside another; then there was a mini-supermarket with some grimy underwear pegged on a washing line outside. Dadong honked impatiently and swerved around cars that got in his way, then we turned a corner into a street where the houses were painted white and set back behind walls with barbed wire on top and guards standing at the gates. A man was pedalling a pushbike with an ice-cream cart behind that was playing a tinkling tune. Dadong nearly forced him off the road as we overtook, but he didn't seem to mind.

We stopped outside one of the gates, Dadong sounded the horn and a uniformed guard peeled back a metal barricade, then we drove up a short lane into a garage and stopped.

'This is your house,' he announced.

A tiny, very pretty woman in a bright pink dress appeared, smiling broadly, and the guard opened the car door. Dadong performed the introductions.

'This is Ali,' he said, 'your guard. He also looks after the garden. And Mimi' – he pointed to the woman – 'looks after the house.'

I shook hands with them both and tried one of the few phrases of Bahasa I'd learned from the travel guide I'd bought. '*Selamat siang*. Do you speak English?'

'A leetle.' Mimi gestured with her thumb and forefinger, while Ali shook his head.

'I can translate if you need me to,' Dadong said. 'Ali and Mimi live here, but I come round every morning, then you can let me know what times you will need me for the day.'

Mimi beckoned me to follow her into the house and we stepped through the front door into a vast low-ceilinged, marble-floored room. My entire London apartment would have fitted inside. In one corner, sofas were grouped in a C shape in front of a television and video. In another, a long dark-wood dining table was surrounded by twelve chairs. Beyond the table, glass doors opened onto a twinkling turquoise swimming pool ringed by grass and more of the spectacular red and fuchsia-pink flowering bushes.

Mimi was waiting to show me another room, this one a huge master bedroom with doors opening onto the pool area. A bathroom the size of my bedroom at home led off the back. The men brought my cases into the room and Mimi gestured that I should continue the tour. On the other side of the main room there was a second bedroom, only slightly smaller, also with its own bathroom.

'Do you sleep here?' I asked, and she shrugged in non-comprehension so I mimed it, pointing at her then bending my head sideways onto my hands.

'Oh no!' she exclaimed, clasping her face as if horrified by the idea. She led me through the kitchen out of a back door by the garage and pointed to a doorway on the other side of a courtyard, then used the same miming gesture to explain to me that that was where she slept. I walked back into the house, noticing the dramatic difference between the muggy air outdoors and the crisp air-conditioned interior. There was a piece of paper on the dining room table, a note scribbled on Medimachines headed paper.

'Dear Dr Drew,' it read. 'I hope you had a pleasant trip and that the house is to your liking. If you're not too exhausted, there's a drinks party this evening not far from you. Just give your driver the address 334 Belanban. He'll know where it is. The party starts around 9. It might be nice for you to meet a few locals but if you can't make it, I'll come by and introduce myself tomorrow morning. Best wishes, Phil Pope.' That was the one Peter had said was his local manager.

I put the note down, pulled back the sliding doors and walked out to the swimming pool. There was a colonnaded area with two cushioned sunloungers. I knelt and trailed my fingers in the warm water and looked up at the rapidly darkening night sky, and for the first time that day, the weighty sadness I'd been carrying around descended again. It would have been so wonderful to arrive in Jakarta with Sedic, to chat to him about the singing children and the transvestites, about Dadong's cool dignity and the splendour of the house we'd been allocated. He'd probably be in the pool already, splashing around childishly. Without him, it all felt unutterably lonely and meaningless. From a wall in the corner an invisible creature called 'e-kko, e-kko,' and it seemed like a comment on the emptiness of my life.

Chapter Eleven

I was tired but my head was buzzing with too many new impressions and sad thoughts to make sleep possible, so I decided after all to call in at the party. Dadong dropped me in the driveway of a house a few streets away. The sky was velvety black now and the air hummed with night insects and smelled sweetly floral. The girl who opened the door had stripy blonde-streaked hair and was wearing round tortoiseshell spectacles.

'You must be Dr Drew,' she smiled.

'Nicola.' The handshake was damp and fleshy.

'I'm Diana Blake, this is my house. Come in, welcome. How was your flight? You must be exhausted, I wasn't sure if you'd make it.' Her voice was quick and breathy, with a girls'-school accent.

The main room was similar to mine but with much more furniture and ornament. Carved wooden animals stood around the walls and beige sofas sprawled in a wide circle. Every surface was covered with trinkets, vases, boxes, and more painted animals: parrots, monkeys, tigers and elephants. About twenty people were chatting in small groups and Diana pointed at each in turn, reciting names that I promptly forgot. I felt shy and awkward in the face of so many strangers but they carried on talking amongst themselves. I gave Diana the bottle of wine I'd brought with me and she glanced at the label.

'Chablis, that's wonderful. You are a darling. It's impossible to get decent wine out here. I'm going to hoard this. We're drinking margaritas, can I get you one?' All her sentences were jumpy, blurring into each other, and she never seemed to expect an answer to her questions.

I perched on the end of a sofa, opposite a dark-haired man who was speaking loudly. His hairy legs were spread wide and his shorts were so brief I could see the shadowy outline of his testicles.

'They're just fucking stupid,' he was saying. 'They're all the same. Yesterday my driver knew I had to get to a meeting on the other side of town by ten on the dot, and what time did he turn up? Half past nine. And do you want to know what his excuse was? The traffic was bad. Well, duh! As if it isn't always bad. And had he put any petrol in the car? Had he fuck!'

Another girl cut in with a story about how she'd bought some terracotta urns for her garden and she got home from work the next day to find the gardener had painted them white. They all laughed.

Diana handed me a drink. 'Phil's not here yet. He called to say he's running late. Trouble with the girlfriend.' She raised her eyebrows at the company and there was a communal snigger.

'Serves him right for going out with a fucking native,' the man in the shorts commented.

What a repulsive specimen he was, I thought to myself. 'Are you a doctor?' I asked Diana, mainly to change the subject.

'No, not me. I work at the British Embassy. Assistant to a junior secretary. It's very interesting, actually. You meet all sorts. You must come to an embassy party some time, I'll put you on the guest list.'

'Where are you going to work, Nicola?' someone asked, and I explained.

'Bloody hell,' the man in shorts commented. 'You'll be treating the natives? I hope you've been vaccinated against all their wog diseases.'

'Hey, Howard,' one of the guys called. 'Did you hear the rumours about the oil merger? I've got shares in Texaco, stand to make about half a mill from this.'

'What's the word on Shell?'

Increasingly improbable figures were bandied around in a

display of macho one-upmanship. I speculated on whether Howard would have tempered his racist remarks if I had brought Sedic with me. My ex-fiancé was one of the 'natives' they were ridiculing. He would have hated these people on sight. I remembered his scorn when I took him to a dinner party given by an old schoolfriend that was full of self-important banker types. We had to leave early before his drink-fuelled sarcasm turned to blatant aggression. I wondered how quickly I could make my excuses to leave tonight.

'It's a bit overwhelming when you first arrive,' an Australian voice remarked. The man was deeply tanned, the rusty colour of a leather handbag, with blonde corkscrew curls springing out of his head. 'Do you know anyone yet?'

'I only arrived in Jakarta about three hours ago,' I smiled, 'so I don't know a soul.'

'Fred Hacker,' he introduced himself. 'I've lived here for five years. If you'd like someone to show you round town, just say the word.'

His bone structure was attractive but his eyes were blood-shot, as though he lived hard. 'Thanks very much,' I said.

'It's a fascinating place but it's virtually impossible to find anything on your own. Are you starting work straight away or would you like me to take you on a guided tour tomorrow?'

'That's very kind. I'm not sure what I'm doing tomorrow but I could give you a call if I'm free.'

'Why don't I call you? Do you know your phone number yet?'

It seemed rude to refuse so I looked it up in my notebook, tore out a page and scribbled it down. 'Where do you work?'

'Unfortunately, not with the big money, like this lot. I was backpacking round Asia when I arrived here and now I make a living as a sub on the *Jakarta Post*.'

'Is that an English-language paper?'

'Sure. We just round up and rewrite the stories from other papers to keep the expats informed.'

'So you speak Bahasa?'

'Yeah, it's not hard to pick up. I'm sure you'll learn it in no time.'

I took a sip of the sickly cocktail. Fred was trying to flirt with me and I knew it would be a long time before I was capable of that again. It was then I noticed my feet. Summer shoes were always a problem for me as they tended to reveal too much but before I left London, I'd found that one of the new season's styles, a clumpy suede slip-on with low platform wedges, disguised my bumpy joints and was comfortable and cool to wear, so I'd bought several pairs in different colours. Somehow I had got muddled and had managed to come out that evening wearing one beige shoe and the other slate grey. I clapped a hand to my mouth and shook my head at my carelessness. What would Sedic have said?

'Have you only just realised?' Fred grinned. 'I noticed when you walked in. I figured it was a new trend in London but from your reaction, I guess not.'

'What an idiot! You must think I'm very strange.'

He touched my arm with warm fingers. 'Quality strange. As it happens, I'm very keen on strange. I'm an expert on degrees of strangeness.'

I shifted so he had to move his hand and took another gulp of the drink.

'Why isn't your fiancé out here with you?' Fred asked, nodding his head towards my left hand, where I was still wearing my engagement ring.

I hesitated. I wasn't sure whether the story would have preceded me. Presumably Peter must have told his manager, Phil Pope, what had happened, but I didn't feel like explaining it to Fred. 'There was a last-minute change of plan and he had to stay in the UK, but I couldn't get out of my contract here. It's all a bit of a mess really.'

'Poor you,' Fred said with what seemed like genuine warmth. 'It must be lonely arriving here on your own.'

'Do you think you could get me another drink?' I asked, in an attempt to deflect the intimacy, and he leapt up and took my glass.

'Nicola,' Diana tapped me on the shoulder. 'Why don't you come out and have a look at my pool?'

I followed her through the doors at the end of the room

and as soon as we were out of earshot, she grabbed my arm. 'I hope you don't think I'm speaking out of turn, but I'd watch out for Fred if I were you.'

'He seems very kind. He's offered to show me round town.'

'Yeah, yeah, that's his usual line with new arrivals. Then as soon as he gets them into bed, they never hear from him again but every other guy in that room knows about their sexual performance in minute detail. He operates an efficient bush telegraph, that boy.'

'Thanks for the warning,' I told her. 'But he wouldn't have got me into bed. Romance is the last thing on my mind.'

Diana patted my arm. 'Phil told me you'd just broken up with your fiancé. I'm so sorry.'

I felt my face go hot and tears well up. 'No, it's fine. Honestly.'

'I'm so glad there's going to be another single girl in town. There aren't many of us so we tend to stick together for safety. You and I will have to do some girls' nights out. I'll give you my mobile number.'

'I'd love to. Meantime, I'm going to have to make my apologies. I think the time zones are catching up on me. Do you mind?'

'But you haven't met Phil yet. I'm sure he won't be long.'

'I'll meet him tomorrow. I'd better go before I fall asleep on one of your sofas, but thanks for the party.'

I waved a general goodbye as I slipped through the room to the front door. Fred looked surprised then mimed that he would call me. Dadong was standing by the front gate, talking to the guard. As soon as he saw me, he walked over to the car and opened the door for me. His movements weren't hurried but there was a formality, like a butler in a stately home.

As we drove off I buried my face in my hands, feeling overwhelmed and very sorry for myself.

'Are you all right, madam?' Dadong asked. I looked up to see him watching me in the driver's mirror.

'I don't think much of these people,' I told him. 'All they care about is money and possessions and status. They talk and talk without listening to each other, just trying to score points and impress.' I hesitated. 'Sorry, I shouldn't be saying all this to you.'

There was a long silence and I wondered if Dadong had understood. Finally he spoke. 'And you? What do you care about?'

'Sedic,' I thought, but stopped myself. 'I care about medi-cine,' I said. 'I care about healing people.'

He nodded and didn't respond. His expression in the mirror was unchanged but I felt as though there was a companionship between us when he dropped me off at home. Maybe I just imagined it.

'I'll be back at nine tomorrow,' he said.

'Don't rush. I'm sure I won't want to go out early. Eleven would be fine.'

He nodded and watched me walk into the house.

I woke to the sound of a telephone ringing somewhere. Pure white light seared round the edges of the curtains and I felt leaden, as though my limbs had melted into the mattress. My travel clock read quarter past eleven but that was the equivalent of quarter past four in the morning in UK time. The ringing stopped, then there was a quiet tap on my door.

'Madam, telephone,' Mimi's voice called.

I pulled on a robe and padded out into the main room then peered round, unsure where the telephone was located in my new house. Mimi pointed towards the corner, where there was a little table with a stool beside it.

'Hallo, is that Dr Drew?' a voice said. 'My name's Linda. I'm Phil Pope's secretary. He asked me to call and see if he can take you out for lunch today. Are you free?'

'Yes, of course,' I said. The next seven months were a blank space in front of me.

'Ask your driver to take you to Café Batavia for one o'clock. It's in Tamar Fatahillah Square. He'll know where that is.'

I got her to spell the names and wrote them down on a notepad. 'I was hoping to go to the clinic today and have a look around. My contract says I'm to start work on the fourth of November, in three days' time, but I'd like to begin earlier if possible. I've got nothing else to do.'

Linda sounded doubtful. 'Phil might have time to take you there and introduce you after lunch but he's got another appointment at three. You'll have to see what he says.'

When I put the phone down, Mimi was placing a platter of coloured fruits on the table: dusty pink papaya, bright orange mango and cool greeny melon, all cut into bite-sized chunks with a tiny fork poised on top.

'You like tea or coffee? Some toast? Some eggs?' She spoke the words like a poem she had memorised by heart but didn't understand, placing the emphasis on 'some'.

'Yes, please,' I nodded. 'Tea, toast and eggs.'

My mouth was furred from travel dehydration but the fruit was succulent and the sweet juices were cleansing. I ate quickly, shovelling back huge slabs of barely chewed toast and egg. My stomach felt hollow and I couldn't remember when I'd ever been so hungry, then I realised the last time I'd eaten had been a snack on the plane the previous afternoon. Everything was upside down. 'The time is out of joint,' I mused.

Mimi reappeared. 'A visitor, madam,' she said. 'Outside.'

'Is it a man or a woman?'

Mimi concentrated for a moment, then understood what I was asking. 'Woman,' she said.

I assumed it must be Diana, since I didn't know any other women in Jakarta. 'I'll just get dressed,' I explained, pointing to my dressing gown. 'Please ask her to come in and wait here.' I indicated the sofas on the other side of the room. Mimi nodded.

I pulled on some clothes, splashed my face with water and brushed my teeth, checking that my shoes matched this time before I opened the bedroom door and emerged. It wasn't Diana sitting on the edge of the sofa, but a diminutive Indonesian woman. She stood up quickly, as if embarrassed, clutching a parcel in her arms.

'Hello, I'm Nicola Drew.' I stretched out my hand and smiled.

The woman seemed very nervous as she transferred the parcel to her other hand so she could shake mine. 'My name is Lila,' she said, in a soft, musical voice. 'I hope you don't mind me coming when I know you've just arrived yesterday but I can't wait to see my son and I've been dying to meet you as well.' I must have looked at her in consternation because she explained, 'I'm Sedic's mother.'

I sat down hard on the arm of a sofa. 'Sedic's mother?' I repeated, stunned.

She nodded. 'But yes.'

All sorts of thoughts were swimming through my brain. Perhaps the word 'mother' was used differently in Indonesia. Maybe she was really an aunt or some other kind of family friend. Or was it a case of mistaken identity?

'There must be some mistake,' I began. 'Who gave you this address?'

'Sedic phoned me about a month ago and said you were both arriving yesterday. He said he'd call to arrange when it was convenient for me to visit but I've been so impatient I couldn't wait. Is he here?' Her eyes travelled towards the bedroom door, which I'd left slightly ajar.

'Are we talking about Sedic Molozzi, the son of Peter Molozzi?'

'Yes, of course.'

It seemed rude to tell her I'd thought she was dead, so I fumbled for words. 'I'm sorry if I seem surprised, but he told me there had been an accident . . . when he was eight . . . I didn't know . . .'

'He didn't tell you we found each other again?'

I shook my head, dumbstruck, and she looked hurt. 'Maybe he planned to surprise you once you got here.' She looked towards the bedroom again. 'Has he gone out this morning?'

'I'm so sorry,' I told her. 'But I'm afraid there's been a change of plan. He's not here. He should have let you know.'

She clapped a hand across her mouth and her eyes filled with tears. I was furious with Sedic. What was he playing at? Did he want to alienate everyone who cared about him in one fell swoop?

As if she could read my thoughts, Lila said quickly, 'It's not his fault. He said I was to wait for him to get in touch after you arrived. He said maybe he'd come down to Jogja to visit. I just couldn't wait.' She struggled to control the disappointment on her face. 'Is he coming later, perhaps? Maybe in a few days?'

I couldn't bear to upset her any more, but it would have been cruel to give her false hope. 'I'm not sure,' I said.

She was puzzled. 'But you are Nicola, the girl he is going to marry? I thought you were both working here for seven months. That's what he said. I've been looking forward to meeting you so much.'

'I'm so sorry,' I said again. 'I don't know what Sedic is planning to do. He broke off our engagement three weeks ago. I came out here alone.'

Now Lila started to cry, her tiny shoulders shaking. 'I brought you a present,' she sobbed, and handed me the parcel. 'To welcome you to our country.' I took it and hesitated, so she added, 'Open it, please. It is for you.'

I unfolded layers of tissue paper and inside there was a length of soft fabric in subtle shades of sea-green, royal blue and dove grey, fringed with a paler shade of turquoise. The pattern undulated like light reflected on the surface of water.

'It's beautiful,' I told her, embarrassed. 'You shouldn't have bought me a present.'

'It's a sarong,' Lila explained. 'Do you know how to tie them?' She wiped her eyes with her knuckles then took the fabric, stood up and stretched it around her tiny frame, demonstrating how it could be tied at the bust or the waist. She must be less than five foot tall, I realised. I couldn't see any immediate similarities to Sedic but maybe the lips were the same – her lower lip was fuller, the top one narrow, just like his.

'I don't know what to say,' I shook my head. 'It's a wonderful present. I'm so sorry that you've travelled all this way and your son's not here to welcome you.'

'I will get the bus back this evening, I suppose. If he comes out later, you could ask him to phone me in Jogja.' She sighed and her eyes filled with tears again.

'You've come by bus from Jogjakarta? That's miles away! You must be tired from your journey. Please feel free to stay here and rest. I have to go into town for a meeting, but we could have dinner together this evening and talk some more.'

She looked shy. 'Oh, I couldn't. This is your house.'

'I insist,' I begged. 'I'd love to talk to you. I hardly know anyone here. Please say you'll stay for a while.'

'Maybe just tonight, then I'll go back tomorrow,' she agreed at last.

I felt dizzy with conflicting emotions. I needed to find out the extent to which he had lied to me about his background and why. Was this really his mother and, if so, when had he found out she was still alive? Or had the whole gas explosion story been fabricated in the first place to win my sympathy? The root of my feelings for him had been based on the little orphan boy story and if he had made that up, what else had he invented? Was there anything left about our relationship that I could trust?

Chapter Twelve

Once again the traffic was slow-moving and as soon as we came to a standstill, children tapped on the window begging for money. Some of them didn't bother to sing, but Dadong gave a few coins to each group. Teenagers in peaked caps blew whistles and stepped out with a hand raised to try and hold up the traffic so cars could pull out of side roads, but Dadong ignored them. The car in front of us stopped to let someone out and they tipped the teenager before continuing. Dadong snorted his impatience.

Just before we turned onto the main highway, he pulled over to the kerb. 'We have to pick up a passenger here,' he explained, and signalled to a boy standing nearby.

I assumed it was a friend of his and wondered if this was acceptable behaviour for a driver. 'Where are we taking him?' I greeted the boy as he climbed into the front seat, but he didn't turn round to look at me.

'Just to the other side of this intersection. It's illegal to travel into the Golden Triangle with less than three people in a car during rush hour. They're trying to reduce pollution by forcing people to share cars.'

'I still don't understand.'

'For a fee of 1,500 rupiah, this boy will be our passenger. It's how he earns his living.'

The boy sat, tense, not looking round or uttering a word, until Dadong dropped him by the roadside about half a mile further on and handed him some coins from the dashboard.

'What happens if you don't have three people in the car?' I asked.

'If the police saw us, we would be fined. It's much less expensive to take a passenger.'

I smiled at this skirting of the law, which seemed to be commonplace. Just behind us another teenager was disembarking onto the hard shoulder.

'What's this road called?'

'Sudirman.' Up ahead there was a roundabout. 'That's the British Embassy,' Dadong volunteered, indicating a large house on a corner surrounded by tall fences topped with spaghetti loops of barbed wire.

I looked with interest. That was where Diana worked. 'Why all the barbed wire?'

There was a pause before he answered. 'To keep out the refugees who seek asylum there.'

'Surely not! If they're in danger, the embassy should take them in.'

Dadong shrugged. 'There are too many, I think.'

'What kind of refugees? From East Timor?'

'I don't know,' he replied, then immediately changed the subject. 'There is Monas, our national monument. Sukarno built it.' It was a towering, phallic column with a gold sculpted flame on top. We passed a large stately building on the left, ringed by rows of guards in grey shirts and black berets carrying semi-automatic guns slung across their shoulders.

'What's that?' I asked.

'The President's palace,' he explained.

The expressions on the soldiers' faces were suspicious, their postures hostile.

We circled round Monas then cut down into an older, scruffier part of town. Streams of men rode clapped-out motor-bikes, nose-to-tail along the kerbside. As we pulled into a square, the bikes clustered in a cycle lane demarcated by ropes. One barrier had fallen over and each successive bike that rode over it pulled down an extra segment of the barricade, so the riders had to slow right down to avoid tangling their wheels.

'That's the Café Batavia.' Dadong pointed at a dark-fronted, pillared building, like some grand hotel in an English seaside town. 'When you want me to pick you up, you ask the doorman to call for Dadong, Medimachines. It's very important that you say "Medimachines".'

I assumed it was a precaution in case I got the wrong Dadong and agreed. Everything here was new and I had to concentrate hard to remember it all.

A wide curved staircase with mahogany banisters led up to a large wooden-floored dining area. The fittings were Art Deco style and the walls were lined with black and white photographs of movie stars of the 1920s and 30s. About fifty tables were set for lunch but only two were occupied. A rotund, balding man stood and waved to me.

'Nicola, welcome, over here. Phil Pope.'

We shook hands and his palm was sweaty.

'It's good to meet you. Sorry we missed each other last night. I'm having a Jack Daniels. Can I tempt you?' He sat down and took a slurp from his glass.

'No, thank you,' I demurred. 'If I drink at lunchtime, I fall asleep immediately afterwards. I'm not very good with alcohol.'

'You'll have to learn,' he remarked cheerfully, 'otherwise you'll never fit in out here.'

'I presumed that most Indonesians wouldn't drink. Aren't they Muslim?'

'The men don't turn down a beer if it's offered. You'll find you don't socialise much with Indonesians though and the ex-pats here are champion drinkers. Your liver toughens up after a while.'

I raised my eyebrows sceptically.

'Of course,' he chuckled. 'I forgot that you're a doctor. Well, maybe it doesn't but the hangovers seem to get easier.'

'Aren't you a doctor?'

'Goodness, no. I'm the sales manager for Medimachines. I cover the whole of the Far East but I'm mostly based here because it's such a huge market. Over two hundred million people and they all need health care. Now what would you like to eat? I can recommend the steak sandwich.'

He had broken veins on his nose and cheeks, reddish skin and trembling hands. I guessed his blood pressure would be dangerously high, about 160 over 95. He didn't look as though he ever exercised.

Waiters brought some bread and a jug of water and Phil began what sounded like a sales pitch for Medimachines equipment, ranging from ultrasound monitors and CAT scanners to resuscitation units. 'We import all the leading brands. Are you familiar with these machines?' he asked. 'Or shall I arrange for someone to give you a demo at HQ?'

'I'm sure they work in the same way as the ones I'm used to,' I said. 'But don't they have trained operators?'

'No, damn locals. They buy these machines and then can't use them, so it's getting harder for me to persuade them they need more. That's where you come in. If you can show them the benefits of new technology in diagnosis and treatment and explain what else is available in our range, we'll make it well worth your while.'

'I'm sorry?' I put my glass of water down. 'What do you mean?'

A hard gleam darted across his eyes. 'I mean up to five percent of the retail price, payable in US dollars, tax free. How does that grab you?'

I sat very still, thoughts fluctuating: surprise, distaste, dismay. It would be too humiliating to have to go straight back to London again if the job didn't work out, but this man revolted me.

'It's all top of the range stuff,' he continued, 'so no one's being ripped off. Medimachines are already the leading suppliers of medical equipment in Indonesia for the basics like sterile-pack syringes and catheters, but there's more money in the larger items, as I'm sure you'll appreciate. We just have to convince them that they need them, especially now they're much more expensive because of the currency collapse. If we can get through this period and continue at the same rate of growth, we'll control virtually all the hospital supplies for this part of the world in five years' time.'

I spoke calmly, although my cheeks felt flushed. 'Let me

get this clear. You want me to act as some kind of sales rep for your equipment?'

'No, no, love. Keep your hair on.' He patted my hand and I pulled it away. 'You'll just advise them about the way you treat certain things in London. They'll listen to you. And if they follow your advice and buy a new machine, you'll find a nice little bonus in your account. That's all. It's how people operate out here, you'll soon find out.'

'I wouldn't dream of recommending any equipment that I'm not convinced they need.'

'Of course not. You've got the wrong end of the stick entirely.' He downed the rest of his drink and motioned for the waiter to bring him another. 'I'm not asking you to do anything unethical. Quite the opposite.'

'I came here to practise medicine. I'm getting the impression that you have a different agenda for me.'

'Not at all, no. Let me level with you.' The waiter brought our lunch: Caesar salad for me and a huge meat sandwich for Phil with plum-coloured barbecue sauce trickling onto the plate. He picked it up and took a bite then spoke with his mouth full, spitting saliva-coated crumbs. 'Your appointment is a goodwill gesture, to convince the Indonesians that we have their best interests at heart. We're asking them to give us exclusive contracts for some products and they have to trust us implicitly. Your role is to help us build that atmosphere of mutual respect and co-operation. Now you can't have any objections to that.' I regarded him coolly and didn't reply. 'While you're here, you'll have a first-class lifestyle and you'll find we're a very friendly crowd of people. What do you think of the house. Pretty nice, eh?'

'It's lovely, but rather too big for me on my own. Perhaps you could enquire about something smaller?'

'Don't look a gift horse in the mouth, that's what I say. You're not paying for it, after all, so if you like it, why not stay there?' He wiped his chin, smearing the white linen napkin with purple sauce.

'When can I start at the clinic?' I asked. 'I wondered if I could go in to meet everyone today and get familiar with the systems?'

'Aren't you keen? More haste, less speed.' He took another bite. 'Just let me finish my sandwich then I'll call Karlina and see if it's convenient.'

'Who's Karlina?'

'Head of the clinic. Brilliant woman. You'll love her.'

My sense of dread solidified. If Phil liked this woman, chances were I wouldn't. I stared out of the first-floor window at the speeding motorbikes below.

Karlina had dark hair streaked with silver, drawn back into a tight bun, and her eyes were framed by thick black-rimmed glasses. A three-inch scar formed a groove down one cheek. I guessed it must have been a knife wound. She was wearing a pristine white coat and her hands were clasped on the desk in front of her.

'We operate as a treatment hospital,' she explained, 'with a walk-in clinic between six and eleven every evening. We either deal with patients on the spot or admit them. Unlike your hospitals, relatives provide the food and bedding, so we can concentrate on medical treatments. Otherwise, I'm sure you'll find our methods familiar.' Her tone was businesslike, not friendly.

I smiled but she didn't reciprocate. 'So when would you like me to start? What hours do I work?'

'That's up to you. You can choose. Maybe you'd prefer not to give up your evenings, in which case you can come to the hospital during the daytime. Expats love the restaurants and bars out here. You should have a good social life.'

I was puzzled. 'Don't you have a staff rota so that you're sure of being covered at all times?'

'Of course we do. But you're not a member of our staff. You're employed by Medimachines. You can come and go as you please.'

I hesitated. 'I'm not sure if I'm clear about how you see my role. Will I be allocated any particular area of responsibility?'

She gave a slight smile, without warmth. 'I think maybe you don't understand how it works here. You can only be an observer in our hospital. We would be happy to discuss our approaches to patient care and hear your views, but under our law you cannot treat anyone unless they have had consultations with two Indonesian doctors first, then request your advice. I made that quite clear when your appointment was first suggested.' Her glasses glinted in the fluorescent light.

I was stunned. 'I'm sorry,' I managed at last. 'But this is ridiculous. I was led to believe I was coming here to treat patients, but you tell me I can't do that.'

'Not unless they've seen two Indonesian doctors first.'

'Well, how . . .' I stopped and bit my lip, unsure what to ask.

'Our doctors are very well qualified. Many of them trained in Europe, Australia or the United States, so it's not as if we're crying out for your Western expertise.' Her tone was sarcastic.

I took a deep breath. 'I seem to have walked into a sensitive situation. I suppose I'd better talk to the owner of Medimachines and see what he has to say.' I decided to try and reach Peter as soon as I got back to the house.

'Meanwhile, since you're here, why don't you let me show you around? You'd be welcome to observe this afternoon. Unless you have other plans, of course.'

'I should tell my driver if I'm staying for a while.'

Karlina laughed. 'He'll be fine chatting to his friends outside, but suit yourself.'

As she opened the door to the first ward, a sickening smell hit me. I'd detected it faintly in the corridors and offices but now I identified it as the smell of pus. It filtered into my taste buds like a heavy cold. There was a disinfectant smell too, but not as pervasive. As we toured round, stopping at individual beds, I saw where the smell came from. In the humid heat, wounds suppurated and oozed like over-ripe fruits; blisters clustered like raspberries and boils bulged like white grapes. Karlina peeled back gauze bandages soaked with greenish-yellow pus and gave sharp instructions to the nurses, while patients looked on unquestioning.

'This man has tetanus,' she explained. 'He had a bad toothache and the village medicine man stuck a rusty nail into his gum to cure it.' The man's face was swollen like a lumpy potato. 'His family wheeled him here, over fifty miles in a cart, when it seemed to be getting worse.'

'Do you treat everyone or do they have to have health insurance?' I asked.

'This is a public hospital. I would never turn anyone away, but sometimes resources are tight. We might not be able to afford the drugs I would like to prescribe in an ideal world.'

'That's the same in the UK,' I told her. 'The big drug companies charge ludicrous amounts for the newest, most successful products, and each district has its own healthcare budget to work within. So you find weird anomalies, like a woman in one street might be prescribed a treatment that someone equally deserving in the next street is not allowed. Or they discriminate by age. Many districts won't put someone on dialysis if they're over sixty or sixty-five.'

'Don't patients figure out what's going on?'

'The press have reported some extreme cases but no one has an answer. The British people are proud of their principle of free health care for all.'

'As they should be.' She swept on ahead of me and I had to hurry to catch up.

There were several amputees and Karlina attributed most to traffic accidents. Three young men with stab wounds and heavy bruising stared straight ahead. I didn't ask for case histories. I was just an observer, after all.

Before we entered the next ward, a nurse handed us protective masks. 'This is a barrier nursing area. We have typhoid, cholera, dengue, malaria. You may not see these so often in London.'

'No, we don't. How do you treat them?'

'Typhoid, dengue and malaria generally respond to anti-biotics but you have to keep watch for complications. They all need rehydration.'

The patients were semi-conscious, feverish, bathed in sweat.

'Do you have many HIV positive patients?' I asked as

we reached a young man's bedside. 'What's your policy on testing?'

Karlina gave me a curious look. 'Officially, there are very few cases in this country. That's just officially, of course. This man is unfortunate enough to be positive. Could you tell?'

'No.' I was startled. 'I was just asking in general.'

'We only test with the patient's permission. Or maybe sometimes without, if the symptoms are suspicious. What's your policy in London?'

'We're legally bound to seek the patient's consent. I would always discuss the test first and arrange pre-test counselling to explain the implications.'

'We're probably further behind because the government refuse to accept that there could possibly be a problem here. We're all supposed to be devout Muslims, so there haven't been any big education programmes.' She shrugged. 'We do what we can.'

'All the London AIDS wards are overflowing with Spaniards and Italians who come to us for treatments their own governments refuse to provide.'

'That doesn't seem fair.' Karlina raised her eyebrows.

'What would be fair? To send them home to die? I don't know.'

We walked along a corridor to a women's ward. One of the first patients was a pretty girl in her early twenties who tried to smile as we approached but her mouth seemed strangely distorted. Karlina said something to her and she opened her mouth, wincing with pain. Her tongue, gums and the back of her throat were coated with tiny white blisters.

'Oh, that must be painful,' I exclaimed sympathetically.

Karlina nodded and examined the chart. I looked over her shoulder and was surprised to recognise the name of the antibiotic metronizadole written on her sheet.

'Does the girl speak any English?' I asked.

'I doubt it.' Karlina asked her then reported, 'No, she doesn't. But why do you ask?'

I hesitated. It wasn't my place to criticise their decisions.

'It's just that I'm pretty sure she's pregnant and metronizadole is contraindicated during pregnancy. You probably know.'

Karlina spoke sternly to the girl, who lowered her eyes before answering in a subdued tone. Karlina called a nurse and gave some instructions, then turned to me. 'Stupid girl! She told us she was a virgin when we admitted her but now she says it's possible she's pregnant.' She breathed a sigh of frustration and we walked on. 'They're so scared of their fathers and brothers. There are some doctors out here who would break patient confidentiality in a case like that so her caution is not ill-founded.' When we left the ward and were alone in the corridor, she turned to me. 'What made you suspect?'

'I don't know. The thought just came into my head.'

'This has happened to you before?'

There was no point in lying. 'Yes, sometimes.'

Karlina considered for a while. 'We'll have to be careful because some people round here believe in evil spirits. If you ever make a diagnosis like that, you must give some physical reasons for it. You could have told me you thought you detected a bulge in her abdomen, or a certain pallor. I don't believe in spirits myself but we'll have to be extremely discreet. Do you understand?'

'But I thought you said that I'm not allowed to treat patients anyway.'

She smiled and patted my shoulder. 'There are always ways round the rules, don't you think?'

She pushed open a set of double doors into a large, swelter-ing hall where every inch of space was occupied by people sitting on the floor, hugging their knees to their chests, or lying back on relatives' laps. Children, teenagers, old men, nursing mothers, every possible age group filled the room to overflowing. The babble of their conversation rose in a blanket of sound.

'These people are all waiting for the evening clinic. It looks as though it's going to be a busy night.' She looked at her watch. 'If I start early, would you be able to help for a couple of hours until the evening staff get here?'

'Of course I would. If that's all right with you, I'd love to help.'

I was assigned a consulting room and a pretty nurse called Yanti who spoke good English. It was rather spartan, with just a trolley, a table and two chairs, a tray of instruments and a sink in the corner. Yanti found me a white coat and stethoscope and the first patient was ushered in.

She was a woman, about thirty years of age I estimated, and she could hardly walk. She hobbled on the bony outside edges of her feet, cringing with each step. I motioned for her to sit on the edge of the trolley and removed the flip-flops from her feet to find huge watery blisters covering the soles. I applied antiseptic and debrided the dead tissue then bandaged them as gently as I could.

'Antibiotics?' Yanti asked, and seemed surprised when I said they weren't necessary. It transpired that industrial doses of antibiotics were prescribed for all open wounds in the tropics. 'Just explain to her that she should change the dressing twice a day, keep her feet clean and try not to walk on them. She should come back if they're not healing in three days.'

Next I diagnosed appendicitis in an old man and Yanti arranged for him to be admitted. I removed a huge wooden splinter from a workman's thigh. I referred several people with digestive disorders for stool samples. I checked for concussion in an old woman who'd been knocked down in the street then asked Yanti to arrange a skull X-ray. I strapped a sprained ankle. No one seemed to mind the slowness of the procedure, with every question and answer having to be translated. They glanced patiently from one to the other of us, waiting their turn to speak.

The pace was unremitting but I was happy to be occupied. As soon as one patient left, the next was brought in and I barely had time to clear up and change my surgical gloves between each. A couple of hours later, Karlina slipped in as I was lancing a boil the size of a gooseberry.

'The patients don't seem to mind being treated by a white woman,' she said. 'They tell me you are very gentle.'

'So I can work here after all?'

'Come back when you like. Maybe tomorrow would be good? Maybe at three? I don't want to put you out at all.'

I realised I was being tested. Karlina was trying to judge how far I could be trusted. It made sense, if Phil Pope was the only other representative of Medimachines she'd come across.

'I'll see you at three.'

Dadong was standing outside and he opened the car door as soon as I appeared. I smiled at him.

'Did you have a good day, madam?' he asked as we drove off.

'It was brilliant,' I exclaimed. 'Very interesting indeed.'

'And now, where would you like to go?'

'Home, please. I have a visitor waiting.'

He glanced at me in the mirror then looked away again quickly. I bet Mimi has told him who it is, I thought. They probably know the whole story. I expect they gossip about me behind my back and feel sorry for me. The thought dampened my excitement about the work at the clinic and we sat in silence the rest of the way home.

Chapter Thirteen

As I walked through the garage to the back door, I could hear Lila and Mimi chatting to each other in the kitchen. Fragrant, spicy, multi-layered aromas permeated the muggy air. I felt uneasy about the evening ahead but curious about what Lila might tell me.

'Sorry I'm late,' I greeted her. 'They wanted me to start work at the clinic.'

'You must be tired,' she said. 'Shall I get you a drink? Why don't you sit down?'

I laughed. 'You're the guest. I should get you something.' I found some wine in the fridge door. 'Will you join me if I open this?'

'No, no, just water for me,' she giggled nervously. 'I am a Muslim.'

I opened the wine anyway and we took our drinks out onto the terrace by the swimming pool.

'Mimi is a very good woman,' she told me. 'Her family also come from Jogja. She will take good care of you.'

'She seems lovely. I'll have to learn to speak more Bahasa so I can communicate with her. At the moment I only know a few phrases.'

The surface of the pool was like glass, hardly a ripple marking it. The stillness was almost eery. Not a leaf ruffled, and the evening felt unusually silent. My ankle itched and I bent to scratch it and felt a small hot lump just above the ankle bone.

'I think I've just got my first Indonesian mosquito bite,' I exclaimed, lifting my leg to try and see it. The itch became fiercer as I rubbed.

Lila leapt to her feet. 'Wait one moment, please. I have something for you.' She scurried into the house and returned a few moments later clutching a little brown bottle with a rubber dropper. 'Let me see.' I extended my ankle and she trickled one droplet of liquid onto the bite then stroked it into the skin with a finger.

'What's in it?'

'Some herbs,' she told me. 'I don't know the names in English. I have a shop in Jogja where I sell herbal potions for treating health and emotional problems.'

'What kind of problems?'

'Everything. Depression, infertility, too much anger, too much fear. We look at imbalances in the body and try to correct them.'

'How do you diagnose what's wrong with people?' I asked. My bite had stopped itching and the skin felt cool around it.

'We talk to them, look at their eyes, their skin, their tongues and nails, ask questions about their general health and their lives.'

'The same way I do, probably. You shake the evidence in a pathological sieve and see what remains when everything else has passed through the mesh.' She looked puzzled. I had reached the extent of her grasp of English. 'Your ointment has certainly done the trick. I can't even see a mark any more.'

She nodded proudly. 'That potion always works. I'll give you a bottle before I leave.'

I kept searching her face and mannerisms for similarities to Sedic and I was aware that she was examining me just as closely. There were so many questions I wanted to ask – when did she last see Sedic? what had happened when he was eight? how had they met up again? – but it seemed rude to launch into them straight away.

Mimi called us in to dinner. The table was spread with multi-coloured dishes: rissoles and patties, rice dishes, bright vegetable stews, little bowls of dipping sauces. I thought I could smell peanuts and chilli, wine vinegar and coriander;

the colours ranged from pistachio to mustard yellow, ochre to seaweed green. Lila threw her hands in the air and exclaimed at the sight.

'Please will you see if Mimi would like to join us?' I asked. 'There's enough food here for ten people.'

Lila passed on the request but Mimi shook her head, shyly. 'She says she's not hungry. I have asked her for some of the recipes. Her nasi goreng looks very good, much better than mine.'

We sat down and helped ourselves from the steaming dishes. I loaded my plate, suddenly starving, but Lila didn't take much. As I lifted my fork, she couldn't hold back any longer and began to ask her own string of eager questions.

'When I spoke to Sedic last month he said he was just getting ready for an exhibition of his paintings. Can you tell me, how did it go? Was it successful?'

'I think so.'

She nodded, excited. 'Were there many people there? What was it like?'

'I was at the opening night. There were a lot of very famous people milling around.'

'And the pictures?'

I paused. 'I didn't notice them particularly. That was the night Sedic and I split up, so I was a bit upset.'

She shook her head and tutted. 'I don't understand this at all. What did he say? I got the impression that he was very much in love with you and couldn't wait to be married. That's what he told me.'

This upset and confused me in equal measure. I tried to be as honest as possible without portraying her son in too callous a light. 'He hasn't explained it to me very well. I don't know what went wrong. Maybe I have some ideas but I'll have to talk to him one day when we've both calmed down. It's hard to . . .' I stopped, with no idea what to say next.

'You must feel very angry with him,' Lila said quietly, watching me.

'I'm not angry. Not at all. I'm sad and hurt, I suppose. It's very recent and I'm still pretty shocked about it.'

Lila was watching me with interest. 'I have some potions for people who don't express their anger. It's very unhealthy, you know.'

I smiled, wondering what she would prescribe. Her dark eyes were unblinking and serious.

'Tell me, how did you and Sedic meet?'

It was easier to talk about that period: the meeting in the bank, how I had fallen in love straight away and broken off my relationship with Geoff. 'We agreed to get married when I'd known him for just six months. I'm very keen to have children but now I think maybe I pushed him too hard. Perhaps he wasn't ready to be tied down. Maybe I was trying to fit him into a mould that he wasn't comfortable with.' I'd been considering this possibility but it didn't quite fit. Sedic had been the one to suggest marriage, not me.

Lila was concentrating, watching my face intently.

'When Peter asked us to come out here, I thought it would be a wonderful opportunity. He offered us a lot of money and arranged this house, the exhibition, a job for me – he seemed to think of everything. Looking back, Sedic was far less keen than me. I knew he was fed up working for Peter but I thought this seemed like such a great opportunity that I talked him into it. Maybe he resented that because among the things that he shouted at me was that I always have to be the one in control.' I'd been considering that comment ever since. It was puzzling, because I'd never felt as if I'd been in control with him, but obviously that was his perception.

'Peter is a very materialistic person. He will always look after his business interests first.'

I frowned. 'Are you still in touch with him?'

'No, of course not. I don't want to be.'

'You dislike him?'

'Sedic hasn't told you any of this story, why Peter brought him up?'

I decided to be honest. 'He told me his mother had died when he was eight and that Peter took him off to live in Italy.'

The hurt was obvious on her face. 'So he didn't tell you that we met up again a year ago?'

'A whole year ago!' I repeated, stunned. 'How could he not have told me?'

Lila looked as though she was on the verge of tears. 'I suppose he was ashamed of me and he was very angry about what I had done.'

I waited, but she didn't seem to want to tell me. 'So you survived the gas canister exploding?'

'There was no explosion. No one died. That was a lie Peter told so that Sedic would accept his new life abroad thinking there was no alternative.'

I stared at her, aghast. How could they have lied to a child about his mother's death? 'Why did you want him to go with Peter?' She didn't answer, gazing down at her lap. 'Was it because you thought he'd have a better life in Europe?'

'Maybe,' she whispered. 'No, not really. In fact,' – she lowered her voice so it was virtually inaudible – 'I suppose you could say I sold him.'

I couldn't make sense of the words. 'You sold him?'

'Peter paid me to raise his child through infancy then gave me a large sum when I handed him over, just after his eighth birthday. Sedic doted on his sister and me so much that I knew he would never have been able to leave, so I discussed it with Peter and we came up with the story of the gas explosion. Peter picked him up from school one day, told him we were all dead, and it was that simple.'

I felt chilled at the callousness. It wasn't uncommon among poorer families in Asia to sell a child, I reminded myself. What was the difference between that and giving up a child for adoption as people did in the West?

'You're shocked,' she said. 'It's a dreadful story. I've never forgiven myself. As soon as they'd gone, I knew I had done something fundamentally against nature. I prayed for help, then I used the money to set up my herbal business in Jogja, thinking it would be some kind of recompense if my skills could heal others. At the back of my mind, I always hoped Sedic would find me again one day, but I never thought he would, because why would he be looking for someone he'd been told was dead?'

I shook my head. 'So what happened? How did he find you?'

'He was in Jakarta doing some business deal for Peter when he saw a photo in the paper of an old schoolfriend he remembered. He got in touch with the man, they had a drink and it all came out. This man phoned his mother, who knew that I had a herbal business in Jogja, and Sedic tracked me down. You can't imagine how I felt when I heard a voice on the line asking, "Did you ever have a son called Sedic?" I crumpled completely and told him the whole story. He came down to Jogja for a couple of days to see me and he was very angry – rightly so – but we've kept in touch since then and I was hoping we would become closer while you were living out here.' She covered her face with her hands.

'I can't understand why he didn't tell me,' I breathed. I remembered the trip he'd made to Jakarta the previous November. That's when he'd bought me the Rama and Sita picture. My head was full of questions. 'Why did Peter want him anyway? He could have got married and had a son to help in the business without all the complications of this arrangement with you. It seems so convoluted.'

'I'm not sure.' She seemed flustered. 'Maybe he thought it would put him in a good light with the Indonesian authorities to adopt a child he'd had with a local woman.' I regarded her curiously. She seemed like a gentle person. Why had she slept with Peter in the first place when she was already married? Had he really paid her for it, this woman who was so religious she wouldn't drink a glass of wine? It seemed incomprehensible that she could just have handed over her son for the price of a new business. What mother could do that? What had her husband and daughter thought about it?

'How did you explain it to his sister when Sedic suddenly disappeared?'

Lila looked distraught. 'Anika? We told her that Sedic had gone off to live with his father and that he'd have a much better life, and she went berserk. I don't think she ever forgave me. Things were never the same between us and soon afterwards she fell in love with a man and ran off with him and I haven't heard from her since. I should have protected her better. I failed with both my children. At least I still have Faisel and I have Allah. They are my only compensation.'

'What did Peter say when he heard Sedic had tracked you down?' Maybe that was the cause of the deterioration of their relationship. He must have been furious.

'I don't know. He didn't say. Peter hasn't contacted me for over twenty years. I wrote to him many times asking for news of my son but he never replied. It was very hard.'

I couldn't think of any words to comfort her. What she had done seemed inhuman from a Western perspective but different cultures set different values. Mimi emerged from the kitchen and began to clear the plates. I lifted the bottle to pour myself another glass of wine and realised I'd consumed more than half of it already. I didn't feel drunk but maybe the alcohol was helping me to cope with the painful topics we were discussing. Lila watched me refilling my glass.

'I've got some photos with me,' I told her. 'Would you like to see them?'

She clapped her hands together and excitement lit up her face. 'Oh, yes please. Very much.'

I went into the bedroom and dug out the packet of snaps I'd brought, a mixed selection of my favourite shots of friends and family.

'Let's move to the sofa. We'll be more comfortable,' I told her, and picked up the wine bottle to carry it across.

The first picture showed Sedic drunk at a dinner party, raising his glass to the camera, with a yellow flower stuck behind his ear. Lila laughed delightedly and examined it for a long time. Then I handed her a happy image of the two of us entwined on the sofa in my living room, taken by his friend Shirley. There were a couple of pictures of him at my parents' house and I pointed out my Mum and Dad. Lila admired the house, pointing at the fireplace, the rug, and she said they looked like very good people. Then I pulled out one of my favourites, showing Sedic sitting cross-legged on the bed in his grey towelling dressing gown, opening presents on Christmas morning.

While she was looking at that, I flicked through the rest of the pile. Most of them showed Anna or Claire, my grandmother and cousins, but towards the bottom of the pack I came across a photo that Sedic had taken of me, displaying some colourful patterns he'd painted all over my body. Blue violin scrolls curved up my belly to each nipple; an elaborate orange garland circled my neck and shoulders; exotic flowers grew from my pubic hair, like a lush garden; ivy twisted up my legs and rambling pink roses trailed up my arms. It was a fantastic creation that had taken a whole Sunday to complete. Surely he must have liked my body then, to lavish such care on its decoration?

Lila was waiting for me to hand over another picture, so I slipped that one to the back of the pile and extracted a couple more family portraits to show her. She was watching me closely.

'How would it be if I telephoned Sedic?' she asked. 'I could call now and ask him what's happening, whether he's planning to come out here or not. Do you think that's a good idea?'

I looked at my watch. It would be early afternoon in London. 'The only problem is that I don't know where he's staying,' I explained. 'He was going to move to a new apartment.'

'Maybe one of his friends would know?' Lila suggested.

I considered for a moment. The idea was very appealing. Maybe he would be more likely to answer my questions in a civil tone if his mother was here, and I was dying to ask why he had never mentioned he'd found out she was still alive. 'Leona, Peter's partner, might know. She runs the gallery where his exhibition was showing. Do you want to call her?'

Lila looked embarrassed. 'It would be better if you call. I have never met her.'

I found my address book in a drawer in the bedroom then perched on the stool to dial the number. There was a long silence before I heard a phone begin to ring on the other side of the world. When it was picked up, the voice was faint and difficult to make out.

'Is that you, Leona?' I shouted. 'It's Nicola. Can you hear

me?' There was an echo on the line and my words floated back milliseconds later.

'Darling, how are you? Is everything all right?'

'It's fine. I need to get in touch with Sedic, though. Do you know where he's staying?'

I couldn't judge whether she paused or if there was an electronic delay on the line as our words bounced off a satellite. 'I've got no idea. I haven't seen him for a couple of weeks.'

'Could you ask Peter if he knows and call me back?'

She said something else but the words disappeared in a static buzz.

'Please try and get a number for me, Leona.' All of a sudden it seemed very important.

The line was fuzzy now and I just heard her saying, 'Don't worry', before we were cut off and a blank hiss emanated from the receiver.

I showed Lila to the spare bedroom and said goodnight, then went to my own room, undressed and pulled on a dressing gown. I didn't feel remotely sleepy so I pulled back the sliding doors and wandered out to sit by the swimming pool. There was a static hum of night insects, the creaky wooden sound of crickets, and the now familiar 'e-kko, e-kko' from the garden wall. Dadong had told me the noise was made by gekkos.

The air was scarcely cooler than by day but the sky was dusty black and starless. Something made me shiver and, moments later, there was a deafening explosion and the garden turned brilliant white. My first instinct was that a bomb had gone off, as I felt shock waves vibrating, but then huge raindrops began to splatter on my arms. I retreated under the shelter of the colonnade to watch as torrents of water were hurled to the ground and sheets of lightning flickered over the rooftops. Great puddles formed in the grass and circular ripples collided on the surface of the pool. Mist rose as water evaporated on the heat of the paving stones, like dry ice in a theatre.

I huddled in the shelter, watching the drama, trying to order the thoughts and questions that cluttered my head. If Sedic had really been in love with me, why hadn't he told me about the reunion with his mother? Had our whole relationship been a farce? Had he never cared about me at all? Was he just using me for some purpose of his own? There was no other logical answer that I could see.

The rain lasted for about half an hour then stopped as suddenly as it had started but the sky was beginning to lighten before I was ready to go to bed.

Chapter Fourteen

I woke around nine, scarcely refreshed, from complicated, stressful dreams that I couldn't recall. The door of Lila's room was open and the sheets stripped from the bed. I looked round the sitting room but there was no sign of her. Mimi was chopping fruit in the kitchen.

'Where's Lila?' I asked.

She pointed towards the garden gate. 'Jogja,' she said, then wiped her hands on her apron and lifted a piece of paper from the windowsill. 'Telephone number.'

I took it and nodded, then went back into the front room to slip it inside my address book. Maybe she was in a hurry to catch her bus home. My immediate concern was to get in touch with Sedic and find out what he had to say about all this. I had no idea how he might attempt to explain it but it felt important to find out. I flicked through the pages, searching for inspiration, trying to figure who might know where he was staying. The book fell open at Claire's name and I remembered that she sometimes bumped into him at music events. It was a starting point anyway.

I dialled the number of my London flat, calculating that it was two in the morning in London, not too late for Claire. The machine clicked on and I heard my voice saying, 'I'm out of the country until June but if you would like to leave a message for . . .' and then it was interrupted as someone picked up.

'Hello?' Claire called brightly.

'Hi there, it's Nicola!'

'Nicola!' She sounded astonished. 'Where are you?'

'In Jakarta, of course,' I laughed. 'Where do you think?' There was music in the background and I heard someone shout, 'Who is it?'

'Jesus, how on earth are you? How's it going?'

'It's OK. I'm staying in an amazing house. You should come out and visit.' There were more voices in the background. 'Who's there with you?'

'Oh, just a couple of friends I bumped into at a gig tonight. You don't mind, do you?'

'Course not. I was actually wondering whether you've seen anything of Sedic? I need to get in touch with him urgently.'

'Funnily enough, yes. I saw him the evening you left. He turned up here while I was unpacking my stuff and seemed surprised you'd gone already. He must have got the dates wrong.'

I couldn't speak for a moment. I'd wanted to see him so badly before I left, and I'd fantasised about him turning up on the doorstep many times. 'What did he want?' I gasped. My tone must have sounded odd.

'Oh, Nicky. Don't be upset. You're so well out of this; you just don't realise it yet.'

'Maybe,' I breathed. 'What did he say when he heard I'd gone?'

'He was horrid. Really cold. He said something like, "Oh well, she's on her own now." I offered to give him a note of your phone number out there and he shrugged as if he didn't care either way, so I copied it out and gave it to him anyway. My theory is that he's upset about you but trying to do the nonchalant-bloke act about it.'

Sedic would never have let Claire see how he felt about anything. 'Did he say where he's staying now?'

'He hasn't found anywhere yet. I asked when he was going to pick up his stuff but he didn't know.'

'So you've got no idea how I could get in touch with him?'

'Uh-uh.' Claire paused. 'But it's not a good idea anyway, is it? You need to move on. Forget about him.'

I sighed. 'It's just that I had an unexpected visitor yesterday. Sedic's mother, the one who's supposed to have died when he was eight, is alive and well and living in Jogjakarta, and seemingly he knows all about it. Why would he have lied to me about being an orphan? Someone who can do that is capable of anything.'

'That's outrageous! What a bizarre thing to do. If I bump into him again, do you want me to ask him to call? He'll have to come back here for his stuff some time.'

I thought for a moment. 'Yeah. Tell him I've been having a long chat with his mother. Let's see how he reacts.'

When I hung up, I felt very isolated. What I really wanted was to sit down with my friends, with a bottle of wine, and talk through the whole mystery. I needed people on my side, supporting me, but out here I was all on my own and life in London continued as it always had without me. Friends were going to the same bars and parties, another doctor was looking after my patients on the ward, my parents were coming home from work and eating supper then watching television together. I was completely dispensable.

Next, I dialled the number for Medimachines. Linda picked up the phone and was very friendly when I told her who it was.

'Is everything all right with the house? You must give me a call about any problems or if there's anything you need.'

'Thanks very much. I wanted a quick word with Phil. Is he there?'

'You've just caught him. He's on his way out. Here you go.' I heard her telling him that it was me, then he picked up the receiver.

'How did it go at the clinic? Isn't Karlina great?'

'She's fine,' I said, 'but you might have warned me that I'm not legally allowed to treat patients. It all seems very complicated.'

'There's some stupid law to that effect but no one pays any attention to it. I wouldn't worry. Are you going back in today?'

'Yes, at three. Meanwhile, I was wondering if you could

tell me how I can get in touch with Peter? I need to speak to him.'

'What about?' He sounded wary. 'If it's anything to do with work or your position here, I'll sort it out for you.'

'No, it's personal. Do you have a number I can contact him on?'

'Nicola, you know what he's like. I don't even know what country he's in just now. Tell you what, though, I'll send him an e-mail asking him to give you a ring at home. How about that?'

'Thanks. Tell him to call in the morning before eleven our time, or after ten at night.'

'Will do.'

Dadong arrived at eleven o'clock, and I was feeling restless and agitated sitting around in the house, so I asked him if he would mind taking me on a tour of the city to help me get my bearings. We pulled out of the driveway and at the end of the road, instead of turning up towards the main highway, Sudirman, he took the other direction along narrow, rutted roads.

Once we'd passed the exclusive houses of the Kemang district, with its barbed-wire-topped walls and deserted streets, we came into a much busier area. There were carts selling all kinds of food: fried pancakes and twisted sugar trellises, sticks of saté and huge bags of nuts. Filthy toddlers played by the roadside; men crouched on street corners, talking and smoking tiny black cigarettes. I saw women on motorbikes wearing the full Muslim dress of long sleeves and head coverings that left only their eyes visible. There were endless dingy apartment blocks festooned with laundry, and families living in flimsy box-like structures alongside putrid canals. Everywhere there was movement. Each one of these people was a human being with needs and desires, lovers and enemies, sadnesses and secrets.

'What's the population of Jakarta?' I asked.

'Nine million,' Dadong told me. 'Seventeen million if you count the outlying districts.'

'How do all these poor people survive?'

'Like anywhere else, I suppose. They beg, go through

rubbish dumps, steal. I think it would be easier to be poor in the countryside.'

'Where do your family come from?' I asked, watching his face in the mirror. His monosyllabic style didn't encourage personal questions.

'From Jakarta.'

'And where do you live? Which part of the city?'

He waved his hand vaguely. 'Over there. It's quite far.'

I tested the ground further. 'Do you have any children?'

'One daughter,' he said. 'That's all.'

'Do you want to have more?'

'No.'

'What about your wife? Doesn't she want more?'

He shrugged as though that was immaterial.

'I want to have children some day. Two maybe, then they'd be company for each other. I was an only child and it can be very isolating.'

He didn't respond. We were stuck in a queue of cars trying to turn onto a main road and Dadong was tapping his fingertips on the wheel impatiently. I noticed that the thumbnail on his night hand was long and neatly filed into an oval.

'Do you play guitar?' I guessed.

'Yes. And I sing.'

'Really! What kind of music?'

'Pop music. I like Madonna, Eric Clapton and Bruce Springsteen.'

I smiled. He was obviously a child of the eighties. 'Are you in a band?'

'No, I don't play that much now.'

'That's a shame.'

There was a sudden lurch as Dadong pulled out into the other side of the road, overtook the cars in the queue in front of us and eased out onto the main road ahead of them. I'd been leaning forward against the front seat but the acceleration rocked me backwards.

'That was a neat move,' I commented, and saw him smiling in the mirror. There was silence for a while, but I wanted to get back to the personal level of our earlier conversation. 'Do you have brothers and sisters?' I asked.

'One brother.'

'Does he live near you?'

'No, I don't see much of him.'

'Why not? What happened?'

He shrugged. 'We have separate lives.'

He was forced to slow down as we approached another long queue. The cars shuffled forwards a few feet then stopped. I looked out the window. 'What does that sticker say on the car in front?' There was a cartoon of a large-breasted blonde woman, with a legend alongside.

Dadong hesitated. 'It's rude.'

'Oh, go on, tell me. I won't be shocked.'

'It says, "I want your bra".'

I laughed and he joined in with a low-pitched chuckle. 'And over there?' I pointed. 'What does that one say?'

He laughed again. '"Who says I have a mistress?"'

I searched round for more car stickers. 'What about that one on the white car two lanes over? Just there.' It was red with black lettering and no cartoon or illustration accompanying it.

'It says, "We are army family",' he translated.

'What does that mean?'

I got the sense that Dadong was choosing his words with care. 'It means that they don't get stopped by the police. People leave them alone.'

'Because they are in the army?'

'Them, or a cousin, or an uncle.'

'The army is much more powerful here than in Britain.'

'Of course it is,' he said quickly.

Some children swerved out into the traffic, tapping on car windows and asking for money, but I noticed that they gave the army family's car a wide berth. So influence permeated down to all levels.

Dadong dropped me at the clinic at around quarter to three and I went straight to Karlina's office. She stood up as I came in and slipped off her white coat.

'You're early, good. Let's go out to a café and get something to drink. I need to talk to you some more before we start work today.'

She led me round the corner and across a road to a glass-fronted café. About twenty white plastic tables were arranged amidst lush greenery but no other customers were there at that time. A waiter rushed straight over with some menus.

'I'm having iced cappuccino,' Karlina said. 'It's very good.'

'I'll have the same.'

She watched the waiter walk back towards the counter before she began to speak. 'So, what did you think of our hospital yesterday?'

'It's fascinating. Very busy, but I loved the work. That's exactly what I was hoping I would be able to do here. I'm worried about this law you mentioned, though. I don't want to do anything illegal or tread on anyone's toes.'

'Most days it won't be a problem. Our country is weighed down by laws that no one ever tries to enforce, unless they want an excuse to intimidate you.' She traced a pattern on the tabletop with her finger. 'But that wouldn't be the case with you.' I waited as she seemed to be working out a way of explaining something. 'There's one nurse, called Rianna, who might be a problem. She believes in rules more than most.'

I smiled. There were types like that in my London hospital as well.

'When she is around, we'll play it safe. Patients will come into my office first, then see one of the other doctors, and then they will be brought through to you.'

'That seems crazy! What a waste of everyone's time, when you seem short-staffed as it is.'

'I know. But if Rianna reported us, there would be all sorts of repercussions. As far as she is concerned, you are an observer from Medimachines and you are here to advise us on the equipment we need.'

'Does she speak English?'

Karlina nodded. 'Very good English. Better than Yanti.'

I decided to level with her. 'I've been offered commission if I persuade you to buy more machinery from Medimachines,' I smiled.

'Of course.' Karlina was unsurprised. 'We don't have much of a budget but you must tell me if you think we should buy something.'

'It looks to me as though you need more drugs rather than sophisticated scanners. You don't have much of a range of antibiotics or anti–inflammatories.'

Karlina looked surprised. 'I didn't think Medimachines sold pharmaceutical supplies.'

'No, I don't think they do. Surely you must have other suppliers?'

'Of course. I would be very grateful if you have time to check our pharmacy and tell me what new drugs we should order. But what would be in it for Medimachines? Do you want a fee?'

'Goodness, no. I just want to be as useful as I can while I'm here.'

She raised her eyebrows. 'In that case, I would be delighted to have your advice. It would also be a good alibi if anyone challenges you working here.' The waiter brought our cappuccinos. I spooned some foam from the top. The taste was mild and smooth, very refreshing, like nutty milk rather than coffee. 'Now tell me, are you married? Do you have any children?'

I shook my head. 'I was engaged back in London but my fiancé broke it off just before I came out here. He's Indonesian.'

Karlina spat. 'Stay away from Indonesian men. How do you think I got this?' She touched the scar on her cheek. 'My husband came home drunk one night and woke me up with a knife in my face.'

'No!'

'It was because I'd refused to let him have his conjugal rights, so the police wouldn't press charges. In their eyes he was perfectly justified. We're divorced now and I live with my daughter. Never again will I let a man into my life.'

'I'm not surprised.'

'But I was asking if you have children because I wondered how you knew that girl was pregnant yesterday. Will you explain it to me? What did you see?'

I'd tried to explain this before, to Sedic, but it was hard to find the right words. 'It's as if I can feel an extra life force. That's how it works with pregnancies. Sometimes, with seriously ill patients, I seem to get a feeling about the strength of their will to live. How hard they're fighting to survive, or if they've given up. I suppose it's as though I sense a kind of energy. But these processes aren't conscious at the time. It's as though the words just form in my head without me thinking them through. "He's dying", "She's pregnant" and so forth.'

'You mean you hear voices?'

'No, it's my own voice and it's not audible, it's just a thought.' I cupped my chin in my hands and stared out the window, trying to find a way to describe it more clearly. 'I don't think I'm so unusual in our profession. Doctors often have to work instinctively.'

'Your instincts are heightened though. Very interesting. I once knew a nurse who had a similar gift but she used to disguise it in case people accused her of witchcraft.'

I nodded. 'I'm very careful who I discuss it with.'

'Good,' Karlina drank the last of her coffee. 'And you'll be especially careful around Rianna?' I nodded. 'I think when we get back I'll ask her to take you on a guided tour of the pharmacies and treatment facilities. You can decide what you think of her as well as our hospital.'

The girl was plain, with small eyes and a pointy face like a vole. Her manner was dour but I flattered her by asking questions about which drugs they used for specific conditions and soon she was showing off, leading me round proprietorially, boasting about the standards of care in the clinic.

'You're much better informed than nurses in England,' I told her and was rewarded with a smug smile.

'The doctors often follow my advice.'

'I'm sure they do,' I concurred.

'Where did you do your training?' she asked, and I told her about the ancient London teaching hospital where I'd progressed through all the painful learning stages from biochemistry and anatomical dissections to clumsy first attempts at bandaging and trotting round wards after the consultants. When I thought back, I could never recall how I'd got through the endless sequences of exams that required regurgitation of screeds of Latin terms, chemical formulae and obscure case histories.

Rianna led me into the X-ray department. I was staggered by the range of machinery they possessed, although, on closer examination, none of it was state-of-the-art.

'When did you get this MRI?' I asked. It was a ten-year-old model that had been superseded some years previously.

'July, I think. Maybe August. The exact date will be in the Medimachines file.'

I nodded, trying not to look surprised. 'And do you use it much?'

She hesitated. 'Not yet. I think we don't have the right kind of computer to connect it to. Mr Pope is going to look into it for us but maybe you could advise.'

I bit my lip. Without the computer, it was pointless, because they wouldn't be able to process any of the images. We continued on the tour, past CT scanners, ultrasound machines and a gamma camera for radionuclide scanning. 'How many radiographers do you employ?'

'Just two, and we share them with some other hospitals, so they come here on Tuesdays and Thursdays.'

'Uh-huh,' I murmured. 'I see.' They could hardly get any use out of their machines if they only had operating staff two days a week. It would have made much more sense to refer patients elsewhere for tests rather than spend all that money.

The biggest surprise was tucked in the corner and had not yet been set up for operation. It was a Parios 539 PET scanner, around six years old, and as soon as I saw the name I remembered all the scandal about this machine. PET scanners are research tools for investigating neurological activity but they're not used in clinical practice for diagnosis or treatment. There seemed no reason for the clinic to have one. I narrowed my eyes, wondering if I could possibly be misremembering the trade press stories from the time of the Parios launch, but I was sure I wasn't. They were too dramatic. Staff operating Parios scanners quickly began succumbing to severe headaches and it was discovered that there was a design fault which meant radioactivity was being emitted into the atmosphere. The model had been withdrawn rapidly amid a flurry of lawsuits that closed down the company. I had never seen one but the name stuck in my head because the potential dangers were so devastating. These machines could have caused radiation sickness, cancers, brain tumours.

'When did you get the PET scanner?' I asked her, keeping my tone level.

'Don't you know? It's just been delivered,' Rianna replied. 'We're the only hospital in Jakarta that has one.'

'But it hasn't been used yet?' I glanced at her anxiously.

'No, Mr Pope is going to come in and give us a demon-stration. I'm not sure when.'

'Leave it with me,' I said. 'I'll speak to him about it without delay.'

'That's very kind of you,' she said, and I glanced at her, wondering if there was a hint of irony in the tone. Was she aware that Medimachines were selling obsolete machines or was she just irritated that they didn't work?

I was profoundly shocked, horrified at what I'd seen, and I considered asking Dadong to drive me straight to the Medimachines offices to confront Phil, but I decided it was better to get the facts straight first. I asked Karlina if I could use the phone in her office and waited until she left the room before I dialled the number of the hospital in London and asked to be put through to Cameron. I explained to him about the scanner and asked him to look up some old articles in the library and check that it was definitely the Parios 539 that had caused problems, then I gave him my home number and told him to call me back there. If Medimachines had sold the clinic a dangerous piece of equipment, I would have to tell Karlina to return it, and my position as a Medimachines employee would be seriously compromised. Better to wait until I had the full story and make sure that no one used the scanner in the meantime.

Chapter Fifteen

My first patient that evening was an elderly woman with a strange poultice strapped around her calf, who walked with the aid of a stick. I peeled back her bulky, makeshift dressing and a sharp stench of garlic filled the consulting room. Underneath an open gash gleamed, full of mushy brown flesh like the insides of a rotting fig; the woman had pressed peeled garlic cloves directly into the wound. I pulled them out carefully.

'The pain must be horrible,' I told Yanti. 'Ask her why she did this.'

Yanti translated and the woman replied. 'She says the garlic stopped it getting infected.'

I shuddered in sympathy, but the woman hardly flinched as I scraped the pulp from inside her cut, disinfected it with harsh purple liquid and threaded four stitches through the flesh to hold it together.

Next I saw a child with glands like a puff adder, a man with a badly scalded hand, and a young woman who had been beaten so severely her face was swollen like a bruised plum, but who refused to say who had inflicted her injuries.

There was something medieval about the wounds and the general stoicism with which they were accepted. Londoners would never have endured such agony. Hands clasped over hot puffiness, shoulders hunched to cocoon pain, feet dragged in silence, poisoned wounds glistened. The smell of proliferating anaerobic bacteria pressed on my sinuses, coated the back of my throat and burned my lips.

Around nine o'clock, Karlina came in waving a piece of paper. 'There was a phone call for you. One of the nurses took it. She didn't catch the name but she wrote down the number.'

I glanced at it and guessed that it was the code for a mobile. Maybe it was Peter. 'Can I use the phone in your office?' I asked.

'Help yourself.'

I dialled, feeling incomprehensibly nervous, but it was a girl's voice that answered.

'Hello, it's Nicola Drew speaking. Who's that?' I asked.

'It's me. Diana. Where are you? What are you doing?'

'I'm working, at the clinic.'

'When do you finish? We're all going to a club called Tanamur. It's a city institution, the most famous club in Indonesia. You have to see it. We'll be there from around eleven. It'll be nice and quiet. It doesn't get busy until around two. Why don't you come?'

I hesitated. 'I'm very tired.'

'You're practically round the corner from it if you're at the clinic. Your driver will know where it is. Just pop in for a quick drink. You don't need to stay all night.'

I agreed, mainly because I felt like some company and the alternative was sitting alone by my swimming pool, feeling miserable about Sedic. More and more I was finding it hard to avoid the conclusion that he'd never loved me. He must have been acting the part of the devoted fiancé all the way through and I'd been gullible enough to fall for it. The range of emotions this thought aroused were too uncomfortable to dwell on.

When I emerged from the clinic at eleven and told Dadong I wanted to go to Tanamur, his attitude was cool.

'Where is it?' he asked. 'I don't think I could find it.'

I dialled Diana's mobile again and she gave him instructions but I could tell from the way he barely listened that he'd known all along. He just didn't want to take me there, for some reason. In fact, the club was only a few minutes away, as she had said.

'I won't be long,' I told Dadong, but there was no reply.

Two doormen nodded as I walked past them into a dim

cavern lit by pink, green and yellow flashing disco lights. The air smelled of warm beer and tobacco and another, sicklier scent, of cheap candy perfume. A steel mesh walkway ran overhead and there were a couple of Indonesian girls on it in high heels and mini skirts writhing to Sister Sledge, but most people were huddled round a long bamboo bar and I spotted Diana near one end. She was sitting with Fred, the Australian journalist, and Howard the racist.

'Nicola, I'm so glad you made it. Welcome!' Diana exclaimed.

'We were beginning to think you were some kind of nun,' Howard remarked. 'Hail Mary.' He crossed himself.

'I hope you haven't been working too hard,' Fred grinned. 'This is Sin City. You have to get out there and sin.'

They clinked glasses and toasted sin, then Fred ordered a drink for me. Howard and he began to argue about whether the original Sin City was Bangkok or New Orleans.

'Phil Pope's over there with his girlfriend, Sanita,' Diana told me. 'But I wouldn't interfere if I were you.'

I followed her gaze and saw him sprawled across a seat with an Indonesian girl on his lap. She wore shiny white trousers and a bright pink boob tube and they looked as though they were gnawing each other's faces like starving lion cubs. Phil's podgy hands were grasping her bottom.

'They've been together about six months now,' Diana told me. 'And she's putting the pressure on to get him to marry her. I wouldn't be surprised if he caved in. He'd never get a girl like that back home.'

'She looks very beautiful,' I said. 'But very young.'

'She's seventeen,' Diana told me. 'Phil's forty-six.'

'She's an expensive hobby, though,' Fred commented. 'While he's at work, she and her sister spend their days shopping, buying up half of Jakarta with his money.'

'You're just jealous because you can't afford one,' Howard sneered.

'Not me, mate. Call me old-fashioned, but I like to be able to talk to a girl afterwards.'

Diana snorted derisively and Fred gave her a warning glare. Howard was smiling into his drink.

'Phil's had strings of other girlfriends before Sanita but none of them lasted as long as her. They'd be hanging off his arm, gazing adoringly for a few weeks then they'd disappear to be replaced by the next.' I was glad to note that Diana obviously disapproved of this behaviour.

'I don't know how he gets rid of them,' Howard remarked. 'Friend of mine had a one-night stand with a local girl and she pursued him for months afterwards demanding money, marriage and all sorts.'

'Maybe he bumps them off,' Fred suggested.

'Look at the man!' Howard exclaimed. 'He's too drunk and podgy, hardly the image of a ruthless killer.'

'He could just lie on top of them and they'd suffocate.'

'Stop it, you two,' Diana interjected. 'Nicola works with the guy.'

I looked round the club and was suddenly reminded of school discos when I was a shy teenager. The girls huddled in groups, giggling and chattering on one side of the dance floor, frequently glancing towards the bar that was lined with overweight men in business suits. As I watched, a girl in a white mini-skirt sauntered over to talk to a man who was sitting on his own. Seconds later, he had summoned the barman and ordered her a drink.

'Sex is their only commodity,' Fred commented. 'Who can blame them?'

'God, no, I don't blame them at all. I just worry that they won't get what they want out of it. Does it ever work the other way round, with Indonesian men going out with white women?'

'I'm sure they would love to. I saw a survey the other week about what they think of us and all the men said they would like a white girlfriend because they see it as free sex. You don't have to pay for it, don't have to marry them. Personally I don't know any girls who're going out with Indonesian men, though. There are so few decent girls here, we tend to keep them for ourselves.'

'What else did the survey say?'

'It was a bit predictable, really. They find it embarrassing

that we talk about sex so openly. They're very private about
their bodily functions. They think we're not as clean as them.
But they also said we don't seem to touch each other much
or show affection. Can't think where they got that idea.' To
contradict it, he slung an arm round my shoulder and kissed me
on the cheek. Diana caught my eye and winked. I shrugged his
arm off.

Phil Pope staggered across, his eyes unfocused and words
slurred. His shirt was unfastened almost to the waist and his
podgy flesh swelled into two pendulous breasts and a stomach
that looked pregnant. Classic heart attack physique.

'Dr Drew, we meet again. How's it going? Can I buy you
a drink?'

'No, thank you, I have one. Did you manage to contact
Peter for me?'

'Not yet.' He clutched my arm for support then leaned
heavily against the bar. 'I'll do it in the morning. Must drop
in and visit you and old Karloff some time soon.' He waved
a barman across and ordered some drinks. 'Going on a trip
tomorrow, though.'

'Where are you going?' I asked, politely.

'Ah-hah!' he slurred and tapped the side of his nose with a
finger. 'Wouldn't you like to know?'

I turned away in disgust at the revolting smell of his
boozy, nicotine breath mixed with stale underarm sweat.
His poor Indonesian girlfriend had my profound sympathy
if her highest ambition was marriage to this stinking whale
of a man.

'Keep up the good work,' he exhorted me, before picking
up two glasses and swaying back across the floor towards
her.

'What are you doing at the weekend?' Diana asked. 'We're
all going water-skiing in the Thousand Islands. You should
come along.'

'I'm afraid I can't water-ski,' I said.

'Neither can I,' Diana admitted. 'I just lie on the beach
laughing at them all trying to stay upright. You need to get
yourself a tan, though. You're very pale.'

'I think I'm working this weekend, but maybe another time.'

'I've got a share in a beach house at a place called Sambolo. It's just opposite Krakatoa, the volcano. It's very pretty there and only a couple of hours' drive from the city. My turn comes up about every six weeks so maybe you can come with me next time.'

'That's very kind. I might take you up on that.'

When I announced to the group that I was leaving, Fred insisted on accompanying me to the door.

'What's your driver's name?' he asked, and when I told him he relayed the information to a doorman who spoke into a microphone on the desk.

'Can I take you out for dinner some time?' Fred asked. 'You must have a night off and there are some fantastic restaurants in the city.'

'I'll see,' I hedged. 'I'll give you a call if I can make it.' I could see Dadong edging the car round the corner of the building and I wriggled free of Fred's arm.

He touched my shoulder with a finger. 'I'd really like that,' he said, then kissed me quickly on both cheeks and followed up with a brief peck on the lips. He gave me a tight hug, his eyes questioning whether he could kiss me more, but I broke away as soon as I could, feeling repulsed. It would be a long time before I felt like kissing another man. How could I ever trust anyone again?

A few feet further back, Dadong was holding the car door open, staring into the distance, his face creamy in the moonlight and his eyes opaque.

'Where to now?' he asked, without looking at me, as we pulled out of the nightclub forecourt.

'Home, of course.' There was silence for a few minutes, but Dadong's rigid posture made it quite clear that he was unhappy with me. 'What's the matter?' I asked.

His voice was cold. 'I thought I told you that you should always ask for Dadong Medimachines when I pick you up.'

I was surprised. 'Fred asked the doorman to call you. Why, what did he say?'

'They just called for Dadong, as if I was a private driver. It made me look foolish in front of the other drivers. If you say Medimachines, then they know I am a company driver.'

'Is that more prestigious?' I asked.

'Of course.'

'I'm sorry, I'll make sure I get it right in future.' I stifled a smile at the complex code I seemed to have transgressed.

The engine screamed as he accelerated through some traffic lights that had turned red, narrowly avoiding a stream of cars approaching from our right. I tried to catch his eye in the mirror but he scrupulously avoided contact.

'Look, I didn't like Tanamur and I don't like these people either, but I don't know anyone else in Jakarta. Do you expect me to go straight home after work every night?'

'It's none of my business who you go out with,' he replied.

'Don't be so horrible to me, Dadong. Don't you understand that I'm lonely?'

He cleared his throat slightly. 'You could go out with some people from the clinic maybe.'

'Karlina has to get back to her daughter and anyway, we're all too tired when we finish. You're not being fair. You have friends and a wife at home but I have no one.'

He didn't say anything for a while. 'Tanamur is notorious. Indonesian girls who go there get a bad reputation. I was just trying to warn you since you don't know the city.'

I caught eyes with him, amused. 'Notorious indeed! Your English is excellent. Have you really never had lessons?'

He shook his head. 'I suppose it's because I'm a good listener.' His eyes in the mirror were friendly now.

Maybe it was the drink, or maybe I was just feeling sorry for myself, but I wanted to tell him more. 'You must know that I was supposed to come here with my fiancé. That's why they gave me such a big house. But three weeks before we were due to leave, he broke up with me. He doesn't want to marry me any more. So I had to come here on my own.' I nearly cried but stopped myself by biting my lip and staring out the window at the blur of lights along Sudirman.

'I'm sorry, madam,' Dadong said.

'Don't call me that. Call me Nicola.'

'I'm sorry, Nicola.'

'Anyway, that woman who arrived yesterday was my fiancé's mother, who lives in Jogja. The weird thing is that he'd told me she was dead then she just turned up out of the blue. I can't understand why he would have lied to me about something like that.'

'He's Indonesian?'

'Yes. And to make matters worse, I seem to be in a very difficult situation at the clinic. I probably shouldn't tell you because you work for Medimachines, but I'm beginning to think they're not a very nice company.'

'What makes you say that?'

When we got back to the house, I asked him in for a beer and we both sat out by the swimming pool. I did most of the talking, first describing my relationship with Sedic and the horrific evening of the exhibition opening, then his brutal behaviour on our last meeting at the studio.

Dadong's eyes flickered. 'I don't understand,' he said. 'How could you have been planning to marry someone like that?'

I shook my head and looked away. 'Maybe I was dazzled by him. He was so exotic and different, and he had so many qualities I lacked, like style, good taste, creativity, confidence . . .'

'These aren't important, surely? You're a good person and it sounds as though he's not.' He stopped abruptly, as if embarrassed to be speaking so personally.

'You don't know me. I have my faults.'

Dadong sipped his beer thoughtfully. 'Do you still love him?'

I considered the question. 'My feelings are very mixed up. Most of all, I feel disappointed in him. Does that sound odd?' Dadong shook his head slightly. 'I opened out my life to him, introduced him to my family and friends, gave him keys to my home, bankrolled him, offered him all my love and support. I really believed in him and I thought we had the same vision of our future. Then, for some reason I don't understand, he threw it all back in my face. He'd just been taking me for a ride.'

'The reason is simple. He's a bad person.'

'Is life really so black and white?'

'I think so,' he replied.

I watched him in the dusky light. He was clear about his opinions in a way I found refreshing. I tended to muddy issues by trying to see everyone's point of view and make excuses for them but he just saw right and wrong.

'Tell me what you think of Medimachines as a company. You've worked for them longer than I have.'

He hesitated. 'It can be easy for sophisticated Western companies to make a profit here because there are so many products we need and can't produce ourselves.'

'But I think Medimachines are selling equipment the clinic doesn't need, which might even be dangerous.' I told him about the scanner that could be leaking radioactivity and he listened calmly, seeming unsurprised.

'What will you do?'

'I'm checking my facts first of all, then I'll confront Peter, since he's the one who hired me.' Putting it all into words helped me to rationalise and order my thoughts.

'It sounds as though you're doing the right thing,' he said, and I was pleased.

A bat swooped down, skimmed the surface of the pool and curved up into the black sky again. The air smelled especially fragrant, with a sweetness like roses in summer rain. My gekko called from the corner, making me smile, and the night insects hummed busily.

'It's strange living on your own in a foreign country,' I said. 'You carry so many thoughts and impressions round in your head and have no one to share them with.'

'Such as what?' he asked.

'Little things. The clove smell of those funny black cigarettes . . .'

'Kreteks.'

'And that horrible fruit that smells like a sewer.'

'Durians.'

'And all the hierarchies you have to learn, about army families and street kids, and company drivers versus private ones.'

Dadong gave a little smile.

Chapter Sixteen

Next morning, I woke early and decided to go out and buy a newspaper. I opened the front gate and stepped into the street, then turned left down the muddy road. There was a clatter behind me and I looked round to see Ali, the guard, following.

'It's OK,' I shouted, and gestured that he should go back. 'I'm just going to the shop.' He hesitated, then continued to follow me, at a distance. I tried again to discourage him, but to no avail.

Beside the ice-cream seller at the corner of the road, there were two soldiers carrying black guns slung across their bodies. They regarded me unselfconsciously, and I gave a little nod as I walked past. There was no pavement as such, and when a car came by, I had to step into a ditch by the roadside. I looked round. Ali was ten yards behind.

It took about five minutes to get to the mini-supermarket beyond 'Best Jeans' and the bamboo shop. I pushed open the door. Two old men were sitting talking to each other; their tone sounded gossipy and personal, like women discussing neighbourhood affairs over the garden fence. There was a newspaper stand just by the counter and I glanced down the titles, but the only one in English was Fred's paper, the *Jakarta Post*. I held out a note to pay for it and one of the men counted out my change without interrupting his conversation. They both looked at me and I knew, from a slight change in tone, that they were discussing me.

Ali was standing opposite, waiting, so I smiled and lifted the paper to show him what I'd come for. He nodded, then followed me back again. It felt silly that he didn't walk alongside me, but we wouldn't have been able to talk to each other anyway. When we reached the gate, I waited for him to catch up and said, '*Terima kasih*', although if my grasp of the language had been better I would have explained that he didn't need to accompany me, rather than thanking him. He pointed at the paper and then at himself, indicating that he could fetch a paper for me in future and I nodded and said, '*Terima kasih*' again.

I sat in the shade beside the pool with a cup of coffee and leafed through the pages. 'Currency crisis deepens' was the cover story. The writer advised that it was a good time to buy up luxury goods, and a table in the corner of the page compared the prices of various items converted into US dollars with their equivalent just six months previously. The price of Cartier watches and Mont Blanc pens had dropped by sixty percent. A weekend break at a five-star hotel near Borobodur was now less than a hundred dollars a head. I pursed my lips, well aware who was making a loss in these transactions. Ex-pats were paid in British or US currency, not rupiah, so their already ostentatious salaries would go even further than before.

On the next page, I read a story about a series of grisly murders near Surabaya, in which the victims were decapitated and had their hands and feet cut off, making identification virtually impossible. It occurred to me that the murderer must have some very efficient cutting equipment. Another story covered a row about an American professor of Far Eastern studies accusing the Indonesian minister of trade of corruption over some deforestation deal. The journalist was careful not to take sides. There was a paragraph about the Middle East peace talks, then a report from the Paris fashion shows that hemlines were rising again. There was a small-ads section at the back of the paper that read like any equivalent in the British local press. Furniture for sale, homes wanted for a litter of puppies, a local writers' group looking for members, even a short and very sad-sounding lonely hearts section.

I shut the paper and lay back in my lounger. The air was

thick and sticky, the sky shrouded in dense grey and white clouds, the heat pressing down hard. The humidity made my joints click like a broken clockwork toy. I considered going to the kitchen for a glass of water but getting up from the chair would have meant pushing through the wall of air. After a while I removed my sarong and slithered into the pool. The water was lukewarm and viscous, like the water that trickled out of the shower, but it helped to lower my body temperature slightly. When I first arrived, I had resolved to swim every morning but there were days when I just couldn't be bothered; sometimes it seemed to require too much effort.

I dozed off, and when I woke, it was almost one o'clock. Mimi was preparing some lunch in the kitchen but there was no sign of Dadong out in the garage. I was surprised, but got dressed for work all the same, and sat down to eat. Two o'clock came and went and at ten to three, when he still hadn't appeared, I rang the Medimachines office. Linda answered.

'Do you have any idea where Dadong is?' I asked her. 'I'm due at the clinic in ten minutes but there's no sign of him.'

'Maybe he's been held up in the traffic,' Linda suggested.

'But he usually comes at eleven. Do you think he might be ill? Do you have his home telephone number?'

'He doesn't have a telephone, but I'm sure he's not ill. He's never ill. He'll turn up sooner or later.'

I wondered if something might have upset him about our conversation last night. Maybe he was uncomfortable that his boss had talked to him about her personal life. 'Is Phil there?' I asked. 'I wanted to remind him to e-mail Peter for me.'

'He's away on a business trip,' she said. 'He's not back till next week.'

'Do you know where he's gone?' I asked, remembering his secretiveness the previous evening.

'I've got no idea. He never tells me anything,' she laughed.

I rang the clinic to tell Karlina I was running late and she sounded annoyed. I worried that she would change her opinion of me if I seemed unreliable. I went out to the front gate and peered up the street. The soldiers were still standing at the end but there was no sign of Dadong. I found a peach in the fridge and ate it as I wandered round the cool marble rooms of my house, peach juice dribbling down my chin and hands. It would have been nice to call Anna for a chat but it was just after eight in the morning and she would be getting ready for work. The emptiness made me jumpy and out of sorts. I hated rattling round with space to fill because it was then that thoughts of Sedic crowded in. Since finding out that he'd lied to me about his mother, I knew it was definitely over between us. There could be no way back after that. All I had to do now was keep myself busy and wait for the wounds to heal. Sometimes I wondered how he was, where he was living and whether he ever thought about me, but I knew I had to stop such speculation. I had to learn to hate him.

The phone rang and I hurried to answer it, convinced it would be Dadong, but it was a long-distance call with the usual fuzzy, delayed transmission.

'Nicola, it's Cameron. Is this a good time? I couldn't figure out when to phone you.'

My thoughts had been so far away that it took me a few moments to remember that I'd asked Cameron to call me back about the scanner. 'Perfect. Thanks for getting back to me so quickly.'

'I looked up everything I could find on the Parios and you're right – the 539 was the model there was a radioactivity scare about. However, it could be that the machine you saw out there is OK. They found a way to correct the fault and tried to relaunch it, but by that time, after all the adverse publicity, no one would touch it and the company went bust. I ran some checks on their liquidation papers and it seems that the existing stock was bought up by a Hong Kong-based company, so that's probably where Medimachines got them from.'

'But how can I be sure the one here has had its fault corrected and won't contaminate us as soon as it's switched on?'

'That's difficult. You'd need to get a technician who knows what he's doing to run some tests. Why not tell your boss at Medimachines about your concerns and they may be able to get some reassurances from the Hong Kong company?'

'Do you know what it was called?'

'Yes, that's the odd thing. The company's called Art Deals International, which is a strange name for a medical equipment retailer, don't you think?'

I didn't make the connection straight away but it was only five minutes or so after I came off the phone that I realised Art Deals International must be another one of Peter's companies, possibly associated with the gallery.

He'd talked about shuffling resources between his various business interests. That was one of Sedic's roles, if I remembered correctly.

Why would an art company buy medical equipment? Surely it would have been simpler for Medimachines to buy it directly? Was Peter up to something duplicitous, some tax dodge or other? I wondered how much the clinic had been charged for old liquidation stock with a flawed reputation? I was willing to bet it hadn't been a bargain purchase. When I finally got hold of Peter, I'd confront him with all this information and see what he had to say for himself but in the meantime, all I could do was make sure that scanner wasn't used until it had been checked out.

It was five o'clock before Mimi came running through to say that Dadong had arrived, and I hurried straight out to the garage. He was standing by the car, pristine as ever in a pale blue cotton shirt and dark grey trousers. We stared at each other.

'What happened to you today? I was supposed to be at the clinic at three.'

'Sorry, madam.' He inclined his head slightly.

'I told you to call me Nicola. But where were you? Why didn't you phone?'

'There was a demonstration in town, so many streets were closed.'

'What kind of demonstration?'

'Pro-democracy.' He looked me in the eye with a peculiar expression and I knew there was something he wasn't telling me.

'So you couldn't get through town and you couldn't phone to let me know what was going on.'

'Sorry,' he said again, but in a tone that made it clear he didn't consider it to have been his fault.

'Let's go now. I'll just get my bag.'

He glanced at my blouse with just a momentary flicker of the eyes but I picked up on it and looked down to see trickles of sticky peach juice on the white cotton. I couldn't help laughing.

'You're always so perfectly dressed,' I said, 'I guess it would embarrass you to be seen with someone messy like me. I'll just go and change.'

He grinned and we were friends again.

In the car, I asked more about the demonstration. 'How many people were there?'

'I don't know. Maybe two hundred, three hundred. Not so many.'

'Are they mostly students? That's what they've been reporting in our newspapers back home.'

He didn't answer for a while. 'Some demonstrations are organised by students. They post details on the Internet and anyone with access to a computer can come along, but it means that the army are prepared for them.'

'It sounds dangerous,' I said. 'Was there any trouble today?'

'I don't think so.'

'So you were there?'

'I told you. I was trying to get past to come and pick you up.'

I decided to let him get away with this for now. 'Another time, please will you phone and let me know if you can't get here on time? I have to be able to rely on you.'

'Yes, you can,' he said. 'There's no need to worry.'

I told him what I'd found out about the scanner. 'I don't think there's any point in talking to Phil about it. He probably doesn't even know where they came from. Besides, he's out of the country till next week on some mysterious business trip.'

'He's gone to Vanuatu,' Dadong told me.

'Where on earth is that?'

'An island in the South Pacific.'

'But why would he go there?'

'I've got no idea. Maybe it's for a holiday.'

'How do you know that's where he's gone? Linda in the office didn't even know.'

Dadong was full of surprises. 'I took him to the airport this morning, first thing.'

Several barriers had been broken down by our talk by the swimming pool. Dadong still had secrets and would resort to monosyllabic answers when I asked questions in an area he didn't wish to discuss, but by the end of November, a month after I'd arrived, there was an alliance of sorts.

We began to tease each other: he would always raise his eyebrows at any stains or creases in my clothes and I'd mock the immaculate perfection of his; I teased him about the arrogance of his driving and he ridiculed my nervousness when he cut across streams of oncoming traffic. Music was a major area of conflict: I told him that Madonna is a terrible singer but when I brought my tapes to play in the car – Catatonia, Blur, Jamiroquai – he'd imitate them in a screeching falsetto or tilt his head from side to side like a metronome to show he found them monotonous.

I discovered a scurrilous side of him that loved to gossip. He told me that Ali was secretly in love with Mimi but she wouldn't let him near her. He told me that Phil Pope's girlfriend slept with two other men friends as well as him. In return, I told him that Diana was in love with her married boss at the embassy and that Howard's girlfriend had just left him for a much richer man who lived in Kuala Lumpur. We became friends of sorts, which was nice considering the fact that given the state of Jakarta traffic we spent at least two hours a day, often more, trapped in a car together.

Phil Pope came back but still I heard nothing from Peter, although Phil swore he'd sent the e-mail now. One night in mid December, the phone rang at about two o'clock in the morning, soon after I'd fallen asleep. I roused myself slowly and pulled on a robe. Mimi couldn't hear the phone at night because her bedroom was too far away. I reckoned it would be someone calling from London, who'd miscalculated the time difference, but there was always a chance it could be Peter.

An American voice asked me if I would accept a reverse-charge call and when I queried where the call originated, she said, 'The Bahamas.' I agreed and there were muffled clicks and buzzing sounds before a voice came on the line, but it wasn't Peter's.

'Nicky, is that you? It's Sedic. Listen, I'm in trouble. Very big trouble. I need ten thousand dollars and there's no one else I can turn to.'

Chapter Seventeen

I sat down on the stool by the telephone and leant my cheek against the coolness of the wall. The sound of his voice shook me badly. I felt a massive rush of mixed emotions, but most of all I was scared that he was going to hurt me again, just when I felt as though I was beginning to get over him.

'Are you there?' he asked.

I whispered, 'Yes.'

'I can imagine what you must be thinking, but please don't hang up until I've had a chance to explain. I'm serious, Nicky. There are two men in the next room who are going to kill me if they don't get that money today.'

'Why don't you ask Peter?' I tried to make my tone icy but my voice was trembling too much to obey me.

'I don't know where he is. I've been trying to find him but I can't get through.'

'But according to your mother, he paid good money for you, so he's unlikely to let you come to any harm.'

There was a sigh. 'I heard from Claire that you met my mother. I can explain all that but not right now, not in present company, OK? I'll call and tell you everything as soon as I get back to London.'

'I don't want to know, Sedic. I don't care any more. I'm beyond that.' I was very close to tears.

'OK, whatever you want, but please just listen. Peter has a casino out here and some local gangsters think he should have been paying them protection money, but he's been wriggling out of it. They've kidnapped me and said I have to get someone to wire a down payment tonight or they'll kill me. Nicky, you have to help. I'm so scared.'

I sighed. 'Why should I believe you?'

'I can't tell you everything right now, but surely you must understand that after all we've been through, I wouldn't ask you if I had any choice. If there was anyone else I could turn to, I would do it.'

'What about Leona?'

'She won't help.'

'Why not?'

'I don't know. Nicky, please. I swear you'll get the money back. It will be in your bank account within a week. But if you don't agree, my body will be found washed up on some Caribbean beach.'

'Maybe that would be for the best,' I said, then immediately retracted. 'You know I don't mean it, but I should.'

'This is probably the last thing you want to hear, but the truth is that I still love you. I've had no choice about what's happened over the last few months. I miss you very badly.'

I clutched my forehead in my hands, trying to think what to do. It was only money, after all. The seconds ticked by. I ran the telephone cord between my fingers, twisting and untwisting the coils.

'Please, Nicky,' he begged, quietly.

'I'll make a deal with you,' I said at last. 'I'll give you the money now and you make sure it's back in my bank account within a week. But after that I never want to hear from you again. I don't want you to phone me, and I don't want to listen to any explanations about what happened between us. This will be the last time we ever speak to each other. Agreed?'

He didn't say anything.

'I can arrange a bank transfer but not until tomorrow morning, British time, so it wouldn't reach you in the Caribbean today. Do you want to explain that to the men you're with?'

'Hold on a minute,' he said, then the receiver was put down and I heard the sound of footsteps and a door opening. A few moments later, Sedic came back on line. 'They said, can you give them a credit card number?'

I exclaimed in disbelief. 'How can gangsters process a credit card transaction? That's weird, Sedic. Think about it.'

'That's what they said.'

I thought hard. My credit card limit was ten thousand pounds and there were already a couple of purchases on it, but there should easily be enough. 'If that's how they want it,' I said. 'Get a pen and I'll give you the details.'

I went to the bedroom to retrieve my handbag and when I came back, I read the card numbers over the line. My hands were shaking so much I could hardly hold it still.

'Thank you,' he said, sounding very subdued.

'Claire has my bank account details so you can give her a cheque when you're in a position to repay it. But don't forget what I said. I don't want to hear from you again.'

'Goodbye,' he said, then murmured indistinctly, 'I love you.' I hung up first.

I sat for a few moments with my head in my hands, breathing rapidly, then I dialled the number of my London flat to see if Claire was there. It was just the answer machine and I hung up without leaving a message. Then I dialled Anna's number. It rang and rang and I was about to give up when she lifted the receiver and spoke, breathlessly.

'Nicola, hi! How are you?'

I told her what had just happened, about giving Sedic my credit card number, and she was stunned.

'You need your head examined,' she exclaimed. 'You'll never see that money again. What on earth were you thinking of?'

'I don't know. I suppose I would have felt guilty if he was found dead somewhere. If he doesn't return the money, I'll just consider it an alimony payment. It will be worth it if he leaves me alone from now on.'

'Are you sure that's what you want? Aren't you secretly hoping this will bring you back together?'

Anna often had a knack of pinpointing my ulterior motives but this time she was wrong. 'I'm tired of it all. He's lied to me so comprehensively and consistently that I feel there's nothing left. The whole relationship was an illusion from start to finish. It took me a while but at last I've realised what a complete creep he was. I feel foolish that I believed in him for so long but I'm definitely over it now.'

'That sounds quite plausible, Nicky. You'd convince me more if you hadn't just given the guy your credit card number. I hope you're going to change it after this so he can't use it again.'

'How did you get to be so cynical?' I asked.

'The school of life. The one you flunked out of.'

After our call, I crawled back to bed, but lay awake wrestling with uncomfortable thoughts and emotions that I couldn't put a name to. Sadness was still among them, but anger was present as well; and maybe a tiny smidgeon of satisfaction that it had turned out that he did need me after all. I was firm in my resolve not to speak to him again, but glad that I was the one in the position of power at the end.

Next morning, Dadong drove me down town to do some Christmas shopping. I decided not to tell him about the late-night conversation. I was certain he would think I was crazy for giving Sedic the money, but it also seemed obscene to let him know that I had access to such amounts, when I knew that his salary was only the equivalent of thirty pounds a month. Mimi got twenty-five and Ali twenty. They were reasonably well paid by local standards but it was still the kind of amount Diana or Howard would spend during an evening's drinking at Tanamur.

'What age is your daughter?' I asked him. He never spoke about her.

'Seven.'

'And what does she like? What games does she play with her friends?'

He had to consider this for a while. 'She likes music,' he said. 'Sometimes I play guitar and she sings.'

'I bet she likes the Spice Girls,' I said. I knew they were popular in Indonesia because the anthems were ubiquitous, in department stores, bars and hotel foyers.

Dadong grunted.

I found a karaoke machine in one shopping mall, red plastic with a microphone and song book, so you could play the backing tracks and sing along to your favourites, and I had them wrap it up securely so Dadong wouldn't see. For my parents I bought a beautiful print of the Ramayana story, showing the Monkey People searching high and low for the missing Sita while her husband Lord Rama paced and fretted.

Prices were so low that I bought much more generous presents for friends at home than I would normally have done – silk blouses, fine woven bedspreads and skillful wood carvings. Diana had told me about a courier firm who would airfreight them back to Britain.

It was strange to contemplate Christmas alone in a foreign country, but too far to fly home for a break so soon after I'd arrived. A few ex-pat bars and shops hung up strands of threadbare tinsel but there were no carols or Santa Claus figures. Diana sent me a gold-embossed invitation to the British Embassy Christmas party, but otherwise it looked as though the festive season was going to pass unmarked for me. The temperature remained constant at thirty-one degrees although it rained most nights, freshening the air but making the garden muddy.

I didn't hear any more from Sedic and I still hadn't heard from Peter. I tried to put it all to the back of my mind and carried on working at the clinic as usual. Sedic had said I would get the money back in a week, so exactly a week after the phone call from the Bahamas, I rang Claire to find out if he'd kept his word. I left a message when I got in from work, then tried again at midnight before I went to bed, but it was the next morning, at one a.m. London time, when I finally got her on the line.

'You're not going to believe this,' she told me, 'but the money's here. In cash in a plastic carrier bag. He brought it yesterday but I haven't had a chance to get to the bank yet. It looks as though it's in a mixture of currencies.'

'Claire, for God's sake! Don't leave it lying around. Anything could happen.'

'I'll take it to the bank today. Who would have thought it, though?'

'What did he say when he gave it to you?'

It was a clear line and I could hear her hesitation. 'I think he's just relieved that it's all settled.'

'Has he moved the rest of his belongings out of the flat yet?'

'No. He doesn't have anywhere else to take them. I can hardly chuck them out in the street. He's been round a couple of times recently when he needed to pick things up.'

'What kind of things? Clothes?'

'No, he was looking through the writing desk. He said some of his papers were missing.'

'Tell him they're all packed into the boxes in the cupboard. But I'm serious. I want him to move everything out before Christmas. This has gone on long enough.'

'I'll tell him. And I'll take the money to the bank tomorrow, definitely.'

'When you drop it off, do you think you could request a statement so I can check that it converts to roughly the right amount?'

'What then? Shall I send it to you?'

'No, just give me a call when you get it and tell me what it says. The credit card company are sending my statements here directly. He'd better have been straight with me this time.'

'It's good to hear you standing up to him at last.'

That was a bit ironic coming from Claire, who would jump in the Thames if Marco asked her to, but I let it pass.

Around two hundred people were gathered in the large, high-ceilinged rooms on the first floor of the old colonial building. Most of them were English, with a sprinkling of Indonesian faces, and everyone wore flashy evening dress: sequinned jackets, satin ballgowns, dinner jackets and black tie. A huge fir tree in one corner was covered with flickering white bulbs shaped like candles. Waiters circulated with trays of bright jewel-coloured drinks: tomato-red Bloody Marys, lurid green crème de menthe and sickly turquoise curaçao cocktails. I opted for a ladleful of mulled wine and the glass burned my fingers.

Christmas-style canapés were served on silver platters: duck and orange rolled in tiny pancakes, turkey and cranberry squares, miniature puddings and mince pies, marzipan holly.

I felt paralysed with shyness, tongue-tied and clumsy amongst the huge gathering of well-to-do strangers, but as soon as Diana spotted me, she swept me into a whirlwind tour of the party, introducing me to one group then whisking me along to the next. She chatted so easily and confidently that I could smile, shake hands and observe without having to dredge up much conversation. If required to speak, I asked people about their plans for Christmas and found that most were returning to their families in Britain. Jakarta would be left to the Indonesians for a couple of weeks.

It was an older crowd than Diana's group of friends. Their children were at university or boarding school while they spent a few years out here reinforcing their pension plans. Some seemed like nice people and I received a few invitations to Christmas dinner from couples who were remaining behind in the city.

'I must introduce you to the Parkers,' Diana announced. 'They're your local wardens.' Before I could ask what a local warden was for, we were shaking hands with a pinched, grey couple in their late fifties or early sixties.

'Dr Drew,' she said, 'I've been meaning to call on you. Our house is right behind yours.'

'Really? Which direction?' The streets were such a jumbled maze, it could have meant anything.

'If you threw a ball over the wall behind your swimming pool, it would land in my rose garden. So don't do it, please.' She smiled at her little joke.

'I'll try not to.'

'Diana's told us all about you. How awful about your fiancé.'

I frowned. 'What did she say?'

'Just that he was supposed to come out here with you and then . . . It must seem very strange being here on your own.'

'It's not too bad. I enjoy the work.' I was momentarily annoyed with Diana for being so indiscreet, but then realised I had no right since I listened to all her gossip about other people. 'Diana tells me you're the local warden in our area. What exactly does that mean?'

'It's in case of trouble. If there are serious riots or, heaven forbid, a military coup, I advise you on evacuation procedures and make sure everyone is accounted for. There are wardens for every part of the city where British people live.'

'Have you ever had to arrange an evacuation or is it just a precaution?'

'Of course we have. I was here in 1965, my dear, when whites were the target of all the local anger. It won't be so dangerous next time because they understand how much money we bring into their country. The new hate figures are the military. And the Chinese, of course. They've always been in the firing line.'

'What do you mean – next time? Do you think there's going to be trouble?'

'Of course there is. Don't you read the papers?'

Diana grasped my elbow. 'Will you excuse us, Mrs Parker? I want Nicola to meet the ambassador.'

'I'll give you a call, Dr Drew,' she said portentously. 'You're on my list.'

'Old scaremonger,' Diana whispered as she pulled me away. 'Don't listen to her.'

The ambassador was disconcerting to talk to because he didn't meet your eye, gazing off into the middle distance throughout our conversation, but he asked intelligent questions and listened to my answers.

'What do you make of health care provisions here?' he asked, after Diana explained about my job.

'The staff are very well trained,' I replied. 'They're short of resources but seem efficient and dedicated.'

Diana laughed. 'I haven't told her about poor old Tony.'

'Maybe you shouldn't,' the ambassador twinkled.

'Who's Tony?' I asked.

'He's an aide at the Australian embassy. He sat on a broken glass at one of their parties and they whisked him off to the nearest hospital to have his cuts stitched up. A week later he had to be rushed to Singapore by air ambulance. He was suffering from acute blood poisoning because they'd managed to sew up his anus at the same time.'

'That sounds like an apocryphal tale to me,' I smiled.

'Yes, really, Diana,' the ambassador interrupted. 'You shouldn't spread these rumours around. Don't you think it's possible that Tony sensationalised his plight somewhat to divert attention from the undignified manner in which he sustained his injuries? Who can say? But what are we doing at a Christmas party talking about an Australian's bottom?'

We all laughed. He asked me more about the set-up in the clinic, how I managed to communicate with patients, and the differences I found between Jakarta and London medical practice. Before we parted, he asked if I would come for dinner in the New Year and said his secretary would contact me.

Next, Diana introduced me to her direct boss, the married one she claimed to be in love with. He was a tall, fit-looking man, the type you imagine rowing for Oxford and shooting grouse at weekends. He emanated flirtatiousness, meeting my eye with amused directness and holding my hand a fraction of a second too long. I imagined he liked to collect admirers and couldn't see a happy outcome for Diana.

'James is going to take me sailing in January,' she beamed.

'Have you done a lot of sailing?' I asked him.

'I've completed the Whitbread and the Americas Cup, if that counts as a lot,' he smiled, arrogantly. 'I need Diana as crew for a trip round Lombok. You can't get decent Indonesian help at that time of year.'

'Why not?' I asked.

'Ramadan,' they replied together, and Diana rolled her eyes. James continued, 'They have to fast between dawn and dusk and nothing is allowed to pass their lips. They can't even swallow their own saliva. You'll find that any Indonesians you work with get exhausted and irritable around that time and standards tend to slip. Not exactly the kind of crew I want for my trip.'

'What, they all fast? All day long?'

'Only the Muslims, of course. You're not Muslim, are you, Diana?' He tickled her shoulder and she giggled. 'I tell you, I can't wait to get away from these bloody speakers echoing the call to prayer all over the city five times a day. There's one just round the corner here and I sometimes feel like marching round there with a sledgehammer.'

'Isn't he gorgeous?' she asked me, once he'd moved on to another group. 'He's so sexy, I can't bear it. I know he'll never leave his wife but she stays back home in Wiltshire bringing up their children. Silly woman. If I had someone like him as a husband, I wouldn't let him out of my sight.'

I liked Diana. She was warm, friendly and generous. But sometimes I wondered if she wasn't just as gullible as me when it came to men. 'He seems very charming, but I hope you're not going to get hurt.'

She giggled and shrugged. 'Better to have loved and lost, I always say. Don't you agree?'

'Frankly, no. Not always.'

'You need a holiday, darling. You're getting jaded. My weekend at the Sambolo beach house comes up over Christmas but I can't use it because I'll be back in the UK. Why don't you take it instead? There are bound to be loads of parties going on down there. Anyone who's not back in the UK will be at their beach houses. Why don't you think about it? Half a mile of white sand, warm turquoise sea, the houseboy catches fish and barbecues them for you and massage girls come by every five minutes. Wouldn't that be better than smoggy old Jakarta?'

'Maybe it's not a bad idea.'

'I'm leaving in a couple of days, but I'll draw you a map of how to get there and call the houseboy – his name is Keri – to let him know you're coming.'

I stayed at the party longer than I'd intended, enjoying the chance to talk about something other than medicine. Some of the older couples had begun to filter towards the cloakroom and Diana was dancing with James when I started to yawn. I glanced at my watch and was astonished to find it was two-thirty in the morning. I wove through the dancefloor to kiss Diana goodbye, shook hands with James, then slipped out of the room and down the staircase to the front entrance.

'They're not all bad,' I told Dadong on the way home.

'Products of their generation and class but some are decent people.' He smiled.

'Diana thinks I should go to her house at Sambolo for Christmas. Would you be able to take me there?'

'Yes, of course.'

'I would only stay for two or three days.'

'I could find a room and stay there as well, in case you need me.'

I'd hoped he would suggest that but immediately felt guilty. 'What about your wife? Wouldn't she be annoyed if you had to spend a couple of nights away from home?'

He shook his head. 'She wouldn't mind.'

I was curious about his marriage but he would never discuss it. 'You can hardly see each other as it is; you work such long hours. I'm sorry you had to wait so late for me tonight.'

'I think it will be good for you to go to the beach,' he said. 'You seem tired. You are working very hard at the clinic.'

I was touched by his concern. 'They're understaffed and I don't have anything else to do with my time.'

'You need a rest, though. Besides, you haven't really seen Indonesia yet. Just this.' He gestured out through the windscreen.

I looked ahead at the dark skyscrapers against a slate grey sky, lights blinking on flyovers and car headlights trailing like comets, and I knew he was right. Little separated it from cityscapes the world over. I needed a change of scene.

Chapter Eighteen

The boot of the car was almost full. Mimi had packed boxes of bread, fruit, vegetables, rice, all kinds of drinks, coffee and tea; a holdall contained sheets, pillows and towels, candles and insect repellent. I hadn't packed more than a couple of bikinis and my sarong, a novel and some sunscreen. Dadong arrived before ten, and for the first time since we met he was wearing a casual shirt with a pattern – black on tan, like the markings on a tree trunk.

'Can I sit in the front?' I asked. 'I want to see where we're going.' He hesitated before he agreed, with an attitude that implied that it was irregular but he would allow it just this once.

We drove down Sudirman for a few blocks then veered onto a flyover heading west, and after twenty minutes or so the landscape was transformed from huddled apartment blocks to waterlogged fields. People in cone-shaped straw hats waded through rows of bright green shoots. In a couple of fields I noticed farmers burning tarry pyramids about three feet tall that gave off thick trails of smoke.

'Is that some kind of pesticide?' I asked.

Dadong shook his head, amused. 'Not at all. It's an offering to the rice gods.'

'Are you serious?' I couldn't tell if he was pulling my leg.

'It's true. Many people worship spirit gods here. In the countryside there are shrines scattered around and you are supposed to stop and leave offerings. It's bad luck to pass them by. Fortunately I don't believe in them, so we don't have to.'

'But I'd like to stop at one. I love visiting churches and

temples when I travel. I always light a candle, if they have them, and leave a donation.'

'Are you superstitious?'

I considered this. 'I just think it's a fascinating insight into other cultures, the way people worship.'

'You're a very strange person, Nicola.' He said this deadpan, staring ahead at the road.

'I'm not,' I began, but couldn't think what to refute it with.

Dadong shrugged, amused. 'Of course not, whatever you say.'

I smiled, enjoying the easy companionship, beginning to relax already.

We passed through an industrial area, with factories set behind high wire fences, then the road narrowed and we entered a village with a market running along either side of the main thoroughfare. Shoppers milled in front of the car and a child sat in the road eating a slice of watermelon. Some scrawny chickens were tied upside down to the awning of a stall, where they hung, clucking and flapping. On either side there were boxes of misshapen fruits and spices. Some I recognised, some I didn't: round black squash-ball fruits; shiny red pear-shaped ones; the bumpy yellowy green surface of the durian; geometrically precise creamy-yellow starfruits; long dark crackly pods and chillies of such a deep red they looked plastic. Suddenly I thought of Sedic's painting of the marketplace, still hanging above my mantelpiece, and a twinge of the old sadness made me shiver.

Dadong slowed to a standstill and beeped patiently until the child scrambled into the gutter. The women looked round and acknowledged us then stepped towards the side, still in mid-conversation. I opened a window to breath the overpowering scent of cloves and sweet decaying fruit and immediately a skinny man appeared dangling an armful of wooden necklaces.

'English?' he asked and I nodded, 'Yes.' Dadong said something that sounded unfriendly and inched the car forward, but still the man followed.

'You like?' he asked, holding out the jewellery. 'Very good price.'

'No, thank you,' I smiled, but he followed us the length of

the market, urging me to take a necklace, poking them into the car so I couldn't close my window without inadvertently acquiring some. I glanced at Dadong but he was grinning to himself, focusing on the road ahead.

'*Tidak mau*,' I said, 'I don't want.' But still the man insisted. 'Very nice, look.'

As we reached the end of the market, he whipped the necklaces out of the car just in time, as Dadong accelerated into the clear stretch of road ahead.

'Thanks for your help,' I said sarcastically.

'You encouraged him by smiling and being so polite and English about it,' he laughed. 'And I can't believe you haven't learned more Bahasa after almost two months here.'

'Everyone speaks to me in English,' I complained.

'It would be a bit of a one-way conversation if they didn't. "Hello." "Thank you." "I don't want." That's all I've ever heard you say.'

I snorted indignantly but he was right. I resolved to buy a book and start learning more vocabulary so he couldn't tease me any more.

The road swung round to follow the coast at this point and pale grey sea glittered under an overcast sky. Beautiful flowering trees lined the route: there were intense coral blossoms with yellow centres, and long, pale yellow ones with black stamens. Inland, mists shimmered over dark green hills, like a fairytale kingdom. We rounded a headland and I could see the distinctive shape of two black islands, with classic flat-topped volcano shapes.

'Is that Krakatoa?' I asked.

'Yes, and Anak Krakatoa. The smaller crater formed after the eighteen eighty three eruption.'

Either streaks of cloud or plumes of smoke were drifting around the top. 'When did it last erupt?' I asked.

'It's erupting all the time, spitting rocks into the sea. Fishermen get hit sometimes. But nothing like the big eruption, when thirty-five thousand people died.'

I gasped at the figure. 'I've never been this close to a live volcano before.'

'If it erupts, you should climb up the nearest palm tree as high as you can go, then maybe the tidal wave won't reach you.'

'That doesn't sound exactly foolproof.' He grinned.

We reached an area where well-kept houses blocked the view to the sea. There was one hotel, a mini-supermarket, and then a string of bamboo-thatched bungalows, each fringed by patches of lush tropical garden. Dadong slowed down, consulted the sheet of instructions Diana had given me, then swerved into a driveway and came to a stop.

'Here we are.'

I got out of the car and walked round to the front of the house. A strip of jaggy grass separated it from a white sand bay that curved round to dark breakwaters on either side. The twin volcanoes puffed on the horizon. A couple were playing with a dog a few hundred yards further along and some fishermen stood on a jetty to the left, but otherwise there was no one to be seen. Dadong appeared with an Indonesian boy, who looked about fifteen or sixteen.

'This is Keri, your houseboy,' he told me. 'He doesn't speak any English.'

'*Selamat siang*,' I greeted him, and he nodded. Dadong went to get the luggage and boxes from the car and Keri pulled back a flimsy screen door to show me around the house. A circle of canvas-covered sofas under the front awning faced out towards the sea, and there was a kitchen and dining area behind. Four doors led off the hall and I pushed them open one by one. The first had a double bed and two others held twin beds; the fourth door led into a tiny toilet with a shower cubicle. I checked the bedrooms again. They didn't have air-conditioning but there were electric overhead fans. I decided to take the one with the double bed.

Keri was unpacking the boxes of food in the kitchen and Dadong hovered awkwardly by the door. I felt uncomfortable suddenly, unsure how this arrangement was supposed to work. He never came into the house in Jakarta except on the couple of occasions when I'd invited him. 'Would you like a drink?' I asked. 'Some tea, or coke or a beer?'

'Maybe a glass of water,' he requested, and I got one for each of us.

'Why don't you sit down?' I asked, pointing at the sofas, but he said 'I'm fine, thank you,' and stood formally, sipping his drink.

'Why don't you stay in the house? There's so much space. I don't need three bedrooms all for myself.'

He wouldn't look at me and I wondered if he was embarrassed. 'No, I can't do that. I'll get a room somewhere nearby. The company will pay.'

'Dadong, it seems crazy.'

'It wouldn't be right for me to stay here,' he insisted. It was obvious that I didn't understand some nuance he considered important. Maybe his wife wouldn't like him staying under the same roof as a single English woman? Somehow I doubted that was the reason. It was much more likely to be a question of status and professionalism. Perhaps a live-in servant had less prestige than one who lived out.

The houseboy asked something and Dadong translated. 'Would you like him to get you some fish for dinner tonight?'

'What kind of fish?'

It was the first time I'd seen Dadong stuck for an English word. '*Ikan laut*. I don't know what you would call it. They're about this big.' He held his hands a foot apart.

'Yes, I'd like that. Thank you.'

The houseboy said something else. 'You should ask him if you want anything. He can get coconut milk, cigarettes, or girls who give massages.'

'*Terimah kasih*,' I told the boy. 'Dadong, tell him I'll let him know if I need anything. Now I think I'm going to swim. Do you want to come with me?'

If I hadn't known him better, I could almost have sworn he blushed. 'I have to go and see to the car,' he said, put his glass down and disappeared round the side of the house.

The water was chalky green and much cooler than my pool in Jakarta. Occasional clumps of bracken-coloured seaweed floated past and shoals of tiny fish glittered. I swam far out from the shore, towards the black craters, then turned onto my back to look at the sky. Wisps of cloud drifted by. It was the twenty-third of December, three o'clock in the afternoon, and I was floating in the sea between Java and Sumatra, two hundred miles south of the Equator. I pictured myself as a microscopic black dot on the globe. The only sounds came from tiny waves lapping against my limbs, rocking me gently. The volcanoes looked benign, seeming further away than they had on shore, but I tried to picture the strength of the explosion that had killed thirty-five thousand people, an unimaginable number. How far had the destruction spread? How much warning did they have?

My reverie was disturbed by a stinging sensation on my thigh, as though it had brushed against nettles. I peered into the water. The jellyfish was almost translucent, its tentacles like trails of saliva. I turned and swam swiftly for the shore but another one caught my calf before I reached the warmer shallow water. When I clambered onto the sand and sat down, my legs were marked with two scarlet welts that prickled and throbbed.

A translucent crab hurried sideways up the sand and I mused on the number of invisible creatures in Indonesia. Mosquitos don't make a noise, although they still bite; crabs and jellyfish are colourless; sometimes you feel imaginary bites and itches on your skin but when you look, there's nothing there. It's as though the air is so dense it plays tricks on your senses.

I walked up to the house and rinsed off under an out-door showerhead, then four women appeared, seemingly from nowhere. They were carrying armfuls of brightly coloured sarongs, ceramic pots and woven bedspreads.

'You want sarong? You want massa? Is my business. Have two children.' The speaker extended her hand at thigh and then at knee level to demonstrate the heights of her children. The others joined in, their voices rising and falling like a song. They were young, maybe in their early twenties, and very pretty, although one had a scorched birthmark on her cheek.

I looked through their wares and selected some sarongs for my girlfriends and a bedspread I liked for myself. I didn't want to buy ceramics and have the hassle of carrying them home but it seemed unfair not to give some money to the fourth woman when I'd bought from the other three, so I pointed at her and asked 'Massage?', and she smiled and nodded happily.

We went into the house and I spread a towel on my bed and lay down on my front. She began to work on my feet, using a lemon-scented oil, digging furrows in my flesh with thumbs so strong it felt as though they could have killed a man. She kneaded tender spots, moving upwards, and as she finished with each area, she cracked the joints like kindling. At the top of my thighs, her powerful fingers slid down between and I became nervous that she would enter me completely, but she moved up to the lower back, pressing down till the vertebrae snapped.

It took about an hour and when she finished, she selected a note from the handful I offered before rejoining her friends outside and they disappeared between the houses giggling to each other. I retrieved my book and sat outside on a sun lounger but I was too lulled and drowsy to read. Around six, the light began to change fast. It was like viewing the world through a series of darkening tinted windshields. The sand turned caramel, the water greenish-gold and the sky was nicotine-stained. Then the raspberry sun began to pulsate, turning the water bubblegum pink. The fishermen on the breakwater stood out like black stick figures in a Chinese painting. The sun slid suddenly beneath the ocean and everything became grey and murky. The progress from bright daylight to night had taken less than half an hour.

Around the garden, a dozen electric lights clicked on simultaneously, and my houseboy arrived, grinning widely, holding up a large, orange-pink scaly fish. 'You like gin-tonic?' he asked, and I agreed, 'Yes, why not?'

I sat at an outside table with my drink while Keri lit the barbecue and marinated the fish in some oils and herbs. There were no other lights visible along the bay and I wondered if Diana had been mistaken in thinking people would come here for Christmas. Maybe I would prefer to be alone anyway. The only sounds now were the crackling of the fire, the hushing of the waves and some crickets in the bush. I went in to replenish my drink and saw a gekko poised high up on the kitchen wall, about four inches long, with mottled green and brown markings and disproportionately large eyes. As I watched, her long tongue shot out and flicked a mosquito into her jaws. Her big eyes half-closed in ecstasy as she swallowed, then she uttered what sounded like a ladylike shriek of embarrassment before the customary 'e-kko, e-kko'.

The second gin made me warm and fuzzy. 'I'm so lucky to be here,' I thought, and realised I felt content and peaceful for the first time since Sedic and I had broken up. Somehow in Jakarta there were constant reminders: the house we were supposed to have shared; meeting his mother; other people enquiring about the whereabouts of my fiancé; then the call from the Bahamas. There was no telephone here, nothing to shatter the tranquillity. It was just me and the sea and the air.

Keri brought a bowl of salad to the table, far too much for one person, and I wondered where Dadong would be eating that night. It would be nice to have company.

'*Dadong di mana?*' I asked him.

'*Ma'af,*' he replied, holding his palms wide and shaking his head.

He must have gone out somewhere. No doubt I'd see him in the morning.

Chapter Nineteen

———◦◦◦◦———

I opened my eyes, suddenly wide awake. The room was pitch black and it took a few moments to remember where I was. Overhead, the fan circulated warm air with a 'fut-fut' sound. I pulled the scratchy bedcover up to my chin and listened.

There was a scrabbling of tiny feet on the bamboo directly behind my head. Maybe a mouse; that could have been what wakened me. I reached out and clattered the glass of water on my bedside table to let the creature know I was there. When the next sound came, I felt very alert, muscles tense. It was a scream of outrage, remarkably like the burst of noise if you stamp hard on a child's squeaky toy. Seconds later, there was a rattling release of air. The scream seemed very close, as if inside the room, but it was impossible to tell. Acoustics are misleading in the tropics and the walls were only made of bamboo thatch.

The next shriek was unquestionably one of terror and the feet scrabbled frantically but now it sounded as though they were on the ceiling. Once again it was followed by a pressurised hissing noise. I tried to decide whether to get up to switch the light on but the thought of putting my bare feet on the floor was a deterrent. There might be something scurrying about down there.

All at once, there was a loud rustling of the thatch, another shriek, and then something long, heavy and unmistakably alive thumped down on top of me, landing diagonally across my stomach and thighs. I yelled hard, flicked back the cover and threw it across the room then leapt from the bed and out of the door, slamming it behind me. I jumped onto a sofa in the living room, sharp involuntary yells bursting from my lungs. My mind was a blank, full of sheer, awful horror, and as Dadong burst through the screen door, I didn't even remember that I wasn't wearing any clothes. He picked up a towel from the back of a chair and wrapped it round me then helped me down from the sofa and I clung tightly round his neck and started crying, great shaky sobs.

'Something fell on me,' I managed to stutter. 'In my bed.'

'How big was it?' he asked, glancing towards the bedroom door.

I held out my hands. The creature had been at least three feet long. 'Oh my God! Oh my God!' I cried, pressing the heels of my hands into my eye sockets.

'Sit down,' he urged. 'You're all right now. I'll deal with it.'

I tucked my feet up and huddled into the tiniest space I could. Dadong disappeared outside for a moment then reappeared with a spade. I couldn't bear to think what the creature might be. It was as if I could still feel that weight on my chest and stomach and thighs and the wriggling movement it made before I flung it across the room. If it was a mouse, surely it wouldn't have been so long? And I hadn't felt the sharpness of its clawed feet. I couldn't stop shaking at the memory of those few milliseconds when it was on top of me.

Dadong opened the bedroom door cautiously and switched on the light, then he crept in and closed it behind him. There was silence for a few moments then the clanging of his spade striking something hard, repeatedly, without mercy. I heard him shout at one point but couldn't make out what he said. The spade struck at least forty or fifty times; I've got no idea how long it took but it seemed an inordinate while before he opened the door again. He was holding a large bundle wrapped up in my bed cover.

I shrank back on the sofa, nervous that it might suddenly leap from his arms. 'What is it?' I squeaked.

'It's better if you don't know,' he said. 'I'm just going to throw this cover out. I don't think you'll want it any more.' He vanished out of the door and round the side of the house but came back less than a minute later and went to the sink to scrub his hands and forearms.

I was gripped with revulsion and a sick feeling in the pit of my stomach, but I had to know. 'Please tell me,' I said. 'It can't be any worse than I'm imagining.'

He dried his hands carefully. 'Maybe I'll make some tea before I tell you.'

That sounded reasonable. I found another towel to wrap around my shoulders, so that I was swaddled tightly, and watched as he boiled some water and put teabags in the pot. I was still trembling when he carried the tray across to the table and sat down, but the flashbacks to the moment when that creature landed on top of me were getting less intense. For the first time, I wondered why Dadong had been close enough to hear me. Where was he staying?

'Nicola,' he began gravely, watching me closely. 'What landed on you was a snake that was trying to swallow a rat. The rat was half in its throat and half out, still attempting to escape, and in the struggle they fell through a gap in your roof where the thatch is torn. That's what happened.'

I pressed my hands over my mouth as my gut clenched and heaved, and then I started to cry. Dadong was embarrassed but once I'd started, I couldn't stop. 'I can't bear it,' I sobbed. 'I can't do this any more.'

He shuffled round the sofa and took hold of my hand, patting it gently and trying to hush me.

'It's no use, I've had it. It's just too much for me, it's not fair.' Tears were soaking my cheeks, dripping off the end of my nose and chin. 'It's Christmas Eve and I want to go home. It's too hard, living here on my own. Too hard.'

Dadong slipped an arm round my shoulder and I snuggled my face into his tee-shirt. I just wanted someone to look after me. He stroked my hair, whispering, 'Calm down, it's all right now.' It felt warm and comfortable and it came to me in a flash of insight that I'd wanted this to happen since the first day we met at the airport. That's why it had always seemed important what he thought of me, why I wanted him to approve. He smelled clean, of soap and fresh cotton.

Tentatively, I raised my face and kissed him quickly on the lips. He pulled away a little. 'You're tired, Nicola. I think you should go to bed in one of the other rooms and I'll wait out here to make sure you're OK.'

I started crying again. 'I can't. There's no way I'm going in there. Let me just sit out here with you. Please.'

Finally we lay down full length, side by side, on the largest of the sofas and Dadong put his arms round me and whispered, 'Go to sleep'. But dawn was streaking the sky outside before I was able to relax enough to give in to unconsciousness. I lay there against his firm, controlled body, listening to the almost imperceptible sound of his breathing, feeling gradually calmer, trying not to think about what the repercussions of the night might be. He's married, I reminded myself. He works for you. But he still felt safe.

I awoke to raised voices, round the side of the house. Dadong was shouting angrily and Keri was trying to defend himself. I adjusted the towels that were draped round me and pulled on some shoes before hobbling to the bathroom. I pushed the door wide and checked the floor, walls, shower cubicle and ceiling before I dared enter.

When I emerged, Dadong was making more tea. Outside it was bright and hazy and I could hear some voices and laughter drifting up from the beach.

'How are you feeling?' he asked.

'Terrible.' I shook my head. 'I'm sorry, you must think I'm pathetic, but that's the scariest thing that's ever happened to me. I guess I've led a sheltered life.'

'It's not pathetic. If you hadn't moved fast, it could have been very dangerous. I've just been telling the houseboy that it's his fault and he says he'll mend all the thatch covering the house today so it can't happen again.'

'I don't think I can stay here anyway.' I sat down and took a sip of scalding tea. 'I'm just too jumpy. Maybe we should head back to Jakarta straight after breakfast.'

Dadong came over and put some bread and jam on the table

in front of me then surprised me by slipping his arms round my shoulders from behind. I leant my head back against his chest.

'If it makes you feel safer, I could stay in the house with you,' he suggested.

'Where were you sleeping last night? Is your room nearby?'

'I was sleeping in the car.'

I swivelled round to look at him and slipped my arms round his waist. 'Dadong, that's stupid! I thought you said the company would pay for a room.'

He spoke very quietly. 'They will.' I was bemused. 'I need the money, so I'll claim for the room. Do you understand?'

'Of course I do. But why don't you stay here and claim for the room?'

'I could do that tonight, if you want to stay here.'

'And today. Please don't leave me on my own.' I stood up, with my arms still round his waist, and pulled him into a hug. We were almost exactly the same height. I was too self-conscious to try and kiss him again, but rested my head on his shoulder and held tightly, feeling ripples of attraction.

He broke away first. 'Do you want me to fetch anything from your room? It would be better if you don't go in until Keri has cleared up.'

'Oh God!' I clasped my forehead. Panic fluttered under the surface. Memories of the grotesque union of creatures locked in a death struggle made me want to retch.

We spent the day lying on the sand, snoozing, the outside world drifting in and out of my unfocused dreams. I swam a little, but not too far out because the sea was rougher and I didn't want to encounter any more jellyfish. Dadong stripped his shirt off but kept his long trousers on. His chest was hairless, more muscular than I'd expected, with cherry-purple nipples. Whenever he closed his eyes, I watched him and wondered what he was feeling about everything. He was attentive to me – bringing cold drinks, pointing out when my shoulders looked as though they were burning, asking how I felt – but there were no other attempts at physical intimacy. He was probably just being nice to me because of the shock last night, I decided. I wanted to touch him but was wary of transgressing any boundaries. He hadn't given any sign that he was attracted to me and I didn't want to risk making a fool of myself.

In late afternoon, we walked right along the beach and clambered over the headland at the end. I noticed the sarong-massage girls giggling and pointing at us.

'What kind of snake was it?' I asked and he glanced round to see if I was all right. 'It's OK, I think I'm coming to terms with it now.'

'It was a cobra.'

'Are they poisonous?'

'Very. Their bite injects toxic venom but they can also spray victims from up to six feet away. It's lucky that you moved as quickly as you did.'

I looked round at the grassy scrub. 'Do you think there are many of them around here?'

He took my hand and squeezed it. 'Some, but you have to remember that snakes will do anything to avoid contact with human beings. If they hear you, they'll get out of the way. You did the right thing last night, rattling your glass, but that snake was preoccupied with its catch.'

'What size was it?'

'It wasn't fully grown. Only about four feet long.'

I sighed deeply.

'I don't think you're pathetic for being scared of it. Anyone would have been. You're very brave.'

I laughed, unconvincingly. 'I must have looked ridiculous, standing on the sofa screaming when you arrived.'

'No, you didn't look ridiculous.' He turned away, seeming embarrassed, but squeezed my fingers again.

We stopped to look out at the volcanoes, growing misty on the horizon as the light began to fade. A little boat puttered past them, with a tiny black figure standing inside.

'There is something I haven't told you yet,' Dadong announced, seriously. 'It's about my wife.'

I stared out to sea, my face twitching inadvertently. I wasn't sure I wanted to hear this.

'Our marriage broke up last year and we are divorced now. I didn't want Medimachines to know because companies like that tend to prefer employing married men. They think they're more reliable.'

'I won't mention it to anyone,' I said. 'I'm sorry to hear about your marriage, though. What went wrong?'

'We are very different people. She likes the country, I like the city; she's not interested in politics, but I am; she doesn't like music, I do. The question is, what we ever had in common in the first place. I can't remember the answer now.'

I felt a glow of excitement to learn that he was single. Was it significant that he was telling me now? What could it mean?

'So where do you live? And what about your daughter?'

'My daughter lives with my wife and I have a room in a friend's house round the corner from them. I hoped I would still be able to see a lot of my daughter if I lived nearby but it doesn't work that way. I'm thinking of moving further into town soon, but in the meantime, I am paying rent for them, and that's why I'm short of money.'

'You could always move into my house,' I said, without thinking. 'There's plenty of room.'

'You're only here for another three or four months,' he pointed out. The words introduced a distance. We could become close in some ways but our lives and future expectations were fundamentally different.

That evening, after Keri had cleared the dinner plates, we sat on the sofa drinking beer and playing a game called Jenga we found in one of Diana's cupboards, which involved removing blocks of wood from a tower one by one without letting it topple over. Dadong's hand was much steadier than mine and he won game after game. Tactically, he had very good instincts about which blocks were loadbearing and which would wriggle free most easily.

'Not very good for a doctor. It's just as well I'm not a surgeon,' I laughed, after the tower collapsed for a third time. I looked at my watch. 'Do you know, back in England, an old man called Santa Claus is flying around the sky on a sledge delivering presents to children by climbing down their chimneys.'

'You forgot about the time difference,' Dadong reminded me. 'It's only afternoon in England just now. Doesn't Santa come at night?'

'How do you know about him?' I asked.

'The same way you know about the Ramayana.' I looked at him quizzically. 'I saw you bought a picture of Rama and Sita the other day when I took you shopping.'

'Are you Muslim?' I asked him.

'Certainly not,' he replied indignantly, as if I had insulted him by asking. 'Are you Christian?'

I laughed. 'No one asks that question in Britain any more. The truth is that I was brought up as a Christian but I'm not sure what I believe now.'

'You hedge your bets by lighting candles in other people's churches,' Dadong teased.

A creature began to purr close to the ceiling, making a 'frrtt, ffrrttt,' sound.

'What's that?' I asked. 'Is it friend or foe?'

'Some kind of lizard, I expect. They make a lot of different sounds.'

I was getting sleepy, but wasn't sure how to broach the subject of the sleeping arrangements. I yawned ostentatiously.

'Keri has cleaned your bedroom and mended the thatch,' he said. 'Nothing will get in there now.'

I slithered round on the sofa and took his hand, sliding my fingers down between his. I tried to think of something seductive to say or do, but instead I just felt shy. What if he wasn't attracted to me? I laid my head on his shoulder and he curled an arm round me. We sat uncertainly, in silence, listening to the lizard in the rafters and the waves murmuring outside. At last, I tilted my face to kiss him on the lips and it turned out that was all that was needed. Soon we were unfastening each other's clothes with impatient fingers, unable to stop kissing. I was dying to feel his skin against my skin, but then I remembered something.

'I don't have any condoms,' I whispered. 'We can't . . .'

'There are many other ways to make love,' he smiled, and his tongue licked my shoulder and slid over towards my breasts.

Chapter Twenty

I woke on Christmas morning with a smile of surprise stretching my skin. No one had ever treated me with such affection and consideration and tactile sensuality. He made love as though he was in love, gently kissing all over my face, stroking my back and stomach and arms with his fingertips, taking care that I was comfortable, arranging a pillow under my head. I felt like a princess, someone special and privileged and feminine.

I turned to watch him sleeping. Morning light shone through the thatched walls and cast criss-cross patterns on the bedcover. Dadong lay on his back, his chest rising and falling slightly. One arm curved behind his head and wisps of purply-black hair lay neatly in his armpit, as if they'd been combed in place. Faint lines creased the waxy skin of his forehead and the corners of his mouth. His nose was narrow and elegant, his eyelashes luxurious. His ear was an orangey-pink colour, the cartilage looping in perfect scrolls. An Adam's apple protruded like a lump in his throat.

I remembered what Fred had said about the attitude of Indonesian men to Western women: you don't have to pay them, don't have to marry them. Was that why Dadong had slept with me? For free sex? Or did he feel sorry for me? Perhaps he'd regret it now. Maybe he hadn't enjoyed it. Maybe I wasn't good enough in bed. I wondered if he'd seen my feet, or all the minor imperfections of my flesh. Would he become cool and distant when he woke up? Maybe this was just a one-night stand for him.

I rolled onto my back. Curse Sedic! I had never been this insecure before he illustrated my flaws in lurid oil paint on a gallery wall. Dadong's hand reached out to turn my face to his and he kissed me good morning, sweetly and passionately, banishing insecurity for the time being.

I slipped out of bed and retrieved two parcels from the wardrobe, where I'd hidden them.

'This one is for your daughter,' I told him, 'and this is for you.'

He opened his daughter's present first, and exclaimed at the karaoke machine. 'Her poor mother is going to have to listen to this twenty-four hours a day,' he said. 'She'll love it. Thank you.'

His present was a shirt, a good one, in petrol green linen. He unwrapped it carefully, without tearing the paper, then held it in front of him.

'They can change it if it doesn't fit or you don't like it,' I said, but he smiled.

'No, I like it very much. You guessed the right size as well.' He kissed me. 'I have a present for you in the car,' he said.

'But you shouldn't have bought something for me. It's not Christmas here.'

He swivelled his legs over the edge of the bed and managed to pull on his shorts while modestly keeping the sheet draped across his lap. His legs were thin and virtually hairless.

'Don't move,' he instructed. 'I won't be a moment.'

I lay back against the pillow and listened to his footsteps tramp round the side of the house, and the boot of the car open at the back. Up above I could see the new area of thatch, lighter than the rest, with a few loose strands curling inwards. Dadong reappeared carrying a foot-long parcel wrapped in newspaper. He held it horizontally, as you would hold a baby, and laid it delicately across my lap.

'What is it?' I smiled. I unfurled the newspaper and inside there was an exquisite *wayang* puppet of a woman in a headdress, wearing an elaborately sequinned and beaded costume. Her head twisted when I turned the pole underneath her skirt and her graceful hands gesticulated in response to tiny movements of the attached sticks.

'Dadong, it's extraordinary!'

'She is Sita, Lord Rama's wife. My brother makes these puppets for a market stall.'

The eyes were slanting and chocolate-coloured with full painted lashes; strings of beads and coloured pom-poms hung by the sides of her face. 'I thought you didn't see much of your brother.'

'Ah, you remember everything. In fact, I visited him not long ago.'

'You're a very mysterious creature. Why is it so difficult for me to find out about you?'

'You are my boss,' he replied.

'Is that going to make things difficult?'

'Of course. Everything will be difficult.'

Over breakfast, we felt uncomfortable with each other in the suddenly altered circumstances. He wouldn't use the bathroom until he was sure I had finished in there; he asked my permission to pour another cup of coffee. But then I spilled some orange juice down my sarong and as he raised his eyebrows we laughed disproportionately, relieved to re-establish common ground with one of our old jokes.

Dadong walked along the beach to find a boy selling newspapers, then we sat in the garden overlooking the bay. The sun was strong so I stayed in the shade of a large-leafed tree with creamy cylindrical pods suspended from its branches. I daydreamed, listening to the waves shushing on the sand and watching the fishermen toil on the breakwaters.

Dadong looked so serious reading his paper. If you put him in a suit, he could easily be the managing director of a computer company.

'Is there anything interesting in the news?'

He hesitated. 'There have been a string of murders near Surabaya and the police have arrested a local shaman. They're saying it's black magic.'

'I read about that. Victims have their heads, hands and feet cut off, is that right? Why do they think it's magic?'

'Eyewitnesses claim the victims are abducted from their houses in the dead of night by figures wearing black cloaks and hoods. They are found in the morning suspended from trees. It ties in with some local superstition about malignant spirits.'

'There's nothing magical about it. They must have some serious cutting equipment and maybe even some medical knowledge. Do you know how difficult it is to cut through those joints?'

Dadong nodded. 'My guess is that they must be professional killers.'

'What do you mean? Some kind of Mafia? Are they targeting businessmen who haven't paid protection money?'

'No. The choice of victims appears to be random.'

'So they're just trying to intimidate the community?'

'Exactly.'

I looked at him. 'You're talking as if you know who's responsible.'

'I have a strong idea, but it probably won't make sense to you.'

'Try me.'

'I think these murders are committed by the army. Professional killers, with the equipment and expertise to carry it out.'

I frowned, trying to understand. 'But why?'

Dadong spoke patiently. 'There are severe food shortages in our country because of the economic crisis. People are blaming the government and, as you know, there have been sporadic uprisings demanding change. Although it's in Java, the people of Surabaya are very superstitious, with complex and deep-rooted spiritual beliefs. My theory is that the army are trying to make the people there believe that bad spirits are causing the food shortages rather than bad government. That probably sounds far-fetched to you,' he laughed, 'but you don't know what our military are capable of. They have never hesitated to kill their own people if they are convinced it will serve the greater good.'

'But who would give the orders?' I asked. 'Does it come from the top?'

'In this case, I'd say it's probably the local military taking things upon themselves, but equally, it could come from the chief of the army. Who knows?'

'Are there no dissident voices on the press or television, or in opposition to the government? Why doesn't someone stand up and say what you've just told me?'

'Occasionally they do, but it's not a very safe pursuit.'

I sighed and gazed down the beach. Dadong picked up his paper again and turned the page with a rustling noise. A middle-aged couple were walking along the shoreline, throwing half a coconut shell for a plump black labrador. The dog's hindquarters wriggled from side to side like a blowsy hooker as she chased it, then she'd engage her owners in a mock struggle before she relinquished it to be thrown again. The woman noticed me watching and waved, then advanced towards us up the sand.

'Are you Doctor Drew?' she called.

I stood up and pulled my sarong around me. 'Yes, I am, how do you do.'

'I'm Alison Green.' She tried to wipe the sand from her hands before shaking with me. 'Diana said you were staying at her place. Merry Christmas!'

'Doesn't it seem incongruous here?'

'This is my husband, Desmond.' She indicated the man with a huge beer-barrel gut who'd followed her up the sand. He waved cheerily.

'This is Dadong,' I introduced him, realising that I didn't know his surname. I'd have to ask some time. Dadong nodded politely.

'I didn't realise you had company. Diana thought you were going to be here on your own, so I came to ask if you would like to join us for Christmas dinner. Turkey and all the trimmings, crackers and hats, Christmas pudding. There'll be about a dozen of us. You must come along, I insist.'

'That's very kind,' I smiled and turned to Dadong. 'Would you like to sample a British Christmas dinner?'

He looked embarrassed and murmured something into his newspaper.

'You'd be very welcome,' she smiled. 'We can easily set an extra place.'

Dadong stood up. 'In fact, I am Dr Drew's driver. I wouldn't like to intrude on your party. If you'll excuse me, I must see to the car.'

I gasped and reached out a hand towards him, but he brushed past. Alison Green was watching me closely. 'I didn't mean to cause any offence. Quite the opposite. Feel free to bring your driver along if you like. Around seven. We're third house from the end, along that way.' She waved an arm.

'Thank you. It's very kind but, to be honest, I've been working very hard and I just need to have a rest here. Maybe we could have a drink another evening.' I was babbling, craning to see where Dadong had gone, and I caught a knowing look in Alison Green's eyes.

'Whatever you like. You know where we are.' They walked off together and as soon as they were out of earshot, I saw her leaning over to whisper to her husband.

I hurried after Dadong, round the side of the house to the courtyard where the car was parked, but he was nowhere to be seen. I walked out to the main road and peered along but couldn't see anyone in either direction. The hissing of crickets in the scrub was intense, like an ancient watertank dramatically refilling through rusty mains pipes. A strong cloud of scent filled the scorching white air. The wasteland across the road was overgrown with tangled plants and bushes interspersed with rocks and I didn't dare go any further for fear of snakes.

I remembered that we had nearly finished the large bottle of drinking water in the kitchen so I pressed the catch to open the boot of the car and retrieve some more. There were a couple of five-litre bottles there, smelling of rubber and hot petrol. A panel along the bottom, just by the spare wheel, had been shifted across and I noticed a compartment beneath it that seemed to stretch under the back seat. That must be where Dadong had hidden my Christmas present because I hadn't seen a parcel like it when we were loading up the car to come here. It was dark in the compartment but I stretched a hand into the gap and my fingers touched a bundle of papers. I stopped and considered whether I should respect his privacy but then I decided I wanted to know everything about him. I'd suffered too much from my last boyfriend's secrecy. I didn't know what was going to happen next between us but I was keen to avoid any more surprises.

I pulled a few papers from the top of the pile. They were leaflets, badly printed, the letters so smudged they almost ran into each other. I only recognised the word '*Merdeka*' and knew it meant 'Freedom' because that was the name of the square in Jakarta where the National Monument had been erected. The leaflets only had type on one side. I reached in and pulled out some more then my fingers closed around some rolled-up tubes. I pulled them out and unfurled one.

Twelve black and white photos stared back at me, of young men with haunted expressions. '*Di mana mereka?*' the legend along the top read in bold letters, and I knew that '*di mana*' meant 'where?' Underneath each photo there was a name and a date then some words. I traced them with a finger, trying to find more words I recognised and get the gist of the poster. A quiet voice spoke behind me.

'It says "Janoceta Letjen, carpenter, arrested twentieth of May 1997, no charges brought. Police say he was released the next day but his family haven't seen him since." They are some of Jakarta's disappeared people, Nicola. I think it would be best if we put this poster back in case the houseboy comes past. You never know. He might be army family.'

'I'm sorry, I didn't mean to pry.' I rolled up the poster and handed it back to him. He nodded but didn't say any more and I hoped I hadn't made him angry. It was almost impossible to read his emotions.

For Christmas dinner, we had roast chicken, rice and mixed salads, cheese and fruit, and I opened a bottle of champagne. We worked side by side, like a proper couple, Dadong carving the chicken while I mixed salad dressing.

'Do you actually organise demonstrations?' I asked tentatively.

'No, I don't even participate. My colleagues and I just observe.'

'Observe what?'

'We try to keep an eye on anyone who is arrested and find out who they are from friends, then we have people who follow up to see if they are released again.'

'What if they're not?'

He was arranging slices of white meat on our plates, far too much for me. I raised a hand to stop him. 'If we have enough evidence we go to one of the international agencies like Amnesty. Have you heard of them?'

I nodded. 'Of course.'

'But often it's difficult to prove that people have been taken into custody at all because the police just deny it.'

'Isn't it dangerous for you to be involved? I mean, won't they target you one day?'

'We try not to be too obvious about what we do. I don't exactly march into Amnesty headquarters or write letters to them signed with my own name. There are more subtle ways of passing on information. I have some contacts.'

I sat down at the table and took a sip of my champagne. It wasn't particularly good, with a slight hint of vinegar, but there hadn't been much choice in the shop round the corner from the clinic. I never asked Mimi to buy alcohol for me. It didn't seem fair to compromise her religious beliefs in that way.

'Why you?' I asked. 'How did you get involved?'

He curved his lips ruefully. 'My brother was arrested ten years ago. At first the police denied they were holding him but we managed to get proof and so they had to press charges and send him for trial. He was found guilty of spreading anti-government propaganda and sentenced to fifteen years. He's in jail near Bandung and I go to visit him when I can.'

'I'm so sorry.'

'I take him materials for his puppets. Bits of wood and fabric, sequins and paints, and that's how he spends his days. Only five years to go!' He turned his head away and I reached out to squeeze his hand.

'Why didn't you tell me before?'

'No one at Medimachines knows I have a brother in jail. Phil would sack me if he found out.'

He was probably right. Phil was too much of a coward to

risk any whiff of scandal. 'But you could have told me. That day when you were late for taking me to work, I guessed you were somehow involved with the demonstration.'

'Yes, I thought you would. I was waiting for you to ask me more.'

I smiled. 'Dadong, I never know what I'm allowed to ask you and what's taboo.'

'You can ask me anything you like.'

'And you'll tell me the answer?'

'Not necessarily.' He gripped my fingers tightly and the engagement ring dug into my flesh.

I extracted my hand and looked at it with a twinge of guilt. It was like a message from Sedic, as if he was trying to prevent me getting involved with anyone else. But I had no reason to be ashamed. Two and a half months had passed since he had dumped me so brutally. I twisted the ring to face inwards, confused by my feelings.

'Are you thinking about your fiancé?' Dadong asked quietly and I blushed.

'Just that I know it's finally over and I'm ready to move on.'

Dadong looked pointedly at the ring then got up to clear our plates away.

Chapter Twenty-one

I knew I wanted more from Dadong than a brief holiday fling but I wasn't sure what he was thinking. Nothing had been said about the future. Maybe, despite my protests, he thought I was still in love with Sedic. I couldn't bear the uncertainty so as the car pulled out onto the road back to Jakarta, I asked, 'What happens now? Between us, I mean.'

'What would you like to happen?'

I watched Krakatoa disappearing on the horizon to my left. 'I'd like to spend time with you and get to know you.'

'I think you know a lot already,' he smiled.

I smiled too, thinking of the intimacy of our lovemaking. It had felt very personal. With other lovers, especially with Sedic, I'd sometimes had visions of them doing exactly the same things with other women – kissing their necks, licking their stomachs, pushing a leg down to roll them over. With Dadong, it felt like a strictly private event, just between him and me.

'Will we be able to sleep with each other in Jakarta? Can you stay overnight with me in the house?'

'Ummm,' he sounded doubtful. 'Mimi would disapprove. She's very religious and she would be offended.'

'Does she have to know? She goes to bed early and she never comes into my room in the morning without knocking. You could get up and slip out through the back gate, then arrive for work round the front as normal.' I stopped, hoping that I wasn't sounding too pushy, but Dadong grinned. I'd never seen him in such a good mood.

'Of course we'll find a way,' he said. 'I don't think we have a choice.' Our smiles were infectious.

I kept the window shut this time as we drove through the street market. A ragged, threadbare goat was blocking the road, refusing to move despite Dadong beeping the horn, so he inched forward carefully and nudged it with the front bumper until it trotted nonchalantly aside.

It was mid afternoon when we arrived home, and Mimi and Ali rushed out to greet us. I had Christmas presents for them: a leather belt for Ali because his trousers were always drooping under his curved belly, and a bright flowered dress for Mimi, slightly too big although I'd bought the smallest size in the shop. She held it in front of her and stroked the fabric, obviously delighted.

'Do you want to go out later?' Dadong asked me and I shook my head.

'I don't think so, not unless you want to. I thought I'd have dinner here. I'm going back to the clinic tomorrow. What about you?' I was gabbling, not sure whether to ask him to join me for dinner or if Mimi would object to that as well. They couldn't understand what we were saying but maybe they would perceive the change of tone between us.

'I wonder if I can take the night off to go and see my daughter?' he asked. 'I could take her the present you bought.'

'Of course!' I exclaimed, too abruptly. 'Of course you can. Do you want to go now?'

'I thought I might, so I can see her before she goes to bed.'

'That's fine, no problem.' I paused, feeling awkward. 'Do you want to come back later?'

'It's too far,' he said. 'They live on the other side of town. I'll come back in the morning to take you to work.'

'No, of course. You go.' We stood six feet apart, acutely conscious of the space each other's bodies occupied.

'I wish I could kiss you,' he said in a business-like tone, glancing at Mimi and Ali.

'I wish you could too. Till tomorrow.'

After he'd gone, I had a swim in the pool, slicing through the warm chemical water that was much thinner than the ocean and an artificial turquoise colour rather than glinting chalky green. I yearned to be back at the beachhouse, snakes or no snakes. It felt as though the honeymoon was over, although we'd only spent three days and two nights together – three if you counted the night of the cobra. Sneaking around to save Mimi's feelings seemed like a juvenile way of conducting an affair. Maybe I should take my chances and, if she left in disgust, ask Linda at Medimachines to find me another maid. But perhaps Dadong didn't want the affair to become common knowledge. It might be embarrassing for him if people knew he was sleeping with his boss, and gossip seemed to spread round this city faster than you could blink.

When I had dried myself and wandered inside to the cool of the main room, Mimi handed me a list of messages and pointed to the telephone. Her handwriting consisted of neat, precise capital letters. There were three names: Mother, Peter and Claire. It was around six in the evening, or eleven in the morning in the UK. I poured myself a drink and sat down at the telephone table.

My mother was chatty, anxious that I might be lonely; my father was concerned about a news report that soldiers had opened fire on a student demonstration in central Sumatra, killing one and wounding over a dozen more. I reassured them that my life was snug and well-protected, with a driver, a maid and a guard to look after me, and I told them about my unusual Christmas on the beach, although not about my new lover. That could wait.

I rang Leona's number and had started to leave a message when a sleepy voice answered. 'Nicola, what time is it?' I told her and she groaned. 'Peter and I are still in bed. We were at a party last night.' I heard his voice asking who it was, and her telling him, then she handed the phone over.

'Merry Christmas,' he said. 'I hope you had a good one.'

'Very good, thank you. I've been trying to reach you for a while, but I guess we keep missing each other. There are a few things I need to discuss with you.'

'No time like the present. Fire away!'

'This is a bit embarrassing, but I have to tell you that I'm not happy about the way Medimachines has been operating. They've been selling obsolete machines to the clinic and one of them's potentially dangerous. I'm going to warn them not to use it but I thought I should tell you first.'

'Have you mentioned it to Phil?'

'Not yet. The machine I'm most worried about was bought by a Hong Kong company called Art Deals International after the UK manufacturer, Parios, went into liquidation. Does that ring any bells with you?'

'How did you find this out?'

'It doesn't matter. Is Art Deals International one of your companies?'

'Yes, it's Leona's, but I can't imagine why it would be buying medical equipment. Darling, did you know that Art Deals International sold Medimachines a scanner?' Leona's reply wasn't quite audible. Peter came back. 'I suppose it was a decision made by the Hong Kong manager.'

'What can I do about this machine, Peter? If someone switches it on, they might get contaminated with radioactivity, so I'm going to have to say something to the staff at the hospital.'

'Give me a couple of days. I'll talk to Phil, we'll find out about the source of the machine and get back to you. If there is anything wrong with it, obviously we'll refund the money or provide them with a replacement.'

'I'm just getting a bad taste about the set-up here. I'm sure it's nothing to do with you,' I added quickly. 'But I'm not happy with the general attitude. It feels to me as though the Indonesians are being ripped off.'

'I can assure you that's not the case. Quite the opposite. You should discuss all your concerns with Phil, though. You'll find him very receptive to criticism and eager to make amends if there are any problems. He's a decent man, Nicola. I know he may come across like a bit of an idiot but he cares about what he's doing out there. We all do.'

'Is there a number where I can contact you if I need to?'

'I'm going to Moscow tomorrow and I've got no idea

where the Russkies will put me up. Leave a message with Leona if it's urgent, but otherwise I'll speak to you in a week when I'm back.'

I took a deep breath. 'That's not all I wanted to talk to you about. I think you should know that Sedic's mother came to visit me and we had a very interesting chat.'

'Good God!' he exclaimed. 'How on earth did she find you?'

'I suppose Sedic must have given her the address. She was expecting him to come out here with me.'

There was a pause. 'Sedic knows about his mother?'

'Obviously. I think he found out about a year ago. He must be furious with you for lying to him all that time.'

I could hear a mumbled conversation in the background as he relayed the information to Leona. 'I wish he'd talked to me about it so I could explain. We did it all to give him the chance of a better future, a good education and all the advantages of life in the West. It may seem odd to you that we lied about his mother's death, but he'd never have come with me otherwise. He'd just have pined for her.'

'She says you bought him, Peter, like a commodity.'

'That's a very emotive way of looking at it. I gave his mother the money to set up her herbal business but I'd have thought that's a perfectly acceptable gift to give an old girlfriend. Have you discussed this with Sedic? What's he planning to do?'

'I don't want to talk to him. That's over now. In fact,' I couldn't help adding, 'I've met someone else, so it's all worked out for the best.'

'Have you indeed! Anyone I know? I've met most of the English crowd out there. Nice bunch of people.'

'I don't think it would be anyone you know.'

'I must say I'm very relieved, Nicola. You're a fantastic girl, far too good for him. That may sound a harsh thing to say about my own son but I've given him everything over the years only to have it thrown back in my face. He's just not worth it. I'm ready to wash my hands of him.'

'I thought you had already. He was trying to contact you a few weeks ago when those gangsters kidnapped him in the

Bahamas. He sounded really desperate and he had to turn to me for help because he couldn't find you.'

'What gangsters? What are you talking about?' He sounded genuinely puzzled.

I hesitated. Why hadn't Sedic told him? I'd assumed it must have been Peter who gave him the money to reimburse me but obviously not. 'I don't know the details. You'd better ask him yourself.'

'He could have found me if he'd rung Leona. She always knows where I am. Surely you've realised by now that you have to take everything Sedic says with a pinch of salt? He's not the world's most honest person.'

Neither are you, I thought. His slick explanations for all the concerns I raised were far from convincing. I felt as though he was just saying what he thought I wanted to hear. 'Will you get back to me about the scanner as soon as you can, Peter?' I finished. 'We're both professional people with reputations to protect and we don't want them to be tarnished by association with a disreputable organisation, do we?'

'Absolutely not. I'll look into it straight away.'

I wasn't reassured, but I'd reserve judgement for another week and see what story came back about the scanner. Meanwhile, I'd remain on the lookout for any other Medimachines transgressions.

I waited till after dinner to ring Claire, knowing she wasn't an early riser. In fact, she was bright and cheerful when I phoned and we talked for half an hour or so about our Christmases. She was excited to hear about Dadong and asked what he looked like, how well he spoke English, was he a good kisser, what was the sex like, how the romance began. I filled her in on the details, and the thought crossed my mind that it would serve Sedic right if she told him I had a new lover. I wanted him to know he wasn't irreplaceable.

'Did that bank statement come through?' I asked, when we'd exhausted all our news.

'Yes, I never realised quite how rich you were,' she exclaimed. 'I'm going to be much nicer to you in future.'

I laughed. 'That's just because Sedic's money is in the

account. I have to repay it to my credit card company. How much did it convert into?'

'The foreign currency I put in the bank for you was about six thousand seven hundred pounds. Is that right?'

'Yep, that's it.' The dollar exchange rate was around one sixty-six.

'That brings the total you have in that account up to just over nineteen thousand pounds. Did you know that?'

'What?' My mind raced through all the people that might have put money into my account. A Christmas present from my parents, perhaps? Surely they'd have mentioned it. Could the hospital in London have made some administrative error with my last pay cheque? 'How long has there been so much in the account?'

'Since the sixteenth of December,' she said. 'Ten thousand three hundred and eleven pounds were transferred into it on that date. It just says "advised" on the statement.'

I called my bank immediately and was put on hold for a few minutes then transferred to an account manager. He asked me the usual security questions then looked up the account on his computer before finding the information.

'The payment was made by a company called Olbisson Computers and it was received in a foreign currency called the "vatu". Do you want me to tell you the conversion rate we used?'

'No, but where does the vatu come from?'

There was a pause while he checked, but I'd come up with the answer myself before he spoke.

'Vanuatu,' I breathed. 'It has to be.' It had been mid December when Phil Pope had made his mysterious trip out there. But why would he have transferred money to my account?

Chapter Twenty-two

———◇◇◇◇———

I called the Medimachines office the very next morning, demanding to see Phil, but Linda told me he wouldn't be back until the fifth of January, so I asked her to book me an appointment at their offices that day. She called again on the morning of the fifth to say that Phil insisted I come for lunch at the tapas bar in the Holiday Inn. I argued that I wanted to keep the meeting strictly formal, but she said Phil couldn't be reached and was expecting to meet me there at twelve.

Dadong dropped me by the wide marble steps and I climbed into a cool, luxurious foyer with lights glittering in tall display fountains. A uniformed doorman directed me to the first floor and along a corridor into a dim, mosaic-tiled restaurant area. Suited businessmen on barstools turned to leer as I walked past. Someone was playing Spanish guitar in the corner and a television mounted on a wall showed silent scenes of bullfighting. It looked like a programme of selected highlights because it cut from one scene of gory death to another, the huge tortured creatures bewildered and desperate.

Phil was about ten minutes late so I sipped a watermelon juice, running through what I planned to say.

'Good Christmas, Nicola?' The voice appeared from behind me. Phil leaned down and kissed my cheek and I noted that he already smelled of beer.

'Not bad.'

He sat down. 'I got back from the UK last night. No rest

for the wicked. Have you ordered anything yet? Shall we share a selection of tapas?'

The thought of eating from the same plate as Phil made me shudder. Who knows what might be transmitted in his saliva? 'I'll just have a portion of Spanish omelette,' I said.

He gave a lengthy order to the waiter, asking for a bottle of Rioja as well as half a dozen dishes, and when the wine arrived, he poured me a glass despite my protests. I deliberately left it untouched.

'I hear you managed to get through to Peter at last,' he said. 'That man's a difficult one to pin down. Anyway, he told me your concerns about the Parios and I've tracked down a certificate which should put your mind at rest. Here.' He bent double to rummage in his briefcase and looked even more flushed than usual when he straightened up and handed me a piece of paper.

I glanced down the page. It appeared to show a series of tests that had been carried out on the scanner, around two years previously. The date of each test was written alongside.

'We knew there had been a problem with Parios scanners years ago, so we had the stock meticulously checked out before we bought it. That's a very reputable lab; I don't know if you've heard of it.'

I looked at the rubber stamp at the bottom, which bore the name of a medical engineering firm near Cambridge. 'Can I keep this?' I asked.

'Oh, drat!' He snapped his fingers. 'I'd have made a photo-copy if I'd thought. I'll get Linda in the office to have one sent over to you. Don't want to risk losing the original.'

I took out a pen and notebook and jotted down the serial number of the machine, the name of the Cambridge firm, and the test dates.

'Nicola, Nicola, Nicola.' Phil regarded me sadly. 'How did we get to this position, where you don't appear to trust us any more? What can I say to convince you that we are a squeaky clean set-up, doing our best to help advance the standards of healthcare in this country? They can't afford brand spanking new machines so we're giving them perfectly functional older models and we're responsible enough to check them out in advance. I don't know where you've got the idea that anyone's being ripped off in any way.'

'Call me cynical, but I don't like the way information has been withheld from me. I'm also deeply suspicious about a certain payment that arrived in my bank account just before Christmas from a company called Olbisson Computers. You wouldn't happen to know anything about that, would you?'

'Of course I do, my love. I arranged it! It's your bonus for convincing Karlina that they need to buy the computer to link up with their MRI scanner. You told them that, didn't you?'

'I told them the scanner would be useless without it.'

'Well, there you go. I explained there would be a bonus in it for you if you got them to buy new equipment.'

'But ten thousand pounds? The computer can't even have cost that much.'

'The rest is your Christmas bonus. We look after our staff out here.'

The waiter was balancing tiny plates of tapas on our table, struggling to fit them all on the mosaic-tiled surface.

'I can't accept it, Phil. I don't deserve it and I don't want it. I insist you take it back again.'

He had ripped off a hunk of crusty bread and was dipping it into an oily sauce round some fatty-looking chicken legs. 'Goodness me, what planet do you come from?' he asked, before shoving the bread into his mouth.

I shook my head. On the television screen a bull sank wearily to its knees, fed up with the struggle, and the matador raised his arms in triumph. 'You're paying me a perfectly generous salary already and I don't want to feel compromised or pressured by some bonus system. I'd rather you sold them the machines more cheaply.'

'That's a bit holier-than-thou, don't you think?' He refilled his wine glass with a glugging sound. 'Let's not argue about this, though. If you want to pay back the bonus, just write us a cheque and it won't be mentioned again. I think you're crazy, but it's a free country after all.'

I scraped my chair back and lifted my bag. I'd brought my

British chequebook, because I'd decided before the meeting that this was what I wanted to do. 'Who shall I make it payable to?'

Phil was gnawing a spare rib, chomping along the edges of the bone. 'No idea. I didn't expect this. I'll check with Peter where he wants it paid in. Why don't you leave it blank for now?'

I hesitated. 'Shouldn't I make it payable to Olbisson Computers, since that's where it came from?'

'Let me think.' Phil massaged his chin with podgy fingers. 'No, I've just closed that account, so I wouldn't be able to pay it in. If you want to wait for a week or so, I'll be able to tell you where I plan to deposit it. Or you can give me a cheque now and leave it blank. Whichever you prefer.'

I sighed noisily. 'Why is nothing straightforward with Medimachines? I'm not a business expert, but you seem to operate in quite unorthodox ways.'

'Nothing could be further from the truth.' He drained his wine and refilled it again, then gestured in the direction of my glass. 'Sure you don't want some?' I shook my head. 'It's not us, it's the countries we're operating in that have unorthodox systems. It's also because we're having to shift resources around to try and stay on top of the currency crisis, which is no easy feat at the moment. You've seen what prices are doing out here.'

I made up my mind that I'd rather give him a cheque and have it off my conscience. I'd be able to find out from my bank where it was paid in, so there was no point in Phil being secretive about it. I wrote out the details, tore it from my book and passed it across. Phil pocketed it without looking.

'I've been hearing naughty little rumours about you,' he said mischievously. 'It seems you approve of the driver I hired to take you around.' He gave me a knowing leer. 'Glad you've got someone to keep you warm at night anyway.'

I considered pouring a glass of wine into his lap but that would have meant descending to his level. I stood up and picked up my handbag. 'Thanks for the lunch, but I have to be going now.'

'Oh, Nicola!' he exclaimed. 'I only meant to be friendly. Will you stop taking everything the wrong way?'

'I'm in a hurry,' I said. 'Another time, perhaps.' Then I strode through the hall and down the staircase. The doorman called into his intercom for 'Dadong, Medimachines' and a few minutes later my car crawled round the corner. I jumped into the back without giving Dadong time to get out and open the door for me. 'Just drive,' I said, and he pulled out into the traffic on Sudirman with a screech of tyres.

'How the hell did they find out about us? I haven't told a soul out here.'

'That woman on the beach in Sambolo must have guessed. If she told Diana, it will be all over town by now.'

'Oh, flip. I don't want them knowing my business. And what about your position? Could this compromise your job?'

He shrugged. 'I don't see why. We're not doing anything wrong.'

I was agitated about the money as well, but I couldn't talk to Dadong about that. I hadn't told him that a mysterious lump sum had arrived in my bank account. The amount was too obscene. Maybe he wouldn't understand why I wanted to repay it.

We stopped for coffee in a quiet bar we sometimes visited near the train station. I ordered tea and he had a cola. Since the return from Sambolo, we'd slipped into a pattern of sleeping together three or four nights a week but he rarely stayed all night. He'd arrive in the early hours, once Mimi was in bed, then leave before I awoke, and when I got up at nine or ten, he'd be out in the garage polishing the car and would greet me formally, with only a flicker of amusement at the illicitness of the arrangement.

I still couldn't make him out. He was sensitive and loving when we were in bed together but he held me at arm's length in most other ways, refusing to talk in any detail about his ex–wife or daughter, his brother or his work with political prisoners. It was as though there was a force field round him that I wasn't allowed to penetrate. Maybe he was holding back because he knew I was returning to the UK in a few months' time. I tried not to think about that. Sometimes I stared into his dark eyes trying to read what was going on behind them, but all I could see were the huge black circles of his pupils.

On the whole, I was happy. The life that had seemed so empty before Christmas was now full and rewarding. The work at the clinic was testing, physically exhausting, but at the end of a shift I felt satisfied, knowing I had made a difference. And the hot still nights of love-making seemed to get more exquisite every time, especially now I'd stocked up on a supply of condoms. I reached across the table and squeezed his hand and he smiled but withdrew his fingers before the waiter could see us.

'I was wondering,' he said, 'if it would be possible for me to go to Bandung to see my brother some time soon. I could arrange for another driver to look after you for a couple of days while I'm gone.'

'Couldn't I come along?'

He regarded me seriously for a few moments, then stared out of the window, considering the question. 'It might be dangerous. I will be watched when I'm there because my brother is an influential prisoner and they worry about my visits. Also, the Institute of Technology in Bandung is one of the centres of political activism and tensions are simmering. I think it would be better if you don't come.'

'What could possibly happen? I haven't done anything wrong. I would be going as a tourist, to see another part of the country. Anyway, surely it would be safer for you to be there as my driver rather than as an independent traveller?'

'Maybe,' he said. 'Let me think about it.'

'Shall I check with Karlina when would be a good time for me to take a break? She said they're not so busy during Ramadan, because no Muslims will take any medicines then. When does it start?'

'Next week. You realise it means that Mimi won't go to bed till late, because she can only eat after sunset?'

I hadn't thought of that. I must have looked gloomy because he laughed. 'Don't worry. It doesn't mean we have to change our arrangements.'

When I got to the clinic, the first thing I did was go through to the equipment room and check the serial number of the PET scanner. It corresponded with the one I'd scribbled down. Phil wouldn't have been so stupid as to try and trick me over something like that. Then I went to Karlina's office to phone Cameron. I described the certificate and told him the name of the Cambridge firm who'd conducted the tests and he seemed to think they were legitimate.

'One more thing,' I said. 'I don't suppose you could get some prices for me?' I gave him the make and model of a couple of the scanners and the new computer that had recently been delivered. 'I just want to see what kind of a mark-up they're adding.'

'You really don't like these people, do you?'

'I've got a very odd feeling about the company but every time I confront them about something, there's a semi-reasonable explanation. Maybe I'm being paranoid.'

'I'll get the prices to you as soon as I can,' he promised.

Chapter Twenty-three

Dadong and I left for Bandung early one February morning, just as the speakers across the city were sounding the call to prayer. The wavering voice sounded like an Eastern version of a Tarzan cry in the Johnny Weissmuller movies. This time we headed east out of the city and the industrial warehouses, foetid slum-lined canals and dingy shops were soon transformed into fantastically green and lush countryside. Blue hills were bisected by terraces of crops, dense forest covered the lower slopes and lavish palm trees stretched out their leaves to wrap around each other. I caught sight of a bird with impossibly long yellow and white tail feathers, like the train on an elaborate wedding dress.

The road wound inexorably higher, the hills got closer and the sky became a clearer blue. My ears popped suddenly, with a crackling sound. Cool mists swirled around jagged ridges and scrubby plains. We talked on and off, but I was happy just to absorb the sheer physical grandeur of our surroundings. After we'd been driving for about three hours, Dadong pointed to some peculiar slate-grey hills to our left.

'These are volcanoes,' he said. 'And the one with the bumpy top is called Tangkuban Prahu. It means "Upturned Boat". Shall I tell you the story?' I smiled encouragement. 'It is said that a young prince had been wandering for many years and when he came home, he fell in love with a beautiful woman. She soon realised that this was her estranged son and couldn't think how to tell him but it was obvious she must break off the affair. So she set him a challenge. He had to build a dam and a huge boat in a single night and complete them before the sun rose if she was to agree to marry him. In the early hours of the morning, it looked as though he was going to succeed so his mother called on the gods to make the dawn break early. Rays of sunshine crept into the sky and the cocks began to crow before he'd had the chance to put the finishing touches to his boat and in fury, because he knew he'd lost the challenge, he pushed it over sideways.'

I laughed. 'Why can't people ever be honest with each other from the start in relationships? She could just have told him.'

'But then there would be no story. If you sat down at the beginning of every relationship and said, "It can't possibly work out because of this and that," and listed all the obstacles in the way, then you wouldn't have the fun of finding out what the story was going to be.'

I leaned over to rest my head on his shoulder and he bent down and touched my lips with a kiss. 'In fact, there is a practical explanation for its peculiar shape, because the centre collapsed in on itself.'

'Is it active as well?'

'Oh, sure. If you open the window, you might be able to smell the sulphur from here.'

I pressed the button to lower the window and was struck by the cool freshness of the air outside compared with the desultory heat of Jakarta. I sniffed deeply and caught an earthy smell with maybe a hint of rotten eggs.

We had booked a bungalow in the hills just outside Bandung, because I didn't want to risk raised eyebrows and shocked expressions if we'd tried to share a room in a big city-centre hotel. As we approached, Dadong pointed to a ridge and explained that, just behind it, hot springs gushed out of the hillside, and people bathed in bubbling hot geysers.

'If you want an egg for your breakfast,' he said, 'you go out and put it in one of the springs for three minutes, then it's ready to eat.'

'So long as it doesn't become impregnated with that ghastly smell.' It was seeping into my nose and lungs now and making my eyes water.

We left our bags at the bungalow then drove on into the town. Dadong wanted to visit the jail and make an appointment for the next day. We agreed that he would drop me at a museum in the centre, but there was a road block halting all traffic on the outskirts of the town. Cars were trying to turn round in the narrow road and snarling themselves in bad-tempered rucks. Dadong lowered his window and shouted to another driver, who replied at length with animated gesticulations. He nodded and put the car into reverse to turn us around.

'What's going on?' I asked.

'Students have occupied one of the university buildings and it's surrounded by troops. The only way into the city will be if we loop right back and enter from the south side.' His expression was grave.

'Why have they occupied it?'

He shrugged. 'The usual reasons.'

'Which are?'

'They're calling for the president to stand down. They think all their problems will be solved with a change of government.'

'You don't?'

'Life is never that easy, I find.'

We zigzagged through narrow streets on the outskirts of the town, then drove down a wider boulevard lined with the pavement restaurants known as *warungs*, where you sit cross-legged on mats on the ground. Dadong had taken me to one in Jakarta once. There was no menu. You were served a heaped platter of whatever was cooking in the pots that day – fried chicken, banana fritters or rice with jackfruit in coconut milk. I hadn't suffered any ill effects from the inadequate hygiene but Diana was horrified when I mentioned it. She said that even the locals got sick from eating at *warungs*.

We turned left onto a main highway. It wasn't as wide as Sudirman in Jakarta, but the traffic moved as slowly, three lanes of cars jostling for slightly preferential positions. I laughed as we passed a Dunkin' Donuts outlet. These were omnipresent in Jakarta, the most prolific Western food chain, and now it seemed doughnuts were popular in other Indonesian cities as well. I knew Dadong was partial to them. 'Look, your favourite restaurant,' I joked, but he ignored me.

'There are some shops here, if you prefer. Or will I take you up to the museum?'

'Museum, I think. I can shop any time in Jakarta.'

He took a turning that led away from the main shopping and restaurant area and suddenly the road was virtually deserted. I glanced at Dadong and saw that he was frowning. Half a dozen policemen stood at the next cross street, watching as we approached, then one of them stepped out into the road and held up his hand for us to stop. Dadong pulled over to the side and wound down his window.

The policeman looked about forty and there was a sly, knowing expression curving his lips and glittering behind his eyes. He peered into the car and his eyes ran over me almost lecherously. Dadong said, something, obviously explaining who I was, and the policeman continued to stare. I met his eye and smiled coolly.

He gestured for Dadong to step out of the car and show his documentation. I remained in the back seat. Two other officers wandered over and perused me, unabashed. The first one had taken Dadong's papers and was talking into a radio. Dadong looked back at me and nodded imperceptibly, as if to say there wasn't a problem. One of the other officers tapped on my window so I opened it.

'Passport?' he asked.

I rummaged in the bottom of my bag, where I kept a photocopy of my passport, and handed it to him. He shook his head.

'No. Passport.'

'This is a copy of my passport,' I explained, speaking slowly. 'I don't carry the real thing in case it gets lost.'

He went over to discuss this with the first officer, showing him the photocopied pages. I was ill at ease with the atmosphere. They weren't distant and respectful of foreigners like the few policemen I'd encountered in Jakarta. This bunch seemed hostile and suspicious.

Dadong had his back to me but his posture retained its usual quiet dignity. I heard him raise his voice at one point and the first policeman snapped at him fiercely.

'What is the purpose of your visit?' one of them asked me, with careful enunciation, as though he didn't quite understand the words.

'Sightseeing,' I said. 'I came to see the city. He is my driver.' I pointed. The policeman nodded and went to talk to his colleagues.

Ten minutes later, I was beginning to get annoyed about the delay. I climbed out of the car and wandered over to stand beside Dadong.

'What's this about?' I asked.

'They're just checking my name with the station. We were heading towards the university campus and it seems they thought we might be involved with the students in some way.'

'Can I do anything? Should I offer them money?' Bribery was the standard way to get out of paying fines for traffic violations. No one was incorruptible.

'How much cash do you have?'

I tried to remember: quite a lot, because I hadn't been sure how easy it would be to withdraw cash in Bandung, so I'd brought enough to cover our stay. 'About five hundred thousand rupiah,' I calculated.

'Offer them fifty thousand,' he said. 'Hand it to the one who stopped us. Don't let him see the rest of your money, though.'

I walked back to the car, reached into my bag and extracted a fifty thousand note from my purse, calculating that it was around twenty-eight pounds in British currency. My hands were shaking. I didn't know how I was supposed to do this, but I sidled up to the first policemen, smiled and handed over the cash. It disappeared into his trouser pocket and he nodded his thanks, with a knowing look in his eyes. Then the whole group of them carried on as before: standing, watching us, talking into their radios or to each other.

'What now?' I whispered to Dadong.

He said something to the first policeman and there was a

firm shake of the head. The radio crackled and a voice could be heard. We waited. Dadong turned to me and whispered, 'I think they have found out about my brother.'

The first policeman said something to Dadong and pointed at the car. He replied, gesturing towards me. I didn't like the sound of it.

When they finished, Dadong explained to me. 'We're going to drop you at the museum as planned,' he said. 'Then they want me to go to the police station for some questions. Don't worry. I'll come back to pick you up within a couple of hours.'

'Are you sure?'

'If not, you know the name of the place we're staying. Just ask the museum to order a taxi and I'll meet you back there.'

'What if you don't come back?' Suddenly, I felt very scared.

'I'll be back. They don't have any reason to detain me.'

One of the policemen motioned that I should follow him to a car round the corner. I looked at Dadong and he nodded that I should do it. The first policeman climbed into the driver's seat of our car and the last thing I saw was Dadong being hustled into the back seat, flanked by a policeman on either side.

There was no conversation. The museum was only two streets away and the police car pulled up outside. I climbed out with a hollow feeling in my stomach and the car drove off immediately.

I wandered round the old colonial building without taking in much information about the exhibits: model volcanoes, fossils, prehistoric remains, displays explaining the geology of the area. It was dusty and smelled of old rotting wood. I only saw three other visitors – a Japanese couple and a tall bearded man in shorts. An hour passed, and then two. By five o'clock, I was tired and hungry, and a sense of dread was weighing me down. I wandered outside and bought a can of Coke and some sugar-coated peanuts from a street vendor. The road was empty in both directions. It seemed the citizens of Bandung were staying at home today, because it was strangely silent for the end of the afternoon on a working day in a fairly large city.

I listened hard but could only hear distant traffic noises hovering in the still air.

I finished my nuts then went back in to the museum shop, where there was an array of books, maps and souvenir lumps of rock on sale. The man at the cash desk spoke English and immediately agreed to find me a taxi. I sat on the steps outside as the light faded to grey and the evening call to prayer echoed round the streets. Occasional police sirens wailed. Every time a car turned into the street, I prayed it would be Dadong, but about an hour after I'd ordered it, a cab pulled up. The driver took me back to our bungalow along a tortuous route through the back streets, and it was seven o'clock when we arrived. Only twelve hours since we left Jakarta, but it had been a very long day.

The back of my arm felt itchy and as soon as I began to scratch, I realised there were other itchy spots on my neck and ankles. There must have been mosquitos in the cab. I unpacked my toilet bag and dug out the brown bottle Lila had given me. Using the dropper, I put a little liquid on each bite and rubbed it in and the itching disappeared in seconds. It would be interesting to know what she put in it.

Next I made a sandwich and coffee from the supplies we'd brought and lay with my feet up on the sofa, trying to plan what I would do if he didn't return. Would Linda at Medimachines be able to help? But then they might find out about his brother and Phil would sack him. I could call Diana at the embassy and ask her advice. That seemed like the best bet. There wasn't a phone in the bungalow but surely there would be one nearby? I hoped the police were treating him well. He hadn't committed any crime; we'd just been driving along a road towards the museum. And then a terrible thought occurred to me. What if they searched the car and found those posters and leaflets? Did he still keep them there? If that happened, I might never see him again.

It was after eleven when I heard a car pull up outside. I leapt to my feet and ran to the front door and there was Dadong, look-ing very small as he climbed out of the car in the chilly night air. I rushed over and we hugged for a long time before he spoke.

'They won't let me see my brother. They said the situation in Bandung is too tense. We have to leave tomorrow.'

'How can they order us about like that? I came here as a tourist to see the area. They can't just tell me to go.'

'No, not you. You can stay if you like, but I have to go.'

I stroked my fingers through his hair. He seemed sad and defeated and I wished there was something I could do to make things better. The sulphurous mists swirled around us and volcanoes loomed on all sides, like some ominous portent in an ancient tragedy.

'Of course I'll come back with you,' I said.

We rose early the next morning and were carrying our cases and boxes out to the car when I saw a figure walking up the hill towards us. He wore a white turban and bright green shirt and was swinging a canvas bag by his side. As he got closer, I saw that his features were rounder, his nose wider and flatter than the normal Javanese appearance. He smiled a wide cheery smile and waved when he saw me watching him.

Dadong walked past me and greeted him with a hug. They spoke for a few moments then he turned to introduce me.

'This is Ibad, a friend of mine. Can I offer him some tea?'

'Yes, of course.' I shook hands with him.

'You are English?' he said. 'I've been to England, to Newcastle.'

'How bizarre! What were you doing there?'

'Working on a boat. Terrible work. Bad weather, too cold. I brought you a present.' He held out the bag.

'Let's go inside first,' Dadong suggested, glancing down the road. There was no one else in sight but we could hear the shrieks of some tourists having an early dip in the geyser.

I boiled water and made a pot of the weak Indonesian tea Dadong liked, and carried through cups, milk and sugar on a tray. Ibad held out a long newspaper-wrapped parcel towards me. 'For you.'

I unfurled the paper and inside there was another elaborate *wayang* puppet, this one a man with an imperious expression.

His headdress curled out at the sides like horns and he wore rich robes trimmed with gold brocade.

'It's Lord Rama,' Dadong said, 'to go with your Sita. I asked my brother to make it. I was going to pick it up when I saw him.'

Ibad grinned. I was speechless with pleasure, examining the beautifully stitched garments and the intricate painting on his wooden face.

'Do you like it?'

'I love it. That's so kind. Please thank your brother very much.'

'Ibad will tell him. He works in the jail.'

'What work do you do?'

'This and that.' He grinned again and said something to Dadong.

I guessed that Dadong would want to ask for news of his brother and that they might feel rude speaking Bahasa in front of me. 'Shall I leave you two to talk?' I asked. 'I might walk to the top of the road and have a look at the view before we go.'

'That's fine. We'll leave in ten minutes.'

The road came to an end just past our bungalow and some steps were cut into the blackened rock, leading to a path up the edge of the crater. The mists had cleared and the light was sparkly, twinkling on outcrops of stone that had a peculiar metallic tinge. Trickles of water leaked out through the earth and the rotten stench was strong, the kind of air that would tarnish silver jewellery and clear blocked drains. No plants grew on this patch, although there were green areas on other slopes nearby. I supposed it must depend on how recent the lava flows were, whether nature had had a chance to regenerate.

The summit was a long way up, but I could see puffs of smoke shooting from the top and there was a muffled roaring mingled with the sound of human voices. I cleared a ridge and saw a group of six Indonesians bathing in a pool from which steam drifted lazily. There was a general giggling when they noticed me then someone waved and I waved back. The next part of the path curved steeply uphill so I decided to return to the bungalow along another path that snaked nearby.

It was a strange feeling, walking on earth that was so alive and volatile. It made me consider how insignificant human beings were in the scale of time. The Earth had been boiling and exploding like this for four thousand million years and homo sapiens had only been around for the last hundred thousand. Most of the other living creatures we shared the planet with had existed for a lot longer and this rock, welling up from the Earth's core, had been there from the beginning, soon after Big Bang.

Ibad had gone and Dadong was standing by the car waiting for me.

'Did you pack my puppet?' I asked.

'It's in that compartment in the boot.'

'Why did you put it there?'

'There might be a message for me inside. I'll check when we get out of here. Are you ready to go?'

He didn't talk much on the road back to Jakarta. I asked if there was any news from his brother but he answered in the noncommittal monosyllables he was so practised in and after a while I just lay back and watched the mountains. When we reached a remote part of the road, without any other cars in sight, he pulled over and walked round to open the boot. I couldn't see what he was doing. A few minutes later, he closed it and got back into the driver's seat.

'Was there anything?'

'Yes.'

'What does it say?'

'Some names.'

I waited, but no more information was forthcoming. The protective force field remained in place.

Chapter Twenty-four

————◆◇◆————

Several weeks passed during which I threw myself into work at the clinic and spent most of my time off with Dadong. I remained deeply suspicious of Medimachines and had an angry exchange with Phil on the telephone because it took them over three months from receiving the order for the computer to deliver it.

'Blame Indonesian customs,' he defended himself. 'They make you jump through hoops to import anything here. Karlina knows that; I'm sure she understands.'

One afternoon in April I treated an unusual patient, who remained in my thoughts afterwards. She was an old woman and she walked into my consulting room clutching the left side of her face. Her cheek was hideously swollen, a growth the size of a small melon forcing her left eye to a slit and distorting her features. She sat down on the chair I indicated and bent her head to one side to support the weight of the tumour in her hand. I got up to examine it more closely. The surface was scabbed and shiny, spreading into her ear lobe and down the side of her neck.

'Ask her how long she's had this,' I instructed Yanti and the answer came back that it was over a year but it was growing all the time.

'Has she seen a doctor? Have they run tests?' The woman supported the growth with her hand as she spoke, her voice muffled as though her tongue was swollen. It must be in her mouth as well.

'She says it's cancer. They wanted to cut it out but she wouldn't let them and now it's too big. She wants your advice, though, because it jolts around when she walks and that's uncomfortable for her.'

'It must be more than uncomfortable. What's she taking for the pain?'

Yanti spoke to the woman for a few moments and with her free hand, she pointed to the bridge of her nose and the ridge of the brow bone. 'She says she gets bad headaches behind her eyes and she takes pills that the doctor gave her.'

I moved her hand so I could feel the weight of the growth. It was surprisingly heavy, a sack full of cells that had gone berserk, dividing and subdividing constantly.

'She not taking any anti-cancer drugs? No radiotherapy?'

Yanti consulted the woman. 'She says she's sixty years old and knows that this is what will kill her. She just wants to be more comfortable while she's waiting for her death.'

I gestured that she should open her mouth and saw straight away where the growth was coming through the palate and spreading down toward her tongue. Soon she would lose the ability to speak and she wouldn't be able to eat for much longer.

'Ask about her diet. Is she able to swallow?'

'She says she sticks to liquid foods, like soup.'

The woman looked at me with her good eye and her tumour twitched and wobbled as she tried to smile. I patted her shoulder. She murmured something to Yanti, who laughed nervously before translating. 'She said it's just as well she's had her children already because what man would look at her now?'

I laughed and shrugged at her. There wasn't a comforting answer.

Yanti fetched some bandages and I looped them carefully round her head, forming a sling to support the growth, then tested to see that it would hold firm. Then I went to the pharmacy to find some drugs. When I returned, Yanti and the woman were chatting to each other. She was a lively soul but it was discomfiting to watch the asymmetrical animation on one side of her face and the hostile invader that had taken root on the other. I handed over a bottle of morphine tablets and explained that she should take one tablet twice a day, then I also gave her a bottle of quick-acting liquid morphine.

'Tell her to have a slug of liquid if she experiences pain between the tablets. There is no limit to the amount of liquid she can take, but if she brings the bottle back in a week, I'll assess how much extra she's needed and increase the dose of the tablets until she is pain-free. She can also come back any time the bandaging needs to be redone. I suspect she'll need to be admitted somewhere soon, though.'

Yanti translated, and the woman replied, sounding adamant. 'She's not going to be admitted to a hospital. She wants to die at home with her family.'

Suddenly the woman grabbed my hand and pulled me towards her, peering hard into my eyes. It felt as though she was trying to scour my soul. I smiled uneasily, then she spoke to Yanti in a slurred but emphatic tone.

'She says you are in a period of great change and you must take care. She sees illness, a death and a baby, all of them very close.'

It was odd, in a patient consultation, to find the tables turned. 'I come across illness and death every day, but tell her that I'm not aware of any impending babies.'

Yanti spoke to the woman again.

'No, it's you or people very close to you. Not patients. She says you could be in danger.'

The woman nodded at me for emphasis and I thanked her, patting her shoulder, then watched as she shuffled out of the room.

'Why do you think she said that? What a strange thing.'

'It used to be her job. Predicting the future.'

'Just by looking at people?'

'I guess so. Why not?'

'No reason,' I said quickly, remembering the number of times I did this myself.

I felt very disturbed after the consultation, not so much because of her gloomy prediction, but because it wasn't going to be an easy death and it would be especially traumatic for her family to watch. I went to Karlina's office to ask if there were any nursing support services that could visit the woman at home but she seemed doubtful that she would be able to arrange anything.

'We're completely broke. I can hardly afford to pay the nurses' salaries or buy the drugs we need.' She was slumped over her desk with her head in her hands.

'Are you OK?' I asked.

'It's one of those days, I suppose. I lost a patient this morning, a little girl having an asthma attack. She went into heart failure on my trolley and I couldn't revive her. She was the same age as my daughter. Some cases just get to you more than others, don't you think?'

'Do you want to take a break and go out for a coffee?' I asked, but she shook her head.

'I've got too much to do today. We're having some kind of an inspection the day after tomorrow and I've got to make sure all the paperwork's up to date.'

'What are they inspecting for?'

'Search me. It happens once every year or so, but there's never any follow-up or feedback. I've got no idea what they're after. Maybe it would be better if you don't come in that day, though. Just to be on the safe side, in case they ask questions about your role here.'

I wondered whether this was a good moment to enquire about the receipts for the scanners. Cameron had sent me some UK prices for comparison but I didn't want to rouse Karlina's suspicions just yet. I asked as casually as I could, explaining, 'I just wanted to check the warranties in case they break down. If you don't have them handy, I suppose I could get copies from the Medimachines office.'

'Surely you are familiar with your company's terms of business?'

I shook my head. 'That's not my area.'

She frowned. 'OK, then. There's a filing cabinet in the main office with a folder on our transactions with Medimachines. Help yourself.'

I slipped upstairs to the office at the first chance I got. No one else was around and I found the file easily, a fat blue cardboard one bulging with documents, some in English but most in Bahasa. The figures were quoted in rupiah, and I didn't have a calculator to do the conversions so I just scribbled down the numbers in my notebook, careful to copy the exact number of zeros as most of the prices were in millions.

I flicked through the pages, looking for a receipt for the Parios, and I noted down the price they'd paid for that. It was such a large number, it looked more like a serial code than the cost of a machine. I checked the bottom of the document to make sure I wasn't missing anything, then turned it over and flinched. I stared at the page for a moment before it sank in properly. My signature ran across the right-hand column.

But how could that be? I hadn't even arrived in Indonesia when they bought the Parios. Confused, I began to flick through all the other receipts, dating back over two years, and on the papers that required a Medimachines signatory, it always seemed to be my signature that was used. It was a very convincing forgery: the loop in the 'l', the curved upright of the 'D' and the way the dot on the 'i' seemed to wander off the letter were exactly as I wrote them.

Panic gripped me. What on earth could this mean? Where could they have got hold of my signature to copy from? It was only last summer I'd signed a contract concerning my work here. If they were forging my signature before then, what had they used as a specimen?

I heard footsteps approaching along the corridor and quickly shuffled the papers back into place and closed the file, but whoever it was didn't come in. What should I do? Who could I talk to about this? I felt completely out of my depth. If I told Karlina the signatures were forgeries, she would have to report it to the authorities so as not to jeopardise her own position. If I rang Phil, he would never tell me the truth; but what could he possibly say to justify such blatant fraud? If I had discovered something like this in a hospital in Britain, I would have gone straight to the police without hesitation. They'd have handwriting experts who could verify that the signatures weren't mine. But if I went to the police here, I suspected the legal process could be complex and the outcome uncertain.

It seemed that I could be in real trouble. The only reason for forging my signature must be because there was something deeply underhand about Medimachines's business methods and they were trying to incriminate me. What was incomprehensible was that it had been going on for almost two years, since just after I met Sedic, long before I ever agreed to come out to Jakarta. But why me?

I put the file back in the cabinet reluctantly. My instinct was to steal it and remove the evidence, but Karlina would remember I'd been asking about it so I'd be the first suspect if it went missing. She must have noticed that I was the signatory on all the Medimachines contracts; no wonder she had been slow to trust me. I couldn't wait for the shift to finish so I could rush out to the car and tell Dadong. In the circumstances, he seemed the only person I could confide in.

He listened carefully as I related the whole story, occasionally stopping me for clarification.

'You have never signed any other papers apart from a contract?'

'No. Nothing else.'

'Was there anything unusual about the contract? Were the terms standard for a post of this type?'

'More or less. I didn't find any clauses suspicious. It just covered the period of employment, the salary and then the expenses they would reimburse, such as air fare, accommodation, staff. It didn't say anything about bonuses or additional payments.' I told him about the money that had been deposited in my account without my knowledge and he seemed concerned.

'You say you've given Phil a cheque to cover the amount, but has it been cashed?'

'I'm going to call and find out as soon as I get back to the house.'

'Because if not – I don't know how these things work –

couldn't you ask your bank to return it to wherever it came from? Surely they could do that?'

'Phil said he was closing the account, but I'll certainly try. What about this inspection the day after tomorrow? I hope there's nothing in those documents that is going to put me under suspicion. Maybe I should tell Karlina everything tomorrow and see what she suggests.'

'Let's sleep on it tonight and talk again in the morning,' he advised.

I called my bank manager as soon as I got in and he confirmed that the cheque hadn't been cashed, so I instructed him to cancel it and arrange an electronic transfer instead to the account where the money originated. Then I poured myself a drink and sat out by the swimming pool under a black, hooded sky feeling shell-shocked about the extent of the conspiracy against me. Someone had set it up to look as though I was responsible for all these machines being sold to the clinic over the last two years and the only reason why they might do that would be because there was something illegal about it.

If I talked to Karlina tomorrow and she reported the forgeries to the police, as she should, then it would be best for me to get myself a lawyer, someone who understood the Indonesian legal system and could argue my case convincingly. It would mean that I'd have to stop working for Medimachines, but perhaps I should resign this evening, to distance myself from them. The problem with that course of action was that they paid for the house and the staff. I'd have to find somewhere else to live and Dadong would no longer be my driver.

It occurred to me that I could just leave the country, go back to London and hire an international lawyer from there, to investigate the fraud and clear my name. But that seemed cowardly. I wasn't ready to leave Jakarta yet. I was too involved in my work at the clinic, for one thing, but I was also becoming very fond of Dadong and didn't want to leave him at a time when we were enjoying each other so much. There were moments when I watched him from a distance – washing the car he was so proud of, or chatting to Ali at the front gate, or concentrating so hard on not giving way to a single car in the chaotic city traffic – that I really felt as though I was falling in love. Maybe it was just a reaction to the life-affirming passion of our physical relationship; but I also loved his calm clear-headedness and the strength of his convictions. I knew that no matter what happened between us, he would never deliberately hurt me.

'This is a holiday romance,' I told myself. 'They write about it in teenage girls' magazines and warn them not to take it seriously. I shouldn't let him influence my decision.'

He hadn't even said if he was coming back later that night. In fact he seldom let me know. I left the pool door unlocked and sometimes I'd be awakened, slowly and seductively, by a shifting of the mattress and a kiss on the back of my shoulder before cool skin pressed against my cosy night-cocooned body and gentle hands began stroking flesh.

Almost overnight, our affair had dissolved the pain of the rejection by Sedic and I still felt surprised when I thought about how quickly I'd got over him. Sometimes I tested the wound to see if there was any residual scarring but I felt only relief and a sense of freedom. With Sedic, I'd been constantly anxious, waiting for criticism, trying to second-guess his moods. With Dadong, I felt cherished and protected, accepted for myself; I didn't have to try to pretend to be someone I wasn't. There had been a way in which my engagement to Sedic had never felt real. Maybe I had sensed his detachment; or maybe I was just imagining it in retrospect. But everything with Dadong seemed straightforward and honest.

What would he advise in the morning? He was the person who had made me cynical about Indonesia's police force, and the incident in Bandung had confirmed their corruption. But surely Westerners would receive better treatment than political dissidents? I had done nothing wrong, but somehow I felt a twinge of guilt. I'd had misgivings about Medimachines from the start. I'd broken the law by treating patients in the clinic; maybe they would be able to compile some kind of case against me. If I was found guilty of a criminal charge, I could be struck off the medical register in Britain and unable to practise any more. The thought was deeply distressing. As the only child of two GP parents, I had never considered any other career, since the days when they used to give me offcuts of gauze bandage to treat my dolls and teddy bears. There was nothing else I wanted to do with my life.

On the other hand, perhaps all my worries were for nothing. Maybe I was completely over-reacting. There could be a practical, although not an ethical, reason for the forgeries. Maybe no law had been transgressed.

My thought processes were circular and contradictory, like a spiral yew-tree maze or a Möbius strip. It was very late when I went to bed and I couldn't sleep for hours as my exhausted brain dreamt up potential but increasingly unrealistic ramifications.

Dadong slipped into bed some time around dawn and we made love first, deliciously, then kissed for a long time afterwards. I was drowsy and when he began to speak I didn't initially understand what he was telling me.

'There was a break-in at the clinic last night,' he cautioned. 'I thought I'd better warn you before you go in.'

'Goodness, was anyone hurt?'

'No. Someone just smashed the glass of the office door and took the cash box. Seemingly it's a bit of a mess, though, and the files are all muddled and scattered across the floor.'

'That's terrible. I hope they didn't lose much.'

'No, not much.'

I surfaced a bit more. 'How did you find out about it?'

'Someone told me,' he said enigmatically.

I scrutinised him, narrowing my eyes. 'This is a bit of a coincidence, is it not?'

'No, it's not a coincidence.'

I sat up abruptly. 'Please tell me it wasn't you who broke in.'

'No, it wasn't.'

'But you know who it was?'

'Yes.'

'And where's the Medimachines file?'

'It's in a safe place.'

I swung my legs round and climbed out of bed, reaching for my robe. 'Dadong, I can't believe you've done this. Before tonight, I hadn't broken any laws – well, not really – but now it will look as though I have. This is not the way to go about things. You'll only make the situation worse. I want you to take that file back straight away.'

'The file will be returned once we've examined it carefully and found out what's going on. A friend of mine, someone we can trust, is going to read it today and make copies of anything compromising.'

'Will it be returned in time for the inspection?'

'I think they will have to cancel the inspection. There is too much of a mess in the office.'

I strode into the bathroom and slammed the door noisily, my emotions in turmoil. What if they suspected me of involvement in the break-in? What a stupid, irresponsible, foolhardy thing for him to do. On the other hand, I was deeply touched that he would go to such lengths to protect me. In the mirror, my cheeks looked pink, my eyes puffy and old. Fear wedged in my throat like a fishbone.

Dadong was dressed and ready to leave when I emerged. 'Are you angry with me?' he asked.

'No. I'm very scared, though.'

He put his arms round me and I rested my head on his shoulder. In the next room I heard Mimi setting the table for breakfast. A vague doubt crossed my mind: could I really trust Dadong? I hadn't known him for long, after all. But seconds later, I knew I was being paranoid. He was the only person I *could* rely on.

Chapter Twenty-five

Karlina didn't seem at all fazed by the break-in. 'It's a regular occurrence,' she told me. 'There were only around ninety thousand rupiah in the cash box, but the way things are around here, we couldn't afford to lose it.'

I felt a muscle twitch under my right eye. 'What about the inspection?'

'I'm glad we can put that off for a few weeks. I wasn't nearly ready for it.'

All day I felt jumpy, as if someone might confront me at any moment, demanding to know where the file was. When I walked past the office, a glazier was replacing the glass and one of the secretaries was sitting on the floor sorting through heaps of paperwork that were piled in a stack in the corner. Rianna was on duty and we weren't especially busy, so I spent a few hours on the new computer, installing software and trying to connect it to the scanner. It was good to have a task that demanded close attention but at the same time wasn't too intellectually challenging.

The instruction booklet was in English. I followed the procedures carefully and everything seemed to work perfectly until it was time to switch the scanner on, at which point the system repeatedly crashed. I rebuilt the desktop and started from the beginning following each instruction exactly, but it crashed again and this time an ominous flashing question mark appeared on the screen. I wasn't experienced enough to judge whether there was an incompatibility or if I was omitting some vital step. They'd have to get a technician to look at it another time.

'Is there a problem?' Rianna asked, hovering behind my right shoulder.

'I expect I'm the problem,' I replied cheerfully. 'I'm probably missing some vital link.'

'You are not an expert with computers?'

'Definitely not.'

'So why do you work for a company that supplies medical equipment?'

'That's just coincidence. They offered me a job out here and I thought it sounded interesting so I accepted.'

Rianna looked puzzled. 'But you were involved with Medimachines in the UK. I thought you had been with them for years.'

I guessed she must have seen my signatures on the receipts and considered my answer. 'No, the owner of the company, Peter Molozzi, is the father of my ex-fiancé. That's the connection.' It occurred to me at that moment that I had never seen Peter's name on any of the Medimachines documents. I'd always assumed he was the owner but he had never confirmed his connection.

'Peter . . . how do you spell the surname?'

I spelled it out for her. 'You haven't met Peter?'

'No, I've never heard of him. Just Mr Pope and you.'

'Peter's an international businessman. He's got companies all over the place. I don't think he comes to Jakarta very often.'

'What other business does he have?'

I told her what I knew, intrigued by her curiosity. Maybe she was just nosey; maybe she was suspicious about Medimachines.

Dadong picked me up early, around seven o'clock, and as soon as I got into the car, I asked if there was any news.

'Yes, some. My friend was astonished that all of the signatures in the file were forgeries because it seems you are a director of Medimachines. Did you know that?'

'That's ridiculous. I can't be.'

'According to these papers you are, and you approved the sale of all the equipment the hospital has purchased.'

I stared out of the window at the headlights passing on the other side of the road. The bit about being a director was a shock but I had been pretty sure the signatures represented some kind of required authorisation. 'So if any of the equipment is defective or dangerous, I'll be held responsible.'

Dadong sighed. 'My friend has recommended that you consult a lawyer. He's given me the name of someone he trusts, who speaks good English. You should commission him to look up the Medimachines records and then he'll advise on whether you should report the forgeries to the police. It makes sense to get all the information we can before making a decision, don't you think?'

'How long will it take, though? I feel as though there's a sword hanging over my head and I could be found out at any time. It would look better if I went to the authorities and told the truth now. Hiring a lawyer seems the action of someone who's guilty.'

Dadong didn't speak for a while. I could tell he was thinking about what I'd said and weighing it up. 'In the best case, this lawyer will not find any illegal trading activities and he will get you removed from the Medimachines board. In the worst case, though, if you go to the police and they find a crime has been committed, you might have to go to jail until the trial.' He was watching my face in the mirror. 'That's what I want to avoid at all costs.'

I leant my forehead against the back of the front seat and closed my eyes. Thoughts of escape swirled through my brain. I should probably get on a plane the next morning. Or I could go to the British Embassy and explain everything to the ambassador. He'd seemed to like me. Surely he would help?

'Why don't we try to see this lawyer tomorrow? If you don't agree with his advice, we don't have to follow it.'

When we got home, I tried to call my parents. I didn't like to worry them when there was nothing they could do from so far away but my father usually dispensed calm, practical advice from a clear moral standpoint. He'd know what to do. Unfortunately, the receptionist at his practice told me he was at a conference until the weekend, and my mother had accompanied him.

'Do you want me to give him a message, dear? Is everything all right out there?'

'It's fine,' I lied, a huge lump in my throat. 'Just fine.'

Edy Mariman was a smart Javanese man in a good suit, taller than average and around fifty, I estimated. Dadong's friend had made copies of all the documents in the Medimachines file and I handed them over, explaining that none of the signatures was actually mine. As he flicked through them, I noticed that his nails were neatly manicured.

He asked questions about my association with Medimachines, the work I was doing at the hospital, and I gave him a copy of the contract I'd signed the previous summer.

'This is your real signature?' he asked and I nodded. He placed it alongside one of the Medimachines documents. 'Not such a good forgery after all. Your handwriting slopes to the left. Look. And the letter "a" is quite different.' He traced the shape with an elegant fingernail.

'Really?' I breathed a sigh of relief.

'You have no idea why anyone would want to set you up like this?'

'None whatsoever. I mean . . .' I'd been giving this some thought over the last couple of days. 'Maybe they thought it would lend their company more legitimacy to have a doctor on the board, so when I got involved with Sedic – my ex-fiancé – they decided to use my name. I'd always assumed that his father, Peter, was the owner of the company. Maybe you'll be able to check that for me?'

Edy nodded, deep in thought. 'They'd have needed your passport and birth certificate as well. Maybe your medical qualifications. Could anyone have had access to these?'

I stared out of the window for a moment. 'Sedic and I lived together. He could easily have borrowed them. If they weren't missing for long, I'd never have noticed.' I'd been trying to avoid the conclusion that Sedic had helped to set me up, but it seemed the most likely scenario.

Edy nodded sagely. 'You said this man, Peter Molozzi, has

several other international business interests. Could you tell me what you know about them?'

I leaned back in my chair. 'He and his partner have an art gallery in London, and a company called Art Deals International in Hong Kong, the one I told you about that sold Medimachines the scanner. He has a casino in the Bahamas, a vineyard in New Zealand . . .' I thought hard, trying to remember any other businesses I'd heard mentioned.

'You say he travels a lot. Which other countries does he visit?'

'He was in Russia recently.' Then I remembered something else. 'Did I tell you that the bank account for Olbisson Computers is in Vanuatu? Phil Pope made a trip out there just before the surprise bonus turned up in my account.' Edy was making notes as I spoke. 'I've been wondering why they would have an account there. I looked it up in an encyclopedia and it's a tiny group of islands whose exports are mainly coffee and timber. Seems odd, don't you think?'

Edy gave a slight smile and I got the feeling he knew more than he was telling me. 'Anything else? Where did your ex-fiancé go when he made trips for the company?'

'He came here, to Indonesia. The Bahamas. Bangkok once. He was trying to distance himself from it all though. He just wanted to be an artist.'

'Uh-huh. And did you ever ask Peter why he has such a diverse range of businesses?'

'I used to tease him about it. He doesn't run any of them himself. He hires local managers for each. I always presumed he just invested his money where he saw a good business opportunity. Why, what do you think?'

Edy spoke carefully. 'I think it sounds like an unusual portfolio and an interesting selection of countries to operate in. But let's not jump to any conclusions just yet.'

'What happens next? What do you think I should do?'

'If you decide that you would like me to act on your behalf, I will go to our records office in Jakarta and find out what I can about Medimachines. I will also run international searches on all the companies you've mentioned and see what comes up. In the meantime, I advise that you should act completely normally. Don't do anything to make them suspicious. I've got a feeling this operation may be more sophisticated than it seems at face value, in which case they will have contingency plans to shut you up if you start making a fuss.'

A shiver ran down my arms. 'What do you mean – "shut me up"?'

Edy smiled. 'I didn't mean to worry you. It won't be anything we can't deal with, but if they're forging your signature on bills of sale, who knows what else they might try to involve you in? It's a stupid ploy because handwriting analysis is very accurate nowadays. No, I just advise that you should act normally until we have all the information we need to take the next step because otherwise they'll have a chance to cover their tracks.' I stared at my lap. 'Of course, you don't have to follow my advice.'

His manner instilled trust but I still wasn't sure. 'How long will it take for you to find out what you need?'

He clasped his hands together. 'I'm in court this afternoon but I can make a start tomorrow. I should have uncovered everything about Medimachines' trade in Indonesia within a week. The international companies may take a bit longer. But we should meet again in a week to talk about the next step.'

'What might that next step consist of?'

'Several things. They've clearly broken the law so there could be criminal charges against the perpetrators, if we can identify them. There's a chance you'll be able to seek compensation for damage to your reputation, but maybe it would be better for you to take such action in London rather than here. There are a number of strategies. We'll know more by next week.'

'How much will you charge for your services?'

'I cost around 700,000 rupiah an hour. Most of my clients are big companies who can afford to pay for good advice. But for you, I will agree a set number of hours – say four – that I will spend finding out about Medimachines in Indonesia. That way you will know what bill to expect.'

'Would you rather I paid you in sterling or dollars, given the currency fluctuations?'

'Absolutely not. Everything between us will be transparent. If you want to proceed, my secretary will type you a letter this afternoon, stating that you have hired me for not more than four hours and confirming the fee. If, after our meeting next week, you want me to continue with the investigations, she will type you another letter. When our business is completed, I will invoice you in rupiah and I will expect payment with a cheque or banker's draft. Is that acceptable?'

His formality was the reassurance I needed. 'Agreed,' I said, and he stood up to shake hands.

'Make an appointment with my secretary for a week today but call me in the meantime if there are any further developments.' I turned to leave the room. 'Dr Drew, one more thing. How many people know that you are worried about Medimachines?'

'My driver, and his friend who recommended that I come to you.' He nodded. 'Peter and Phil know that I'm concerned about the scanners and the bonus that appeared in my account. And a friend of mine in London found out about the Parios for me.'

'Make sure your friend doesn't say anything, and don't mention it to anyone else. The fewer people who know, the better. OK?'

Dadong was waiting outside. 'He's nice,' I told him. 'In some ways he reminds me of my father. He's not emotional, just clear and practical.'

Dadong nodded. 'Good.'

The week passed slowly. I met Diana for lunch on Saturday in a café in Kemang and she teased me remorselessly about my affair with Dadong. It seemed he'd been right about the way news leaked out. Alison Green had been suspicious about the way we behaved together at the beach, and since then we'd been spotted several times around town. I couldn't make Diana understand that it was more than purely sexual. She seemed to find it impossible that we might have anything in common and her jokey innuendo annoyed me so much that I resolved not to see her again for a while.

I went for a coffee with Karlina and she chatted about her daughter, whom she hoped to take on holiday to Bali the following month. I felt guilty in her presence, conscious that it was because of me that the clinic's files were still in disarray. Work had returned to the usual frenetic pace once Ramadan was over, and it was usually close to eleven o'clock before we'd worked through the queue of outpatients.

Dadong took me to a *wayang* show on my evening off and I marvelled at the skill of the old man who manipulated all the puppets in front of the screen and gave each one a different voice, while the gamelan orchestra players sat cross-legged by their instruments, smoking kreteks, hooting and commenting on the action. The story was complex and dramatic: characters were killed or banished from the kingdom too frequently for me to keep track of them, although Dadong whispered a running commentary in my ear.

One evening, as we pulled into the garage around midnight, Mimi came hurrying out to meet us. It was later than her bedtime, so I immediately worried that something was wrong. She seemed very agitated, wringing her hands, looking from one to the other of us.

'What is it, Mimi? What's the matter?' I asked and Dadong translated.

'You have visitor,' she said, pointing into the house.

'Who is it?'

She seemed embarrassed, as if unsure whether to beckon me into the kitchen and talk to me privately. She glanced from Dadong to me and back again and I realised at that moment that she'd guessed about our relationship. Of course she had. How arrogant lovers can be, thinking they're discreet when their emotions are a visible aura around them, etched on every gesture.

Dadong spoke to her in Bahasa and I couldn't catch the words as she answered him, but he turned to me with his eyebrows raised and an opaque expression in his eyes. 'Well,

well,' he said. 'It seems as though your "fiancé" has turned up. He's brought a suitcase and Mimi says he's in the pool having a swim.'

At some deep level I'd been expecting this ever since he phoned me from the Bahamas, but it still came as a shock. The timing couldn't have been worse. 'Will you come in with me and meet him, Dadong?' I pleaded. 'I don't want to see him on my own. Please stay here tonight.'

'I don't think that's a good idea,' he said. 'I might want to kill him.'

I sighed heavily. 'What am I going to say? I just want him out of here.'

'Say that then. I'll be back in the morning.' His tone was curt.

'Dadong, don't be jealous, please. I hate him. It's you I want to be with.'

He kissed me quickly on the cheek then walked down the path and out of the front gate and the security mesh sprang shut behind him. Mimi touched my arm in a gesture of support and smiled sympathetically at me before turning to go up to her bedroom.

Chapter Twenty-six

Sedic waved when he noticed me standing in the doorway then swam to the side and hoisted himself up to sit on the edge of the pool. He'd turned the floodlights on, which I never did because they attracted mosquitos, and his skin gleamed pale in their artificial shimmer. He'd lost weight, I noticed. His waist was narrower and the line of his ribs sloped round his sides. There was no attraction left; I just felt annoyed that he had disturbed my evening with Dadong.

'Hello,' he said, his eyes big and black. I was wearing a baggy cotton dress that I knew he wouldn't like. 'Do you think I could have a towel, please?'

I walked through to the cupboard in my room and pulled one from the top of the pile, then I closed my eyes and stood still for a few moments trying to find some self-control. It was important that I stayed calm and considered every word carefully. I mustn't say anything to make him think I knew about the forgeries and had hired a lawyer. When I got back outside, he was splayed on a sun lounger, dripping water onto the cushions, a glass in his hand. I threw the towel at him roughly.

'Your maid offered me a drink.' He raised the glass. 'Why don't you join me?' His voice was uncertain.

I folded my arms. 'You can't stay here. If you haven't got anywhere else to sleep, I'll phone a hotel and book you a room.'

'It's a bit late for that.'

'It's a bit late for everything.'

He was staring at me but I refused to catch his eye. 'Please can I stay, just for tonight? I only landed a couple of hours ago. I'll find somewhere else tomorrow.'

I kept my voice low. 'What on earth did you think you were doing, arriving here without arranging accommodation first or warning me that you were coming? You can't just presume like that, not after what's happened. You promised me, when I lent you the money, that you'd leave me alone.'

'I know.' There was a long pause. 'I'm sorry.' He rubbed his hair with the towel. 'I just couldn't leave it at that. I had to see you again.'

'Why? Do you need some inspiration for your next exhibition?'

He looked startled. I'd never spoken to him like that before. He hung his head, as though he was about to cry, in a posture I remembered well. In the past, it had always made me melt with sympathy for the poor little boy who'd been shunted from stepmother to stepmother and school to school, but now I felt steely. He was a consummate actor, a con man who'd turned my life upside down and implicated me in a sinister, criminal plot that could destroy my medical career. I had to remain very clear-headed. Maybe if I let him talk, he'd give me some idea of what I was involved in; or maybe he would just heap further lies on top of the rest.

Sedic leaned back in the lounger and huddled inside the towel. The hairs on his legs were flattened in streaks against his skin and rivulets of water trickled onto the cushions, creating a dark patch on the canvas. The nightly call of 'e-kko, e-kko' came from the back wall, behind the plants, and he glanced across trying to identify the source.

'That's my gekko,' I told him.

He nodded. I sat down on the edge of the other lounger. 'So are you going to tell me why you've come?'

He mumbled something but the words caught in his throat. He coughed slightly and turned his head away. 'You're not going to believe me but the truth is that I've come because I miss you.'

'Oh, fuck off!' I shouted, and he jumped with shock. I don't think he'd ever heard me swear before. 'We're not going to have this conversation unless you're going to be honest. I don't want to hear any more bullshit or I'll waken my guard and ask him to throw you out on the street.'

'I don't know where to start,' he whispered.

'Let me help then. Why don't you start by telling me about the fact that you found out a whole year ago that your mother was still alive and it didn't occur to you to tell me, the woman you were planning to marry? What was that all about?'

'There are complications you don't know about, Nicky. I wanted to stop Peter finding out that I knew and . . . I don't know. I wasn't sure if I could ever forgive Lila for what she did. I certainly can't forgive Peter. And I knew you would urge me to have some big reconciliation scene. I just needed time to figure out how I felt about it before I told anyone else. Do you understand?'

'I'm afraid I don't. I'm not secretive like you. I believe in sharing my worries with the person I love. But since it turned out that our whole relationship was based on a lie, it seems I'm well out of it.'

Sedic was frowning. 'Have you spoken to Peter since you found out?'

'I certainly have. His explanation about wanting to do the best for you and give you more chances in life was very slick.'

'Shit!' He chewed his lip, then drained his glass and set it down on the table. 'I'm not prevaricating. I'll tell you everything. I want you to understand. I can't bear for you to hate me.' He hesitated. 'But do you think I could have another drink first? For Dutch courage.'

I stood up and held out my hand for the glass. 'What are you drinking?'

'Gin and tonic. Why don't you join me?'

I went through to the kitchen and prepared his drink, slicing a crescent of lemon and clattering some ice cubes into the glass. When I poured the gin on top they crackled and spat. I moved slowly, feeling tired and numb. Maybe we should talk in the morning; I wasn't sure if I could face it tonight. But then I remembered Dadong. I wanted everything resolved and for Sedic to be on his way before he came back the next day. I couldn't let anything jeopardise my new relationship. I topped Sedic's glass to the brim with tonic then prepared another glass for myself, exactly the same but without the gin.

On the way back through, I noticed that Mimi had left Sedic's bag outside the door of the spare room. The poor woman couldn't have known what to think when he arrived.

'Thanks,' he said as he took the glass, then he grabbed my hand. 'Ah! Look! You're still wearing your engagement ring.'

I glanced at my hand, surprised. It had become a fixture, not something I noticed any more. 'I just like it as a ring,' I said. 'I'd give it back to you but you didn't pay for it in the first place.'

'I'm glad. I want you to keep it.'

'In that case . . .' I said. I slipped the ring over my finger joint, raised my right arm and tossed it as hard as I could over the garden wall. ' . . . I don't want it any more.' There was a muffled tapping sound as it hit the ground on the other side.

He took a large slug of his drink. We were both silent for a while then he began to talk.

'You're right to hate me. I've behaved abominably towards you, but I'm just hoping that you might not detest me so much when you hear the mitigating circumstances.'

'I'm listening.'

'Peter is not a nice human being, Nicky. He didn't pay Lila to raise his child out of any great paternal instinct, to propagate his genes or whatever. There's a lot more to it than that. He'd have wriggled out of a financial commitment if he could. He only brought me to Europe because he wanted a minion to help with all his dodgy businesses, someone who would obey without asking questions. I'm supposed to be so grateful for the wonderful life he's given me that I'll be eternally loyal, but you of all people know how little I get in return. A few hundred quid and a pat on the back alongside veiled threats about what might happen if I rock the boat.'

I was watching his body language and it was very nervy. He was pulling at his finger joints compulsively and wouldn't meet my eye. 'What would happen?'

COMPULSION

Sedic looked away. 'Peter has little schemes set up to incriminate everyone that works for him if they start asking too many questions. He's got loads against me but I don't think he'll ever risk having me arrested now because I know too much.'

'Are you saying you think your own father would be capable of harming you?'

'Christ, yes! He's never treated me as a son. I'm just an employee that he doesn't have to pay when he doesn't feel like it. Expats here treat their servants much better than he treated me. The number of times I sat in a car outside a restaurant while Peter and Leona had dinner, or slept on a floor because they were too cheap to get me a hotel room . . .'

'So Leona was as bad as Peter?'

'She's a bitch! An evil, nasty cow.' He gulped his drink. 'I don't know if I can bear to tell you the next bit.' He rubbed his chin. 'But I have to, because it explains what happened to us in London.' I waited. 'Leona used to make me sleep with her, then she'd threaten to tell Peter about it. I didn't know what to do.'

'Don't lie to me,' I snapped. 'How could she make you?' It was a shock, but somewhere in my head, this confirmed an unacknowledged suspicion. An image sprang into my head of an afternoon on Leona's roof terrace when she'd asked Sedic to rub some sunscreen into her shoulders and, as he did so, she glanced at me with a triumphant look in her eyes. If they were lovers, that would explain the peculiar tension between the two of them and her hostility towards me, but the idea that she could have forced him was ludicrous.

'She just did. One time Peter was away she asked me to bring her a cup of tea in bed then she pulled me down beside her and – I didn't know what to do. Anyway, it happened; then she said I had to do it next time, or she'd claim that I raped her. It was a mess.'

Watching him, I realised he was remarkably easy to read. When he was lying, he shifted around more, touching his face, switching his focus.

'So how long did this go on?'

'It stopped when I met you. There hasn't been anyone else

239

for me since then.' He turned to look at me directly but there was a flicker in his gaze and I nearly laughed at the attempted sincerity.

'How did she take it when you said you'd got a girlfriend?'

'Leona was furious. That's why she was always so rude to you. Peter was annoyed at first but then he decided it would be a good idea for me to settle down with someone respectable.'

'So he told you to marry me?' This made sense. I'd been astonished when he proposed. He hadn't struck me as the marrying kind and the proposal had seemed to come out of the blue. It was probably around that time they made me a director of Medimachines.

Sedic shivered and pulled the towel more tightly round his shoulders. 'I have to admit that I felt trapped at first. But as the months went by, you were so sweet and generous to me that I began to think maybe there could be a way out of Peter's stranglehold. You were on my side, encouraging me to paint, looking after me. And I knew,' – he glanced at me sideways – 'or at least I was pretty sure, that you really loved me.'

'But it was all based on a lie,' I said coldly.

He stared at his lap. 'It could have worked out, you know. I still think we could have overcome all the problems, if it hadn't been for Peter proposing this plan that we both came out to Indonesia. That sent me into a complete tailspin of panic. I was scared he would drag you into one of his illicit deals as well, then he'd be able to blackmail us both and we'd never break free of him. I tried to talk to you loads of times but you seemed to be so set on the idea. I was going mad last summer. I didn't know what to do. I was too scared to level with you because I thought you would throw me out when you knew the mess I'd got myself into, then I'd be completely at Peter's mercy.' He clutched his hands to his cheeks. 'But I really loved you by this time and I didn't want to ruin your life as well.'

He was lying again. I kept my face deliberately expressionless. 'So you decided the easiest thing was to get rid of me by painting crude, humiliating pictures of me and displaying them to the London art world?'

He was really uncomfortable now, folding his arms across

his chest, shaking his head, not meeting my eye. I felt as though I was assessing a patient, as though I wasn't directly involved. 'It wasn't that straightforward at all. I was in such a state, I couldn't think clearly. But no. First of all, I have to explain that before Peter suggested the exhibition, I'd been working on some big coloured abstract bodies, looking at the different shapes you can make with limbs and altered perspectives, in a kind of Picasso-esque fashion. I wanted to do something similar but with a bit more realism and eroticism.'

He emptied his drink but held onto the glass, running his finger round the rim. 'After that dinner, Leona came over to the studio to see them and she was scathing. She said they were derivative, childish and not even well executed but that she'd have to let me exhibit them because Peter had promised me. It was a very unpleasant meeting. She told me I had no talent, that I was weak and gullible and would never amount to anything.'

I could imagine her delivering these words, and how devastated he would have been by them.

'I was furious, incandescent with rage, after all she'd done to me. I felt disgusted that I'd ever slept with her. She has withered, scaly skin with all these sacks of loose flesh hanging off her bones, like a badly stuffed skeleton.' He shuddered. 'Anyway, I started painting her body into the pictures: the way her tits slide down into her armpits and her stomach sits in rolls. You saw the results.'

'I thought they were me,' I breathed. This bit was a revelation.

'But how could you? There's no way . . . Nicky, I loved your body. How could I have made love to you the way I did if I saw you like that? Come on, you *know* how much I fancied you. You have a fantastic figure, nothing like the ones in the pictures.'

I bit my lip. 'But my feet? You painted my feet.'

He frowned and swivelled round in the chair. 'In the strappy sandals? They're not your feet.'

'No, in the "Site of Outstanding Natural Beauty".'

'But that was a landscape!'

'It looked like my feet.'

'I promise you it's not. How could you think that?' His tone was reproachful. 'The landscape pictures in the exhibition were of nuclear wildernesses. They were supposed to be barren scenes representing the ugliness of what we're doing to the planet. It was all part of the "Moments After" theme.'

I thought back to the picture but the details were hazy in my memory. I was sceptical of his explanation but let it pass. 'Anyway, you used my face in some of them: that one in the little black dress, for example, then told me to wear it to the opening. That was the cruellest bit, I think.'

He exhaled a great weary puff of air. 'Leona saw the pictures as I was hanging them the week before the opening and she went berserk. She attacked me, tried to push me down the stairs in the gallery, screamed and cried and cursed like you wouldn't believe. If Peter had seen the pictures as they stood, it would have been obvious that she and I had slept together and she claimed he would kill us both.'

I considered the jovial, demonstrative side Peter always presented to me, which I had never trusted, and wondered if he was capable of murder. I didn't know him well enough to judge.

'But then, Leona started threatening you. She was raving, clutching at straws and I stormed out. When I came back the next day, she presented me with an ultimatum. Either I adjusted the pictures to look like you instead, or she would implicate you in an illegal scheme in Indonesia and tip off the police about it as soon as you arrived out here. I wasn't sure if she was bluffing or not, but I had to try and stop you coming out.'

I was scarcely breathing, concentrating so hard my eyes hurt. 'What scheme?'

'I told you Peter has set up a number of traps to catch me if I ever turn against him. Leona pointed out how easy it would be to make it seem as though you were involved as well. We were engaged and soon to be married. Just a couple of adjustments could have made it look very bad for you.'

I frowned. 'But I wasn't involved. I could have proved that in a court of law.'

'Not necessarily. They work in very devious ways. Once I

came across a shipping document they'd forged your signature on, and I was furious and made an almighty fuss about it. Peter swore to me it would never happen again. But then, when Leona began threatening you before the exhibition, it occurred to me that I was putting you in danger by being involved with you at all. If we'd got married, it would all have come out at some stage and your career would have been ruined. They'd always have been able to blackmail me with that. You'd have ended up in jail, Nicky, and I couldn't bear to be responsible for that.'

'What shipping document had they forged my signature on?'

'Something for Medimachines.'

I turned my head away, worried that he might be able to read my expression and tell that I knew about this, but he didn't seem to notice.

'I probably wasn't thinking straight but it seemed to me that the only way to protect you was to break up with you very publicly, so we were clearly no longer together in the eyes of the world. And I decided the best way to do that would be to follow Leona's plan — adjust some of the pictures to look like you and give a press interview about our breakup. Do you have any idea how much it destroyed me to do that?'

'No,' I shook my head. 'I don't. All I remember is the callousness of you asking me to come to the exhibition wearing that black dress, the one in the picture, and refusing to speak to me when I got there.'

He covered his face with his hand. 'I decided that if the ending was brutal, you would get over it more quickly. You would be so horrified you would just want to forget all about me. I never dreamed you would come to Indonesia without me and when I heard you were leaving I came to see you, to warn you, but you'd left already. Leona lied to me about your departure date.'

'What would you have said?'

He shook his head. 'Just enough to stop you going. I hadn't really thought it through.'

A strange bird squawked loudly somewhere on the rooftop

and when I looked up, I saw that the sky was beginning to lighten a fraction. I had no idea what time it was. I'd gone into this conversation feeling separate, cocooned from hurt by my new love affair with Dadong and the suspicion that Sedic had been using me from the start, stealing my passport and papers to enable them to register me as a director. Somehow along the way it had got to me, though. I felt raw and vulnerable, but I still had enough distance to judge that he wasn't telling me the whole truth. Bits of it were probably true; others had a cosmetic gloss; some may have been total fabrications.

'What are you thinking?' he asked, tentatively.

'That I'm not sure I believe you.'

'How could I make this up? I don't understand how you could think the bodies in those paintings were you. There was no similarity whatsoever. Nothing.'

'I'm going to ask you some questions, Sedic. A kind of truth or dare. But in this case it'll be truth or I'll throw you out of this house right now and never speak to you again. I want you to answer quickly. No hesitations or pausing to think up lies. OK?'

He was holding his cheeks in his hands again.

'I'm going to know if you're lying to me, so don't even think about it.'

'OK,' he whispered.

I didn't plan the questions, just asked them as they came into my head.

'Why have you come out here now?'

'I've got some business of my own to take care of and I'm going to make some enquiries to try and make sure Peter and Leona haven't been tying you up in any schemes of theirs. I want to protect you.'

'If they have, I'll take care of myself.'

'You don't understand. Honestly. This is much more serious than you seem to think.'

I folded my arms. 'But why should I believe you're on my side after all you've done to me?'

'Because I still love you,' he whispered.

I shifted angrily, and the legs of the sunlounger scraped on the marble floor. 'Sedic, I've got a new boyfriend now so if you were hoping for a reconciliation, you can forget it.' I glanced across and he was staring at his hands. 'Next question. What was really going on in the Bahamas and why were you associating with gangsters that take credit cards?'

He exhaled loudly. 'The story I told you about the protection money was true but it was me who used the credit card details. I needed cash to get myself out of there. These guys would never have let me off with ten thousand dollars but I reckoned that was the most you'd be able to raise straight away.'

'I checked my statement afterwards. It said the money was paid to a company called Asteroid Finance, whatever that may be.'

He nodded. 'That's a company I've set up in the Bahamas that Peter doesn't know about. It's just a way that I can get access to some funds.' He looked worried. 'You haven't mentioned this to Peter, have you?'

'Yes, of course I did. I asked him why he hadn't been around to bail you out.'

'Did you tell him about Asteroid?'

I shook my head and he was visibly relieved. 'So what did you do with the money?'

'I got an old guy to take me on his yacht to Freeport because I knew they'd be watching the airport in Nassau, then I jumped a flight to Miami. But you got your money back. I would always pay you back, Nicky.'

'What do you mean – always?' There was something about the way he said it.

'I'm sorry. I had to use your card again to pay for my flight out here. I'll reimburse you within a week when I sort out my business.'

I slapped the canvas seat of the lounger in fury. 'How dare you!' I was angry with myself. I'd meant to cancel the card after the Bahamas transaction had gone through, as Anna suggested, but it had seemed too complicated to arrange from Jakarta. I didn't have any other cards with me and wasn't sure how quickly they'd have been able to get me a replacement.

He fingered his chin. 'I just need access to some funds until I can sort a few things out. It won't be for long. I didn't know what else to do and you know you can afford it.'

'I'm going to cancel that card first thing in the morning. You'll have to get your funds elsewhere. Why don't you ask your friends? Shirley and Tom, or Henry? Or what about Celia Wing?' I watched him closely.

'She's not exactly a friend of mine.' He looked away.

'So what is she then?'

'I can't tell you, Nicky. Someone I'm doing some business with.'

I thought back to the woman with the bleached pony tail and smudged makeup. 'How can you possibly be doing business with someone like that? She's a mess. I don't believe you.' I waited but he didn't respond. 'Is she involved in one of Peter's businesses?'

Sedic was picking compulsively at a piece of skin on his finger. 'I will tell you about Celia, I really want you to know, but there are a few things I have to sort out first. Maybe I can explain in a couple of days if all goes according to plan.'

He got up from his lounger and came over to sit on the edge of mine. I curled my legs away from him. 'I've been as honest as I can about the bits that concern you, but it would only get you into trouble if I told you any more.'

'We couldn't have that,' I said sarcastically and he looked puzzled.

'I swear I came here to protect you,' he protested. 'If you make Peter angry by poking your nose into his interests in a way that doesn't concern you . . . Just don't forget that he's much more experienced in international law than you are. You wouldn't win. If I'm around, I can advise you about how to deal with him.'

I narrowed my eyes. 'Tell me, Sedic, do you really think, after everything we've been through, that there is any possibility at all we could patch up our relationship and get back together again? Honestly?'

He took my hand and began to trace the outline of the fingers. I didn't resist, just watched to see what he would do next. 'I suppose not. In my dreams, yes, but I can't imagine how I could ever make you trust me again,' he said, and I restrained myself from snorting. I struggled to keep my expression neutral. 'As far as I'm concerned, I'll always love you, but I'll understand if you can't reciprocate any more. I always felt that you were too good for me. You are, Nicky. You're the best thing that ever happened to me.'

I got the impression he was going to lean forward and try to kiss me, so I stretched and twisted my legs round onto the floor to stand up. 'I'm going to bed now. You can stay in the guest room tonight but I want you to look for somewhere else tomorrow. Maybe there is a way for us to – I don't know. But it will be a very long, slow process. It can't be mended overnight.'

'Sure, darling. I understand.'

I felt sick with disgust but I let him kiss me briefly on the cheek before I went into my bedroom and shut the door.

Chapter Twenty-seven

It was only a few hours later when I wakened to the sound of the telephone ringing in the other room. Mimi picked it up and I heard her talking in Bahasa, so I assumed it was a friend of hers, but then her feet pattered across to my bedroom door and she tapped softly.

'Madam, Dadong is on the phone.'

I pulled on a robe and went to pick it up, glancing at a clock as I passed. It was only just after nine.

'How is everything?' he asked first of all.

'It's very difficult,' I whispered, not sure if Sedic would be able to hear from his room.

'Is he still there?'

'Yes, in the spare room. But I've told him he has to leave today. Are you coming at eleven? Maybe we could go for coffee somewhere.' I desperately wanted to discuss it all with him.

'I can't come today. There are a few scattered demos in town and I want to be around. You should be able to call a taxi and get them to take you round the back way to the clinic. Or maybe you should stay at home. These ones could be unpredictable.'

'It's not just the clinic.' I hesitated. 'I have a meeting with our friend at twelve thirty.' I didn't want to say his name in case Sedic was listening. Dadong knew who I meant, though.

'The lawyer? I wonder what he'll have found out?'

'Will you call me later at the clinic? I want to be sure that you're safe.'

'Of course I'll be safe. I'll try and phone, but if I don't manage it, then I'll just see you tomorrow morning. OK?'

I felt very lonely when I hung up, a gnawing ache that made me restless and out of sorts. I knew I wouldn't be able to sleep any more so I pulled on a bikini and went for a swim in the white morning sun. Ali had picked up the *Jakarta Post* but there was nothing in it about the demos. I was sitting at the table flicking through the pages when Sedic emerged, puffy-eyed, just wearing boxer shorts. A crease in the sheet had marked a groove down his cheek and he looked young and vulnerable.

Mimi had gone out shopping so I made him some coffee, and it was strange piling three heaped spoons of sugar into the mug, just as I always used to when we lived together. He never had breakfast, just his hot, sweet milky coffee.

'I'm going into town in an hour,' I told him. 'I'm calling a cab because there are some demos so my driver's not working today. Do you want me to give you a lift in?'

'OK,' he said, 'But why don't I drive you in your car? I could pick you up and bring you back later as well.'

I shook my head emphatically. 'No, I told you. I want you to find somewhere else to stay. You can't come back here tonight.'

He sat down at the table. 'Listen, it would be a big help if I could borrow your car just for a couple of hours, to take my bag to a hotel and make a few arrangements. Then I could pick you up from work later, bring you home and get a cab back to stay at my hotel. How about that?'

'I'm not happy about you driving the car.'

'Why not? It's a Medimachines car, not yours personally, and I've driven in Jakarta loads of times, so I know the roads.'

I still felt reluctant – it was as though Sedic was trying to usurp Dadong – but when I rang the two main cab companies, they told me they wouldn't supply any cars till late afternoon when the demos were over. The other complication was that I had to prevent Sedic finding out that I was visiting a lawyer before work but I decided to ask him to drop me at the clinic then walk the few blocks to Edy Mariman's office.

As we pulled out of the drive, I saw a group of four soldiers at the corner of the street, black semi-automatic weapons slung across their shoulders. Sedic pulled up alongside them and lowered the electric window then spoke to them. They were jumpy. Two of them shifted their guns toward firing position. One spoke into a hand-held radio, before replying.

'They said we should go along the airport road,' he reported. 'It seems one lane is open and traffic is moving slowly. The other routes could be more erratic.'

The queues began before we turned out of Kemang onto the main stretch. Cars clustered in a knot, jostling for position, moving painstakingly slowly, as if headed for some bitterly sad funeral.

'So tell me about your new boyfriend,' he asked.

'No, I'd rather not.'

There was a silence.

'Have you made many friends out here?' he tried again.

'Not really. I've mostly just been working.'

We pulled out through a tangle of ropes and traffic cones into the airport road. The carriageway in the opposite direction was closed completely and the pedestrian flyovers were deserted. Nothing was moving except for one slow procession of cars.

'Have you met any of the ex-pat set? Haven't you been to the famous Tanamur?'

'Yeah, I hated it.'

He grinned to himself. 'Nicky, can I take you for dinner one night? Maybe tonight? Just to talk. No strings.'

'I'm not sure. I'll see. Not tonight anyway.' I felt ever more strongly that I just didn't want to see him any more, that I wanted to get free of the situation I was in, then tell Sedic, Peter, Phil and Leona to get lost.

After more than a mile of the strange procession, I saw a crowd in the distance. What was odd was that they didn't seem to be moving. Soldiers stood stock still outside a building that Sedic told me was the House of Representatives, and a mass of people stretched in front, some holding placards like a freeze-framed video scene. There was no sound, so I pressed the button to open my window, but the air was utterly silent. A wave of stale heat shimmered into the air-conditioned interior.

'Why aren't they shouting?' I asked Sedic.

'They must have been told not to.'

Our car reached the edge of the demo and I scanned the figures, half-wondering if I would find Dadong among them. They were mostly young men, but some looked older than students. They wore ripped tee-shirts and scarves and their placards were written in heavy black capitals.

'What do the signs say?'

'They want the government to resign.' He sounded bored.

A protestor with nervous eyes turned to look at me. He wore a turquoise Che Guevara tee-shirt and his hair was tied back in a mini ponytail. There were no women, I noticed suddenly. I tried to estimate how many were there. Five hundred? A thousand? More? They all seemed the same height, all dark-haired, all unmoving. I looked out of the back window at the line of soldiers with their guns trained on the demonstrators. It felt tense, as though anything could happen at any moment.

Suddenly the car in front of us stopped and Sedic braked. Four cars ahead, the soldiers were holding up traffic and, as we watched, a gate into the compound opened and a black car drove out. The demonstrators turned to watch as it was directed through a cordoned channel towards one of the empty lanes. A murmur travelled through the crowd and Sedic had just hissed at me to close the car window when a protester broke away, ducked under a rope and ran after the black car shouting wildly. I couldn't make out any of the words but the tone was anguished, desperate. A single shot rang out like a firecracker or a car backfiring, and I saw him fall forwards. I'd never heard a gunshot in real life before but there was no doubting what had just happened. Time speeded up. The black car disappeared over the horizon and the cars in front of us began to inch forward again. I leant on my door handle and opened the car door to get out but Sedic grabbed my skirt and tugged viciously.

'Get back in,' he snapped.

I tried to pull away from his grasp. The protester had been surrounded by a group of soldiers but he appeared to be lying still on the ground. I was too far away to make out if there was any blood. '*Saya doktor!*' I shouted into the crowd, then repeated myself, louder. Up ahead a soldier turned to look at me then gestured with his gun that I should get back in the car. Sedic was still tugging my skirt. '*Saya doktor!*' I shouted again but Sedic leaned across and grabbed my waist and pulled me physically into the car. My head struck the door frame.

'For crying out loud, Nicola, the guy's dead. Do you think they want a Western witness? Shut your fucking door!'

The protesters nearest to us had turned to watch and I felt the weight of their eyes upon me. 'He might not be dead.'

'If he's not now, he will be by the time they've finished with him. You're so naïve.' He started inching the car forwards and I was forced to close my door to stop it hitting some demonstrators standing just ahead of us.

'I can't see someone being shot in the street and leave the scene without trying to help.' I scanned the group of soldiers guarding the body on the ground. They were huddled so tightly around, it was impossible to see the protester any more. The soldier who'd noticed me said something to a colleague and they both stared into the car. I glared back. 'Sedic, please stop and let me go and talk to them.'

'No way.' He shook his head and accelerated to catch up with the car in front. Soon the last of the demonstrators was behind us. I turned and surveyed the scene again. Had Dadong been there? Had he seen what happened? My hands were trembling and I clenched them together. Sedic was talking, his tone gentle, but I couldn't listen to the words. It felt obscene and wrong and profoundly disturbing.

Edy seemed very pleased with himself. He was smiling broadly as I walked into the office and shook hands, but he soon noticed that my composure was rattled – I was still trembling, I think – and he asked what was up.

'I've just seen someone shot,' I told him. 'At a demo.'

'By soldiers?' he asked and I nodded. 'Were they using rubber bullets or live?'

I considered this. 'I don't know. I don't have any experience of these things but the force knocked the guy to the ground.' I tried to remember the way he fell, whether it had looked as though the bullet had entered his back, but I'd been too far away to judge.

'It's a bad business,' Edy said, shaking his head. 'It's going to get worse before it gets better.'

'I was wondering if I should report what I saw? To the international press, maybe, or some kind of civil rights organisation?'

Edy shrugged. 'I think it would be a very poor idea to draw attention to yourself just now. It's up to you, of course, but I was going to suggest that you keep a very low profile until we've resolved the company problems you're involved in. I'm sure someone else will report it to the press.'

I sighed and sat down. 'It's horrible to feel so powerless after seeing an event like that.'

He regarded me calmly. 'Everyone who attends a demonstration here knows that they're risking their life. It's just something you accept.' He paused. 'Anyway, let me tell you what I've found out about Medimachines and your friend Peter Molozzi.'

I nodded.

'I suspected as soon as you told me about the list of companies you knew he controls. They're all businesses with high turnovers, generally located in countries that have less than rigid banking systems. Each one of them will have different directors, and although financial transactions will sometimes be traced between the companies, no one will find enough to prove the links. Do you see what I'm getting at?'

'I suppose Peter is moving money around between them all. But why?'

'I'm almost sure he's money laundering but we'll never be able to prove it. You said he was in Russia recently, and a lot of business comes from the criminal gangs there. The Bahamas used to be an important banking centre for money launderers and Vanuatu is a reasonably new location that's gaining in popularity because its regulations are so lax.'

'So what does Peter actually do?'

'First of all, I'd be extremely surprised if he is identifiable as the owner of any of the companies in the group. He's far too clever for that. He'll get his minions to feed the criminal money into one of his less salubrious enterprises, like the casino, then it will circulate around until it reaches his wholly legitimate companies, by which time it will be untraceable. It sounds to me as though your ex-fiancé is what is known as a "smurf".'

I frowned 'What's that?'

'Just a courier. He takes money in and out of countries one way or another, so it's not going through official channels.'

This sounded entirely plausible. All the facts seemed to fit. 'So why am I a director of Medimachines?'

Edy took his glasses off and rubbed a speck from one lens with a handkerchief. 'All his businesses will have local managers to take the rap should any illegal activity be uncovered, so that nothing is ever traced back to him. You have a co-director, by the way, an Indonesian woman called Sanita Katoppo. Do you know her?'

'Sanita?' I screwed up my eyes. The name rang a bell.

'Having a local person as a director will have helped them to avoid some of the more stringent checks on foreign companies. She's only been on the board for about six months. Before that it was a woman called Linda something.' He reached for a notebook on his desk to look it up.

'Linda works in the Medimachines office. Hang on!' I remembered. 'I think Sanita is Phil Pope's girlfriend.'

He nodded. 'That makes sense.'

'So is there any kind of illegal activity I should be aware of?'

'Masses!' he exclaimed. 'Good grief, it's a nest of vipers. You don't have import licenses for any of the equipment, they haven't filed any accounts or paid any tax since the company was founded and there haven't been any government inspections.'

'But how can that be?'

'I expect there was some serious greasing of palms. Isn't that your phrase in Britain?' I smiled gingerly. 'It's easy to pay off customs officials at the airport, and tax inspectors have some schemes all their own. One example. A client I now represent wanted to avoid having his books examined. The officials turned up at his office one day and he said it wasn't convenient and asked if they could come back another time. The officials produced a cheap old plastic clock and suggested that he should buy it from them. 'It will look very good on your office wall,' they said. He asked how much it cost and they said a million rupiah. He paid them a million for the clock and he was never inspected. That's how it works.'

I was astonished. 'So do you think Phil Pope has been bribing officials not to look into Medimachines business affairs?'

'Oh, definitely. But meanwhile, if anyone did come to inspect one day, you and Sanita would be the guilty parties. My theory is that if Mr Pope finds out you know about all this, he might call in the authorities. Although that would mean implicating his girlfriend, so maybe not.'

'I'm sure he wouldn't hesitate,' I said cynically. 'But what can I do?'

Edy grinned and rubbed his hands together. 'You've come to the right person. I've been pondering this for the last couple of days and I've come up with a scheme that will solve everything. The first option is to go to the authorities and tell the truth, claiming the signatures are forgeries, but the onus would be on us to prove it, which could be expensive and time-consuming. I've got a feeling that's what Peter will expect you to do and that's why he's piled on evidence like the bonus going into your bank account, and maybe other things we haven't uncovered yet. So I don't favour this option.'

I stared at my lap, feeling sick with worry.

'You could just resign from the Medimachines board, as of today, but you would still be held responsible for any past irregularities. No, what I suggest is a very simple, straightforward solution. You can tender your resignation but backdate it. Because they haven't filed any papers since the company was founded, they can't prove you didn't resign ages ago. I've drafted a rough outline. Here.' He passed me a typed sheet. 'Obviously you can adapt it if you like, but this is what I suggest.'

It was addressed to Linda, my co-director, but copied to

Phil Pope and Peter Molozzi, and stated that I was resigning my position as a director of Medimachines forthwith. I was sorry to let them down but I found my other work commitments too heavy to allow the extent of the involvement such a responsible position would require. I would therefore be grateful if they would remove my name from any Medimachines stationery or documents with immediate effect and it should not be used in connection with the company thereafter.

Edy watched me as I read. 'I am suggesting that we date the letter roughly a month after Medimachines was founded, before any of the equipment had been sold or imported. We lodge your resignation in the companies register here, making it look as though it's been there all along.'

'Isn't that fraudulent? Won't they be able to prove when it was lodged?'

'Not if I just slip it in. These things happen in Indonesia. If they had filed six-monthly accounts, as they're supposed to, we wouldn't have been able to backdate it, but they didn't. So we can.' He locked his fingers, very self-satisfied.

'But what about the forged signatures on all the sales certificates for the medical equipment?'

'Once you are no longer a director of the company, these have no legal weight and don't incriminate you.'

I rubbed my nose. 'Am I not accepting some responsibility by admitting I've been a director at all?'

'Only for a period in which there were no transactions.' Edy smiled gleefully.

I tried to think through the ramifications. 'If I do this, Sanita will be left as the sole director and I don't want her to get the blame for everything. She's only seventeen years old.'

'Ha!' Edy clapped. 'In that case, she won't. She's too young to be a sole company director, so she'll get off. It's a shame we can't slip Peter Molozzi or Phil Pope's names into the records, as they did to you, but that would mean committing forgery. It's too risky.'

'Are you sure there won't be any repercussions if we follow your route?'

'Absolutely not. I can go down and lodge the letter tomorrow morning and then you will no longer be a director of Medimachines. It's as simple as that.'

I shrugged and made up my mind. 'OK, let's do it.'

Edy nodded, pleased. 'My secretary will send you an invoice tomorrow for the amount we agreed.'

'Why don't I write you a cheque now? I've got my chequebook with me. Otherwise, I would have to put it in the post and it's not very reliable over here, I've noticed.'

He thought for a moment. 'I don't want to take your money until I've completed the job, but maybe if you put tomorrow's date on the cheque, that would be OK.'

I laughed. 'What a strangely scrupulous creature you are, for a lawyer!'

'But of course,' he said seriously, and I got the impression I might have hurt his feelings by impugning his profession in any way.

I felt jumpy all day at the clinic and found it hard to concentrate. I willed the time to pass quickly until tomorrow afternoon when I would be free of this legal nightmare. Every time I thought of Sedic and Peter, I was engulfed with rage that they had cold-heartedly implicated me in it all. I was nervous, despite Edy's assurances, that someone might question why he was lodging a resignation dated two years previously. So much could go wrong, it seemed. And I was still shaken by the memory of the shooting I'd witnessed that morning; Dadong hadn't phoned and I worried that something might have happened to him.

We'd agreed that Sedic would pick me up at nine o'clock and I felt increasingly tense as the hour approached. It was as though something was shifting inside me and all the repressed emotions of the last few months were forcing their way to the surface. When it reached half past nine and he still hadn't arrived, I knew it was going to be difficult to restrain myself. Rather than hang around waiting I called a cab, and as I climbed in I peered up the street searching for the dark green people carrier Dadong was so proud of. What would he say if it hadn't been returned by morning?

The roads were clear but unusually quiet. I turned on the television to a news channel as soon as I got home, but the Jakarta demonstration wasn't mentioned. After listening to the world headlines, I wandered outside to the garden. A stinging chemical smell drifted from the pool and I guessed Ali had treated the water. My gekko was missing from the garden wall; perhaps it didn't like the astringent scent in the air. The phone rang and I hurried back inside.

'It's me, Sedic,' the voice said.

'Where the hell's my car?' I snapped. 'I had to get a cab home.'

'I'm really sorry, Nicky. I'm trying to meet up with someone who's going to straighten everything out. After that, I'll be free of Peter and so will you. Just bear with me for a few more hours.'

'You've really got a nerve. Even while you're begging me to give you a second chance, you're still messing me around.'

'I know that's how it must look, but remember appearances can be deceptive.' His voice sounded excited and edgy.

My irritation intensified. 'I don't want you to straighten things out for me with Peter. Why on earth should I believe you're on my side rather than his? All the evidence points the other way.'

'Such as what?'

'Documentary evidence.'

'What do you mean?'

'Somehow Peter and Phil got hold of my passport and other private documents almost two years ago now. I can only assume they had inside help at the time.'

There was a gasping sound. 'I swear it wasn't me. Peter's got loads of employees who could have managed that. But how do you know about it? What have they done?'

'Oh, never mind.'

'Tell me. It's important. I might be able to resolve it for you tonight.'

'I don't want your help. I want you out of my life.'

'Please stop this, Nicky. There's some stuff I haven't told you yet, but I'll explain as soon as I get back tonight and I promise you'll see things differently. You've got no idea how much you mean to me, how much you've always meant.'

I shook my head in disbelief. 'I'll tell you what, Sedic, I know exactly how much I mean to you. I'm fully aware of it and that's why I don't want anything more to do with you.'

I slammed down the receiver and unplugged the phone from the wall so he couldn't ring back. That pleading tone had worked on me in the past but he was dealing with a different person now. There was no going back. Not any more.

Chapter Twenty-eight

———◆◇◆———

An arm curled round me from behind and without looking I snuggled back into the curve of Dadong's body. From the first night, we'd slept together easily, limbs fitting neatly around each other, with no awkward angles. It all felt natural and snug and utterly comfortable.

'Nicola, wake up,' he whispered, his breath tickling behind my ear.

I realised he was lying on top of the sheet, still dressed, and I roused myself and wriggled round to face him. Our lips touched with the usual acute sensitivity and he stroked a finger along my eyebrow.

'I've got bad news for you,' he said gently, his dark eyes watching me, unblinking.

My mind leapt first to the company problems. Someone had uncovered Edy's plans; I was going to be arrested. 'What's happened?'

He stroked the palm of his hand across my temple before he spoke. 'Sedic's dead. He was stabbed last night.'

I sat up abruptly. 'No! It can't be true.'

'He was found in the car. Perhaps he was going to try to drive himself to the hospital but he'd lost too much blood and he didn't make it. If only the streets hadn't been so deserted last night, someone might have found him earlier but it was only around half four this morning when a policeman glanced into the car and saw him.'

'What time is it now?'

'Nearly ten.'

I clasped my hands to my face. 'He called me last night and I told him I never wanted to see him again.'

'Whoever it was, I don't think they meant to kill him. Maybe it was a scuffle of some kind. From what I heard, they stabbed him in the thigh, not the neck or chest. It was just bad luck that he didn't get help in time.'

'The femoral artery.' I felt unreal, sick and ghostlike. 'Are they sure it's him? Who identified him? How do you know about this anyway?'

Dadong took my hand and squeezed it. 'One of our people saw the car being towed into the police yard and heard there had been a body in it. They were worried it might be me but someone came to my friend's apartment and found me there alive and well. We investigated through our contacts and it seems Sedic's papers were found on the body. I came to tell you as soon as I heard.'

I shivered and hugged my arms round my chest.

'The police will probably come here this morning to inform you and I suppose they may ask you to identify the body unless there's someone else who knows him in town.' I couldn't think of anyone, and shook my head. 'But there is another problem, Nicky.' I had started shaking and he wrapped his arms round me on top of my own. 'There were some leaflets in the car yesterday about a political prisoner the police are denying they're holding. They're in the compartment in the trunk and I'm worried they will be discovered when the police search the car. I'm going to have to go underground for a while. I'm so sorry.'

My mind was racing. 'I could say they were Sedic's,' I suggested.

'You can try. But it won't be long before they find out about my brother and they'll know the leaflets are mine. I can't risk it.'

I clung to him, threading my fingers through his spiky hair. 'But where will you go? What am I going to do without you?' I started crying and he pulled my face down to rest against his shoulder.

'If you need to get in touch with me, Ali knows how to get

a message through. It may not be for long. Things are changing very fast in this city.' I sniffed loudly. 'I can't hang around here this morning, though, because they might arrive at any time.'

'Don't go. Please don't go.'

He disengaged and stared at me intensely, as if memorising every last eyelash and pore. 'I'll see you very soon,' he whispered, then he got up from the bed and disappeared through the sliding door.

I rose to follow, pulling on my robe, but the back gate had already closed behind him. My legs felt wobbly and I sat down hard on one of the sun loungers. The heat was oppressive and I remembered Sedic splashing around in the pool just thirty-six hours previously. Maybe the body in the car wasn't him, but who else could it be?

Just then I became aware of a buzzing sound, like the singing of power lines, and noticed a huge bee, the size of a child's fist, hovering blindly across the grass towards me. I huddled my legs to my chest, hoping it wouldn't come any closer.

'Sedic's dead,' I said out loud in its direction and it hesitated then turned and veered back towards the fuchsia-coloured bush in the corner. Suddenly I remembered the bee in the back of my car when I was driving through Soho all those months ago, and the way the rear window had been slightly ajar. And I thought about the time I'd accidentally locked the keys inside the car and a mechanic from one of the hospital labs had rescued them by sliding a thin steel ruler through the top of the window and easing it down. Was it possible that someone had broken into my car that day? If so, could they have found my handbag under the seat? I'd always been stupidly careless about leaving things there. In that case, maybe Sedic hadn't been responsible for borrowing documents to incriminate me. Perhaps it was another one of Peter's employees and Sedic hadn't known anything about it. Maybe it was true that he'd never betrayed me. I'd never find out for sure now.

I was dressed by the time the police arrived. There were three of them. The spokesman, who obviously understood the most English, was a small flabby man in rectangular dark-rimmed glasses, called Major Toemion. I reacted gravely but calmly to the news.

'Do you have any idea who might be responsible?' I asked.

'Not at the moment, but we'll find them. Your friend had wandered into a bad area of town. There are a lot of prostitutes there and petty street crime. Maybe it was just a random mugging.' He peered at me through his bottle glasses. 'Do you know if he was in the habit of . . .' he glanced around the room, 'frequenting such areas?'

'Not to my knowledge,' I replied coldly.

'Of course not, no.' He cleared his throat.

'I spoke to him on the phone last night but he didn't mention where he was.'

'What time did he call you?'

I thought back. 'About eleven. Not late.'

'And what did he say?'

'To be honest, we had a bit of an argument.' Immediately I wondered if it was wise to say that about someone who'd just been murdered.

'What about?'

'He'd been supposed to pick me up at nine but he didn't appear so I had to get a cab. He just said he had one more meeting to go to but he didn't mention who it was with.'

His expression didn't change. 'I need to inform his next of kin. Do you happen to know how I can contact his parents or nearest relatives?'

I nodded. 'I'll give you their numbers. But shouldn't I come and identify him first in case it's the wrong person? It would be terrible to upset his mother unnecessarily.'

There was no doubt it was him. I've seen hundreds of dead bodies in my life, but never someone I used to be in love with, and the experience was surreal. I felt as though I was watching myself through a fuzzy screen; my emotions were unconnected. I pulled back the sheet and for a few moments I just stared. His skin was a pure creamy white, like moulded candlewax, sharply contrasting with the darkness of his underarm and pubic hair.

His penis was shrivelled, like a wrinkly thumb, not far from the black-encrusted gash that had killed him. They'd cleaned up the worst of the mess but I could see dried-in streaks of purply-black blood matting the hairs on his legs and congealed under his toenails.

I spent a long time examining the body, trying to think clinically about what had happened. He wouldn't have realised he was dying. He probably thought he could drive the car but then felt tired and decided to have a rest. He would have drifted gently into semi-consciousness as the blood pumped down his leg, soaking into his trousers, draining his system. I wondered how long it took him to die. Three hours for a slow bleeder? Could have been less.

Although there was already some evidence of rigor mortis, I pulled out my stethoscope and began the legal ritual for confirming death, just so that I would always be sure. I listened to his silent heart for a minute, then listened to his chest for a minute; I checked that his pupils were fixed and dilated with no response to light, then I pressed on his nailbed to confirm that there was no response to pain. Finally, under my breath, I murmured the standard formula: 'Confirmed dead. May he rest in peace.'

Major Toemion cleared his throat.

'Yes, it's him,' I told him. After one final look, I turned away. They led me up a wide flight of stone steps worn concave by decades of tramping feet, then along a corridor and through an archway to a room with a wooden desk and plastic-covered chairs. I repeated my story and they wrote it all down, then I signed some forms and answered their questions automatically.

'I'm afraid it will be some weeks before we can return your car,' the Major told me. 'We'll need to do forensic tests.'

'I don't want it,' I said. 'Anyway, it belongs to Medimachines, the company I work for.' I gave him Phil Pope's name and number. As he wrote it down, I glanced at my watch. Two-thirty. Edy should have lodged my resignation by now, so with any luck, I was no longer a director.

'We will also need to keep your friend's clothes and personal possessions.'

'That's all right,' I nodded. No one mentioned the leaflets in the back of the car, so I supposed they hadn't found them. Maybe they'd overlook that compartment and Dadong would be able to come back to me soon. Somehow I doubted it. Everything seemed to be falling apart in this city.

It occurred to me that maybe, if I asked to have a look at the car, I might be able to sneak the leaflets out. But seconds later I realised it was a stupid idea. They'd never leave me alone with it.

'Do you want to inform his parents, or will we do it?'

I realised I would have no idea what to say. I'd broken bad news to parents of my patients in hospital any number of times, but this would be different. 'You do it,' I said and gave him a note of Lila's number in Jogja and Leona's in London, feeling distant and chilled. I was going through the motions without any sensation.

I'm not sure what the time was when I found myself walking down the steps of the police station but the sun was blinding, like a slap in the face. I dug in my bag for some sunglasses and my hands were shaking as I put them on. Two policemen brushed past me, dragging a young boy whose arms were twisted tightly up his back, so that he was bent double, face downwards. I stood on the pavement looking around, glanced right and then left to get my bearings, then set off to the right in the general direction of the clinic.

I'd been walking for some minutes before the cacophony of my thoughts subsided into a recognisable refrain. 'Sedic's dead. I'm free.' It was a terrible, senseless end to a life, but he had been living so dangerously it had been bound to happen sooner or later. 'The stupid fool,' I said out loud, then glanced round to see if anyone had overheard me, but the street was empty. Unnaturally empty. There were no motorbikes trundling down the narrow street and no people standing around on corners. I listened carefully and detected a noise hovering in the air like a crowd at a football match, a blanket of human sound that rose and fell slightly as though wafting in the breeze. A scrawny cat slunk past, its bony fur hugging the building to the left. Up ahead two soldiers stood at an intersection and as I approached they turned and motioned that I should go back.

'*Merdeka*?' I asked, pointing past them in the direction of the square. I just had to walk diagonally across it then beyond the mosque to reach the clinic.

The soldiers yelled something, shaking their heads, and one of them pushed me on the shoulder.

'*Saya doktor*,' I said, but still they indicated that I should go back the way I had come.

'*Demonstrazione*,' I caught at last. Another wave of sound shimmered in the heavy atmosphere and the soldiers tensed. I realised there was no way I was going to be allowed to proceed, so I turned and walked back the way I'd come. The cat was sheltering in the shade of a doorway and mewled at me as I passed.

It was good to walk, letting the emotions jolt around inside my head, judder down my spine and pound into the pavement. Sedic had behaved with appalling disregard for my feelings, no matter what excuses he made, so why should I care about him now? But I knew I was lying to myself. I wasn't like him. I couldn't close the door on the two years we'd spent together and all the happy memories. I couldn't help feeling desperately sad that such a tragedy had occurred and that the last words I spoke to him were harsh and angry. Grief hovered on the outside edges of my brain and I knew I would have to confront it one day, but in the meantime, I still felt cold and removed.

I was in a street lined with restaurants now but although it was just after lunchtime, they were shuttered closed. They must have known in advance about the demonstration. I turned the corner and found myself in front of a western-style hotel with a uniformed doorman standing outside the glass and bronze entrance. I nodded as I walked past him into the foyer and up to reception.

'Good afternoon, do you think you could call me a taxi, please?' Staff in these hotels always spoke English.

The girl looked worried. 'It's very difficult today. There's trouble in the town. Where do you want to go?'

I gave her the address and ordered an iced coffee to drink

while I was waiting, then I went to the ladies' room and gaped at the dishevelled sight in their full-length mirror. Sweat had soaked dark patches under my arms, beneath my breasts, around my hips and across my shoulder blades, wherever the fabric touched my skin. I must have lost a pint of fluid, walking in the sweltering afternoon heat. I stood under the hand dryer trying to evaporate the moisture but the furnace-hot air only made me perspire more. With any luck, it would dry out in the hotel's air-conditioned lounge.

Next I tried to call the clinic to say that I was running late but, oddly, no one answered the telephone. Maybe there was a fault on the line. It was after four o'clock when a taxi arrived for me.

'*Demonstrazione*,' the driver reiterated, as if worried that I hadn't heard, and he frowned when I handed over the address of the clinic, then nodded. He headed way out east first of all, through Menteng towards Pulo Mas, before looping round through Senen and back in to the northeast side of the city centre. I knew we were almost there when we passed the tall verdigris-green statue of a man bursting loose from chains around his wrists and ankles, known as the Free Irian Jaya monument.

There were crowds of people standing in huddles outside the clinic and they all looked round as my cab pulled up. I leapt up the steps to find more groups of people talking amongst themselves in the entrance hall. The waiting areas were stuffed full and overflowing.

I stuck my head round the door of Karlina's office and she looked up and scowled.

'What's happened?'

'It's the demonstration. We're getting lots of head wounds from the baton charges and broken limbs from water cannon, but I've been ordered not to treat anyone because the hospital has run out of money.'

I gasped. 'We can't not treat them. What are we going to do?'

'If it weren't for your stupid company selling us dozens of machines that don't even work, I might have a bit more cash left

GILL PAUL

to play with.' It was the first time she'd voiced any resentment about Medimachines.

'I'm so sorry. I agree they've sold you some useless equipment but maybe there's something we can do about it.'

'What do you mean – "we"? It's you that sold them.'

'Karlina, it wasn't. I can't explain, but I genuinely knew nothing about Medimachines until the first day I started work at the clinic here.'

She frowned. 'But you're the founder. You're in their advertising. What about all these leaflets?' I must have looked aghast. She opened a desk drawer and began to rummage through papers. The patient she was talking to, an elderly man, sat watching us, bemused. He could surely tell from our tones that there was an argument going on. Karlina pulled out a glossy colour leaflet, slightly creased, with a picture on the front of me smiling, wearing my white coat and stethoscope. The text was in Bahasa.

'What does it say?'

'That as a leading doctor at a London teaching hospital, you wanted to make sure that the latest technology reached the rest of the world at prices they could afford, and that's why you founded Medimachines. Haven't you seen this before?'

I shook my head and turned it over. 'Karlina, they've been conning me the way they've been conning you.' I stared at the photo, trying to think when it could have been taken. My hair was quite long, so it must be a few years old. Just visible in the background there was a gold plaque and I remembered the day the prime minister's wife came to open our new children's ward. There had been a lot of photographers around, so it could have been taken then and Peter would have got it from some press archive.

'Isn't that your signature?' She pointed to the bottom of the sheet.

'No, it's a forgery.' I glanced at the patient. 'Look, I'll tell you about this another time, but I was going to suggest you return a couple of machines, especially the PET scanner. You'll never use it and it's a discredited model, so we can build a good case for Medimachines reimbursing your money.'

'That was a very expensive purchase.' Karlina looked thoughtful. 'If I could tell the head of finance that the money will be coming in, maybe he'll give me permission to continue treating patients today.' She picked up the phone and within minutes had persuaded the person on the other end. I heard my name mentioned several times.

'Can I take a copy of this leaflet?' I asked, and she handed it over. 'When we have time, I'll explain everything. But, in the meantime, please will you just trust me? Believe in the way you've seen me acting since you've known me, rather than any fake documents?'

'OK,' she shrugged. 'For now.'

I pulled on a white coat and hurried down the corridor to my surgery. Rianna was on duty but there was no question of me pretending to let patients see two Indonesian doctors first. She worked alongside me most of the day, translating between me and the patients, cleaning and bandaging wounds, while I administered stitches and splints, tested for concussion and gave tetanus shots. We made an efficient team, and I was relieved to have such challenging, non-stop work to distract me from my thoughts.

The numbers began to drop off as night fell. 'People don't want to be out after dark,' Rianna explained.

'You've been fantastic today,' I told her, sincerely. 'You really should train as a doctor. I'm sure you could do it.'

'Maybe one day.' She looked doubtful but pleased.

'No, I mean it. If there's anything I can do to help, just let me know.'

Karlina had left already so there was no chance to talk further. I took another cab home and the driver skirted way out west this time, avoiding Merdeka Square and the airport road, so I had no way of knowing if the protests were still continuing. It was after midnight when I got into the house. Ali opened the gate then locked it behind me and clipped on an extra padlock.

On the dining table I found a list of phone messages Mimi had left. I'd been expecting calls from Peter and Sedic's mother, but the list was much longer than that: my mother, Anna, Phil

Pope, Mrs Parker, Cameron, Fred, my father, Diana, Leona. I was puzzled for a moment then realised that the troubles in Jakarta must have reached the news broadcasts back home. I switched on the television to CNN and went to the kitchen to pour myself a drink. When I got back, there was a busy airport departure lounge on the screen.

'The US embassy is advising all Americans to get out of Jakarta and Surabaya as soon as possible. Contact the embassy for information about prearranged meeting places and special flights. Other countries advising their citizens to leave include Australia, China, Japan and France. Britain is telling its six and a half thousand nationals in Indonesia to stay indoors until arrangements can be made for evacuation. Many expats have now checked into luxury hotels near the airport until they can get on a flight, but we're told that most are fully booked for the present.'

I sat down, stunned. The picture switched to show the scene on the darkened streets of central Jakarta. Young men with scarves tied round their faces were throwing petrol bombs at a line of troops with shields, helmets and batons. The camera focused on one face; his scarf had slipped and his expression was fierce, utterly committed. They'll get him, I thought. One way or another.

'So far it is known that nineteen civilians have died in the rioting and three soldiers have been injured, but it is feared that the actual figures might be a lot higher.'

I stared at the screen as the story switched to a finance meeting of European leaders. So the demonstrations were serious this time. The chill that went through me was mainly fear but there was also a kind of tingle of premonition. I felt that this was meant to be and that I was meant to be a part of it. The phone began to ring and I rose to answer it.

Chapter Twenty-nine

———◦◦◦◦———

The rest of the evening and most of the next day I spent on the telephone. I tried all the cab companies I knew of but they weren't even answering so there was no way of getting to the clinic. As soon as I hung up from one call, the phone rang again with ever-increasing urgency. Some calls were from friends and family back home, seeking reassurance, but most were from Diana, Fred, even Howard, checking what I was doing, letting me know where they were. Every time I picked up the receiver I was praying that it would be Dadong, and his silence felt ominous and alarming.

Diana was trapped inside the British Embassy, right in the heart of the worst-affected area. Outside their windows, soldiers stood in lines and occasionally charged if the protestors seemed to be advancing. She giggled excitedly as she described the scene, talking rapidly without pausing for breath.

'It's really embarrassing because the British line is that we condemn the killing of innocent protesters, etcetera etcetera, and meanwhile we all know that the soldiers out there are armed with British-made weapons. There's a water cannon outside the gates that was made in Tyneside and we're hoping none of the TV cameras focus in on it. I didn't tell you that, OK?' She laughed.

'Aren't they going to evacuate you?'

'We're not in any real danger, but I'm sure they'd send in the cavalry if they thought we were. Seemingly the airport road is closed today and no one's getting through. Anyway,

I'm enjoying myself here. Siege mentality is doing wonders for my relationship with James.'

'You're not! Have you?'

'I certainly have. There's nothing like the overthrow of a government to help romance thrive. We've been raiding the cellar for champagne and eating tinned oysters, snuggled in an upstairs office. It's ever so exciting.'

'Aren't you scared at all?'

'I'm probably in the safest place in the whole of Jakarta, to be honest.' I could hear a man's voice in the background. 'OK, I'll finish now. Anyway, I'd better go because I'm jamming up one of the phone lines. You can call me on my mobile. Let me know if you're getting out or anything.' She hung up abruptly.

Linda rang from Medimachines. 'Peter's arriving on the flight that gets in early evening and he wants to meet you for dinner. I told him he's going to have trouble getting into town from the airport but he thinks he can manage. Honestly, he must be the only person on an incoming flight today. I've rung around and I've booked you a table at the Orient Express restaurant in Kebayoran Baru. Do you know it?'

'No.'

'It's far enough away from the trouble, I think. I'll arrange a car to pick you up at eight, if that's all right.'

'I've been trying to get a car to take me to the clinic but I can't find any. Do you think you could arrange that?'

'No way. I don't think any drivers will be willing to go into the centre today.'

I was apprehensive about seeing Peter but felt I owed it to him to explain what little I knew about the circumstances of Sedic's death. Presumably he was coming out to make the funeral arrangements. I'd tried to ring Lila a few times but there seemed to be a problem with the lines to Jogja. I couldn't get through to the clinic either, but from what I could make out, it was right in the midst of the trouble spot now. Television pictures showed protesters climbing the statue of Irian Jaya man. I scrutinised every frame, looking for Dadong. There had been no word from him since the visit the previous morning.

I kept CNN running as I talked on the phone, and Mimi came in to watch, pretending to dust round the bookshelves. 'Sit down, don't worry,' I motioned, and she perched on the arm of the sofa. 'What are they saying on Indonesian TV?' I asked, pointing in the direction of the old set she and Ali watched outside the kitchen. Mimi shook her head and spread her hands. Ali popped his head timidly round the door and I gestured that he could come in and watch. It was their city, after all. They spoke to each other anxiously, seeming scared, pointing at images on the screen, although they didn't understand the commentary.

My mother rang again because there had been a report on British TV that the rioters were looting the houses of ex-pats who had left already and she worried that they might be reaching my district.

I explained that I had a guard and security gates. I didn't mention that my guard was now sitting watching a television screen that had switched to showing American football.

When I picked up the next call, a stern English voice exclaimed, 'Dr Drew, I've been trying to get through to you for the last three hours and I have better things to do with my time.'

'I'm so sorry, Mrs Parker, what can I do for you?'

'It's what I can do for you. I've got a spare seat on a British Airways flight to Heathrow tomorrow evening and I'm calling to offer it to you. Mr Parker and I will be on the same flight.'

'Tomorrow! I don't want to go tomorrow!'

'You may not have any choice. The rioters are spreading out and the Foreign Office line was changed this morning to advising all British citizens to leave. I got a phone call from them at eight o'clock,' she added, self-importantly.

I imagined myself packing a bag and stepping onto a plane, but it felt wrong. My contract here was nearly over, but I wanted to finish my stretch at the clinic and see if I was able to help in the current crisis. I didn't feel as though I'd personally be in any danger.

'I think I'll give it another day or so and get a flight out at the weekend if things are still bad.'

Mrs Parker snorted. 'You'll be lucky. Plane tickets are like gold dust. Just don't come back to me if you change your mind because I've got queues of people who'll thank me for this ticket.'

'I'm grateful that you offered it to me. Is there anything I can do for you? Can I keep an eye on your house while you're away, or are you leaving your staff there?'

'No, we're locking it up and sending the staff home. Who knows what they'd get up to without me there? With any luck we'll be back in a few weeks when things settle down.'

When we hung up, I felt a clenching in my gut. I wasn't a physically brave person. The closest I'd ever come to violent conflict was when a psychotic patient punched me as I tried to take blood from his arm. Surely my status as a doctor would earn me some protection, so long as the violence wasn't entirely indiscriminate? If looters came to the house, I'd invite them to help themselves. The TV, video, stereo and furniture all belonged to Medimachines, after all.

Fred rang from the *Jakarta Post* offices. 'I thought I'd be safer here than in my flat so I slept under my desk last night. There are four others doing the same.'

'Shouldn't you be out on the streets investigating the inside story and writing first-hand reports?'

'Piss off! I'm not that kind of journalist. What about you? Are you planning to leave?'

'Not yet. I'm playing it by ear.'

'Good for you. This kind of thing sorts the men from the boys. Howard's flying out tonight and Phil Pope was off to Bali this morning like a bat out of hell, the big coward.'

'Did he take Sanita?'

'Yeah, but I doubt he'll take her along if he has to go back to the UK. At the end of the day, she might be a great lay but to him she's just a native, after all. Anyway, keep in touch. Let me know what you're doing.'

The constant phone calls, nervy voices and the blur of CNN in the background made me tense and alert. There were updates every hour when they read the international headlines and casualty figures were creeping higher. I was glad when evening came and it was time to go and meet Peter. At least it gave me something to do.

Orient Express was an ex-pat hangout with polished wooden floors and chrome banisters, set on three different levels with a huge glass frontage. There were only two other tables occupied when I arrived and no sign of Peter, so I chose a central table and ordered a glass of wine. The menu ranged across Indian, Chinese, Italian and French dishes. I skimmed it, not feeling remotely hungry.

I'd been there for an hour and had almost finished a second glass of wine when Peter trundled in though the door, looking flushed and irritable, carrying a canvas travelling bag. Looking at him, I felt cold fury. It was going to be difficult hiding my emotions about this man who'd set me up, but instinct warned me that confrontation wouldn't be a good tactic. I rose to give him a perfunctory kiss on the cheek.

'The bloody driver Linda had arranged didn't have air-con in his car, can you imagine? What's this city coming to? And we had to head miles in the other direction because he said the airport road was impassable. I thought I'd never get here.'

His suit was crumpled and the armpits looked damp. I poured him a glass of water from a jug on the table but he called the waiter across and ordered a gin and tonic.

'I don't trust the bloody water here. They've probably filled that jug from the tap. These people have no idea how much damage they're doing to their country's infrastructure. I bet at least half the ex-pats who've left this week don't bother coming back and loads of businesses will pull out, costing them jobs and revenue. They need to sort themselves out.'

I sat back and watched as he arranged his bag in a corner, pulled off his jacket and draped it over the back of the chair. Images of other bereaved parents I'd known flashed in front of my eyes, with their mixtures of guilt, shock, anger, bewilderment; but this was not the face of a man who was grief-stricken. Could it even be that he was in some way responsible for Sedic's death? I remembered what he had said, that Peter would never risk him being arrested.

'I'm so sorry about Sedic,' I began. 'You must be devastated.'

'Terrible news.' He shook his head. 'It hasn't really sunk in
yet. The message I got was very fragmented. They just said he
was stabbed in the street and bled to death, but I can't understand
it. Who was he with?'

The waiter brought his drink and I didn't reply until he'd
set it down and left again. 'He was in a red–light district. He'd
told me he was meeting someone but he didn't mention who.
I thought he might be working for you.'

The denial seemed genuine. 'I didn't even know he was in
Jakarta. We haven't been in touch for a while. The first I knew
of it was when the police called Leona to say he was dead. We
assumed he must have come out to see you.' He frowned and
took a large slurp of his drink. 'Leona's distraught. She fell apart
when she got the news.'

I considered telling him about their relationship then and
there. It felt as though this was a time for honesty, when it
couldn't hurt Sedic any longer. But what good would it do? I
decided to wait and see how the conversation progressed. 'It
must have been a terrible shock for you both.'

A sly look flickered behind his eyes. 'You know Sedic and
I hadn't been getting on very well recently, and that's going to
be the hardest thing to bear, that we'll never have the chance
to resolve our differences. He must have been furious with me
about that deception regarding his mother. I think the last time
I saw him was at that dinner last summer, with you and Leona.'
He looked thoughtful. 'Yes, I'm pretty sure that was it.'

'So what are your plans now? Did you come out here to
arrange his funeral?'

Peter cleared his throat. 'I think we should let Lila take care
of that, don't you? Whatever she wants to do is fine with me.
I came out to see if you were all right. I know how much he
meant to you.' He gripped my hand and I pulled it away. 'That's
why I wanted to see you as soon as I arrived, to ask what I can
do to help.'

'I'm OK. Shocked and very sad, but I'm also keen to find
out who killed him and why.'

'Of course,' he said quickly. 'I'll be putting all my efforts into that. I'm going to the police station tomorrow morning to see how I can co-operate with their enquiries.'

'You weren't aware that he knew anyone who worked in a red-light district here?'

'Absolutely not. My son was an attractive man. He didn't need to go to places like that. I wondered . . . I mean, Leona and I wondered, when we heard that he'd come out here, whether there was any chance that you two might have been reconciled. Did you have a chance to talk about it?' He was peering at me through his mean little eyes and I realised that's why he had come: to find out whether Sedic had told me anything compromising.

I wasn't going to make this easy for him. 'We had a long talk the night he arrived, when he explained to me about the exhibition and being reunited with his mother. Yes, we cleared the air between us but I didn't give him any hope of getting back together. I think I told you I'm seeing someone else now.'

'This new man – he's Indonesian, isn't he?'

I nodded.

'And it's going well?'

'Very well.'

'So did you think about my offer to extend your contract here? I believe you've made a big hit at the clinic.'

I pretended to be surprised. 'Will you keep the company open with all the unrest and uncertainty here?'

'Oh sure. Medimachines is a solid company. They're always going to need medical supplies in Indonesia and it's good that we're winning their trust. With your help, I might add.'

I smiled wryly. 'I can't imagine why they should trust you when half the machines you've sold them don't work and the other half are unnecessary. I've told them they should ask for a refund of the money they paid for the PET scanner. They just don't need it and were badly advised to buy it.'

'I'll look into it, if that's how they feel,' Peter mumbled.

I continued. 'They can't use the scanners because they don't have the right kind of computer to link them to and the one Phil supplied from Olbisson Computers is incompatible or faulty,

I'm not sure which. If you want to keep getting business here, someone should go and fix that for them.'

'But of course we will. That's the first I've heard of it.'

'I told Phil weeks ago and nothing's happened.'

'You didn't exactly hit it off with him, did you?'

'That's an understatement.'

'To be honest, I'm not sure that I'm going to keep Phil here. If I replaced him with someone you found more sympathetic would that persuade you to stay on? It would give you more time with your boyfriend and you could keep your house and the same staff.' His expression was knowing; Phil must have told him that their driver was my new boyfriend.

I pondered my reply. If I said I planned to leave when my contract expired at the end of the month, he might become suspicious and expedite his plans to incriminate me. What if there was some illegality that Edy Mariman had overlooked? 'I'll have to think about that, Peter. It depends on whether the hospital in London would extend my sabbatical.'

'Is there anything I can offer to persuade you?' He'd never looked more ugly, I thought, with a gleam of corruption in his pupils. 'I know money is not the way to tempt you because Phil said you tried to return the bonus he slipped into your account. Don't you remember the deal we made last summer? I said I'd give you and Sedic a quarter of a million pounds if you both came out here for six months.' I nodded. 'I think you should let me give you a part share. It's not your fault Sedic didn't keep his side of the deal.'

'Give me a week,' I said. 'I'll speak to the hospital and let you know my decision by then.'

Peter had opened his mouth to reply when we heard a motorbike screech to a halt outside the restaurant and a scruffy Indonesian boy burst through the doors and ran up the stairs to the first level. He stopped by the cloakroom and spoke to the woman working there and we turned round as she gave a brief scream. The boy hurried on up the stairs, followed by the cloakroom attendant and they spoke to a waiter, then all three continued up a flight of stairs by one wall that led towards a roof terrace.

I looked round for our waiter and signalled him across. 'Is everything OK?' I asked, pointing after them. 'What's going on?'

'I'll just go and see,' he said quickly. He made for the stairs and a couple of diners followed him.

'Something's happening,' I told Peter. 'Do you mind if I go up? I'll just be a minute.'

I climbed the steps two by two with a weird prickling sensation on my skin and I knew it was something bad. Around a dozen people were clustered on the roof, gazing northeastwards towards the city centre, and I saw straight away what they were looking at. Clouds of smoke were rising into the sky, which was a surreal flickering orangey colour.

'Where is it?' I asked.

The boy who'd arrived on a motorbike replied in English. 'It's a shopping centre in Glodok and some houses alongside.'

'Is anyone hurt? Was the centre open?'

He looked at me strangely. 'Hundreds are hurt,' he said. 'The streets are full of bodies.'

The cloakroom attendant was sobbing loudly, wringing her hands, tears flooding her cheeks.

'I'm a doctor,' I said. 'I work at the Jalyan clinic. I need to get down there now. Do you know anyone who could take me?'

'We could go on my bike,' the boy replied. 'You could sit on the back.'

'OK,' I said. 'Let's go now.'

I can't say my motives were entirely altruistic. Foremost in my mind was the thought that Dadong might well have been there, and if he was injured, I would find him and save him, if it was humanly possible. That's what I remember more than anything.

'You're mad,' Peter yelled, and grabbed my arm. 'You can't go into town tonight. It's mayhem. You'll get hurt. Don't do it, Nicola.'

'I have to,' I said, pulling away from his grasp. 'I care about these people. Something you would never understand.'

Chapter Thirty

It was a derelict excuse for a motorbike. A hollow metal pole protruded at the place where a seat used to be. The boy untied a parcel from a rack that was screwed precariously above the back wheel and indicated that that was where I should sit. I slipped my shoulder bag diagonally across my body and tucked the hem of my cotton skirt into my knickers so it wouldn't catch in the spokes, then I straddled the rack. The boy struck one of the pedals with his foot. A hiccup. Again. A gurgle, and it caught. He swung his leg across and jerked the bike off its stand and there was a lurch as we began to move. I searched frantically for something to hold onto and grasped the loops at the waistband of his jeans.

The metal spars of the rack gnawed my buttocks. My feet were balanced on a couple of narrow pipes along each side. Something scorched my calf and I guessed it must be the exhaust. Whenever we hit a bump in the road, I clutched the fabric of his trousers so tightly I was afraid they might wriggle down over his skinny hips. I knew to lean my weight with the weight of the bike when we cornered but every instinct urged me to pull the other way for balance. He shouted something and the words blasted past. Seconds later we dipped into a large hole in the road and I bounced high above the rack before descending hard, bruising my coccyx.

In this part of town, the roads were largely unsurfaced. Few houses and apartment blocks had any lights showing. We didn't pass any other vehicles or see any pedestrians, which felt increasingly peculiar. My heart was thumping with apprehension. Maybe we'd get there and the clinic would be shut. Maybe we wouldn't be able to reach that part of town. Maybe I wouldn't be needed.

We bumped round a corner onto a road strewn with loose chippings. The back wheel tipped sideways and, as if in slow motion, we toppled onto the ground. I slid for a few feet and could feel sharp stones embedding in my knees and elbows. I felt like crying. By the time I picked myself up, the boy had lifted the bike upright and was signalling that I should remount. His hand was bleeding and I pointed to it, but he shrugged and said it was nothing.

We were skirting round the edges of the town centre now. The boy stopped at an intersection to listen, then continued. The distant sounds became sharper in the stillness of the night air and I could smell smoke. He braked sharply at a corner and, glancing far down to the right, I saw a long black chain glinting across the road. We appeared to be behind a line of riot police. A few blocks further on, we came across two men carrying a wounded friend, one holding his shoulders and the other his knees, so his body slumped in a V shape between. The boy shouted something to them, pointing at me, but they replied that they were all right and continued on their way.

The sounds of shouting were becoming more distinct, like patterns emerging from a blurred design, and my eyes began to water with the acrid fug in the air. I lost my sense of direction as we zigzagged from street to street but then we crossed the railway line to the north of the clinic and suddenly the streets were full of people staggering, lying on the pavement, helping each other along. Their faces and clothes were blackened and eyes and teeth gleamed. There was no sign of police or army here. The bike wove through the lurching figures and pulled up outside the steps of the clinic.

I climbed off stiffly, my grazed knees stinging. 'Thank you, thank you so much,' I shouted above the background noise of hysterical voices, but the boy just nodded and drove off again. I'd never discovered his name.

I stepped over two men sprawling on the front step and as

I opened the door, the first thing I was aware of was a smell that I recalled from somewhere back in the distant past: the hot, surprisingly sweet smell of burnt human flesh. I swallowed hard to stop myself gagging. In the entrance hall, men lay on the floor and Rianna was offering them sips of water.

'Where's Karlina?' I yelled above the voices, and Rianna pointed down the corridor to one of the medical wards.

Karlina was attaching a drip and didn't notice me approaching. I looked at the patient, his face and chest scorched, one arm charred through to the bone and the familiar giant hand squeezed my chest. He had no hope. I knew he was going to die. His life was ebbing away by the second, almost tangibly. I felt as though I was going to cry and squeezed my eyes shut tightly. I wouldn't be any use here if I got upset.

Karlina turned and saw me. 'Waiting room,' she said. 'We've set up emergency beds in there and Yanti's working on her own. There are just four of us.' Soot smudged her lab coat and smeared across her cheek and her topknot had almost collapsed.

I hurried down the ward to the door at the end. There was a curious murmuring sound. Some of the patients appeared to be talking to themselves, teeth chattering, lips moving incessantly. It was the same in the waiting room, as if they were trying to make sense of what had just happened to them.

Yanti shrieked when she saw me and ran across, flinging her arms round my neck. 'I can't believe you're here,' she said, almost in tears.

'Of course I'm here. I came as soon as I heard. What's going on? How are we coping?'

'We're running out of intravenous fluids. All the phones are down so Karlina's sent some people to try and get more from the other clinics but I think they have the same problem.' Her voice was cracking with nerves.

'How much do we have?'

'There're about fifty litres left but at the last count we had over a hundred burn victims.'

'Fifty? Five oh? That's crazy! What does Karlina want us to do?'

Yanti covered her eyes with a hand and shook her head. 'We have to make decisions about who needs it most.'

Patients with burns covering more than ten percent of their body will be in a state of shock, caused by the loss of fluid from the affected area. If they're not given intravenous fluids as soon as possible, it can be fatal. There's a rapid way of calculating how much of the body surface area is affected, called the 'rule of nines': each arm is equivalent to nine percent; each leg is eighteen percent; the back and front are each eighteen percent; the genital area is one percent and the head is nine percent. It's important to measure this area in order to calculate how much fluid needs to be replaced. In patients with very extensive burns, it's often simpler to measure the unburned area and then subtract from a hundred.

For each patient, I had to check their breathing, measure arterial blood gases, assess the surface area affected and the thickness of the burns, estimate their age, weight and fitness level and then evaluate their chances of survival. If I thought they would make it, I inserted an intravenous line and urinary catheter. If not, I didn't. My instincts had never been so clear, like shouts echoing round my head. It was obvious without any hesitation which patients had a chance and which would die anyway. I had inside knowledge, the voice in my head, the hand on my diaphragm. With each man, I could sense how strong the system was and how desperately it would battle to keep going. On top of the physical horror of the night, it was this knowledge that I had been judge, jury and executioner that would haunt me ever afterwards.

The first bed I approached was a hopeless case. He was conscious and murmuring behind an oxygen mask, but his head, chest and arms were seared and strands of bright pink muscle gleamed through. Forty-three percent. Blood trickled down his scalp. He'd been wearing a nylon shirt of some kind and it had melted into the open wounds. Yanti began to snip at it with her scissors but I raised a hand to stop her.

'Cover it with a moist dressing. How much Cyclimorph has he had?'

Yanti showed me a hastily scribbled chart.

'Give him the same whenever he seems to need it. We're not short of morphine, are we?'

'I don't think so.'

At the next bed, a boy who looked about sixteen grabbed my arm urgently, trying to tell me something. His eyes flickered from Yanti back to me, willing us to understand.

'What's he saying?'

'I don't know, I can't make him out.' Yanti listened hard. 'I think he might be Dayak, from Borneo anyway.' She listened again and shook her head.

The boy spoke faster and louder, desperate to communicate. I watched him and waited till he finished then nodded and spoke reassuringly, as if I understood, and he sighed and shut his eyes. The worst of his burns were to the legs but his pulse was rapid and his skin cool and clammy.

'You dress his legs and I'll set up a drip,' I said. 'Can you get me a litre bag?'

He opened his eyes to tell me something else and seemed to become calmer as I pretended to understand again.

The next patient was dead when we reached the bedside.

'I was talking to him just before you arrived,' Yanti exclaimed tearfully as I followed the ritual procedures to confirm death, then closed his eyes and pulled the sheet over his head.

'Is there anyone here to move the bodies? The stench is going to be awful if we don't get them to the morgue soon.'

'Karlina sent the porter to look for fluids but I hope he'll be back soon.'

With all these open wounds, unprotected by skin, the risk of life-threatening bacterial infection was high.

One patient pointed at me and uttered something that sounded like an accusation. 'What's he saying?' I asked Yanti.

'He says he knows what you're doing,' she translated.

'What am I doing?'

Yanti asked him then passed on the reply. 'He just repeated

that he knows what you're doing. He's in a morphine daze, don't pay any attention.'

I looked into the man's eyes. Could he possibly know that I'd written off his chances of survival? Or did he mean something else entirely?

I made treatment decisions for the thirty-two patients in the waiting room then left Yanti to do the follow-up checks on urine volume and colour, arterial blood gases and ventilation. Rianna was working with the walking wounded in the hallway and I stopped to help her for a while. Soon Karlina emerged and asked me to keep an eye on her ward while she ran out to try and find a functioning telephone.

I walked round slowly, evaluating the treatment decisions she had made. In seven cases, I disagreed. Three of the patients Karlina had hooked up to a drip were dying anyway, and four that she hadn't prescribed fluids for might have a chance. I called Yanti to help me set up the extra drips. The babble of voices seemed to be getting louder, more insistent.

'What are they all saying?' I asked.

Yanti looked scared and glanced towards the door. 'They're telling their stories,' she said, 'What happened to them. I suppose they want it to be known in case they don't make it.'

'What do they want to be known?'

Yanti moved into the centre of the ward, away from the beds, and I followed.

'They're saying the army did it,' she hissed. 'They set the fires then locked all the exits of the shopping centre so no one could escape.'

'Do you believe it?' I whispered, horrified.

'They all have roughly the same story.'

I looked round at the wild eyes set in charred and blistered skin and listened to the frantic chattering. 'I think we should write them down,' I suggested. 'Especially the ones who won't make it. We owe it to them, they deserve to be heard.'

Yanti looked panicky. 'I can't. I don't dare. I have to live here.'

'I'll take responsibility. Just note down names, addresses, occupations, ages, next of kin, then whatever they witnessed this evening. It will help them to have a focus and it might bring a sense of peace for the dying. If anyone asks questions, you can say you're noting down last messages for loved ones.'

'But what will I do with them?'

'I'll be with you. As you finish each one, give it to me and I'll take it through to the office and hide it in my bag. After that, we'll see. But I'll make sure that it never comes out that you helped.'

'What if Rianna sees us?'

'I think you misjudge her. I worked with her the day before yesterday and I'm pretty sure she's trustworthy.'

Yanti still looked worried. 'She's told stories before.'

'OK, I'll make sure she doesn't see what we're doing. Karlina doesn't even have to know.'

At last Yanti agreed. I found a loose-leaf notebook in a cupboard and gave it to her, then we moved from bed to bed. While I checked clinical responses to treatment, Yanti took down their words. A rectangle of light flickered on the floor and I glanced out the window, surprised to see it was morning. When we'd taken a couple of testimonies, I wandered through to the office and tucked them deep inside my handbag where the cloth lining had parted company with the leather.

As I walked back, I saw Karlina slumped in a chair next door. 'They've promised me more fluids by twelve noon. I hope it's true. We have fifty-four patients who need it.'

'How many have we treated altogether?'

'Twenty-eight deaths. Seventy-three still occupying beds. God knows how many outpatients. Rianna says she wasn't counting.'

'Twenty-eight dead isn't as bad as reports suggested. I'd heard it was hundreds.'

Karlina sighed. 'That's just the ones who managed to get here. We're a mile away from the fire.'

'Oh.' There was nothing else to say.

'There are some soldiers in the hall. They want to come in and interview the patients, but I'm trying to stop them because it will cause panic, the last thing we need.'

I leapt to my feet. 'Can you give me some warning if they're coming in? I'd like to prepare the patients so they don't get over-anxious.'

Karlina gave me a questioning look. 'I'll try,' she promised.

I hurried back through to check on Yanti. 'How many statements have you taken down now?'

'Fourteen,' she replied.

'Maybe you should stop. There are some soldiers in the hall. These should be enough to make the point anyway.'

Yanti tore the latest pages from the notebook and handed them to me. 'I'll see,' she said. 'If anyone has any new information to add, I'll make sure I record it.'

'I think you should take a break now. Go and get something to eat. I'll look after things here.'

I hurried back into my office and folded the latest reports to stick them in the lining of my handbag.

'Can I get you a drink, Dr Drew?'

I looked up to see Rianna watching. 'Not just now. Yanti's taking a break so I'll have one when she gets back. How are you coping?'

'I'm fine,' Rianna said, then turned abruptly and left the room. There was something odd about her lack of friendliness after the camaraderie we'd shared two days before.

I hesitated for a moment then an instinct made me remove the statements from inside my handbag, fold them as tightly as I could into a small pad, then stuff them into a surgical glove. I considered hiding the package somewhere in the office but it seemed better to keep it with me so I could take sole responsibility if it were found. After checking the door, I tucked the package inside my knickers, where it felt bulky and strange, but my skirt and lab coat were loose enough to hide the shape. Then I found a few Medimachines price lists in my desk drawer and folded them into the handbag as a decoy.

I walked back through to the ward and spotted a patient whose drip tube had come out. I removed the needle and fixed up a new one. Bubbles formed in the bottle as the liquid began to drip through.

The ward door opened and two soldiers marched in waving

their guns. I hurried towards them. 'Can you put those away, please?' I asked, pointing. 'Our patients are very ill.'

'Dr Drew?' one of them asked. I nodded. 'You are under arrest. Come with us.'

Chapter Thirty-one

One of the soldiers clutched my elbow and they marched me down the corridor. Karlina emerged from her surgery to remonstrate with them but they wouldn't reply.

'What's going on?' she asked me.

'I'm under arrest. I don't know why. I'd better go with them but I'll call you later.'

Karlina shouted something at them but once again they didn't respond.

'Can I get my bag, please?' I asked.

'We have it already,' one of them replied.

'Will you be all right?' Karlina called. 'Is there anything I can do?'

The soldiers pushed open the swing doors and I screwed up my eyes against the midday sun. 'No, I'll be fine. Don't worry.' The last thing I saw as I glanced back was Rianna's pointy face watching us, expressionless.

The streets were cleared now and groups of soldiers stood on every corner. An army truck was parked opposite and they motioned for me to climb into the back then they both sat in the front. I saw my handbag, balanced on the dashboard. Rianna must have told them she saw me putting something in there. Would she really have betrayed me? It was a disturbing thought, but seemed the only explanation in the circumstances.

'Where are you taking me?'

'Police station.'

Suddenly I wondered if this was something to do with

Medimachines rather than events in the clinic. What could they be arresting me for? Maybe I should try to jettison the package in case they searched me at the station? But the soldier in the passenger seat swivelled round to watch me the whole way there so I didn't have an opportunity.

After a few minutes, we pulled up right outside the old colonial building and they led me up the stone steps to an upstairs room close to the one where I'd given my statement the other day after identifying Sedic's body. I stood and looked out of the window, waiting to see what would happen next. Two men were crouched on the corner opposite, smoking kreteks and chatting as if everything was normal in this city, as if the army hadn't set fire to a shopping centre full of people the night before.

The door opened and Major Toemion walked in. His tone was abrupt. 'Sit down, please, Dr Drew.' I obeyed.

'We have received a report that you were treating patients in the clinic last night without them seeing two Indonesian doctors first. Is that correct?'

'Of course I was!' I exclaimed. 'There were only four of us working, two doctors, two nurses, and over a hundred patients. Of course I helped!' Exhaustion combined with fury at the stories I'd heard from patients made me reckless.

'You realise that you broke the law?'

'It was hardly normal circumstances. I did what any doctor would have done.'

'Nonetheless you broke the law. This alone gives me cause enough to have you deported. I am going to set in motion the formalities and until the order comes through, you will remain in your home under house arrest. You may not make phone calls or have any contact with the outside world.'

I gasped. 'Isn't that a bit of an over-reaction? What's really going on here?'

'Why don't you tell me?'

'What do you mean?' He knew something but I had no idea what.

'Don't you think it's rather bad manners to visit another country and then take sides with some violent rebels who are trying to overthrow the government? I'd say that's not the action of someone on a goodwill mission.'

Had he found Dadong's leaflets in the car? Or had Rianna seen us taking down the testimonies of the injured men? I played the innocent. 'Major Toemion, I can only assume you're referring to the fact that I made the patients in the clinic as comfortable as I possibly could last night. It may be that they are enemies of your government but to me they were just men with serious burns to be cared for.'

His eyes glittered behind his spectacles and he tapped a pen on the wooden tabletop. 'I think we both know there's more to it than that, Dr Drew. I have received another report, just this morning, that you have been trading illegally in our country. I will be investigating this further and I hope you know we take such matters extremely seriously. If I find this report to be true, you can be sure that we'll press charges.'

I started. It sounded as though Peter might have set in motion his plan to incriminate me. I must have made him suspicious the night before.

Normally I'm a terrible liar – I turn red and stutter – but irritation made me fluent. 'I'm afraid I have no idea what you're talking about. I haven't done any trading in your country whatsoever. I'm a doctor, not a business person. I would like to speak to a lawyer. I don't think you have any right to deport me or charge me.'

'Do you have a lawyer?' he asked, and I hesitated. It seemed too compromising to give Edy's name. They might ask questions about why I knew him.

'If you contact the British Embassy and speak to Diana Blake, she will organise a lawyer for me.'

'We will inform the embassy of your arrest in due course.'

'Can I talk to them?'

'No. You can't talk to anyone.'

'Can I have my handbag, please? Your men took it.'

'It will be returned to you at your house. We will keep your passport until you leave Indonesia.'

'I don't want to leave. You're being totally unreasonable.'

'I'm too busy to argue with you, Dr Drew. One of my

men will drive you home and guard you there until we decide what action to take. You have admitted breaking the law. End of story. Goodbye.' He rose and picked up his papers from the desk.

'It was a pleasure to meet you, Major Toemion,' I said sarcastically.

'Of course.' He nodded and left the room.

Shortly afterwards a soldier arrived, a smooth-faced boy with blank eyes. 'Come with me,' he ordered.

I followed him down the stairs, walking carefully so as not to dislodge the package in my knickers. We descended the steps and he motioned that I should get into a truck parked right outside the door but another soldier shouted something and extended a hand to stop me. The second soldier pointed to a truck further down the street and the first one began to argue.

I glanced across at the two kretek smokers and realised with a shock that one of them was staring directly back at me. It took a few seconds before I recognised that it was Dadong and a rush of emotion made me giddy. Far from the neatly pressed impeccable appearance I was used to, he looked dishevelled, unshaven, older. I clapped a hand to my mouth. He nodded and smiled quickly then turned and said something to his friend, who made a tiny mark on the wall behind them with a piece of stone.

Moments later the two soldiers reconciled their differences and I didn't dare look backwards as I was led down the street towards the second truck. It was enough to keep me going, though. Dadong was alive. He knew I was in trouble. He was watching out for me. It had all happened so quickly that it was only during the drive home that I pieced together the implications. What was he doing there? Surely it was dangerous for him to be so close to a police station? Then I remembered the mark his friend made on the wall. They were counting people in and out. That's how they could keep tabs on who disappeared. I thought about the men pictured on his poster, who'd been arrested and had never returned to their families. That's the only way they could be sure how many people had been taken into custody. By counting.

His smile lingered in my mind's eye like a warm caress as we drove along the airport road. The streets were clear of protesters and the whole town seemed eerily quiet. Most of the vehicles were army trucks. The House of Representatives was surrounded by hundreds of soldiers, even more than at the demonstration just a few days ago. None of the beggar children were about. The traffic would have been too fast-moving for them to ply their trade. We turned off into Kemang and I noticed that all the shops were shuttered, the bamboo furniture safely locked inside. Most of the ex-pat houses were locked and barricaded. It had the air of a ghost town.

The soldier knew exactly where I lived and he honked his horn outside the gate. Ali opened it hurriedly, saluting awkwardly when he saw it was an army vehicle, but the soldier ignored him and drove straight into the garage. I swung my legs round and climbed out carefully. Mimi came running from the kitchen, her eyes red with crying, and flung her arms round me.

'I have been ordered to search your house,' the soldier said tonelessly. 'Come inside, please.'

The television was switched to CNN. Mimi and Ali must have been watching it in my absence. I sat down on the sofa to look, but foremost in my mind was worry about what to do with the parcel. It seemed too dangerous to keep it in my knickers in case the soldier decided to search me. Where could I hide it that he wouldn't look? Kitchen cupboards, down the back of the fridge, inside a book? Perhaps I could bury it in the garden? Nowhere seemed safe enough. The soldier unplugged the phone from the wall and began methodically checking my bookshelf. I peered outside at the swimming pool. Would the surgical glove be watertight? What if I slipped it into the drainage pipes at the side? But it would shift along and block the filter and then it would be discovered.

The theme tune sounded the hour and the news presenters shuffled their papers to read the headlines. 'The latest estimate is that three hundred and twenty rioters died in a department store fire in Jakarta last night. The city is quiet after the president called for calm. And the Far Eastern economy has taken another tumble in response to the developing crisis. Your newsreader is Angela Capon.' The figure catapulted in my skull as I watched the images of firefighters training their hoses on the vast smouldering building and the city centre streets lined with soldiers carrying shields and batons. Could it really be so many? Our clinic had seen only a small percentage, in that case, and there were no figures about the number of critically injured. 'The dead are believed to be looters who took advantage of the riots to help themselves to goods. It is unknown how the fire started but it is believed the death toll is greater because several emergency exits were impassable.' The president was shown making a brief statement then the picture moved to the Tokyo stock exchange where some worried-looking dealers were trying to sell stocks. Seconds later, they switched to news of a light aircraft that had crashed in Oklahoma in what appeared to be a freak tornado.

The soldier barged into my bedroom and I got up to stand by the door and watch as he opened cupboards and lifted piles of tee-shirts to check there was nothing beneath them.

'I have to go to the bathroom,' I told him and pointed. He went in first to search the room then motioned that I could go inside. At first he hovered as though he planned to accompany me but then let me pull the door shut and flick the lock.

I sat down on the cool edge of the bath and regarded myself in the mirror. I was grubby and gaunt, my face etched with frown lines. I looked down and was surprised to see that my elbows and knees were grazed and smeared with dried blood, then I remembered the fall from the motorbike, several lifetimes ago.

I turned on the shower and undressed, removing the package from my knickers. I placed it at the end of the bath while I stood under the warm water, letting the grime trickle away down the plughole. These testimonies weren't worth getting into further trouble for. Surely other people who escaped from the fire would tell the same story? But many would be too scared and it hadn't yet made the international news. The world had to know that the Indonesian army had massacred their own people by burning them alive, but did I have the right to publicise these accounts and risk incriminating Yanti and the men concerned? If they were used, it would have to be anonymously.

I flicked back the lid of the shampoo and squeezed out a palmful then rubbed it into my hair. The suds streamed down my breasts and stomach onto my bony feet. There was a little window set high in the wall above the shower and I looked out of it as I leaned back to rinse away the soap. Outside, a narrow passage ran round the side of the house, then there was the tall, white-painted wall that separated my garden from the Parkers. I remembered Mrs Parker saying that if you threw a ball over the wall behind my swimming pool it would land in her rose garden. This wasn't much further along. And they'd sent their staff away so there wouldn't be anyone around until the troubles were over and the Parkers returned.

I pushed the window open and the sweet smell of flowers seeped in, mingling with the artificial scent of the shampoo. I listened carefully for a moment, picked up the parcel and flung it neatly over the wall. There was a rustling sound as it hit the ground. If it was in a bush or some undergrowth, that was all the better. Immediately I felt more relaxed. A reflex shudder shook my shoulders.

After stepping out of the shower, I soaked a cotton pad with antiseptic and began to clean my grazed knees and elbows. I had to scrub to remove the tiny stones embedded under the skin and blood began to ooze. I brushed my teeth and rubbed some moisturiser into my forehead and round my eyes.

There was a knock on the door. 'What are you doing?'

'I'm nearly finished.'

I pulled on a towelling robe, combed my wet hair back from my face and, just before opening the door, I remembered to close the tiny window above the shower again.

The soldier seemed embarrassed to see me in a robe, although it was a perfectly decent one. It was the first emotion I'd seen him betray and it made me realise that he was at least a decade younger than me, maybe more. He walked to the bedroom doorway and turned his back.

'I'm going to get dressed. Do you mind?'

After a few moments' hesitation, he stepped outside, shutting the door behind him. Instead of going to the wardrobe, I lay down on the bed. Now I stopped to think, all my bones and joints were aching and a headache was pounding behind my right eye. I felt heavy and bleary, but that was only natural after missing a night's sleep. I glanced at the travel alarm beside the bed. Half past five in the afternoon. Maybe I'd nap for a couple of hours before dinner. I should dry my hair first because it was soaking the pillow, but my limbs were already sinking deep into the mattress. It would take a massive effort to get up again, so why bother?

Chapter Thirty-two

White light pierced my eyelids, causing a sharp hammering on the back of my eyeballs like nothing I'd ever experienced before. I twisted my head away from the light and something vicious shifted inside my skull. My brain felt bruised and swollen and it hurt whenever it jarred against its bony covering. As I awoke further, I realised that I was shivering violently, suddenly freezing, and huddled the bedcover around me and it was only then I realised I must be ill. A foggy blanket of fever pressed me to the sheets. There was no choice but to give in to it. I couldn't have raised myself from the bed if I'd tried. If only Mimi would come in, I could ask for some painkillers and a glass of water. My lips were dry and parched and my teeth began to chatter.

I woke again some time later with an unfamiliar hand on my forehead and opened my eyes to see the soldier looming overhead, silhouetted against the window.

'Water,' I whispered, but my lips wouldn't move properly.

He disappeared and a minute later Mimi came into the room. I reached out and took her hand. 'Oh, madam,' she said sadly. Her cool fingers felt good on my forehead and I wanted to cry. 'Water,' I said again, a little clearer this time. 'Aspirin.' I turned and pointed to the bathroom and the poisonous pain made me gasp and clutch my temple. A couple of tears trickled down my cheek. Mimi would take care of me. It was going to be all right.

There was something seductive about being quite so ill. It relieved me of any responsibility to think or make decisions.

Would they call a doctor? In the back of my mind I remembered that I was a doctor. Tropical parasite, I thought, but changed my mind because there wasn't any diarrhoea. Or was there? Maybe I just wasn't aware of it. This body didn't belong to me any more.

One time when I woke, it seemed to be night. Ali was sitting in a chair by my bed and I felt worse than ever. When he saw me opening my eyes, he picked up the glass of water by the bed. I nodded, but although I strained my neck muscles, I couldn't lift my head from the pillow so he used a teaspoon to trickle it slowly between my lips. It was the most delicious water I'd ever tasted.

'OK?' he asked quietly.

'I'm dying,' I said. The words just came out of my lips and I stopped, stricken with horror. I knew what that meant. The same voice in my head told me when other people were dying and now it was my turn. I began to sob bitterly, gasping for breath. It was so unfair. I was too young to die. There was too much I still wanted to do.

Ali was speaking slowly in Bahasa, willing me to understand, but I was too distressed to follow his words. He repeated one word and after a while, I realised he was saying Dadong, and stopped crying.

'Where is Dadong?'

Ali pointed outside, in a gesture that indicated he wasn't far away.

'Tell him to come and see me, please,' I begged, then remembered that wasn't possible. 'Does he know I'm ill?' Ali looked blank and I searched my memory for the words. '*Saya sakit*,' I remembered.

He nodded vigorously, then began a complicated little mime. He pointed at me, then moved his forefingers up and down against his thumb, then pointed to himself, then made the finger motion again, then he pointed towards the window and said 'Dadong'. I closed my eyes with exhaustion. Ali touched my arm to make me open them again and repeated the mime.

'Oh,' I cried, and two tears slid down my cheeks. 'You're

saying that you'll take messages to Dadong for me.' I'd forgotten about that and began to cry again, feeling overwhelmed. How desperately sad that I was going to die before Dadong and I could find out whether our relationship would have worked. It had felt so different and special. He would be devastated by my death. Then I thought about my parents and my friends in London. Would they fly my body back to Britain for a funeral? The sobs shook my body.

Ali scraped back his chair, alarmed, and the soldier appeared in the doorway.

'What is it?' he asked in English.

'*Saya sakit*,' I kept repeating. '*Saya sakit*.'

The next time I awoke, it was light and Mimi was stroking my forehead. She had found a thermometer in my first aid kit in the bathroom and placed it between my lips. I asked to see the result and screwed my eyes to read the scale: forty degrees. Far too high.

'Doctor?' I asked.

'Madam,' Mimi whispered. 'Army, he say no doctor.'

'It's OK,' I slurred, 's'OK.'

'Madam, Lila is outside,' she told me. 'You want to see?'

'Lila?' I couldn't place the name for a moment.

'You want to see?' I wrinkled my brow, trying to think. Mimi disappeared and came back a few moments later with a tiny Indonesian woman and I remembered: Sedic's mother.

The soldier appeared in the doorway, yelling and waving his gun, barking that they should both get out of the room, but Lila turned and berated him in a rapid outburst, pointing at me, shaking her head, shooing him away. He tried to argue back but his conviction had lessened in the face of her frenetic delivery and finally he was cowed into retreat. She came over and touched my forehead.

'Lila,' I whispered, 'I'm sorry about Sedic.'

'Don't worry. He's at peace,' she said gently. 'I came to get my boy and take him home to Jogja. I can look after him now. But what's happened to you?'

'I feel as though I'm dying,' I whispered and a tear squeezed down my cheek.

Her fingers touched the carotid pulse in my neck then she peered into my eyes. 'Let me see your tongue.'

My lips were so dry, they cracked as I opened them. Lila looked at my tongue for a while then lowered the sheets and rested her palm on my abdomen then my diaphragm. She extended my left arm and pressed hard between the thumb and forefinger. I closed my eyes, giving in to her examination. Next I felt a cool lotion being stroked onto my skin.

'What . . . ?' I asked, but my brain wouldn't form the rest of the sentence.

'This will bring out the sweat. We need to lower your temperature.'

Lila continued smoothing on the lotion that smelled of babies. I fell asleep again.

I surfaced as a bitter liquid touched my tongue and I licked my lips trying to work out the source, unsure whether I was awake or dreaming.

'This is good medicine,' Lila's voice said. 'I mixed it myself. It's time for me to go now but Mimi will give it to you every three hours.'

'Medicine?' I asked groggily.

'It's herbs. Very powerful. You are very sick but they will make you well again. Trust me.'

'I'm sorry. About Sedic, I mean. I'm so sorry.'

'It's not your fault.'

'I should have believed him.' I felt very tearful.

Lila regarded me sadly. 'I want to ask you one thing only. When you are well again. Last time we spoke, Sedic told me that he knew where his sister Anika was. Maybe he told someone – one of his friends perhaps. Will you ask them? Find out for me? I need to get my little girl back.'

'His sister?'

'I've brought a picture. Look.' She held out a photograph of a pretty Indonesian girl. 'Please try. For me.'

I nodded, but didn't have the strength to raise my arm to take it from her. She placed it on the bedside table and kissed me quickly on the forehead. 'I'm going to get my son now. You take the herbs and you will recover.'

'Thank you,' I whispered, and then she was gone.

The next time I woke, the room was empty and it was night. The bedroom door was open and I could hear snoring. I turned onto my back and noticed that the evil pain in my head had lessened slightly but the bedcovers were drenched with sweat and they felt clammy and uncomfortable. I touched my forehead and could tell my temperature had lowered a bit.

I ran through the symptoms I could detect, trying to see a pattern, but it was as though my brain wouldn't function properly. Had I been in an accident? I struggled to remember and the smell of smoke came into my head. Of course, the fire. The events of that night came back to me as though I was watching a movie on television then suddenly realised I'd seen it before.

I pressed my tongue against the roof of my mouth and tasted the strange liquid Lila had trickled through my lips. Should I be taking it? Could it possibly poison me or make things worse? I just didn't know what or who I could trust in this alien country, but she'd said her lotion would make me sweat and it certainly had.

Then I remembered Dadong crouched outside the police station and thought about what message I should send to him through Ali. I'd have to do it in a mixture of Bahasa words and sign language. Soon I dozed off again.

The next time Ali came to sit with me, I forced myself to waken and concentrate. There was a television blaring in the next room so I guessed the soldier was watching it. I raised myself carefully on an elbow.

'*Kamar mandi*,' I whispered and pointed to the bathroom. Ali slipped an arm round my shoulders and helped me to raise my weight from the bed. He pulled my feet round to touch the floor but my knees collapsed when I tried to put any weight on them. Ali supported me and we staggered clownishly to the bathroom. He pointed at the toilet but I shook my head no and pushed the door shut behind us.

'Ali,' I whispered, then mimed as well as I could, saying any words I knew in Bahasa. 'You tell Dadong. Very important papers. Fire.' I indicated the shape of the package, watching his expression. He nodded and seemed to understand. I turned and took an unsteady step towards the bath then pointed at the little window and mimed throwing the package out of it. Ali looked out then mimed the question, 'Over the wall?' I nodded.

'You tell Dadong.'

'OK.'

He would know what to do. 'And Ali.' I held up a finger. 'One more thing. You tell Dadong—' I clasped a hand over my heart. 'Tell Dadong I love him.' Ali grinned but tears came to my eyes and began to spill down my cheeks.

'OK,' he said, embarrassed.

I splashed some water on my face then Ali helped me back to bed. Mimi brought the little brown bottle and filled the dropper to place some liquid on my lips. I was too exhausted to protest and, curiously, I was beginning to like the bitter taste more. I licked my lips then sank into a long, deep, unbroken sleep.

A loud English voice was shouting just outside my bedroom door. I realised it had been going on for a while in my dreams. 'You bloody idiot, she could die. Don't you understand? Get the hell out of here, I'm in charge now.'

'Diana?' I tried to call but it came out as a husky whisper. A face popped round the door.

'Nicola, how are you feeling? I'm going to knock some bloody heads together here. How long have you been like this?'

'I don't know,' I said.

'Mimi says your temperature is through the roof, but don't worry, a doctor will be here any moment now.'

'I'm under house arrest,' I whispered.

'They can forget about that for a start. What a piece of nonsense. We're getting you out of here as soon as the doctor says you can be moved.'

Tears welled up in my eyes. This illness was making me very weepy. I wondered whether to tell Diana I was dying but decided it would sound odd. 'Where are you taking me?'

'The first plane I can get a seat on that's going somewhere civilised. Nothing but the best, darling. The hospitals here are full to overflowing so we'll never get you the treatment you need. It looks as though the president's going to stand down, so God knows what will happen next. You're better out of it in this condition.'

'So they won?' I asked.

'Kind of a Pyrrhic victory, since the army's still in charge.'

'I don't want to leave. Not now.'

Diana sat down on the edge of the bed and stroked the hair back from my forehead. I could feel how hot it was in contrast to her fingers. 'Sorry, old bean, you don't have a choice. You seem to have done something to upset them so it's better if you leave anyway. It'll be deadly dull round here, I swear, because none of the ex-pats will come back till the new government's in place, maybe not even then. Still, I've got James to keep me company.' She winked.

'They aren't pressing charges against me?'

'Goodness, no. They just want you out. Something to do with your work at the hospital.'

I closed my eyes again, worn out with the effort of conversation.

The doctor was a smart Javanese man who spoke fluent English. He took my temperature, palpated my spleen, checked my heartbeat, glands and throat.

'No gastric upset but severe headache and fever,' he repeated.

I nodded. 'And I feel terribly weak.'

'Have you been outside Jakarta at all during your stay?'

'I went to Sambolo at Christmas then I was in Bandung a few weeks ago.'

'I'd need some blood samples to confirm,' he said, 'But I suspect it's malaria. Have you been taking anti-malarial drugs?'

I told him the brand and he nodded. 'Some strains are resistant to that.'

'Oh, shit.'

'There's a chance the fever's not over yet and I'd like to get you admitted to a hospital in Singapore before another wave hits.'

I hesitated before asking the next question. 'Am I going to be OK?'

'You should be, once we get you on the antibiotics. There's some enlargement of the spleen but you don't appear jaundiced. They'll look after you in Singapore.'

I lay back and breathed in this reassurance. Was he definitely right? Could my famous instincts have been wrong? Maybe he was missing some crucial symptom. 'Couldn't I go back to Britain?' I asked.

He shook his head. 'I don't want to risk you having a crisis on the flight. I'll write a letter of referral to Singapore and give you some drugs to keep you going. Make sure you keep the fluid intake up.'

I saw the brown bottle sitting on the table by the bed. 'Someone gave me herbal medicine,' I told him.

He picked it up and frowned at the label. 'And you took it?'

'Mimi fed it to me.'

He put the bottle down again. 'I wouldn't recommend that you take any more. Who knows what side effects it might have?'

'Maybe I would have died without it.'

'I doubt that.' He packed up his bag and patted my arm through the cover, and his smug dismissal of any alternative to allopathic Western methods irritated me. Maybe Lila had saved my life. He hadn't seen me at the height of the crisis. How did he know otherwise? Malaria killed over a million people a year worldwide, many more than died of AIDS.

Diana was speaking on her mobile, bustling around, giving orders. After the doctor left, she and Mimi came into the bedroom and began packing up my clothes and belongings.

'When am I going?' I asked.

'Maybe tonight. I'm just trying to arrange it.'

I lay back against the pillows, trying to think of everything. 'There's some money in the safe, Diana. About five hundred pounds. Will you give a third of it to Mimi and two thirds to Ali and ask him to pass on a share to Dadong?'

'That's a lot of money. You don't have to give them that much.'

'Who knows when they'll get their next job? I want to

make sure they're OK. And please can you pack that photo?' I indicated the picture Lila had left, and Diana swept it into the case she was filling without looking at it.

Ali came in later to thank me for the money. 'Is Dadong OK?' I asked him and he nodded. 'Will you tell him I'm going to Singapore? To the hospital?' I didn't know if it would be possible but maybe he'd be able to come and find me there. Maybe not. He seemed to understand.

Diana helped me to wash and dress then some men arrived with a folding wheelchair. 'I'm coming with you to the airport,' she explained. 'I've got your handbag but Major Toemion refuses to hand over your passport until you're boarding the flight. What a nightmare that man is.'

I lay down along the back seat of the people carrier. The air-con made me shiver and Diana pulled a blanket round my shoulders. She spoke in a continuous stream about James and Howard and Fred, but most of it washed over me.

'I'm coming back to England in July for my brother's wedding so we'll have to meet then. Maybe we could have dinner.'

'I'd like that.'

'What a rotten end to your visit. It won't put you off coming back here in the future, will it?'

'Am I allowed to come back? I thought I was being deported.'

Diana chuckled. 'I didn't let them. I've persuaded them to list you as an emergency evacuation for medical reasons, so you won't have anything in your records to stop you coming back. We'll all meet up for a reunion in Tanamur one day.'

I smiled and closed my eyes.

The last bit happened very quickly. Faces stared as I was wheeled through the airport terminal still wrapped in a blanket. My passport was handed over by a policeman. Diana somehow accompanied me into the departure lounge and only kissed me goodbye when they were ready to wheel me out onto the tarmac. I climbed the steps of the aircraft with the help of a member of the cabin crew and turned for a final look at the black skies and flickering lights. I took a last breath of moist, dense Jakarta air then stepped unsteadily into the cabin where a stretcher was waiting for me.

Chapter Thirty-three

The sheets were startling white and every surface looked smooth. Greyish-white light filtered through the blinds, highlighting minute specks of dust in a diagonal beam. The air was an inconspicuous temperature with a sterile scent. I stared at the ceiling – pure white, without any cracks or discolouration – and tried to figure out what day it was.

The fire had been on Wednesday night; on Thursday I was arrested and fell ill; but how long had I lain in bed before Diana arrived? A day, two days, even three? So it could be Saturday, Sunday or Monday. There was a television attached to the wall at the foot of my bed and a remote control on the cabinet. I thought about switching it on to catch up with the news, but didn't move.

Beside the remote, there was a jug of water and a glass, and beyond that a telephone. Carefully I raised myself on my elbows. Sudden movements could still provoke a toxic headache. I should call my parents, I knew I should. Instructions were clearly printed on top of the phone: press 0 for reception, 9 for an outside line. They must be sick with worry. I last spoke to them on Wednesday and since then the phone at my house had been unplugged. They'd have no way of knowing I was safe, but the effort of explaining what had happened in the interim seemed herculean. Maybe I could just say, 'I'm OK, I'll be home soon,' and leave it at that.

I picked up the receiver and dialled and after a few clicks, I could hear the ringing in their Norfolk home. There were three phones, in the bedroom, the kitchen and the study. It should be the bedroom one they picked up because it was the middle of the night in Britain. I rehearsed my opening lines as I waited and it took over a minute before I realised there was no one there. I redialled in case of a misconnection but still there was no reply. Where could they be? My arm ached from the effort of holding the receiver so I put it down again and lay back on the pillows.

What a terrible thing I had done, to put them through this anguish. My friends must be worried as well. Fluttery anxiety descended like a cloud of moths. I'd got everything wrong, interfering in a country I didn't understand, possibly ruining people's lives. Inside my head it was dark and horrible. What if Dadong got caught in possession of the testimonies? They'd throw him in jail alongside his brother, and they'd persecute Yanti and all those men who'd told their stories so trustingly. I'd been messing around with people's lives, all the while knowing that I could wave my British passport and disappear at the first sign of trouble, but my Indonesian friends didn't have that opt-out clause.

I remembered I hadn't called Karlina; the last time she'd seen me I was being arrested, so who knows what she would be thinking? And then the memories of the night of the fire, that had been clamouring in the background, closed in and I could detect the singed barbecue smell of flesh in my nostrils. I thought about the clinical decisions I'd made in such a rush and wondered if I had condemned anyone to death who might otherwise have lived. Did I rely too much on my quasi-supernatural sixth sense? Who was I kidding? I thought I had all the answers but maybe Lila knew more about healing than me. There were no certainties in medicine.

And then I thought about Sedic, bleeding to death alone in the car, with my angry words in his head. I'd been selfish, foolish, naïve, ridiculous, and my actions had caused profound damage. My heart was beating fast and I found it difficult to breathe. I clenched the sheet in my fists as beneath the guilt and anxiety, another unfamiliar emotion pounded my temples and pulses, gradually getting more strident. The emotion was anger: pure white anger in a pure white room.

Doctors and nurses came and went, taking blood smears and temperatures, administering pills and fluids and urging me to eat. 'You're seriously underweight,' one told me, and I looked down surprised. I hadn't noticed any weight loss but my hip bones jutted sharply through the sheet and my stomach felt concave.

'What day is this?' I asked a pretty nurse with huge bush-baby eyes.

'Tuesday,' she said. 'Tuesday the twenty-eighth.'

The blood tests would take a few days, they said, but meanwhile they administered precautionary antibiotics and intravenous fluids to rehydrate me.

As evening descended in my white room, I asked the nurse to help me get up and sit in a chair by the window for a while. Loneliness engulfed me like an icy fog. I felt totally isolated, a pinprick on the globe again, but whereas in the sea off Sambolo I'd been a significant black dot, now I felt like nothing, as if I didn't exist at all. Down below the city was darkening and floodlit skyscrapers were linked by join-the-dots streetlights leading down towards the glittering waterfront. A helicopter hovered overhead and further away I could see planes swooping in and out of the airport. It was too high up to make out individual figures but I sat and stared at the lights until their halos blurred into an indistinct mass.

There was a tap on the door behind me then a creak as it was pushed open and I twisted round expecting to see a nurse with my supper tray but instead, unbelievably, there stood my mother and father, looking pale and old and overdressed for the equatorial climate. They were clutching travel bags and smiling anxiously.

'What have you been doing to yourself, you silly girl?' was the first thing my mother said. I was so choked up, I couldn't reply.

It seems all my friends had been looking out for me. As soon as I was arrested, Karlina had called the British Embassy to let them know.

Diana had phoned back and kept her up to date with

GILL PAUL

developments. When my parents couldn't reach me at home, they tracked down the number of the clinic and called to ask where I was, and Karlina was able to tell them.

Diana had phoned them when I was airlifted to Singapore and they'd got on a flight from the UK that evening.

'We've come to take you home,' my father said gruffly. 'How did you manage to catch malaria?'

'I guess it was one of my mosquito bites.'

'I thought you'd be sensible enough to wear insect repellent in the evenings.'

'Everything's been falling apart, Dad. That was the last thing on my mind. Sedic came out last week and the day after he arrived, someone murdered him.'

My mother clutched her throat and Dad sat down abruptly on a chair. 'What on earth . . . ?'

'He had told me he was meeting someone he had some business with. Next thing I heard, he'd been stabbed in the femoral artery and bled to death in my car.'

'Do they think it was just a random attack? Or connected with his business dealings?' Mum asked and I shrugged. 'Are you all right, darling? It must be awful for you.'

'I wasn't in love with him any more. That was all over. But it's still dreadful that someone you've cared about can die in such a senseless way.'

'Was that connected with the police detaining you at your house and cutting off the phone? Your friend Diana wasn't sure why they did that.'

'I'm not sure either. The reason they gave me was that I was illegally treating victims of the department store fire.' I told them about that night and the stories told by survivors.

'I read that in the Sunday papers,' Dad said. 'Eyewitness reports spoke of soldiers barricading the exits and throwing in petrol-soaked rags.'

Tears came to my eyes. I wondered if these derived from the testimonies we'd recorded in the hospital that night or other sources. It didn't matter, after all, so long as the truth came out.

'They've appointed an interim president and say there are

310

going to be democratic elections next year. Things are moving forward anyway.'

My father picked up my chart from the end of the bed and examined it for a moment. 'Your temperature's still on the high side. I think I'll just go and find one of the doctors and have a word.'

Mum and I smiled at each other. He liked to be in control. We chatted for a while about insignificant things: my aunt's new car, a neighbour's daughter's wedding. I got tired quickly and she helped me back to bed, tucking the sheet round my chin as though I was five years old again.

The second wave of fever rolled up the next morning. It began with a tingling in the calf muscles and an itch at the back of my neck, then a blanket of exhaustion began to dull sensation. It was an ancient tiredness in every cell. I was vaguely aware of Mum holding my head while Dad trickled water into my lips. Blurred pains nagged in my hips and neck and there was a grinding in my skull but the fierce pain of the previous bout was held at bay by the medication. I could remember it, and sense the shadows lurking, but this was a more muffled illness. Sleeps were long and dream-filled. Mum gave me a sponge bath and I felt as though I was floating above my body watching the limbs being washed without being able to feel the cool dampness of the sponge touching my skin. In a few more lucid moments, I retrieved the brown bottle from my handbag and swallowed a couple of drops of Lila's elixir. Maybe I was hedging my bets; I remembered Dadong's accusation when I told him about lighting candles in foreign churches.

The doctors insisted that I stayed another four days after the second bout of fever, to make sure I wouldn't relapse on the flight, and then at last they pronounced that I was able to fly home. I dozed most of the way, unreal and cocooned with a parent on either side. On arrival at Heathrow, I was taken straight to the Infectious Diseases Unit at Northwick Park for further tests and observation. By now it was getting tedious sitting in a bed all day long. As the mugginess of illness retreated, my emotions were less easy to bear. It was hard to switch my thoughts from life in Jakarta. It felt wrong to have left so abruptly without being able to say goodbye to any of the people who'd been so important to me.

I tried to phone Mimi and Ali at the house, but the number just rang and rang without answer. I tried calling the Medimachines office to speak to Linda, but that line seemed to have been disconnected. In desperation, I phoned Fred at the *Jakarta Post*.

'Do you remember Dadong, my driver?' I asked. 'How can I find out what's happened to him? I'm worried he may be in trouble. Problem is, I don't know where he lives. All I know is that his brother's in jail in Bandung. If you could find out what happened to Ali, my guard, he might be able to contact Dadong. Give him my phone numbers and tell him to get in touch, would you?'

'I'll do my best, sweetheart, but you come back here soon and then you can see everyone for yourself.'

My father went back to run the practice in Norfolk, but Mum decided to stay until I was released from hospital. Claire was the first of my London friends to visit, breezy and energetic, and as chaotic as ever. Cameron stopped by to fill me in on the hospital news and even Geoff came over for a quick, slightly awkward chat. Anna brought photos of her new baby son to show me and I had to swallow my envy. He looked healthy and perfect, with alert little eyes. We hugged tightly and I realised that although we might have our differences sometimes, I'd missed her most of all.

I followed the conversations as best as I could but felt fuzzy and detached from the lives people led there. Every remark had me making comparisons in my head. Claire complained that she owed the taxman a thousand pounds and I calculated how many years an Indonesian family could have lived on that amount. Cameron had cut two fingers doing some DIY at the weekend and I told him that I'd seen a patient of mine in Jakarta die after an injury like that went septic. Anna was wearing makeup and earrings and it seemed decadent; I remembered that it was a long time since I'd bothered with such vanity. Dadong didn't approve of girls who wore makeup, he'd told me.

It was good to recall that I'd had a full life before I went away and that it was still waiting for me to return to but in the meantime, I inhabited a limbo that was neither one culture or the other.

The test results were rushed through, partly because I was threatening to discharge myself. The diagnosis of malaria was confirmed but they also found that I was suffering from amoebiasis, which accounted for some of the weight loss. I hated the thought of amoebic parasites living in my intestine and was glad to start the course of drugs that would kill them in a few weeks or so. Maybe I should have listened to Diana's warnings about the standards of hygiene in pavement *warungs*.

The day I was released from hospital, Mum picked me up in a taxi and brought me home to a flat full of flowers and a long list of phone messages. I skimmed it quickly, praying that Dadong's name might be there: Diana, Fred, various British friends, but the only Indonesian caller was Edy Mariman. I checked the time: it was one o'clock in London, so it would be eight in the evening out there. Presumably he'd have left the office, but I decided to try anyway.

It was picked up on the sixth or seventh ring. 'Edy? Mr Mariman? It's Nicola Drew. How come you're still there?'

'Working, always working,' he sighed. 'Everyone's trying to clean up their act in case the new government starts enforcing the anti-corruption laws, as promised. Do you know, there was a fire at one of the city banks yesterday. A very mysterious fire. The only floor that suffered any damage was the one where all the banking records were stored, and that was completely destroyed.' He laughed, cynically.

'Do you think there will be a lot of changes out there with the new government?'

'Oh maybe, maybe not,' he said. 'There will be a flurry of activity for a while and some cosmetic reforms, but the real power won't change hands. That's my view, at any rate.'

'What about justice? Will the soldiers who set fire to the shopping centre be prosecuted?'

'Almost certainly not. Goodness, no.'

'So the witnesses who risked their lives by telling their stories may as well have saved their breath?'

There was a pause. 'These matters can have a drip, drip effect, do you know what I mean? Things might not change in my lifetime, but maybe they will in yours. There are many very brave people out here. I was talking the other day to your colleague at the clinic, Karlina. She told me you are much missed there, that the patients still ask after you.'

'That's nice.' I smiled. 'So was it she who gave you my number here?'

'Of course. I wanted to talk to you about something.'

'I hope there aren't any problems with the Medimachines business you sorted out for me?'

'No, but thank goodness we did that, because the Medi-machines records are being turned upside down now. Wait till I tell you what's happéned!' My mother placed a cup of tea on the counter in front of me and I nodded my thanks. 'I saw a report in the local press maybe three or four days ago that they'd arrested the man who killed Sedic Molozzi, and I remembered that he was your ex-fiancé, the one who'd got you involved with Medimachines in the first place. It's an odd name, that's probably why it stuck in my mind. Anyway, according to the story in the paper, the man who stabbed him was none other than Phil Pope.'

'Good grief!' I shrieked. 'Are they sure? I thought he was in Bali at the time.'

'He flew to Bali the morning after the attack. They found his mobile phone at the scene and it didn't take long to piece together some forensic evidence. He's claiming it was self-defence.'

'But that's ridiculous. Phil's an overweight, middle-aged boozer and Sedic was young and fit. If they'd had a fight, Sedic would have won.'

'Hmm. Except it seems that Phil had a knife and Sedic didn't.'

'What on earth would he kill Sedic for?' My mother looked round, worried.

'Phil's not talking at the moment but seemingly his ex-girlfriend Sanita is squawking to anyone who'll listen that it's all Peter Molozzi's fault. She's got a bizarre story about them running some kind of prostitution racket, exporting Indonesian girls to work in the West. She says she was nearly taken in but another of their employees warned her about it. Anyway, her story is that Sedic had found out that they'd abducted a member of his family and he was out for revenge.'

I gasped. 'It must be his missing sister.'

'I don't know about that. Sanita overheard Phil talking to Peter on the phone and she says Peter told him to take a knife along to their meeting in case Sedic got rough. That won't give the police enough to make a case against Peter, though, and there's a good chance that Phil's self-defence argument will get him off. I just thought I'd call and pick your brains to see if you can come up with any other angles. It would be good to see them both behind bars, don't you think?'

I thought quickly. 'What about the money laundering? If we presented all the evidence we came up with, couldn't the police start investigating that?'

'It's virtually impossible to make an effective prosecution case against money launderers because they'll have buried their tracks in mountains of paperwork and endless trails of bank accounts and companies. I was wondering about the prostitution racket, though. If it's true, and we could tie them to that somehow, the authorities here would descend on them like a ton of bricks. Isn't that what you say?'

'I'll rack my brains. I'm sure I can come up with something more. I'll call you back, Edy.'

I put the phone down and buried my head in my hands. Could it be true that Sedic had found out his sister had been forced to become a prostitute? Maybe that's why he was in the red-light district that night; perhaps he was trying to rescue her.

'What's going on?' my mother asked. I looked round. She was chopping vegetables for soup.

'A lot. Maybe the edifice is starting to crumble.'

Had Phil been running a prostitution racket all along? I remembered Diana, Dave and Howard's conversation in Tanamur when they said that Phil seemed to have strings of girlfriends and they all disappeared when he broke up with

GILL PAUL

them. Was that because he'd shipped them overseas? Sedic's
mother had told me that Anika ran off with a man she was in
love with, but could it be that she got sucked into that nasty little
business instead? I could imagine Phil doing something like this.
He was sleazy enough to enjoy it. He probably slept with them
all first, and told them they'd make a fortune overseas. But was
Peter involved as well? Had he really allowed his son's half-sister
to become a prostitute?

I had to try and find Anika, as I'd promised Lila I would
do. But where could I start looking?

First I went through to the bedroom and began to flick
through the papers Diana had shoved in the pocket of my
suitcase. Old air tickets, address book, bank statements, some
postcards I'd never sent, the programme from the *wayang* puppet
show, and there, buried amongst them all, was the photo Lila
had given me. It was a Polaroid with fading orange colours. The
girl had long, straight black hair, a round face, a pretty smile. She
was wearing a blue pinafore dress with a short-sleeved white
blouse underneath, sitting primly with her hands folded in her
lap. The only resemblance to Sedic was in the eyes, which were
rounded, heavy-lashed and intense. Her arms were plump with
a teenage fullness. The edges of the picture were slightly creased
with age. I turned it over but there was nothing on the back.

I sat and stared at the photo for a long time, looking
for clues. The chair in which she sat was covered with a
lime-green batik cloth and there was a reddish cotton rug
on the floor. I kept returning to the eyes, as if there was
some message lurking beneath the smile. It was as if she
was trying to tell me something from across the years. And
then, in a flash of lucidity, I realised there was an acquaint-
ance of Sedic's who might be able to help, someone who
looked as though she might know something about that
industry.

I took the address book back through to the kitchen, looked
up a number, and dialled. I hadn't planned exactly what to say
but I knew I had to catch her interest quickly before she hung
up on me.

'Yes?' the voice answered.

'Celia, this is Nicola Drew, Sedic Molozzi's friend. I need to talk to you about his murder.'

There was a long silence. I listened hard but the line was too crackly to make out any clues to her reaction and I began to wonder if we'd been cut off. 'Hello, are you still there?'

'Is he really dead?' she asked at last, and I realised from the broken, gaspy voice that she was crying.

'I'm afraid so. He was stabbed two weeks ago, in Jakarta.' She was crying noisily now, with great choking sobs. 'Do you want to meet to talk about it?' I asked gently.

'I'll come to you,' she said, and hung up.

Chapter Thirty-four

———◦◦◦◦◦———

Mum had gone out to pick up some shopping when the doorbell rang a couple of hours later. The voice on the intercom said, 'It's me,' and I buzzed to let her into the building then stood at the door of the flat waiting for her to come up.

The bleached hair was still scraped into a ponytail on top of her head but she looked younger than she had at the exhibition, maybe mid forties. Perhaps it was because she wasn't wearing the heavy eye makeup and garish lipstick I remembered; maybe it was the trim blue jeans and bright pink tee-shirt. We both hesitated at the door, unsure whether to shake hands or not, then she reached out to pull me into a hesitant hug. She started to cry, with the acuteness of fresh grief, then struggled to control herself.

'I'm sorry,' she said, pulling away and smearing her eyes with the back of a hand. 'I can't believe he's really dead. I mean, are you sure? There can't be any mistake?'

'There's no mistake. I identified the body.'

Her shoulders trembled and tears spilled silently down her cheeks. 'What did he look like?'

I put an arm round her shoulder. 'Come in and sit down. Let me get you a drink. What would you like?'

'Do you have a gin and tonic?' she stammered. Sedic's favourite drink. I decided to have one as well. When I brought them through to the sitting room, she was huddled on the sofa by the window, her arms round her knees, looking small and vulnerable.

I pulled a chair over and sat down then I told her everything about the night he died, and seeing the body in the police morgue the next morning. She listened quietly, absorbing every last detail.

'You're a doctor,' she whispered. 'Tell me, do you think he would have suffered? Surely when he was stabbed . . . ? It must hurt.' She broke down again. Her grief vibrated round the room, cracked and jagged, utterly raw. I contrasted it with Peter's cool acceptance and lack of emotion when we had met the night after the murder.

'I've heard stabbing victims describe feeling as though they'd been punched rather than cut. It's probably not as painful as we imagine.'

'And you're sure it was him?' she asked again.

I nodded. I couldn't stop staring at her. When I phoned, it had been with some wild inspiration that she might know something about Sedic's sister but looking at her now, I wondered if hers might not be the eyes in the Polaroid photograph. Without makeup, her skin colour was similar to Sedic's but somehow the yellow tint of her hair gave it a greenish tinge.

'Who did it?' she asked, with a steely edge to her voice.

'A man called Phil Pope, an employee of Peter's.'

'I knew it. I just knew it. It's all my fault. I was sure they'd get into a fight this time.' The words were muttered.

I watched her, puzzled. 'Why is it your fault?'

She was rocking back and forwards now. 'We were so close. It would all have been sorted. Bloody Sedic couldn't leave well alone. He couldn't just wait. So Phil stabbed him? I'll fucking kill him now, if it's the last thing I do. I don't care, you know. I've been a prisoner all my adult life, so it wouldn't make any difference to me.' She was mumbling, as if she'd forgotten I was there.

'Are you Sedic's sister, Anika?' I asked abruptly.

She laughed, with an eerie, echoing sound. 'They told you that, did they? And you bought it?' I just stared at her. 'So did Sedic, all his life until just over a year ago. Oh, I'm Anika, all right. But I'm not his sister. I'm his mother. How does that grab you, Mrs Doctor with your middle-class values?' She gulped her drink, almost emptying the glass.

'How can that be?' I exclaimed, rushing through the mental arithmetic in my head.

She intercepted me. 'I was fourteen when Peter seduced me. Not a very bright fourteen-year-old. Mum was his housekeeper and Dad was his gardener so we lived in the servants' quarters of his house in Jakarta. When he told me I was pretty, that he liked me and wanted to make love with me, I thought if I let him do what he wanted, he would marry me. I mean, for God's sake.' She laughed again and drained her glass.

I got up immediately to fetch the gin from the kitchen. Maybe alcohol wasn't the best idea but it was the only anaesthetic I had in the flat. The whole story became much more understandable now. Peter had impregnated a teenage girl then bribed her family to bring up the baby pretending he was Lila's son. I hurried back through and topped up Celia's glass and she nodded her thanks.

'So what did they tell you when Peter took him away?'

She shrugged. 'That he'd have a better life in the West – all that crap. I didn't accept it, though. I wanted to go with him and I refused to let go of my little boy. Mum wouldn't give me Peter's phone number or even tell me which country they were in, but I'd met a couple of Peter's business contacts and I tracked down Phil Pope. I worked on him for weeks, persuading him to get me to Europe to be reunited with my son. At last he agreed, but he told me it had to be a big secret, that Mum must never know or she'd stop us. Christ!' she snorted, rolling her eyes. 'There's one born every minute.'

I had goosebumps on my arms, anticipating the next part of her story.

'Anyway, it was the oldest scam in the book. Phil had me shipped to Amsterdam first of all, where I worked my butt off – literally. Then on to London. I was an illegal immigrant, locked into a contract that meant I always owed money to my employers and had to keep working. I didn't have any cash to run away.' She was relating events factually, in a monotone, still rocking back and forwards on the seat. 'The only thing I could do was work hard until they trusted me more. I got promoted to special services and, now I'm a bit older, I act as a mentor for the younger girls, which is good. It means I can look after them when they arrive, in a way that no one ever did for me.' She raised her eyebrows. 'Am I shocking you, dear?'

I was wondering what 'special services' might entail. 'I saw your card in Sedic's wallet once. It said you were a party organiser.'

She gave an echoey laugh. 'Just one of the services we offer. You know, nice parties for fat business types. Look, I've made the best of things.' She ran her fingers through her hair and wisps of it came loose from the ponytail. 'I had a boyfriend for a long time, one of Peter's employees, but he was a decent chap. He really liked me but they'd never have let him marry me. So there I was. And all the time I was searching for Sedic, asking everyone, checking every lead I could come up with. Then I'm reading a magazine one day and there's a tiny item about an art exhibition by someone called Sedic Molozzi and my heart just leapt out of my ribs. I mean, who else would have a name like that?'

'That was the East End exhibition?'

She nodded. 'I went along on the last day and just wandered about, shaking so much I couldn't breathe, and I recognised him straight away. He was on the phone and he was laughing and he looked so beautiful. You were there, talking to some friends, and he came over and kissed you at one point. Afterwards a group of you went off down the road to an Indian restaurant and he had an arm round your shoulder. I just stood on the corner and waited until you all came out again a couple of hours later then you got in a car and drove off without noticing me.'

'Oh Celia, why didn't you come and introduce yourself?' I remembered the evening well. Sedic had been in a brilliant, sparkly mood. Shirley and Henry had been there as well. It was a good night.

'Can you imagine?' she squeaked, making a horrified face. 'No, I just came back to the gallery the next day and they were packing up. I hung around until he appeared on his own and then I approached him. At first I told him I was his sister, because that's the story he'd always been fed when he was younger. It was a dreadful shock for him, but although I'd changed a lot physically,' she pointed to her hair, 'I knew childhood memories that no one else in the world could have known. Games we played, nicknames we had for people. We used to paint pictures together.'

'He told me about that,' I smiled.

I was trying to remember that period and whether I'd sensed any change in him. If I had, I'd probably attributed it to a sense of anticlimax after the exhibition failed to make him famous overnight.

As if she could read my thoughts, Celia said, 'I always told him he should have confided in you. I could tell you were nice. He was so bloody angry, though, all he could think about was getting revenge on Peter and Phil, and rescuing me from my contract. He became obsessed and started taking stupid risks.' Tears sprang to her eyes again and she rubbed them fiercely.

'He never breathed a word to me. The first I knew about any of this was when your mother came to visit me in Jakarta.' I told her about my meetings with Lila and how she'd asked me to try and find her daughter. 'Will you go back and see her?'

Celia twisted round to stare out of the window. 'Maybe some day. I don't bear a grudge against her. She thought she was acting for the best.'

'Are you still bound by your contract now?'

'No, thank god. Sedic bought me out. It's cost him tens of thousands over the last year, I mean literally, but it was the only way.'

'No! Where did he get the money?' I thought about my credit card bills and the few unexplained items that cropped up from time to time, but nothing like the level she was suggesting.

'He'd been skimming it off the top of Peter's businesses, getting himself into all sorts of shit, like that situation you rescued him from in the Bahamas. I knew it was all going to catch up with him. You don't fuck with Peter Molozzi like that. If it had just been the money, that's one thing, but he'd been copying documents and stealing letters, trying to put together the evidence to get his revenge. He had this plan that he could get Phil to testify against Peter by threatening to go to the police about the prostitution racket. There are any number of witnesses to Phil's involvement.'

'What about Peter? Wasn't he responsible as well?'

'Nah. That was Phil's little sideline. Peter never interfered, not even after he heard I'd been abducted to Amsterdam. No one can tie Peter to that business. It's impossible to find anything you can tie him to.'

'The night he died, Sedic told me he was having a meeting that would resolve everything. I presume it was with Phil.'

Celia sighed. 'I suppose Sedic thought he could win him over, but Phil would never have done it. Peter looks after him too well. Sedic was hopelessly naïve.' There was a soft smile behind her eyes when she talked about him that reminded me of the days when I loved him like that; when I wanted to enfold and protect him and make his world a happy place.

'There was a time when I thought you were . . . I don't know what. You left a message for him once saying a service had been rendered and he had to pay up.'

She cocked her head to one side and stared at me, challenging. 'And you thought what?' I shrugged. I'd never been sure what I thought. 'No, maybe it's better if you don't say. What had happened was my ex-boyfriend had stolen some documents Sedic needed for his great plan and he wanted to charge a fee for passing them on. Just a thousand pounds. Sedic was arguing that he should have done it for nothing, to help destroy Peter, and Muggins here was stuck in the middle.' She shook her head.

'What happened to all the documents he was collecting?' I interrupted. 'Because, don't you think the best revenge would be for us to use them the way Sedic intended and get them both thrown in jail?'

Celia splayed out the fingers of her right hand and contemplated them. The fingers were stubby, the nails short and painted with a chipped magenta varnish. She wore a huge yellow-glass ring on the middle finger and a silver band round her thumb. 'The papers are in the studio,' she said. 'I guess it's worth a try. Maybe in a day or so. I'm not feeling up to it just yet.'

Just inside the wooden door, my foot kicked against something and it skittered down the dim stone hallway then ricocheted off the bottom stair. In the light filtering through a frosted-glass window on the half-landing, I looked down to see a syringe.

'Careful,' I warned Celia, worried she might jab one of her toes in their strappy sandals.

The general air of dereliction had increased – empty boxes and broken glass littered the landings – but the sewage smell was more distant, less foetid. I guessed the landlord had given up on the property. We climbed over obstacles, glass crunching underfoot, to the top floor where the door to the studio stood slightly ajar. Cautiously I pushed it open and gasped in horror at the sight.

Inside was chaos. The sofa had been turned upside down, paintings tipped over on top of each other and someone had been covering the walls with graffiti: 'Fuck You' in dark purple; a huge red Anarchy symbol; a heart enclosing the words 'Rosie and Dennis'. I felt a sense of overpowering revulsion. It was as though Sedic's memory had been desecrated.

Celia stood by my side, clutching my arm, as we surveyed the destruction. More syringes littered the ground by the sofa, alongside a piece of rubber tubing, some silver foil and a heap of spent matches. 'Lovely class of squatters you get round here,' she commented wryly. A half-eaten kebab wrapped in newspaper was covered in a swarm of ants, moving busily all over the surface then hurrying in single file towards a crack in the skirting board, each one carrying a morsel that was almost bigger than itself.

I stepped over the ant trail and walked towards the other end of the room, the part where Sedic used to paint. The statue of the lovers sat on the floor, almost exactly where I'd last seen it, but someone had crudely defaced it with red paint; now the figures had an oversized penis, large nipples and protruding satyr tongues, and I cried out at the obscenity.

'How could they do this?' I felt close to tears.

Celia came over and picked it up, scratching at a fleck of

paint with her fingernail. 'Maybe it can be cleaned up. You should keep this, you know. It meant a lot to Sedic. After you two broke up, he used to stroke it really sadly and I knew he was thinking about you. Your relationship was the most beautiful thing he ever had in his life, and he blew it good and proper.'

'If he cared about me, he had a funny way of showing it.'

'Yeah, I know.' Celia stroked my arm. 'But look at what was going on in his life at the time.' She raised her eyebrows. 'I always told him he idealised you too much – you know how blokes do that. He saw you as being utterly perfect and he was terrified you'd notice his imperfections and get fed up with him. I used to say to him, "She probably farts, sweetie. No one's that perfect." But he wasn't having it.'

I made a face. 'The funny thing is, it seems we hardly knew each other at all. How could I have been living with him and not noticed the emotional turmoil he was going through? What a waste!'

Celia put the statue down on a bench and walked over to the jumble of paintings by the back wall. The sun suddenly emerged from behind a dark cloud and a laser beam pierced the skylight.

'Sort out the ones where he's stretched this hessian stuff across the back,' she instructed. 'That's where everything's kept.' She located a Stanley knife on the bench and clicked to release the blade, then ripped through the back of one of the paintings. Inside the gap, behind the canvas, a hessian pocket held several sheets of paper and Celia extracted them and handed them over to me. I flicked through.

There was a photocopy of a cheque that Leona had written to Sedic from a Swiss bank account; shipping documents for a number of paintings being exported from Leona's gallery to the States; a printout of an e-mail from Peter to someone at the casino in Nassau instructing them to make monthly payments into a particular bank account; an electronic transfer form moving money from Olbisson Computers to Art Deals International, signed by Phil; a note to Peter from a legal firm in Vanuatu asking that he sign the enclosed form. Sedic must have thought these were all significant.

There was a tearing sound as Celia ripped the back of another painting. This one held a sheaf of bank statements for Asteroid Finance, a company based in the Bahamas; I remembered that was Sedic's company, the one that had taken the money from my credit card account. Some fairly large sums had travelled through it, according to the statements, but soon after being credited, the money would be withdrawn again.

I found a bashed cardboard box and knocked it into shape, taping the bottom with brown parcel tape, then Celia and I worked for an hour or so, sorting through the forty-odd paintings, extracting the documents and piling them in the box. It was more than half-full by the time we finished.

'What will we do with his stuff?' Celia asked. 'I can't bear to see it abused like this.' One of his shirts, the flame-orange one, was stranded under the bench and she picked it up and inhaled as if trying to catch a last whiff of his scent.

Neither of us had room to store the paintings so I ran down the street to a hardware store at the end of the market and persuaded one of the men who worked there to come back and fit a sturdy security bolt across the studio door to stop the junkies getting back in. We tidied the room, restacking paintings by the wall, throwing the rubbish into bin bags, turning the sofa rightway-up, folding his clothes in a pile. The electricity had been disconnected but we carried on working for as long as we could make out dim shapes in the half-light. When we left, I carried the statue of the lovers with me, and Celia clutched an armful of his shirts. Neither of us spoke as I drove her to her Soho apartment and dropped her off.

Later that evening, my mother and I sifted through the boxload of documents, sorting them into date order. It was impossible to decide what each one proved or how damning they might be as evidence. Sedic would have been able to explain why this bank account was significant, or why that transaction broke the law, but I had no way of knowing. It sounded as though he'd been close to compiling a case but he still needed Phil's testimony to wrap it all up. I decided to make photocopies of everything then airfreight them out to Edy. He would know whether there was enough to prosecute Peter and, if so, whose attention to bring them to.

'I still can't believe you got involved with people like this. Anything could have happened.' Mum's lips were pursed. I knew she was seething with rage at the way I'd been endangered.

'You and Dad always had misgivings about Sedic, didn't you?'

She carried on sorting the papers. 'I suppose I found him a bit supercilious and detached. It all makes sense, of course, when you understand his background. We doubted whether the marriage would last, but you have to let your children make their own mistakes.'

'And I made some pretty drastic ones.'

'Hmm.' So far she had restrained from criticising me. Maybe she was still making allowances for my illness.

'At least some good will come out of it all if we can bring these people to justice. I just wish there was someone who could help us make sense of all this lot.' I gestured at the heaps of paper littering the rug.

'One thing I've been wondering about,' my mother asked, putting her finger on an idea that I'd been playing with all day. 'Who was the Medimachines employee who warned Sanita not to let Phil Pope send her overseas?'

'Celia mentioned something about that. She knows another girl who was warned but disregarded it.'

'Did the girl tell her who it was?'

'I'm pretty sure I know, Mum. I've been leaving messages for him all over Jakarta but he hasn't called me back, so I don't know what else I can do. Just keep trying, I suppose.'

The next morning, Celia rang me at around eight o'clock.

'You'll never guess what I've just done,' she said, sounding gleeful but with a nervous tremor in her voice.

'What?'

'I called Peter in Jakarta. I knew he always stays at the

Hilton. I've been trying for ages but I only caught him ten minutes ago.'

'What on earth did you say?'

'I started by saying that I thought it was time we had a little heart to heart since our son had just died. He didn't want to talk about that, it seemed. He asked how I was getting on and I said, "As if you don't know", and that was another conversation stopper.' She chuckled. 'Then he really riled me. He said, "Are you calling to extort money out of me? Because it won't work." And so that's when I told him what I was calling about.' She paused for effect.

'Which was?'

'Leona and Sedic. I thought he should know about their little affair, because I want to see that woman destroyed and he's the best person to do it. He didn't say much, just listened, but I had plenty of details to add authenticity to my story, right down to the paintings at the exhibition which she tried to pretend were you.'

'Jesus!' I breathed. 'What do you think he's going to do now?'

Celia laughed hoarsely. 'He didn't exactly confide his plans but I would imagine he'll crucify her. No one's allowed to betray Peter Molozzi. I'll be fascinated to see what happens next.'

Retribution came more swiftly and more publicly than either of us expected. It was just three days later when the London news headlines reported that a West End gallery owner had been arrested for dealing in stolen paintings. The police had been given information relating to several million pounds' worth of pictures sold by a Hong Kong-based company called Art Deals International, of which Leona was the sole director. The ruthless efficiency of Peter's scheme left me breathless and anxious. Could he still pull the rug from under my feet in the same way?

When the phone rang a few days later and I picked up to hear Peter's voice on the line, I was instantly alert. His tone was jovial, friendly, exactly as it had been at our dinner the summer before when he first suggested the Jakarta trip.

'I was so sorry to hear you caught malaria. It can be a nasty business. Are you fully recovered now?'

'I'm not back at work yet but the doctors are pleased with my progress. I've just heard about Leona's arrest. I'm sorry, it must be a terrible shock for you.' Sarcasm seemed to come easily to me these days.

Peter's voice didn't give anything away. 'I still can't believe it. I'm sure there must be some mistake. I'd never have guessed Leona was the type to mix with criminals. I haven't managed to speak to her yet to hear her side of things because they haven't awarded bail, but I'll make sure she has a good lawyer, of course.'

'And how about Phil? Your friends are proving very unlucky with the law at the moment.'

'Terrible business. I can't understand it at all. I've known him for years and never thought he'd be capable of violence.'

'It won't have done Medimachines' reputation any good in Jakarta. Will you continue to trade out there?'

'No, not now.' He paused. 'It seems we don't have any directors left. It was a surprise to find out you'd resigned. Surprising and rather embarrassing. I found myself being interviewed by the police about some illegal trading by Medimachines. Of course, I knew nothing about it and don't have any formal links with the company but seemingly you'd told a police informant called Rianna something-or-other that I was the owner. I can't imagine where you got that idea.'

I blinked. Had Rianna been reporting to the police all along? 'I can't imagine why you thought I would want to be a Medimachines director in the first place. It's funny, but if you offered me the role and I agreed, it's completely slipped my memory now.'

Peter laughed, drily. 'So who advised you to resign? Clever idea on their part.'

A suspicion crossed my mind that if I gave him Edy's name, he might subpoena him and try to prove the resignation was more recent than stated in the file. 'It was a personal decision. As I explained in my letter, I just didn't have time to take on the responsibility.'

'You must have had a lawyer to draft it and file it in the records office.'

'It's such a long time ago, Peter, I really can't remember.'

His tone became sharper. 'In that case, I'm sure you do remember the bonus that Phil transferred to your account. He did that in the belief that you were still a director, as a loyalty payment, and since you weren't, I would appreciate its immediate return.'

I had him rattled. 'I tried to return it before, but Olbisson Computers no longer exists and Medimachines doesn't have an owner, so who would I return it to?'

There was a long pause. 'We should work together, Nicola. We'd make a good team. Why don't I buy you dinner next time I'm back in London?'

'Stranger things have happened,' I replied. 'But I doubt that one will.'

Chapter Thirty-five

Three months later, Celia and I flew back to Jakarta for Phil's trial, at which we were both due to testify. Celia had dyed her hair back to its natural black and she looked more like Sedic than ever, very close to the girl in the photograph but with older skin and careworn eyes, and without the teenage plumpness.

She was fidgety and distracted on the flight, and didn't sleep as we passed over Turkey, Iran and India. It was the first time she'd been to her homeland in over twenty years and tomorrow she would see her mother for the first time since then. She kept raising the plastic blind, letting in the piercing light of foreign dawns, and I knew she was willing the hours to pass more quickly, impatient to be there already.

I felt excited too but with a tinge of apprehension. The documents Sedic had collected painted a picture of global collusion and corruption on a massive scale but not enough of them personally incriminated Peter. He was under strict investigation but remained a free man, and I was nervous about what would happen if he was at the court for Phil's trial. How would he react if Celia and I bumped into him?

I was also saddened because there had been no word from Dadong since I'd left Jakarta. He could have obtained my phone number from several people – Diana, Fred, Karlina, Edy – if he'd wanted to, so I could only assume he wasn't interested in me any more. I knew from Edy that he was well, and that he was going to stand as a witness at Phil's trial, testifying about all sorts of business transactions he had witnessed, journeys Phil had made and the young girls he knew of who had become friendly with Phil and had subsequently disappeared. So I supposed we would see each other at court, if not before.

The charges against Phil had snowballed from grievous bodily harm to illegal trading, living off immoral earnings, abduction of minors and premeditated murder. It transpired that Rianna had been reporting to the authorities about Medimachines' transactions since long before I appeared; other witnesses against him included Linda, who was going to cast some light on the unorthodox banking methods the company had used; and Sanita was confirming Phil's movements in the crucial last hours of Sedic's life, as well as his plans to send her overseas.

When we landed in Jakarta, Celia blazed past customs officials and porters with the air of a seasoned traveller, although this was only the second aeroplane she'd been on in her life. Outside the terminal building, in damp, heavy twilight, she marched up and down arguing with the taxi drivers who were leaning against their cars, smoking kreteks and gossiping, until she selected the one who offered the cheapest fare to ferry us downtown.

Nothing seemed to have changed; the temperature was thirty-one degrees, goats grazed on the central reservation, overcrowded buses sped past us in the fast lane, rice growers burned tarry pyramids in their waterlogged fields. But as we reached the city, I could see beyond the flyover to some boarded-up shops and smoke-blackened apartment blocks. Traffic flowed smoothly along Sudirman and it looked as though the tambourine boys had been forced to find another location to ply their trade.

Our cab curved into the forecourt of the Holiday Inn, where I'd booked rooms for us. Diana had invited me to stay at her house but I felt awkward about asking if Celia could stay as well and I suppose I wanted to maintain my privacy and independence on this trip.

As we walked across the marble hallway to the reception desk, there was an excited shriek and Lila came running across the floor. 'I'm so sorry, I couldn't wait. I was meant to come tomorrow but you know me.' She giggled nervously.

I put my arms round her and hugged her first, while Celia stood back, observing.

'You've aged a lot,' Celia said at last.

'And you?' Lila giggled. 'Where's my little Anika gone?' They embraced briefly and then began to chatter as if someone had turned on a tap and twenty years' worth of news was flooding from their lips.

I went to the desk to complete the check-in formalities. There was a message from Diana insisting that I should join her that evening in Tanamur and I smiled and decided to go. Celia and Lila needed time on their own and I was mildly curious to hear the latest gossip on the ex-pat scene.

We ate supper in the tapas bar where I'd argued with Phil, but now the television screen was blank and the barstools empty of the row of corpulent, leering business types. Lila and Celia hardly ate, just picking at hunks of white crusty bread heaped in a basket in the middle, without interrupting the flow of conversation. I drank half a bottle of Rioja, suddenly feeling lonely and anxious, although I couldn't have begun to explain why.

At eleven o'clock, I made my excuses and left them dawdling over coffee. I walked down the marble steps and asked the doorman to call me a cab then I was being driven through the black, peopleless streets of the capital, streetlights blurring past, my driver serious and competent. We drew up outside Tanamur and I could see yellow and pink flashing lights through the doorway. I nodded to the solitary bouncer then walked down the long corridor into the smoky cavern. Two girls danced on a walkway overhead but the dance floor was empty and only around twenty people lined the bar.

'Nicola,' Diana screamed, hurtling over to hug me. 'You're late. Where have you been? We had some champagne but we drank it while we were waiting, so now we'll have to get some more.'

As she talked, she was guiding me towards the bar and I made out Howard sitting with his arm round a pretty brunette,

Fred talking to an Indonesian man who had his back to me, and another girl I knew who was a friend of Diana's. When he saw me, Fred grinned and held out his arms for a hug and, as he did so, the Indonesian man turned round and I jumped with fright.

'Dadong!'

He nodded formally. 'Hello. How are you?'

'My turn first,' Fred smiled and squeezed my shoulders, kissing me on both cheeks.

Regaining my composure, I leaned over and kissed Dadong on each cheek. 'I'm fine. What are you doing here? I thought you hated this place?'

'It's better now it's emptier,' he gestured. 'I was just having a drink with Fred.'

'You two know each other?'

Fred grinned. 'We work for the same human rights organisation. I was Dadong's contact for passing info to the outside world. Sorry we couldn't tell you before, Nicky.'

I glared at Dadong. 'You kept it a secret from me all that time?' I remembered his frostiness the night he'd seen Fred kissing me outside Tanamur but there had been no indication that they had known each other.

He just shrugged. Our eyes locked for a moment.

There was a loud pop as the barman opened more champagne and Diana began handing round the glasses. There were toasts, then Howard introduced me to his new girlfriend. Diana told me that James had gone back to the UK for a couple of weeks and she was hopeful that he would ask his wife for a divorce this time. I kept feeling as though Dadong was watching me but when I turned to look, he'd be facing in a different direction or glancing coolly past my shoulder. I felt shy, as though he was a stranger, but at the same time immensely drawn to him.

It was almost an hour later before I was able to lean against the bar beside him, out of earshot of the others, slightly relaxed by drink, yearning to touch him but managing to restrain myself.

'Why didn't you phone me?' I asked.

'You have your own life in London. What could I have said?' His eyes were steady and I found it impossible to judge his feelings.

'I was dying to hear from you. We had so much to talk about and we never had a chance to say goodbye.'

Dadong shrugged. 'I knew you were all right. That was the main thing.'

'I see. So that's it? Nice knowing you?' I couldn't keep the hurt out of my voice and he blinked hard.

'I knew you would have to come back for Phil's trial and that we would see each other then. Why do you think I came along tonight? Fred told me you would be here.'

'You were happy to wait three months to see me?'

'Are you drunk, Nicola?' he asked, smiling, and I blushed. He touched my cheek quickly with a finger. 'I've been in Bandung. My brother was released from jail a month ago, as part of a general amnesty for political prisoners, and we had a lot of catching up to do.'

'That's brilliant news.' I squeezed his forearm. 'What will he do now?'

'Make puppets, I think. He's through with politics.'

'And you? Are you through with politics?'

Dadong scratched his head. 'My interest has always been in justice. I don't think one political party or another makes much difference but I don't like to see individual liberties abused.'

'Was it you who tipped off Sanita about the prostitution ring?'

'Of course.'

'And there were others too?'

'Yes, many.'

'How did you know about it?'

'I overheard a lot. Phil was never aware how much English I speak. Sometimes when he was talking to people on his mobile in the back of the car, he'd spell out words he didn't want me to pick up, as if I was an ignorant native or a four-year-old child.' He grinned, his eyes crinkling at the corners. 'At least we've got him now. The evidence against him is overwhelming.'

'But we haven't got Peter,' I sighed. 'In many ways I feel he's caused more damage.'

'His businesses are being investigated and some of them have been closed down already. All the Medimachines resources have been impounded because of tax and import licence irregularities and several hospitals have complained about malfunctions in the machines they sold.'

'It's not enough. I wish we could do more.'

Dadong touched my waist lightly. 'You are so idealistic, Nicola. You always want to change the world, cure everyone, find the equation to wipe out poverty. You like numbers and controlling things, I think.'

'No, I've changed. I learned some lessons out here.'

'Some things never change,' he quipped. 'You're wearing makeup and it's smudged under your left eye. And there's a stain that looks like red wine on your skirt.'

I put my arms round him and laid my head on his shoulder. He responded by circling his arms round me and we stood like that for a moment then I whispered. 'Dadong, please can I be with you tonight? At your room or at my hotel. Anywhere. I don't care, I just need you.'

He cleared his throat and I realised he was trembling. 'Of course,' he replied.

The lovemaking was fundamental, like coming home from a long dangerous journey, as though it had always been meant to be this way. Afterwards, I lay with my head in the crook of his shoulder, tilted so I could watch his face, our fingers intertwined. I listened to the steady rhythm of his breathing, watching his eyes flicker from one to the other of mine.

'Where are you working now?' I asked.

'My real job is with the human rights organisation. It has been all along. But I've taken another driving job, for a French company. The pay is better and I've learned quite a lot of French already.'

'Have you taken lessons?'

'No, I just listen to what they're saying in the back seat

and memorise the phrases I understand.' He raised my hand to his lips and kissed it. 'And you? You are back at your London hospital working with sick children?'

'I haven't been able to settle very well back in London,' I told him. 'It all seems – not trivial, but too easy. The colours are muted, the sky's overcast and everything's mundane. Do you know what I mean? I don't have a gekko in my garden. I don't even have a garden.'

Dadong nodded and gripped my fingers sympathetically.

'I don't know if it will be possible but I'm going to see Karlina tomorrow and ask if she can think of a way I could come back to work here legally. Maybe she could put me in touch with a charitable organisation who'd pay me a salary to help out here. I'm sure there must be a route to skirt round the law and I know she wants to have me back.'

'In Indonesia there is always a way round the law.' His expression hadn't changed but he was gripping my hand very tightly.

'Anyway, if I was coming here, I would have to find somewhere to live, and I thought it would be nice to find someone to share with.' I stopped, flustered. 'That's not what I meant to say. In fact, I wanted to ask if you would consider living with me. Just to see how we get on.'

Dadong began stroking my back with his free hand but he didn't respond for a while. 'Do you mean you want me to be your driver?'

I sighed in frustration. 'For God's sake, no. I want you to be my lover.'

'How could it work, Nicola? You have so much more money than me.'

'Does that have to be an issue?'

'Of course.'

'Then I'll live somewhere that you can afford.'

He laughed and wrapped his arms round me for a hug. 'You don't know what you're saying. You couldn't survive in a single room, sharing a bathroom with eight other families.'

'I'd be willing to try if it was the only way you would consent to live with me.'

We made love again, with a tenderness and ardour that left me mellow and smiling all over, then we slipped into our special way of arranging our arms and legs round each other and fell asleep.

Around nine the next morning, there was a knock on the door and Dadong leapt out of bed, grabbed his clothes and disappeared into the bathroom like some errant husband in a West End farce. Smiling at his modesty, I opened the door to find Celia standing outside.

'We just wondered if you wanted to join us for breakfast?'

'I've got company,' I whispered, pointing at the bathroom door.

'Good for you!' She winked, mischievously. 'I'd better check him out for you. Who is it?'

'It's Dadong, the one who was warning girls not to be taken in by Phil Pope.' I was still whispering.

'I want to meet him,' she said out loud. 'Where was he twenty years ago when I needed him?'

There was a cough, then the bathroom door handle turned and Dadong emerged, fully dressed. Even his shoelaces were tied. I marvelled that the shirt I had stripped from him last night still looked pristine and freshly pressed. How did he manage it?

I performed the introductions and they smiled and nodded, then I left them chatting about the forthcoming court case while I took my clothes into the bathroom and got dressed. When I emerged, Lila had joined them.

Dadong smiled at her. 'You're Sedic's mother, the one who saved Nicola's life?'

'Who told you that?' she asked, obviously pleased.

'My friend Ali, the guard at the house, says she would have died without your help.'

'Did he?' I asked with interest. Ali was no medical expert but my own instincts still told me that I'd been close to death during those fever-filled days.

'She's not Sedic's mother, though,' Celia interrupted. 'She's his grandmother.'

I saw the same look on Dadong's face that must have

crossed mine when I first heard the news. A rapid arithmetical calculation was taking place.

'I was fourteen when Peter seduced me,' Celia helped him.

Dadong frowned. 'This may sound like a strange question, but can you prove that you're his mother?'

Celia looked at Lila. 'We have a birth certificate somewhere. I've always kept it.'

Dadong was drumming his fingers on a little side table. 'Does it name Peter as the father?'

'No, no!' Lila exclaimed. 'But Peter never denied fathering Sedic. He just paid me to say that I was the mother.'

Dadong continued, thinking out loud. 'I expect it could all be proved with blood tests. They took Sedic's DNA profile to link Phil to the forensic evidence at the murder scene. If they take tests from Celia and from Peter, that should prove who the parents were.'

'There's no question who the parents are!' Celia snapped. 'I was only a child. I didn't sleep with another man until they got me to Amsterdam eight years later, when I was twenty-two.'

I was watching Dadong, trying to see where his train of thought was leading.

'It's better than nothing,' he said. 'Two years is the mandatory sentence, I believe.'

'For what?'

'Sexual intercourse with a minor. They don't look too kindly on foreign nationals impregnating our young women, even if it was almost thirty years ago. I think you should consider pressing charges, Celia.'

She bit her lip. 'I never knew that. What a good idea! Can you imagine Peter's face when they arrest him?'

I stepped back and looked at the three of them as they processed the idea: Celia was grinning, Dadong serious, Lila looked alarmed.

'It wouldn't be fair,' Lila complained. 'I took his money and promised I'd always keep the secret. We had a deal . . .' Her voice trailed off because no one was paying any attention.

'Who shall we report it to?' Celia's eyes were sparkling.

'Leave it to me,' Dadong said. 'I can have a word with someone.'

I gazed at him, thinking what an intrinsically good person he was, how strong and capable and sure of himself. I was proud to be with him. And as I sat on the edge of our bed, watching, a very curious sensation came over me. In my mind's eye, I saw two cells merge into one and an energy being created. It gave off a strong glow and made me feel profoundly peaceful and contented.

'Oh, my god!' I realised, with a mixture of wonder and shock and stirrings of excitement. 'I know what that was. I just became pregnant.' In the sheer joy of our reunion, contraception had been the last thing on my mind.

I tried to analyse the sensation. It was as if I had experienced the actual moment of fertilisation, the creation of a new life force. I could feel it pulsing with energy and I knew the cells were strong and viable. Suddenly I remembered the woman with facial cancer who'd foreseen illness, a death and a baby. She must have had a very special gift.

I looked round at the faces of the three Indonesians in the room and decided not to tell them immediately. No one would believe me. It sounded too weird. I'd keep the news to myself for a few weeks before letting anyone else in on the secret. Dadong gave me a concerned look and I smiled back, very happy.

GILL PAUL

ENTICEMENT

'A sexy, pacy, thoroughly modern story.'
Ham & High

Jenny is a successful career woman with a passion for ill-advised affairs. When she meets the intriguing French-American Marc at a party, she's immediately involved in an intoxicating sexual fling.

Impulsively accompanying him to France, Jenny finds her blissful adventure darkens. She can tell that Marc is hiding something and curious events deepen her suspicion. Then, on the way home from a perfect evening, he simply disappears.

Angry and mystified, Jenny returns to London but her missing lover and memories of the spectacular sex continue to haunt her. Why did Marc abandon her? And why does she get the uncanny feeling that she's being watched? Her need to uncover the answers leads her on an increasingly dangerous trail from London to New York and back to Brittany, towards a horrifying revelation that threatens her life.

HODDER AND STOUGHTON PAPERBACKS

NATASHA MOSTERT

THE MIDNIGHT SIDE

A phone call from the dead. Lucid dreaming. A ghost manipulating the London stock exchange. And a seductive woman, who even from the grave is able to direct events to her satisfaction.

Isa is not surprised by the late night telephone call from her cousin Alette – until she discovers the next morning that Alette has been dead for two days . . .

Alette has left behind three envelopes and a request. The envelopes contain instructions on how to bring about the financial ruin of the man who made Alette's life a misery while she was still alive.

But as Isa sets out to exact revenge on her cousin's behalf, she is in peril. Unbeknownst to her, Alette was murdered, and now it is Isa's turn to be drawn into the killer's world of dark fantasy and lethal obsession.

HODDER AND STOUGHTON PAPERBACKS

ELIZABETH IRONSIDE

A GOOD DEATH

'Elizabeth Ironside joins those few mystery writers you unreservedly look forward to reading.'

Harriet Waugh, *Spectator*

Theo Cazalle has come back from the dead: from a 'good war' spent fighting with the Free French against the Vichy regime. Unannounced, he arrives at the farm of Bonnemort, eager for a reunion with his wife, his daughter. And discovers, instead, that his wife has been denounced as a collaborator, the lover of an SS officer. The same officer who was found naked, his throat cut, in front of Colonel Cazalle's house.

But what really happened? There are dead Frenchmen – but were they betrayed to the German occupier by their own carelessness or by jealous villagers, cynical comrades? There are two disturbed little girls – but were they terrified into silence by the horrors of the occupation or hurt by people they should have trusted? Was Ariane Cazalle a traitor – or the bravest of heroines?

As Theo Cazalle picks his way through contradictory stories of how their victims were betrayed to the Germans, he comes ever closer to the truth about the dead man at Bonnemort.

HODDER AND STOUGHTON PAPERBACKS

A selection of bestsellers from Hodder & Stoughton

Enticement	Gill Paul	0 340 76669 7	£6.99	☐
The Midnight Side	Natasha Mostert	0 340 76798 7	£6.99	☐
A Good Death	Elizabeth Ironside	0 340 71687 8	£5.99	☐
The Art of Deception	Elizabeth Ironside	0 340 71685 1	£5.99	☐
The Accomplice	Elizabeth Ironside	0 340 64037 5	£5.99	☐

All Hodder & Stoughton books are available at your local bookshop or newsagent, or can be ordered direct from the publisher. Just tick the titles you want and fill in the form below. Prices and availability subject to change without notice.

Hodder & Stoughton Books, Cash Sales Department, Bookpoint, 39 Milton Park, Abingdon, OXON, OX14 4TD, UK. E-mail address: orders@bookpoint.co.uk. If you have a credit card you may order by telephone – (01235) 400414.

Please enclose a cheque or postal order made payable to Bookpoint Ltd to the value of the cover price and allow the following for postage and packing:
UK & BFPO: £1.00 for the first book, 50p for the second book and 30p for each additional book ordered up to a maximum charge of £3.00.
OVERSEAS & EIRE: £2.00 for the first book, £1.00 for the second book and 50p for each additional book.

Name ....

Address ....

....

....

If you would prefer to pay by credit card, please complete:
Please debit my Visa / Access / Diner's Club / American Express (delete as applicable) card no:

Signature ....

Expiry Date .. / ....

If you would NOT like to receive further information on our products please tick the box. ☐